Richard Gordon was born in 1921. He qualified as a doctor and then went on to work as an anaesthetist at St Bartholomew's Hospital, and then as a ship's surgeon. As obituary-writer for the *British Medical Journal*, he was inspired to take up writing full time and he left medical practice in 1952 to embark on his 'Doctor' series. This proved incredibly successful and was subsequently adapted into a long-running television series.

Richard Gordon has produced numerous novels and writings all characterised by his comic tone and remarkable powers of observation. His *Great Medical Mysteries* and *Great Medical Discoveries* concern the stranger aspects of the medical profession whilst his *The Private Life of...* series takes a deeper look at individual figures within their specific medical and historical setting. Although an incredibly versatile writer, he will, however, probably always be best known for his creation of the hilarious 'Doctor' series.

D1642818

The Invisible Victory

Richard Gordon

HOUSE OF
STRATUS

This edition published in 2001 by House of Stratus, an imprint of Stratus Holdings plc, 24c Old Burlington Street, London, W1X 1RL, UK.

www.houseofstratus.com

Typeset, printed and bound by House of Stratus.

A catalogue record for this book is available from the British Library.

ISBN 1-84232-510-8

Author's Note

Who discovered penicillin? Fleming or Florey? Would either have seen its possibilities, had not the sulpha drugs come from Nazi Germany? And who was the sulpha drugs' begetter? Gerhard Domagk, awarded the Nobel Prize? Or an unknown German professor, at the same time on trial for his life at Nürnberg for complicity with Hitler's SS?

My research in London, Oxford and Wuppertal gave fresh knowledge about the discoverers of these drugs, which have benefited almost everyone alive today. This is a novel, but its historical and medical facts stay close to the truth. The scientists Colebrook, Wright, Hopkins, Freeman, Raistrick and Hörlein all lived. Chain, Fletcher and Heatley happily still do.

A note about microbes. The sulpha drugs and penicillin kill the dangerous germ *streptococcus* in the body. The equally deadly *staphylococcus* is killed by penicillin, but not by the sulpha drugs.

1

You could see the whole of Wuppertal from the Schwebebahn. That was the famous overhead railway, its green-painted girders bestriding ten miles of the River Wupper like an angular centipede. Its neat red-and-white aerial tramcars, suspended from their monorail, gave the entrancing feeling of floating in the gondola of a low-flying Zeppelin. The first ride had been taken on October 24, 1900 by Kaiser Wilhelm II, wearing his field-grey military cape and spiked helmet. The only accident in its history, as everyone in Wuppertal told you sooner or later, was a baby elephant involved in a circus stunt falling through the floor into the water.

Wuppertal was a snake of a town, twisting along a steep wooded valley in places barely quarter of a mile across, lined with narrow slate-roofed tenement houses rising on each other's shoulders. Its headlong outdoor staircases suggested Old Edinburgh, the abuttal everywhere of man's ugliness on Nature's beauty reminded me of the mining towns in South Wales where I had gone bicycling during the Cambridge vacations. The river banks were settled by weavers in the eighteenth century, their linen yarn covering the green fields like snow, and its only event to impinge on the outside world was the birth there in 1820 of Friedrich Engels. Wuppertal was synthetic, like the compounds which I created from elements in my chemist's test-tubes. It had been formed from six Rhineland towns breathing the same acrid air – Elberfeld, Barmen, Cronenberg, Ronsdorf, Beyenburg and Vohwinkel – like Arnold Bennett's Potteries. That was three years before my arrival. I came to work there on January 1, 1933, a perfectly ridiculous moment for a particle of the British Empire to settle on the feverish face of Germany.

In Elberfeld — everyone of course still used the old names — which formed the north-west corner of Wuppertal, the Schwebebahn bisected the factory of I G Farbenindustrie Aktiengesellschaft, the huge chemical combine which made dyes and anything else profitable to come out of a test-tube. It was a vast, straggling disarray of red-brick buildings the size of warehouses and long wooden sheds, the river a squalid ditch canalized by the factory walls, rainbowed with oil and overhung with a web of cables and pipes, smoke pouring from a dozen tall brick chimneys and steam escaping from myriad valves. The conscience of the world had not yet stepped so inconveniently between a manufacturer and the cheap disposal of his waste. I worked at the far side of Wuppertal in the old district of Barmen, but that morning I had an appointment at I G Farben. The Schwebebahn was crowded. It was eight-thirty on the last Saturday of January, in an age when men got up six days a week for work — if they could find it. From the factory station, a floorless shed suspended in mid-air, I retraced my route to the gates off the main road leading west towards Düsseldorf. It was a bitter day, the grey sky threatening imminent reinforcement for the black-speckled, iron-hard snow swept into gutters and corners.

I was directed across a triangular yard cut by railway tracks, where a gang of workmen in leather aprons and shiny-peaked caps were loading a dray with carboys of chemicals in straw nests, every man's breath a cloud, the four horses pawing the icy cobbles and smoking like dragons. As I crossed the river by a footbridge of railway sleepers I caught the familiar smell of phenol. All Wuppertal stank. Any town making its living from chemicals in those days suffered its nose to be corroded. The factory was the pharmaceutical division of I G Farben, the works strung along the river in the 1880s by the old Bayer drug company, which still gave its name to the medicaments. From phenol, the Germans were making aspirin to soothe the headaches of the world.

The six-storey research block was modern, a cleanly contrast to the industrial jungle. I was making for the pathology department on the fourth floor, where I found a door to the left of the short corridor ajar, and walked in. I discovered myself in an amazingly luxurious laboratory. It was light and airy on the corner of the building, with white-tiled walls, white desks and swivel chairs, a telephone, even a refrigerator. The bench was separated from a huge window by a shelf of plants in pots, the elaborate microscope was far beyond the pocket of the Sir William Dunn Laboratories at Cambridge, which I had just quit. Its only occupant was a girl in a white coat, busy over conical flasks with cotton-wool stoppers. She was pretty, round faced and dark-haired, her eyes murmuring a hint of the Slav.

'Yes? What do you want?' she asked sharply.

I must have appeared a freak. At Cambridge I had learned, like Michael Arlen's Gerald, to despise the genteel habit of wearing an overcoat, whether it blew, rained, snowed or froze. My twenty-two-year-old frame was hung with grey flannel 'bags' and a brown Harris tweed jacket, a long knitted blue-red-and-gold Trinity College scarf tucked into the lapels. My fair hair was disarrayed. I was red-nosed and raw-handed. One fist carried a brown cardboard attaché case from Woolworth's, which contained principally rye bread and sliced sausage for my lunch, the other clasped a flapping umbrella. God knows why I perpetrated the image of a typical Cambridge undergraduate going about his business in an obscure Rhineland industrial town. Perhaps it was patriotic bravado, or insularity, or 'bohemianism'. Or perhaps I couldn't afford a change of clothes.

'I have an appointment this morning to see Professor Dr Domagk,' I replied in German.

'I'm sorry, mein Herr, but it is strictly forbidden to enter the laboratories.'

My English accent made her more agitated, and I thought prettier. At that age I had a pressing interest in women. (Perhaps it persisted. I have had more wives than usually allowed a Professor of Biochemistry.)

'*Streng verboten*,' she repeated, torn between duty and courtesy. In the Europe of those days, even neighbouring foreigners enjoyed the rarity and mystery of Turks to the Elizabethans. 'Please wait outside.'

This was strange. The Dunn Labs were as open to visitors as Cambridge railway station, and far more convenient than those famously remote platforms. I was about to comply when a door in the far corner opened to admit two men in white linen lab coats.

The first struck me as a younger copy of the Republic's President, Field-Marshal von Hindenburg. He was fiftyish, square-built, bull-necked, bushy eyebrowed, his hair iron grey, his moustache close-clipped, wearing circular horn-rimmed glasses (but everyone's glasses were circular then). The other's lab coat was too long in the sleeves, unbuttoned to display brown trousers badly in need of a press. I recognized him at once from my German host's description as Professor Gerhard Domagk.

'Quite obviously, you are Herr Elgar,' said Domagk in German, taking in my appearance.

Domagk was in his late thirties, tall and spare, with thinning dark hair cropped so close that the sides of his head appeared shaven. He had a neat triangle of clipped moustache and a pin through his soft white collar under the knot of his tie, American style. The little I knew of him suggested that he might begrudge spending even the small change of his time on me. He was a bacteriologist, a doctor specializing in germs, a study initiated by the Germans themselves in the 1870s. He held the title of Professor from the University of Münster – the nation which makes much of such labels has the pleasant custom of applying them without the accompanying trials of office. He had been Director of Experimental Pathology and Bacteriology at I G Farben for the past five years. I needed to dig my youthful fingers deep into my pockets of self-confidence to announce, 'Sir Frederick Hopkins asked me to pay you his respects, Herr Professor. Until last summer I was one of his students in the Biochemistry Department at Cambridge.'

'So Dr Dieffenbach explained, when he telephoned. Well, I'm sure we're honoured to welcome Sir Frederick's emissary.' I sensed no tinge of sarcasm. 'Had there been no Hopkins, our babies might still be misshapen from rickets and our sailors still dying from scurvy.'

Sir Frederick Gowland Hopkins – 'Hoppy' – was President of the Royal Society, great-grandson of a captain at Trafalgar and a relation of the Jesuit priest whose poems combine subtle conciseness with eccentric metre. He was the doctor who in 1898 attended the unexpectedly early arrival of Ramsay Macdonald's firstborn in the flat downstairs at Lincoln's Inn Fields. He was also the man who discovered vitamins.

'My correspondence with Hopkins was a couple of years back, when we synthesized vitamin B_1 here in these laboratories,' Domagk explained to his companion. The girl with the Slav eyes was concentrating on her flasks. She seemed of slight importance. I judged her a technician, not a chemist. 'Some people in Germany said that Hopkins was forestalled in his discovery by the Dutchman Christian Eijkman. You know, when he observed that natives eating polished rice went down with beri-beri. I wanted to tell Hopkins how I disagreed with that view. Anyway, he was always generous in his praise for Eijkman's work. *Fair play*,' he added in English.

The Hindenburg-like man grunted. 'Didn't the gateman send a porter up with you?' he enquired of me. When I shook my head he remarked resignedly, 'Oh, they're too comfortable drinking coffee in their lodge this weather. Visitors aren't supposed to come unescorted,' he added as an apology. 'We are a commercial undertaking, not a university, and a company must guard its secrets like its marks in the bank. Where did you learn your German?'

'There were lectures at Cambridge for scientists. A knowledge of German is of course essential to keep up with modern chemistry.'

'I am a chemist, so I savour your compliment.'

I became aware while we talked of the unmistakable smell emitted by laboratory mice. Somewhere beyond the door which they had left ajar would be an animal house, its shoebox-sized cages stacked the height of a man, each floored with straw and sawdust on which scurried, in various states of ill health, lapping their cunningly doctored bowls, the invaluable and involuntary martyrs to man's easeful supremacy on earth. Through the opening I glimpsed something like an oversized biscuit tin on legs, which from my earlier days working in the Inoculation Department of St Mary's Hospital in London I recognized as an incubator for growing bacteria. For all their secrecy, I gathered from the combination that something was going on involving the experimental infection of living beings with germs.

'If Professor Hörlein will excuse me for a moment,' said Domagk affably, turning to the other, 'I shall install our Englishman across the corridor.'

'You are lodging with Dr Dieffenbach?' remarked Hörlein. I enjoyed the hospitality of Dr Dieffenbach's chalet-like roof in Elberfeld – literally, my freezing bedroom being under the rafters. He had made my appointment. Domagk lived in the same smart residential area near the Zoo, at No 11 Walkürenallee, but it appeared seemly for one of my insignificance to be received in his laboratory. 'We all know him well. A very agreeable man, and an excellent doctor.'

'How did you come across him?' asked Domagk with a look of curiosity. I noticed a habit of inclining his head to one side as he spoke. 'To my knowledge he has never visited England, except as an involuntary guest during the War.'

'He is an acquaintance of a family friend, Sir Edward Triplady – '

'Ah! The physician who attends your King?' Hörlein exclaimed, recognition in his eye.

I nodded. I had mentioned two knights in almost as many breaths. They must have thought me splendidly connected, the Germans taking the English aristocracy completely seriously.

2

I concluded from his spacious Arbeitszimmer, in which Domagk left me alone on the other side of the building, that all the facilities provided by I G Farben compared with those of the Cambridge Dunn Labs as the Ritz to the Little Rose pub in Trumpington Street. The furniture was plentiful, though with the unrelated look of institutional buying. The flat roll-topped desk was piled high with typewritten papers, coloured cardboard folders and neat piles of scientific journals, and against the four tall windows were more of those indoor plants which attract such quaint English names, like mother-in-law's tongue or busy lizzie. Outside was a bare cherry tree, the grey sky and the Schwebebahn.

Decorating the white walls were framed photographs of middle-aged or elderly gentlemen, mostly looking down microscopes. I recognized Professor Paul Ehrlich from Frankfurt-on-Main, bushy haired, neatly bearded, unaccustomedly smart in wing collar and spotted tie and broadcloth cutaway, with his soft mouth and his glasses halfway down his nose, looking up amiably from some chemical tome as though surprised at someone snatching the habitual box of cigars from under his arm and taking his portrait. In 1909, Ehrlich exploited the German genius for systematic chemistry by testing 605 compounds of arsenic before discovering 'Salvarsan' or '606', which killed the treacherous spirochaete *Treponema pallidum*. He cleared syphilis from the veins of the world, many of them blue-blooded.

On a table against the window a microscope stood tilted for the eye. I idly turned the knurled fine-adjustment screw, focusing the fuzzy blue circle on the glass slide.

I am a biochemist, a student of the molecular mechanism of life, but I had worked on bacteria and recognized a specimen of human pus. I saw the globular scavengers of the blood, resembling the pond amoeba, the simplest of God's creatures, which expresses the mystery of existence in a single cell. Among them were twisted minute, dark, exactly similar dots, some in chains of twenty or more, some in fives and sixes, others in pairs, like broken beads on a ballroom floor. They were *Streptococcus pyogenes*, an enemy of mankind only less deadly than man himself. Some of the chains had penetrated the blood cells, to lie against the blobs of a nucleus deep stained by the blue dye. The streptococcus germs were winning this complex and subtle battle. They were killing the body's scavengers, on their way to killing the body itself.

I straightened up, noticing with surprise that the colourful, bold landscape which had already caught my eye on the wall above was an original painting. It was an unusual find in the study of a scientific professor.

'You like my picture?' Domagk entered unexpectedly, still in his white coat. From the warmth of his greeting I had been caught at a fortunate moment. I politely asked the artist.

'Otto Dix. I was going to say that he's one of our younger painters, but of course now he's about forty. He teaches at Dresden. He's a disciple of "The New Objectivity" ' – Domagk repeated *Die Neue Sachlichkeit* in English. 'That's an artistic movement derived from the "Bridge Group" formed early this century in Dresden,' he continued in an explanatory way, 'but after the War some rather crazy people joined it. His work is taken to express a realistic disillusionment with life in Germany today – or by that do we mean a disgust?'

He waved me to a low chair, sitting behind the roll-top desk, crossing his long legs. Unwinding my Trinity scarf, I handed him from my breast pocket a glossy pamphlet entitled,

LES PRIX NOBEL EN 1929
The Earlier History of Vitamin Research
Sir Frederick Gowland Hopkins FRS

On the day I had packed up my luggage, my ambitions and my illusions to leave Cambridge for good, I had taken a self-consciously sentimental breakfast-time walk along the river. It was a December morning which sharply reminded the University that it was but an intruder in the Fens. The Backs wore their midwinter splendour, trees ghostly with frost under the bleary eye of a newly awakened sun, even the incorrigible mallards dulled with cold on the steely waters of the Cam. On Trinity bridge I encountered 'Hoppy', long moustache covering the angles of his mouth to bestow a look of everlasting pondering, his eyes mirrors of infinite shrewdness. When I disclosed I was disappearing to Wuppertal he was amazed and shocked. 'Going over to the enemy,' he called it. But with his usual kindness he suggested that I carried the signed reprint as an introduction to Domagk, who might perhaps be useful to me.

Domagk offered a packet of Juno cigarettes – *Berlin raucht Juno*, said the advertisements – but I have never smoked. 'The vitamins may be a simple idea,' he said, turning Hoppy's few pages, 'but simple ideas need genius to see them. I have often to remind myself that a scientist must view the world through a telescope as well as a microscope. Though sometimes even a telescope is unnecessary, because the most useful ideas stand on the horizon like mountains and we never see them.'

There was a silence. The conversational possibilities between us seemed swiftly exhausted. Perhaps thinking it churlish to evict me so promptly, Domagk added, 'I understand from Dr Dieffenbach that you're working for the Red Crown brewery across at Barmen. That's the American concern, isn't it? Do you find the job interesting?'

'Not in the slightest.'

Domagk gave his shy smile, tossing the spent match into a large glass ashtray. 'Well, I prefer wine myself. And so does Dr Dieffenbach.' I had already found the cellar no disadvantage in my lodgings. 'We don't see many Englishmen or Americans in Germany. It's understandable. The War was hardly a tennis match. You were lucky to go through it as a child, Herr Elgar. I had to leave Kiel University after my first semester to join the colours as a grenadier. I celebrated my nineteenth birthday in a dugout on the Belgian coast at Nieuport, fighting the Tommies. The Tommies wounded me in 1915, so I was posted to the Medical Corps.' He imparted all this with his usual quiet voice. 'In a *most* lowly capacity. The upshot was my qualifying in medicine at Kiel five years later than I expected. Well, I shouldn't complain. Most of my academic brothers lost their lives.'

I felt somehow personally responsible for these misfortunes, and for some reason quoted H G Wells, 'It was the war that will end war.' But Domagk only smiled again and diverted the unpleasant subject by asking, 'Have you done any research yourself?'

I nodded. 'I held a six months scholarship at Cambridge after taking Tripos. I studied the affinity of bacteria for dyes.'

I was startled at the effect of this scientifically inconsequential information. Domagk stiffened in his chair, staring at me for several seconds frowning and half-smiling, like a man suspecting you are pulling his leg. Embarrassed and puzzled, I explained, 'Just the usual bacteriologist's dyes, gentian violet, methylene blue, carbol fuchsin and so on.' They were used to stain bacteria to make them visible under the microscope, a notion which had come from the German Karl Weigert in the previous century. 'I was investigating the chemical reaction behind the colouring effect.'

'I see.' After another moment Domagk said, 'As you can imagine, we're always investigating the properties of dyestuffs in the labs here. I G Farben manufactures drugs, fabrics, a hundred things, but we're essentially a dye-making concern. The company is inclined to see itself as God, creating the colourful dawn and rainbows to please His fancy. You're familiar with that passage in Goethe's *West-Östlicher Divan?*' I shook my head. 'At present I'm investigating a series of dyes, to discover if they've any therapeutic effect against various bacteria.'

It struck me as curious that I G Farben should dissipate its scientists' time seeking remedies in the colours of curtains and girls' dresses. The only dyestuffs I recalled being used as medicaments were the bright yellow proflavine and the brilliant green which had disfigured my adolescent face worse than the impetigo spots they were applied to cure. While speaking, Domagk had taken from a desk drawer a reprint of his own, on which he scribbled and handed to me with a dismissive, 'Please pass that on to Sir Frederick, with my regards and respects.'

I saw the paper was entitled in German, *The Destruction of Infectious Agents.*
The date was 1926. It must have been among the first scientific papers
Domagk wrote. He seemed an early recruit in man's battle against
infection, which progressed with the gloomy indecision of any which had
lurched upon the Western Front.

We rose. I nodded towards the photograph of Paul Ehrlich, remarking,
'*Geld, Geduld, Geschick, Glück*' – money, patience, skill and luck, his four
ingredients for successful research.

'Who taught you that?' Domagk asked as we reached the door.

'When I was seventeen, I worked in the Inoculation Department of St
Mary's Hospital in London…'

'So young! You will soon be a professor,' he exclaimed humorously.

'I was only a technician.' I had been the lab boy, the equivalent of an
office boy, who washed the glassware, prepared the flat round Petri dishes
for growing bacteria, and of course made the tea. 'Before Professor Ehrlich
died during the war, he had been on very friendly terms with one of the
bacteriologists at St Mary's – Professor Alexander Fleming. Perhaps you've
heard of him?'

Domagk shook his head. 'I only know the chief of the Inoculation
Department, Sir Almroth Wright. He came to visit us here at Elberfeld,
you know.' That must have been after my time. Knowing Wright's disdain
for chemistry, and particularly the systematized German variety, his
reflections on Domagk's lavishly-equipped labs would have reverberated
throughout St Mary's. 'By the way –' Domagk nodded towards Ehrlich's
photograph. 'It's a myth that he had to investigate 605 arsenicals before
discovering "Salvarsan". But he examined a good number, and
slaughtered whole armies of mice.'

In the corridor outside we found Professor Hörlein emerging from the
lab where we had met. From the way Domagk stepped back I sensed
Hörlein was an important person in the factory. But he said to me
pleasantly enough, 'You've come a long way to our city of Wuppertal, Herr
Elgar. I hope you'll find it an interesting place.' Everyone seemed to damn
Wuppertal with the faint, non-committal praise of *eine interessante Stadt.* 'The
Elberfeld Rathaus has an excellent museum, and there is a remarkable old

church in the Kolk. You have already visited our splendid Lauretuiskirke, doubtless.'

Domagk smiled. 'Wuppertal cannot offer a great deal of amusement for a young man. It's hardly Paris, *nicht wahr*? There's the cinema. And I expect you enjoy the company of Fräulein Dieffenbach.'

Professor Hörlein shook hands. 'I expect we shall see each other again.'

But we did not, until he was on trial for his life at Nürnberg.

3

'Well, what do you expect?' Fräulein Dieffenbach used an unnaturally sharp voice for arguments, or when she was embarrassed or chiding me about the puddles I left on the bathroom floor. 'We supposed everything would be settled in accordance with the famous Fourteen Points, because after all, President Wilson was a lawyer, so he could produce a just agreement in an intelligent way, without emotion or malice.'

'Whoever heard of a lawyer stopping a battle?' I asked – in German, because she spoke hardly any English.

'The Americans, obviously,' she replied primly.

'The Americans think you can fix anything if you hire a smart enough attorney.'

'That's *exactly* the remark I should have expected from you, Herr Elgar.' She was a schoolmistress, and she reproved me in her best schoolmistress manner, which sat on her as grotesquely as the broad-brimmed flat black hat she was in the act of unpinning. Her hair was so blonde it suggested an albino, and she wore it coiled in plaits over her ears, resembling a telephone girl's headphones. 'Like any educated young man who can't take things seriously, you imagine that you are a…a Rochefoucauld,' she said flatteringly, not being able to think of anyone else. 'President Wilson was a great idealist.'

'On the contrary, he was only a great optimist.'

'Well, what's wrong with that? Relying on the best in people?'

'But it's disastrous! Every leader who's tried has been painfully disappointed. Ever since Jesus Christ.'

'Now you've gone too far.' Gerda Dieffenbach was a Catholic, unlike most inhabitants of Wuppertal, renowned in Germany as a nest of stinging Protestant sects. She was a year or so older than me, tall and grey-eyed, always in appalling long serge skirts and a plain white blouse freshly laundered every day. She never used cosmetics or scent or even bath salts. She smelt wholesomely of household soap. She argued with me because I was the first Englishman she had met in her life, and because argument is flirtation with intelligent young women who are not sure of themselves. I did not really argue at all. I teased, enjoying the delicious spectacle of her pink with indignation, her soft mouth open breathlessly.

It was early evening that same Saturday, and we were in the shabby room where everyone ate and sat at the front of Dr Dieffenbach's house near the Zoo. It was not a large house, and her father had to have his surgery, the waiting room and his small library, aromatic with cigars. The Gesellschaftszimmer across the narrow, tile-paved hall was filled with massive dark furniture and curtained with crimson plush, even the subjects of its solidly-framed family portraits looking uncomfortable. It was kept shuttered and unheated, mercifully reserved for important visitors, who by German custom always occupied in solitude the ugly horsehair sofa. Gerda had just come in from shopping. Her father was attending a patient, her mother gone visiting and her twelve-year-old brother Gunter somewhere out of the way. I could smell our evening meal cooking behind the double doors leading towards the kitchen, and faintly hear the wireless and the two maids calling to one another.

'Germany accepted the Fourteen Points on October 23, 1918 so that the bloodshed might be ended,' Gerda continued relentlessly. 'Then you dictated whatever terms you felt like at Versailles and tried to ruin us in the name of "Reparations". Well! How could you expect Herr Hitler to like that?'

'Why shouldn't you pay reparations? The Kaiser had planned the war for twenty years.'

'Oh, the Kaiser,' she dismissed him impatiently. 'I can't understand why you English never saw through him. He was a braggart, who simply faded

14

out during the War. We looked to Hindenburg and Ludendorff, who ran everything.'

'It was the Kaiser's U-boat campaign –'

'It was England who first made war by starving little children, with the blockade. Admit it, now – go on! I can remember perfectly well not getting enough to eat, Mama standing for hours on end just to buy a cup of watery milk or a spoonful of jam made from beetroot. We had to take down all our net curtains and cut them into bandages for the wounded. You've been reading too many English papers, *Mister.*'

She shut her lips firmly, sitting at the large circular table covered by a pink chenille cloth. Taking a pile of exercise books from the black leather bag she had brought home that Saturday lunchtime, she put on a pair of gold-rimmed glasses and started to correct the children's answers. Gerda was unusual in earning her living, in a land which preached the doctrine of *Kinder, Kirche, Küche* – children, church and kitchen – to its womenfolk as sternly as ever. Only one German woman in five worked, and they mostly toiled on the farm or in the homes of others. And to be a teacher of history in a girls' elementary school was a position of high importance and respect. I sat and opened the *Wuppertaler Zeitung* in deferential silence.

It was less than a month since I had left a nation of three million unemployed for one of five million. It had been an act of dizzy sophistication to take the boat train at Charing Cross and plunge across the Channel in a wretched little steamer with its midwinter handful of nauseated passengers. I had never been abroad before, nor even lived away from my parents, except in the narcissistic air of Cambridge. I had travelled overnight and through Ostend, as a few shillings cheaper. The Belgian train had smelt excitingly of coffee and strange tobacco, and even the direction *Do Not Lean Out Of The Window* written in French had a worldly ring I encountered before only in the library novels of Somerset Maugham and Dornford Yates.

I had sat on a wooden bench in a cramped third-class compartment like a prisoner in a black maria, face pressed against a dark window running with sleet, imagination making do for the passing countryside. I knew nothing of Belgium, except that Nurse Cavell was shot there. At

Aachen I crossed the frontier of Germany, the land to whom Nature gave no frontiers, displaying my brand new passport signed by Sir John Simon, observing, 'That faintly sinister air of leisure which invests the movements of officials at frontier stations,' which struck Christopher Isherwood. But Isherwood went to wicked, delicious Berlin – or invented it. Wuppertal was as staid as a dishful of dumplings.

I reached the Rhineland on the last afternoon of 1932, the cafés glowing yellow and people starting to toast *Prosit Neujahr*! I knew I should need strenuous and painful mental gymnastics, seeing war and peace from the opposite side of the North Sea. The Great War had stamped British thought with a black edge, like the writing paper then fashionable for proclaiming bereavement. Massive monuments had been built above the gently rolling graveyards of the Somme and the Menin Gate in Ypres, both encrusted with thousands of names, all that was left of men lost in the battlefield for ever. At home, the village war memorial shared the green with the oaks, and men doffed their hats passing the Cenotaph in Whitehall, or had them knocked off from behind. Everyone shared an experience lost with the Middle Ages, of knowing a countryman who had died untimely. My uncle Jim had been fragmented at Hazebrouck in the last German push of 1918. A regular soldier, he had survived four years so promising of promotion without even rising to the rank of Adolf Hitler.

We British wanted to hang the Kaiser for it all. But this war aim was unachieved, like all the others. Kaiser Bill was securely in exile in Doorn, peacefully reading P G Wodehouse aloud to his family and repeating all the passages which struck him as particularly funny. I knew the Germans had suffered as badly, or worse. But they did not want to hang anyone, because they did not know who to hang. They went into 1933 confused and helpless, as bitter with old leaders as old enemies.

'What were you doing, going to see Professor Dr Domagk this morning?' asked Gerda, unable to suppress her curiosity any longer.

'Don't be nosy.'

'Oh! I'm sorry.' She looked so crushed that I felt ashamed. I was learning how tender she was. She was aggressive only in her defencelessness, she feared to slacken the tight rein on her emotions lest they drove her headlong.

'I was bringing him a present from another professor,' I told her, relenting.

Her face brightened, all women being interested in presents, even for other people. 'Something nice?'

'A long lecture, reprinted as a pamphlet on best quality paper and signed by the author.'

'That doesn't sound very exciting.'

'Academic personages often exchange their lectures, with a great flourish of politeness. It's like gentlemen with their visiting cards.'

She returned her eyes to her work. 'I thought you might be seeing Professor Dr Domagk to find a better job.'

'Why? I'm perfectly happy where I am.'

'I can't understand how an intelligent chemist like you can bring himself to work in a brewery,' she said with contempt.

'Louis Pasteur worked with fermenting wine, and now there's statues of him all over France.'

'The American pays you a good salary, particularly with the rate of exchange,' Gerda said thoughtfully. She had quickly ferreted the figure out of me. I could not decide whether her serious-minded concern for my welfare was flattering or irritating. 'But why come to Germany? You could have sailed to India, like all the other English. Or Australia or Africa. There's no future in Germany, not if things go on as they are.'

'I don't fancy myself as a pukka sahib with a topi and a fly whisk.'

The Empire provided the British nation with easygoing if warmish jobs, cheap food and a sense of purpose. Though it was a cardboard palace, glittering and showy in the sunshine, artfully realistic with its plumed hats and gorgeous uniforms and battleships firing ceremonial salvos of blank ammunition, doomed since it saw defeat down the rifles of a few Boer farmers. Hitler never realized this before the day he shot himself.

'I don't know that I should like to meet your friend Herr Beckerman,' she went on. 'He sounds like a gangster.'

'You'd find him charming. He's more like an All-America footballer. I'm lucky to work for him.' Jeff Beckerman had been looking for a reliable chemist in London on his way from New York, and Sir Edward Tiplady had mentioned my name while treating him for some small ailment at the Savoy. Young Jeff always selected the best hotels as well as the best doctors.

'I hope none of the beer reaches America. Then you would be participating in something illegal.'

'Prohibition's on its way out,' I reassured her. 'It was futile of President Wilson, trying to save the American people from the horrors of drink by passing a lot of laws in 1917. Just as futile as trying to save the whole world from the horrors of war by passing a lot more in 1918. Don't tell me I'm a cynic.' I wagged my finger. 'I'm a chemist, so I look at life practically. Talking about Americans, there's a super musical film on next week called *Blondie of the Follies*. It's got Marion Davies in it. How about coming along?'

This invitation caused her schoolmistress' red-ink fountain pen to pause in mid-air and her cheeks to turn the colour of the tablecloth.

'Whatever made you think of such a thing?' she reprimanded me.

'Professor Dr Domagk. He said the only items I could find amusing in Wuppertal were the cinema and your company.'

'The professor would *never* make a remark like that.'

'Ask your father to telephone and find out.'

'You mustn't mention a word of this to Papa,' she exclaimed, delightfully flustered.

Gerda saw my invitation as a serious matter with serious implications. She seemed not to have – or she did not dare to have – any casual men friends. She was thought in the tail of childhood, in an age when marriage was an excitement preserved until the third decade, when contraception was unreliable, unobtainable and unmentionable, when abortion carried a prison sentence and the maidenhead had not yet suffered the fate of much else and become disposable. Relations between men and women were wary and ceremonious, sex a delicate dish rather than a staple diet. Such attitudes were particularly strong in the middle-classes, in Catholics, in Germany and in girls like Gerda.

She added, 'Of course, Herr Elgar, I enjoy discussing international politics with you, because you are intelligent and have been to Cambridge University. But I thought you regarded me as a sensible woman, whom you could talk to in a dispassionate way.'

'That's precisely why I want to ask you to the pictures.'

'But I almost never go the cinema,' she said, by way of another objection.

'In one so seriously-minded as yourself, Fräulein Dieffenbach,' I countered, 'self-denial is but another pleasure.'

'As you insist, I shall ask Mama if it would be all right,' she said more cheerfully, shifting responsibility.

I was calmly confident. I had noticed how she generally contrived to take the same Schwebebahn to work every morning as myself.

4

This is a story of drugs, not politics. I am a biochemist, not a historian. But it is also the story of a coincidence, which occurred in Germany over thirty-seven days astride Silversterabend, New Year's Eve, 1933.

The second of these dates was Monday, January 30, 1933. The better schooled of my present biochemistry students in London can identify it as the day which ushered Adolf Hitler to power, and so comparable with St Peter's Day 1338, when the buboes of the Black Death first festered upon Englishmen among the sailors of Melcombe Regis in Dorset. The earlier date was December 24, 1932. Even my fellow professors can remember nothing in particular about that Christmas Eve. Which suggests that the evil of the 1930s lives after them, the good was interred with the hurried riddance of their bones.

The cauldron of German democracy, which had been simmering fitfully for fourteen years since its flame was lit in the haunts of Goethe and Schiller at Weimar, came furiously to the boil that Saturday when I first met Gerhard Domagk. And nobody realized that the brew was already poisoned. No party had a majority in the Reichstag, though the Nazis – which was slang, to match 'Sozi' for Socialist – were the biggest, after advancing sensationally to 230 seats in the elections of the previous July. They always seemed to be having elections in Germany. During the past year, the Rhineland had seen five – two for the reinstatement of President Hindenburg, another for a Prussian parliament which vanished almost immediately in a local *coup d'état*, and two more for the Reichstag. They were neither the decorous cricket match contests of England nor the raucous carnivals of America. They were violent, bloody and murderous.

Since the collapse of Hermann Muller's coalition government in 1930, there was still democracy in Germany. But it was democracy gone mad, like a man gripped with mania, who performs life's normal functions of sitting, standing and speaking with a fury which seems liable to tear him to pieces.

Over the same period, Berlin had seen three Reich chancellors. The austere Catholic Heinrich Brüning had been ousted in May by a fifty-four year old political dilettante, the 'gentleman showjumper' Franz von Papen, lion faced and serpent hearted. His name was already known to the world, from being thrown out of Washington early in the Great War, a neutral diplomat trying to blow up the United States railroads. The gentleman showjumper recruited other gentlemen to his 'Barons Cabinet' from the fashionable Herrenklub in the Vosstrasse of Berlin, as British prime ministers enlisted their school friends from Eton. But before Christmas, sly von Papen was outfoxed by the affable, sharp-nosed, portly 'Socialist General' Kurt von Schleicher, whose name in German meant 'Artful Dodger', very appropriately.

To discredit his predecessor, Chancellor von Schleicher fired the haystack of the *Osthilfe* scandal, which had diverted millions of marks for agricultural relief in East Prussia into the pockets of the estate-owning Junkers. But as so hearteningly happens in politics, the flames had blown back on him. That Saturday morning he had resigned after fifty-seven days of office, in which he complained he had been betrayed fifty-seven times. The same Saturday the Government of France fell too, even more precociously, a sinister coincidence for the sore continent of Europe.

All weekend Berlin wriggled with intrigue like a fisherman's tin of worms, from which a new Imperial Chancellor had needs to be pulled by the President. Field-Marshal Paul von Hindenburg was phlegmatic, narrow, devious, benevolent, fearsomely moustached, the eternal victor of Tannenberg over the Russians in the first months of the Great War, the heroic embodiment of *Militafromm* – his countrymen's exasperating awe of the sword. Hindenburg had displaced the first President of the brand-new Republic, Friedrich Ebert. He was put up to the job by his old crony Grand Admiral von Tirpitz, who felt the country would be better presided over by a shade from the Hohenzollern monarchy than a saddler from Heidelberg. Hindenburg was voted to power by Germans with no love of a republic at any price, he had officiated for eight years impartially, incorruptibly and ineffectively, and his mind was now dimmed with the mists of eighty-six winters.

At eleven-thirty on the Monday morning – half an hour late through a last-minute squabble over the tantalizingly ripened fruits of office – a ragbag of politicians trooped from the room of State Secretary Otto von Meissner to the audience chamber of the Presidential Palace in Berlin. Only three of the dozen were Nazis, all subdued in dark suits. There was the beetle-browed shy policeman Wilhelm Frick, who had spied on his own headquarters at Munich. Hermann Göring, with a pearl tie-pin. And Adolf Hitler, displaying nothing more minatory than a party badge in his lapel.

The gentleman showjumper Franz von Papen did the honours of introduction. The President leaning on his stick, grown pettishly impatient, vitalized the new Imperial Cabinet by breathing upon it a few platitudes. He had still to appoint his new Chancellor. The office had been the gift of Kaiser Wilhelm, the Weimar constitution had subjected it to the Reichstag, but there were hands ready to twist the constitution into any desired shape. The appointment was open to doubt until sealed by the oath of office. Göebbels and the other top Nazis were waiting in the nearby Kaiserhof Hotel, extremely nervously. Only the previous Thursday, Hindenburg had sworn again that he would never invest with the mantle of Bismarck a Bohemian corporal. He never even offered Hitler a chair when he called.

But Hindenburg saw the corporal as a prisoner in a coalition. He would be defused. He would be disposed of. Only a fortnight previously, von Schleicher had declared Hitler no longer a danger, nor even a political problem, but a thing of the past. So had the Socialist messiah Harold Laski in London. The corporal became the Chancellor. Later, he became the President. He was the last before Adenauer. In between, the world entered times when God and his saints slept, as men once said about those of King Stephen.

I was unaware of stepping across three days which shakily bridged the new Europe from the old. I was far more concerned with taking Gerda to the pictures. This was partly because the trivia of human existence continue with the resilience of human life itself. And partly because citizens of the British Empire had the reputation for walking the world with an air of supreme indifference towards the natives.

We went to the cinema the following Thursday night. Gerda changed from her habitual serge to a blue and white cotton dress in bold stripes reaching almost to her ankles, which I self-flatteringly suspected to be new and perhaps even bought for the occasion. A small round fur-trimmed hat turned her disquietingly from a good-looking schoolmistress to a pretty girl. The family and the two maids gathered in the hall to wave us off. We might have been starting on our honeymoon.

We took the Schwebebahn for ten stops to the Old Market station across at Barmen. We found the market square itself packed with an excited crowd. There was another Nazi demonstration, a march of the Sturmabteilungen, the SA, Hitler's Storm Troopers, the Brownshirts. Germany had been locked for years in a brawl of private armies, the Sturmabteilungen against the Communists' Rote Frontkampfer, squads of the ex-Servicemen's Stahlhelm and the Social Democrats' Reichsbanner Schwarz-Rot-Gold waiting to be at somebody's throat in the sidelines. The Storm Troopers of 1933 well outnumbered the troops of the German army. They were recruited from street corners and given clothing, food and a sense of identity, when the Government signally failed to provide all three. England had luckily rid herself of such bands with the fifteenth-century Wars of the Roses. America escaped them – the Civil War was a far more official affair. Ulster suffers them to the day I write. Much that I then saw in Germany reminded me of Ireland during the worst of the Troubles, which coloured the daily papers of my childhood.

We could hardly move in the square. Everyone was shouting and jerking their right arms into the Nazi salute. The Storm Troopers wore brown shirts, breeches and jackboots, the Sam Browne leather crossbelt of British officers and the peaked cap of American baseball players. Germans bathe voluptuously in the warmth of crowds, losing their identity and insecurity. They love and honour uniforms, they instinctively obey rank. I stood on the pavement, tucking my Trinity scarf into my lapels against the cold. I remembered the story about the extras in a German war film, lunching in the AGFA studio canteen, automatically dividing into actors playing officers at the head of the table and other ranks below the salt.

The Brownshirts were of course nothing like the clean-cut stern-faced ranks of the party photographs and posters. In common with the rest of mankind, Storm Troopers came in all sizes, skinny and paunchy, lanky and dwarfish, adolescent and middle-aged. People in the crowd were singing snatches of the *Horst Wessel Lied*, the Nazi anthem written by a Berlin pastor's son who went to the bad and got himself killed in the streets, and achieved like many other stupid people only martyrdom. The tune's one virtue seemed to me a capability of being sung by absolutely everybody, like *It's a Long Way to Tipperary*.

They tramped in columns of four, at their heads drummers and flags. The swastika had been familiar enough in German streets since the summer of 1920, when it was suggested to Hitler as an emblem by his dentist, and run into a flag on a housewife's sewing-machine. As Gerda half-saluted and half-waved, I noticed her eyes wide and brilliant in the gaslight. 'You see,' she said excitedly, stimulated by the show and infected with the surrounding emotion, 'now we can start taking pride in our country again.'

My only feeling was pain that foreigners behaved in so exaggerated a manner. It occurred to neither of us that the force embodied in that procession would shortly leave Europe strewn with corpses like autumn leaves, as casually to be gathered and burnt.

We pushed our way through the onlookers. I bought Gerda some chocolate. We sat at the back of the cinema and she let me hold her hand, which soon became very damp. She stared at the Hollywood musical with the same innocent admiration as at the marching Storm Troopers. Anonymous and unseen in the darkness, she became unnaturally – or perhaps naturally – girlish. It may have been *Wirklichkeitsflucht*, a flight from reality, from the joyless and inhibited life of an ill-paid State employee in the rigid society of Wuppertal, forever whispering over its fences and peeping through its lace curtains. Nazism itself had foundations of the same fantasy.

Then something happened, an incident so trivial and unhurtful in its gruesome context that it invited only forgetfulness. But hair-triggers fire heavy charges in the human mind. Perhaps it saved a ripe soul from the Nazis.

The Nazis disapproved of *Blondie of the Follies*. It was American, it was bourgeoise, it was degenerate, it had the fingerprints of Jews all over it. They had a well-tried technique for exhibiting such displeasure. In summer, they loosed moths which flew into the limelight. In winter, they let free mice or rats. We were in for a different demonstration. Two men in raincoats, to which they had added swastika armbands, jumped to the stage with its screen amid the potted palms, and ripped the material to ribbons with sheath-knives. The projector flickered out. The house lights went up. Everybody fell dumb. Once visible, the pair appeared as barely grown boys, who contented themselves with flinging jeers at the heads of the audience and made off. Within a month or two, such cinematic entertainments were to be banished from German soil, until Betty Grable arrived on the heels of the American Army.

I turned to see what Gerda had made of it. She was in tears, biting her knuckles, shaking with anger. 'Oh! The swine,' she cried in disappointment. 'The swine, spoiling my evening.'

'Perhaps we can get our money back,' I suggested, taking the practical view.

'Why did they want to do that? *Why did they*? I was so enjoying it.'

'Let's go and have some coffee instead.'

'It was all so innocent, so nice. Why did they want to spoil it?' she repeated furiously.

'The film doesn't fit in with their politics, I suppose.'

'What have politics to do with going to the cinema?' she demanded. 'I've been looking forward to this evening, ever since I first thought you were trying to ask me.'

We had a cup of coffee and went home. Naturally, we never got our money back. But Gerda remembered the evening. She laughed when I reminded her last summer, in the little gravel and shrub garden of her house near the Zoo at Wuppertal, a town now as bright and glittering in the smokeless air as Wordsworth's London, the Wupper between banks of well clipped municipal grass beneath the Schwebebahn as sweetly flowing as Edmund Spenser's Thames. Wuppertal has become so clean and odourless she says it is like living in a convalescent hospital.

5

The big black dog became a monster with eyes of firelit emeralds, the white steep-roofed cottage which it guarded dazzled us for a second then reeled into the darkness. We sped through a cramped village with an angular, elegantly spired church and past farmhouses cheerlessly black, countrymen the world over turning their backs on the night. On a hill I caught the turreted outline of a schloss, ahead wet bare trees, snow falling thinly between them and swirling on the ground as it never did in England, broad sheaves of telephone wires undulating gently from post to post as far as we could see. It was about eight in the evening of Monday February 27, a fortnight after my excursion with Gerda. Jeff Beckerman was taking me for a night out in Cologne. The distance was about thirty miles, the road running south along the River Wupper through Solingen, a town famous like Sheffield for scissors and knives. The autobahn still lay in the mind of Germany's new ruler, with a lot of other things.

Jeff Beckerman laughed. 'You're scared.'

'I'm not used to motoring,' I said shortly. My father could never have owned a car, even when Mr Morris of Oxford was putting wheels under the British masses.

'She could do a hundred miles an hour, if the road was good.'

I watched uneasily as the speedometer needle hovered round sixty. Jeff drove a car which I had never heard of before nor seen since, a Cord L29 Phaeton which he had shipped extravagantly from America in contempt for the Bugattis and Bentleys, the Delahayes and Alfas, which fulfilled the need for mobility and cutting a dash among Europe's young bloods. It was long and white, its silvery headlights a foot across, its running boards merging into a pair of front mudguards as elegant as an actress' eyebrows. I am a mechanical ignoramus, but I gathered that it was designed by a man called Erret Lobban Cord to be propelled through the front wheels, and that our whitewall-tyred spares were strapped either side of the enormous flat bonnet because these front wheels had a tendency to fall off.

'Berlin was *fantastiche*, utterly *fantastiche*.' The word had just superseded *wunderbar* in Jeff Beckerman's conversation. 'Berlin's nothing like Wuppertal. It's nothing like the rest of Germany. It's like America, only more like America than America could ever dare – you get me? Berlin's *real*. The skin's torn off, you can see the raw flesh and nerves underneath. I had the feeling that no one was playing a part, not the girls in the cabarets, the pimps and the crooks, they *revel* in what they're doing. Even the whores put their heart and soul into their job.'

My employer did not spend much time in Wuppertal. He preferred leaving his brewery to Herr Fritsch, the grey-faced elderly manager in his pince-nez and 'butterfly', as the Germans called a wing collar. Jeff was interested in Germany, in the bouncy way he was interested in women or his car, He regarded his exile as an educative jaunt before returning to New York and getting down to the serious business of making a million. 'What about our brownshirted friends?' I asked. 'Didn't they spoil your fun?'

'Why should they, old man?' Jeff often used this expression which is sprinkled on English conversation like salt, but always getting it a little wrong by putting the emphasis on the end, sounding slightly sneering. 'You don't have to walk into trouble, neither in Berlin nor Chicago.'

'You don't rate Adolf Hitler's gangsters more dangerous than Al Capone's?'

'I don't. Capone runs a gang of crooks, Hitler's are disciplined like the Army.' With his teeth, he pulled off his leather gauntlet, a reflector of chiselled red glass on the back – the latest thing for displaying driving signals. From the pocket of his ankle-length black leather motoring coat, a trophy from Berlin, he produced a packet of Chesterfields. 'What are the newspapers saying about Hitler in England?'

'I don't know. My mother sends me the *Sunday Graphic* every week, but it seems filled with pictures of the Royal Family.'

I lit the cigarette jutting from his full lips. Jeff was five or six years older than me, red-faced and too fleshy, but still giving the impression of an athlete. He wore his brown hair *en brosse*, his heavy eyebrows transecting his face as a single bar. He enjoyed a long-standing intimacy with money, which reduced it to a reckoning in his daily plans no more intrusive than breathing. Like many Americans, his life was a tropical sea of hedonism traversed by occasional icebergs of Puritanism. His father owned chemical companies in New York State – but of course he was making a fortune from bootlegging. The Beckermans brewed beer long before dropping their final 'n' en route from Hamburg to Ellis Island, and would brew it again when American thirsts might be legally slaked.

Jeff enjoyed a simultaneous reverence and contempt for academics with First Class degrees like myself. He respected me as the only man in Wuppertal with whom he could hold an intelligent conversation. But he would have offhandedly packed me home with barely the fare in my pocket. He could be very simple or very shrewd, equally infuriatingly. He might have inhabited the America of Scott Fitzgerald, which vanished in a similar puff of misunderstanding, ridicule, nostalgia and shame as the British Empire. *The Great Gatsby* had been on bookshelves for seven years, but I doubt if he had read it. Jeff only read books which helped him to get on.

The journey was bone-shaking, snow seeping round the celluloid side-screen. Jeff had lent me his raccoon coat, and I still wore my Trinity scarf. The road ran close to the huge pharmaceutical works at Leverkusen, a blue circle in the sky as tall as the factory chimneys which supported it proclaiming twice BAYER, the words crossed at the Y. KÖLN glittered in the diamonds of a road sign. I had not returned there since New Year's Eve, when I had changed trains at the Hauptbahnhof in the shadow of its dazzling skyscraper of a cathedral. Jeff took the Hohenzollern Bridge across the Rhine, the river which flows through the German soul.

He cursed. The far end of the bridge was blocked by another of the uniformed processions which crawled like worms over the body of Germany. This one presented 'the torchlight red on sweaty faces'. The Brown Shirts were stamping between the Cathedral and the Tankgasse, small knots of spectators in the falling snow raising arms through enthusiasm or prudence, while flankers pressed pamphlets upon them.

Jeff had to stop. The ends of the bridge, the walls everywhere, were plastered with posters. Hitler had dissolved the Reichstag, there was to be yet another election the following Sunday, March 5. As a foreigner, I found neither significance nor even identity in the dreary gallery of political faces – except Adolf Hitler's, as instantly recognizable today, with his lower middle-class, Austrian 'little man' moustache, which you still see decorating street cleaners and tram conductors in Vienna. *Deutschland Eswache!* cried the Nazis' posters. They had stolen the vivid red of their Communist arch-enemies, their message in Gothic type always angry, vituperative and vile, and always highly effective.

Waiting patiently, I recalled how Cologne had recently shone in the political news. The gentleman showjumper Franz von Papen had craftily made a secret rendezvous there with Hitler behind the back of Chancellor 'Artful Dodger' Kurt von Schleicher – who got wind of it, planted a spy with a camera, and had it over the next morning's newspapers. Hitler anyway regarded the gentleman showjumper as a joke. So absurd a joke that he later planned to provoke his invasion of Austria in 1938 by having Ambassador Papen in Vienna spectacularly murdered.

'There doesn't seem to be any trouble.' Jeff tapped the steering-wheel with his reflecting gauntlets. 'The Jews keep well out of sight, and the Communists choose their own time and place to trail their coat. I guess everyone else is too cold or too scared, and staying home. This sort of game is played in Berlin every night – you should have seen it when Hitler became Chancellor, the SA in thousands, parading in the Tiergarten and marching in columns through the Brandenburger Tor and along the Unter den Linden. There was nothing of a rabble about it. Everything was very military, bands playing and the marchers singing their heads off.'

'What was the reaction?'

'Rapturous. You know how the Germans love a torchlight procession.' He flicked up another Chesterfield. 'And they say old Hindenburg looked down from his window muttering "*Du lieber Gott*, I never knew we'd taken so many Russian prisoners".'

We were making for a cabaret called the Sphinx, of which Jeff had heard from some *fantastiche* girl called Heike in Berlin. It was hardly the famous Parisian Sphinx, where I went – off limits – with the Americans after the Liberation, and where girls did strange things with cigarettes. We discovered a narrow dark doorway, a sequence of white electric bulbs writing *Sphinx* continually above. It was somewhere in the old town within the elbow of the Rhine between the Hohenzollern Bridge and the suspension bridge to the south, near the Gurzenich, the building where laws were made for the Holy Roman Empire. Through the unhappy propensity of Europeans for blowing up each other's cities, the whole area is now replaced by orderly pedestrian precincts providing all services from supermarkets to sex shops.

The lobby was flanked with panels of coloured glass depicting palms, pyramids and camels, symbols of greater romance and mystery to the Germans than the British, who policed them. Jeff's brow clouded. It clearly was not a patch on *fantastiche* Berlin. But I was excited enough, never having been inside a cabaret before.

Down a narrow staircase hung a crimson plush curtain guarded by a German in fez and tasselled uniform, suggesting an advertisement for Abdullah Turkish cigarettes. The management tired abruptly of Eastern pretence. Beyond was a long brightly-lit basement resembling a teashop, with wall mirrors and small wicker tables under white fringed cloths, each with a numbered card in a bamboo holder and an old-fashioned telephone. At the far end, the curtain was down on a small stage, and two men in tails played *How Deep is the Ocean* on piano and drums as though it were a march. Attendance was thin, the weather and political turmoil not being conducive to carefree nights out.

'In Berlin, there's men dressed as women and women dressed as men,' complained Jeff.

The waiter in a floor-sweeping apron suggested champagne. Jeff ordered beer. He sat back in his fragile-looking gilt chair, lighting another cigarette and scowling. His black and white check tweeds came from Savile Row, his silk shirt from Florence, his foulard tie from the Rue de Rivoli. He dressed his part as man of the world. 'If you want a girl, you call up her table number,' he explained, nodding towards some gaudily dressed women sitting alone or in pairs against the walls.

But my attention was diverted by waiters equipping the patrons at tables near the stage with long bibs of red rubber. I was speculating what fancy dish might be on its way, when the curtain rose to a roll on the drums, revealing a small roped boxing ring, a mirror sloping above, into which a melancholy man in a long white coat was tipping buckets of greenish mud.

Jeff stuck his thumb in his top waistcoat pocket. 'We're going to see a couple of girls wrestling in mud.'

'Why mud?' I asked in surprise. 'Girls wrestling would be unusual enough for me.'

'It has to be in mud. The Germans have a genius for the extreme.'

It was a coy, even lugubrious entertainment. One girl was fresh-faced and solidly-built, good looking in a farmyard way. The other was pale and sad, seeming in need of a square meal. Both were dressed for the beach, in white rubber bathing caps and ankle-length robes of dazzlingly patterned towelling, removed to reveal swimsuits demurely skirted across the tops of their thighs. They climbed into the ring and braced themselves against the ropes, like the prize-fighters in the newsreels. The band broke into Franz von Suppé's *Light Cavalry*. They fell upon each other, standing in the mud with their breasts pressed together, slapping each other's buttocks.

'This election's going to be a walkover for Hitler.' Jeff was affecting intense tedium. 'He's got big business in his pocket – I heard in Berlin how Sacht and Göring fixed it.'

The music stopped. The wrestlers separated, standing in their corners glistening with green mud, their heaving breasts decrying any sham in the struggle. Jeff lit another cigarette. 'Hey, have you read Hitler's book, *Mein Kampf*?' I shook my head. 'This *fantastiche* girl Heike translated bits for me.'

'You talk politics with whores, do you?'

Jeff looked offended. 'She's a student learning English.'

I have since smelt through its flatulent pages. They expose the author's contempt for the mass of his fellow-Germans and his greatest respect for the English – so much for our Great War Prime Minister, the reader might imagine that Lloyd George knew Hitler's father. It spelt out the Führer's plans with such determined precision, it is unfortunate that it was not translated in bed to an English statesman by some other wayward student of his language.

The bout restarted, the girls entwined on their floor of mud, flicking the rubber bibs of the nearest spectators. 'Only the Army can stop Hitler now,' Jeff continued.

'Why should they? He's hardly a pacifist.'

'But he's an upstart, and the Germans are even worse snobs than the English.' The pale girl grabbed the larger one between the legs, tipping her overhead into the mud then sitting astride her waist. The pair were barely distinguishable, covered with green slime. One of the big girl's breasts plunged free from her slippery bathing-suit. 'That was as rehearsed as the gestures in Hitler's speeches,' observed Jeff.

I quoted Comte de Mirabeau, ' "Other states have an army, in Prussia the army has a state".'

Jeff countered this with a grin. 'What do you expect, in a country which calls war the continuation of foreign policy by other means?'

'Clausewitz' remark was irresponsible and immoral.'

'At least it was logical.'

The thin girl was acclaimed the winner. Both disappeared for a shower. The waiters began untying the red rubber bibs. Within six months, this entertainment would be banned in Germany, along with the music of Mendelssohn and the novels of Thomas Mann.

Then I noticed at a table against the wall the dark Slav girl from Professor Domagk's laboratory.

6

'She looks a pretty thing, why don't you call her up?' Jeff indicated the telephone.

'Don't be ridiculous! She'd be dreadfully embarrassed.' I had recounted our meeting in the laboratory at Wuppertal.

'She's peddling her ass, she isn't in the position to be embarrassed about anything. You're not a sissy, are you?'

'Of course I'm not!' Jeff was 'kidding', as an Englishman 'chaffed'. But I could never be certain how thick his cushion of amiability was between jest and truth. In the end I thought it wise to invite her. She rose wearily, not recognizing me until about to sit down at our table. I introduced *Herr Beckerman aus Amerika*, and asked, 'What's your name?'

'Magda.'

'You're not from Cologne, surely?'

'From Vienna.' She crossed her hands modestly in the lap of her mauve shot-silk dress. I noticed how much more heavily made up she was.

'Don't I G Farben pay enough?'

She gave an unfriendly look. 'I'm of a large family.' She added, as though she were moonlighting as a respectable waitress or shopgirl, 'Everyone has to take a second job in Germany.'

'Ask what she wants to drink,' interrupted Jeff in English, impatient at exclusion from the conversation.

'Champagne,' Magda said automatically.

We held a three-cornered conversation in English and German over the bottle. Jeff never learned German, partly from impatience and partly because he feared the natives could outsmart him in their own language.

Magda smiled as I translated his gallantries, but she struck me as acting badly the *fille de joie*. 'How much does she charge?' Jeff enquired abruptly.

Magda told me fifty marks, about four pounds.

'Why don't you go with her?' asked Jeff amiably. He took out his wallet and fluttered a fifty-mark note on the table. 'I'll grub-stake you – if that's the correct expression.'

'Don't be ridiculous! I couldn't possibly pick up a girl so blatantly.'

'A man who goes off with a whore in secret is like a man who goes off drinking in secret. If I kept either from my friends, I'd be ashamed of myself.'

Jeff's tone had become abrasive, but I was more frightened of the girl than of him. Two years ago, incited by the easygoing tales of fellow-undergraduates at Trinity who were richer and worldlier than myself, I had shopped along the gaudy pavements of London's West End and picked up a tart near Marble Arch. Though I had saved for three months, I could not afford the best, and in my subsequent remorse feared that I had picked the worst. I had sponged the parts involved with dilute hydrochloric acid, which suggested itself to a chemistry student as a promising antiseptic. The result was a raw redness for which I dared invoke neither medical advice nor friendly sympathy, and I had no wish to find myself repeating the experiment. But Jeff pressed me, with the amiable wickedness of a man watching another slide into his own sins. I gave in.

Magda told us that she lived beyond the Hohenstaufenring, the first arc of boulevards and squares which spread round old Cologne like the ripples from a stone. Jeff offered us a lift. Magda suddenly became animated as she climbed into the Cord, lightly touching the steering-wheel, the shiny instruments, the gear lever and brake in open-mouthed reverence. It struck me that she had never before been in a car at all.

'*Ein wunderbarer Auto,*' she breathed.

'*Fantastiche,*' Jeff corrected her, glowing with satisfaction as he pulled on his gauntlets.

Magda stopped us at the corner of Mozartstrasse, a broad and prosperous street, saying we could walk the rest. She clearly did not wish to arrive in such grandeur. Jeff said he would find a bar, and call Heike in Berlin. He had an extravagance towards the telephone which I thought admirably American. 'I'll be back in half an hour – have a good time,' he called, roaring away and leaving a smell of high-grade petrol.

I self-consciously took Magda's arm, in equal parts aroused and ashamed. Without speaking a word, she led me towards a narrow side-street lying in the glow of a sickly gas-lamp. I had imagined our destination some disreputable small hotel or bug-infested lodging-house. As she opened the green door in a four-storied narrow terrace dwelling, I realized with alarm that I was being taken home.

The tiny hallway was unlit. I followed her towards a narrow flight of stairs with broken banisters. In gaslight seeping from a door above, a small boy and girl were grinning at me

I stopped. Desire fled. Vice in such domestic surroundings was ridiculous. 'I don't want to,' I said.

Magda turned. 'You'll still have to pay me.'

I pushed at her Jeff's fifty-mark note, which she folded carefully and put in her large brown handbag. I turned to the door, eager to be out of the place. Then I imagined myself standing half an hour on a freezing street corner. 'Could I have some coffee?' I asked plaintively.

Silently, Magda led me to a kitchen downstairs at the back, stone-floored and lit by the glow of the stove. An old man smoking his pipe rose and left at once, bowing to me with a deference which doubled my feelings of guilt. Magda removed her imitation leather overcoat and lit the gas mantle. I heard scuffling upstairs. The house was as crammed with humans as a warren with rabbits. 'You've a large family, you said?'

'Four brothers.' She added sourly, 'All out of work.'

'Was that your father?'

'Yes.' She moved a saucepan of coffee on to the black iron stove. 'He's an engineer, but he lost everything when the mark fell to zero. So did everyone else, of course.' She spoke as if describing a bad summer which had ruined their holidays.

I sat at a small, rough wooden table which smelt of onions. 'How long have you been at I G Farben?'

'Since the summer. I should have been a chemist, you know. I'm well educated. But in Germany today, nobody can achieve what they deserve. All I do is keep the place clean and look after the laboratory animals.'

'What's Professor Dr Domagk like to work for?'

'He likes to keep himself to himself. He's all right, except when anyone makes a mistake. Not just me, one of the other doctors or chemists. Then he just blows up.' She screwed a finger-tip against her temple. 'His mind works so fast, he's always a jump ahead.'

'What sort of dyes is the professor trying to turn into medicines?' I asked, partly from curiosity, partly from mischievousness over their secrecy.

She replied in her dull way, 'How should I know? Almost every day another compound comes to be tested from Dr Mietzsch and Dr Klarer.'

I had the feeling of meeting an acquaintance in a foreign land. I had heard at Cambridge of Dr Fritz Mietzsch, the chemist who in 1930 had synthesized a drug for the treatment of malaria. The disease had formerly been dosed with quinine, Nature's product from cinchona bark in Peru – the 'Jesuit's bark', which the ague-racked Oliver Cromwell stoutly refused to let stick in his throat. Sitting in Magda's kitchen, I remembered that the name of Mietzsch's new anti-malarial chemical was mepacrine hydrochloride, but that I G Farben had dressed it in the fancy title of Atebrin'. I also recalled that mepacrine hydrochloride was an acridine derivative, a bright yellow synthetic dye. Was Domagk trying to cure other tropical infections? I wondered. But Domagk had spoken to me of using dyes against 'various bacteria', which to the precise scientist did not mean the parasites causing malaria or other tropical diseases, but the streptococcus and staphylococcus and tubercule bacillus which swarmed so richly round mankind everywhere. I repeated, 'What dyes?'

'Why are you so interested? Were you sent to Germany as a spy?' She poured the coffee into a pair of enamel mugs.

'Secrets and cheese go bad with keeping, Fräulein. People begin to smell them. Are they yellow acridine dyes?' I persisted as she sat beside me. 'Remember, I've given you fifty marks tonight.'

'It makes no difference to me if I spend half an hour with you down here or upstairs.' She jerked her head upwards. 'I'm forced into it by the system,' she continued bitterly. 'By what's happening in Germany. Everyone at each other's throats and the politicians in Berlin squabbling like washerwomen. Perhaps everything will change with Hitler. He certainly seems to know what's wanted.'

'But I *admire* you. Doing that to provide for your family.'

'What's admirable in degradation?'

'It's a matter of motives, *nicht wahr*? Killing people was widely advertised as highly admirable during the war.'

She sipped her coffee for some time in silence. 'Well, *Mister* Englishman, sympathy's not something I enjoy every day, I assure you. I don't suppose it makes much difference if I tell you they're red azo-suiphonamide dyes.'

That was interesting. I was familiar enough with sulphonamide, but I had never heard of its use for killing bacteria. 'They don't work like ordinary disinfectants,' she said. 'They're not like carbolic or formalin. Professor Domagk injects them into infected mice.'

'Do the mice live or die?'

'Die. Have you got a cigarette?'

'I don't smoke.'

As she felt in her handbag for a packet of cigarettes, she produced a folded sheet of paper. 'Have that, if you like. The mice don't always die. There was a lot of excitement in the lab just before Christmas. One of the dyes which Dr Mietzsch and Dr Klarer sent up to be tested was very successful. That chit will tell you all you want. Don't let anyone see it. I should never have taken it.'

She lit a cigarette. We talked for some time about the coming election, German politics, Lloyd George. She rose, and thrust into the stove a piece of jagged wood from a pile apparently scrounged from fences or dilapidated buildings. I had a moment to open the paper and observe a printed list of different bacteria down one side, scrawled writing down the other. 'I was intending to sell it,' Magda said frankly, 'but I should never meet anyone who might be interested. The American will be back,' she added, reaching for her coat.

Magda turned out the gas. As we left I could see the two children again, eyeing us from the stairs and whispering excitedly over our parade of wickedness. We walked arm and arm to the street corner. The snow had stopped. 'You are a chemist, mein Herr?' I nodded. She made a circular gesture round her face. 'You have the look of an English lord.' I laughed. 'Where do you live? In London?'

'Yes, in a big house in Harley Street. You've heard of that?' She shook her head. 'You travel to Wuppertal every day?'

'On the train. It makes a hole in my pocket.'

'Couldn't you find a job nearer home?'

'Is that a joke?'

'Perhaps you're right, and life will get better under Hitler.'

'That's what people are saying. Some don't care for him, of course, the Jews and the profiteers. But Hitler means business, you can tell that from the way he speaks. He's the only one up there in Berlin with the welfare of the ordinary people at heart. What do you suppose Schleicher and Papen and the rest are interested in? Lining their own pockets. Look at that disgraceful Osthilfe affair.'

'What about the Communists?'

'Oh, the Communists! They take their orders from Moscow. Hitler will soon put paid to *them*, thank God. They frighten the life out of me.'

She threw her half-finished cigarette into the gutter as we reached the main road. Jeff was in the Cord just round the corner. 'Hey, do you know what?' He opened the driver's door. 'I just got through to Berlin. The Reichstag's gone up in smoke. The whole town's out in the streets looking at it. It started around nine this evening, the sky's as red as dawn and they're expecting the dome to fall in any minute.'

I translated the news to Magda. 'A pity the deputies weren't all inside,' she said.

We dropped her at the Sphinx, Jeff not bothering to switch off the engine. She hurried inside to find another customer. As she waved from the doorway with its camels and palm trees, I raised my right arm and called jokingly, 'Heil Hitler'. She returned a smile, the first I had seen from her. I never encountered this early supporter of Hitler again. But she was a Slav, and doubtless ended with a red line ruled through her name in a concentration camp.

7

The Red Crown Brewery was in Barmen, the opposite end of Wuppertal to the I G Farben works. It was a much smaller but equally hybrid collection of wood and red brick, exhaling the same black smoke from its tall chimneys. The brewing was done in a tall narrow building with Gothic windows and turrets, like a self-confident chapel in South Wales. It had been there since the 1870s, breathing its spicy smell over the area like a genial benediction.

My cupboard-like laboratory was on the top floor of the administration block, over the office which Jeff Beckermnan shared with Herr Fritsch, the manager in the butterfly collar. When I arrived at eight-thirty the morning after our jaunt to Cologne, I was surprised to find Jeff in the lab already. He was smoking a Chesterfield and holding a bottle I recognized as a famous brand of London gin.

'Hey, that Reichstag fire's sure started something,' he greeted me excitedly. 'I've just been on to our agent in Berlin. They've got the man who set it alight. He's a Dutchman, called van der Lubbe or something – a Communist, well known to the police. That's raised hell, naturally. The Storm Troopers are out everywhere, rounding up the Communists and shouting the State's in danger. There's a rumour that the police have already got Torgler.' He was the leader of the Communist party in the Reichstag. 'They reckon to lay their hands on the other ringleaders before the day's out.'

I unwound my Trinity scarf. 'So, the Communists have obliged Herr Hitler as the Jesuits obliged King James.' Jeff looked puzzled. 'The Gunpowder Plot – Guy Fawkes,' I explained. 'It needs a genius for mismanagement, starting out to blow up the seat of authority and ending up being burnt annually in effigy.'

'It won't be effigies of the Communists going up in smoke. Hitler's been waiting his chance to rub them out ever since he took over. My God, how Germany fascinates me! Like I was fascinated by a nigger's corpse they fished out of the Hudson one day when I was a kid. It was bloated, looking like it might explode any minute, with slugs crawling out of it.' As he spoke, Jeff was swilling out a laboratory beaker under the tap of my square sink. 'I want you to try this gin.'

'It's too early.'

'Only a sip. Take it neat.' He handed me the beaker.

'God, how foul!' I spat the mouthful into the sink. 'It tastes like petrol.'

Jeff was amused. 'Maybe it is. I got it off one of your countrymen. It *looks* like the genuine article, OK? I guess a lot of people in the States would have paid good money for it. That's the racket. They reckon only one bottle of smuggled gin in a hundred is real.'

Times were hard for bootleggers, like everyone else. Jeff's father had bought the Red Crown Brewery in May 1931, and a fair share of the brew went by dray to Rotterdam and Hamburg then Toronto or Tampico, bribery greasing a path for it across the frontiers. A bottle of Red Crown in New York must have cost more than a bottle of good claret in Wuppertal, but Americans relished a wholesome German beer. It amuses me in America today seeing imported Red Crown advertised in the colour supplements as indicating the educated taste of its drinkers.

'You know my old man's permitted to handle alcohol by the United States Government, because he runs a chemical plant,' Jeff continued, while I rubbed my smarting lips with a handkerchief. 'A lot of it's on the level, he sells his products dirt cheap just to keep the Federal permits going. Of course, the Government puts all sorts of crap in the alcohol to make it undrinkable. You've heard of "boiling"?' I shook my head. 'You redistill the industrial alcohol, but it doesn't always work out. I want you to find a way of redistilling what's in this gin bottle, so we can get ninety per cent pure alcohol from it.'

'You've a delicate consideration for the health of your customers.'

'Oh, bull!' He laughed. 'We make better gin, we charge double price. I can pick up these bottles and forged labels anywhere.'

I objected. I told him I wasn't a bootlegger. There was always the chance of blindness or death from drinking impure alcohol, a possibility I did not want on my conscience. Jeff coloured, his thick bar of eyebrow drawn into a scowl. I always felt nervous of courting his anger. But he unexpectedly gave a nod and said, 'You're right, I guess. I pay you. Hitler pays the SA. But it's no excuse for them giving him value for his money.' He stared at the deceptive bottle in his hand, ending from the doorway, 'Anyway, it's a sure bet they're going to repeal the Eighteenth Amendment, Roosevelt's saying it's a cause of the Depression.'

He left me to work. My job was to analyse samples of beer for sugars, chlorides, contaminants like copper or iron from the pipes and vats, for acidity and of course for the degree of alcohol. I usually started my morning by lighting the pair of Bunsen burners to reinforce the sluggish central heating, but the weather had turned mild overnight and everything was dripping. 'Hitler's weather,' Gerda had observed on the Schwebebahn. 'It's always fine when he wants to make a big speech. People will think he can order that about, too.'

That morning I had something more important in mind than the analysis of beer. I pulled up a tall stool and sat at the lab bench, spreading on the heavily stained wood the sheet of paper I had taken from Magda. It was headed in Gothic type, *Nr. des untersuchenden Laboratoriums Prof. Dr Domagk.*

Scribbled figures gave the reference number of the experiment. Underneath came a printed table.

Giftigkeit pro 20g Maus

a)	intravenos	%	lebt	tot
b)	subkutan	%	lebt	tot
c)	per os	%	lebt	tot

More figures had been scribbled to show the percentage living and dying after Domagk had dosed his infected twenty-gram mice – either intravenously, subcutaneously, or through a minute stomach-tube, as I had seen performed in the labs at Cambridge. Below was a list of twenty-five common bacteria, the causes of diseases like pneumonia, TB, gonorrhoea or meningitis. Top of the list was the streptococcus, the germ in beadlike chains which I had seen down the microscope in Domagk's study. A pencilled note against its name said in German, *Organisms taken from patient dying of septicaemia. Given in dilution 1:1000 in broth. All twelve treated mice alive!!* At the bottom came *Wuppertal-Elberfeld*, 24 Dez 1932, the Unterschrift a large scrawled initial D.

It was a jotted laboratory note, intended for eyes which had read a thousand similar, discarded after incorporation in the report on a string of experiments. I doubted if anyone had missed it. So the mice in Domagk's cages, suffering the equivalent of fatal human blood-poisoning, were being saved by the red azo-sulphonamide dye mentioned by Magda. I was getting to know more that was going on inside I G Farben than any inhabitant of Wuppertal.

There were some reference books left by my predecessor, an elderly chemist with Franz-Josef mutton-chop whiskers who had dropped dead in the laboratory two years previously. I was not hopeful of finding much to brush up my knowledge of the sulphonamide compounds. Oppenheimer's *Der Fermente ihre Wirkungen*, published in 1928 at Leipzig, yielded only the pleasant discovery of Frederick Gowland Hopkins writing about *Das Schwefel-System* – Hoppy on sulphur. Then I opened a book I had hardly noticed. It was a lucky find. It bore an inscription on the flyleaf to my predecessor from a brother-chemist working across town at the Farbenfabriken, and was on the chemistry of dyes.

I translated to myself a section headed *The Sulphonamide Group*, which started, *P Gelmo of Vienna in 1908 synthesized 4-aminobenzene-sulphonamide* (J prakt. Chem. 77,372).

There followed the formula. This was basically a benzene ring, the familiar six-sided lozenge. At its north point, hydrogen and nitrogen combined as a 'radical', written in chemist's shorthand H_2N. At the south, hydrogen and nitrogen were combined with oxygen and sulphur as a 'sulphamino radical', SO_2NH_2. The reference was to the German *Journal of Practical Chemistry*, which I could easily look up at Cambridge – if I ever got back there. I had never heard of the Austrian chemist Gelmo. But now I knew that he had invented sulphonamide when Gerhard Domagk was still a child.

A familiar name illuminated the next paragraph.

In 1909, H Hörlein of I G Farbenfabriken patented the first azo dyestuffs, which contained the sulphonamide group. These dyes showed remarkable fastness in the repeated washing and milling of the material. Hörlein attributed this to a strong affinity between the sulphonamide dye and the protein of the wool.

No wonder the Hindenburg-like Professor Hörlein had been in Domagk's lab, watching over the progress of his protégé launched on a new career. The article continued about chrysoidin, a reddish, dye popular at the time in gargles and for cleaning up wounds. A Dr Eisenberg in 1913 had shown that it might kill bacteria on the surface of the body, like carbolic or any other disinfectant. But not inside it, as quinine killed the parasite causing malaria.

The section ended,

In 1919, the Americans M Heidelberger and W A Jacobs independently found that azo compounds could be effective against bacteria in vitro. (J Amer. chem. Soc., 41, 2145) Their paper noted that azo compounds were being further tested for their action against bacteria by their co-worker Wollstein, whose report would be published later.

It never was. Scientific enthusiasm is as volatile as many of its products.

I straightened up on my stool. Now I had a chain of facts. The obscure Viennese chemist Gelmo had invented sulphonamide in 1908. The following year Professor Hörlein turned it into a red dye of laundry-defying tenacity. A German scientist just before the Great War and a pair of American ones just after it had half-heartedly tried sulphonamide to kill germs in test-tubes. And now Professor Domagk was using it to kill germs inside living mice.

If there is a tide in the affairs of men, which, taken at the flood, leads on to fortune, there is an ebb which must be philosophically faced as final. Had I seen the significance of those twelve mice – had I also seen the significance of a spore which my own carelessness once left growing on a plate of bacteria – I should have been acclaimed for the benefaction of both sulphonamide drugs and penicillin, noosed by my Sovereign with the blue and crimson ribbon of the Order of Merit, and presented with the blue and gold folder of the Nobel Prize, which resembles the menu of a de luxe restaurant. I did not see Domagk's mountains towering on the horizon. I thought it simply a clever experiment to show that dyes could kill bacteria. The concept of everyday 'chemotherapy' was then as difficult to grasp as everyday flights into space. That Christmas Eve of 1932, when Gerhard Domagk saw his mice were alive and jotted down double exclamation marks, was a day God shifted a piece upon the chess board of the world. On January 30th, it was the move of the Devil.

I was certain that I G Farben would have patented the drug derived from their dye. Or rather, all possible processes of its manufacture, German patent law protecting neither our beer nor I G Farben's chemicals in themselves. Before leaving for the day, I found the list of newly registered patents which Jeff kept in his office. I ran my finger down the columns until struck by the word 'Wuppertal'.

Nr. 607537, Patentiert im Deutschen Reich vom 25 Dezember 1932. Dr Fritz Mietzsch in Wuppertal-Barmen unde Dr Josef Klarer in Wuppertal-Elberfeld. I G Farbenindustrie Akt.-Ges.

They had patented sulphonamide, but this told nothing to me or the rest of the world. I G Farben patented every brainchild born in a fragmentary caul of exploitation.

I joined the crowd flooding from the brewery, lunch tins over their shoulders, starting through the gathering darkness on foot or bicycle, lighting their pipes and cigarettes – smoking at work being forbidden on pain of instant dismissal. The newsboys were yelling. On my way to the Schwebebahn I paid my fifteen pfennigs for a special edition of the *Wuppertaler Zeitung.* There were big black headlines. There seemed to be big black headlines every day in Germany at the time. They announced that President Hindenburg had signed a decree to defend the Reich against Communism. The German people were to be saved from this peril by suspending those sections of the constitution which guaranteed their civil liberties. Germans were henceforward forbidden to express any opinion they cared to, and so were their newspapers. Meetings of any kind were banned. Letters could be opened, telephones tapped. The police could arrest and search as they wished, the courts could condemn to decapitation any armed disturber of the peace. After the night's outrage of the Reichstag fire, these measures were pressed upon the President as essential by his new Chancellor, Adolf Hitler.

8

Campaigning from inside the Government, Göebbels exploited the State radio to the last decibel. From the wireless set at home, from loudspeakers rigged to lamp-posts in streets thick with red-white-and-black swastika banners, the Nazis blared their simple election message – a Vote for Hitler was a vote for the glorious tomorrow which belonged to Germany, a vote against was an invitation to the Communists to lay hands on every German and all his property. This was despite Communists being arrested by the lorry-load, to be beaten, tortured and slain, along with anyone else the Nazis did not care for. The Reichstag fire singed everybody in Germany.

But the German electorate was ungrateful for the energy which the Nazis expended on it. Hitler neither lost the election nor won. He had 288 seats in the Reichstag, needing the cohesion of his 52 German Nationalist allies to scrape a miserable majority of 16. The Catholic middle classes in west and south Germany had deserted their old parties for the Nazis, but still only 44 per cent of Germans voted for him. Those who did, through their good or selfish reasons, had to accept – and accept responsibility for – his policies to their gruesome limits. In Parliament, opposition to Hitler was divided, jealous, bitter and irreconcilable. Along these fatal flaws, democracy in Germany disintegrated.

I should have noticed one change in the Dieffenbachs' household. Most people read the local papers in Germany, but the Dieffenbachs' *Kölnische Zeitung* became replaced by the *Volkischer Beobachter* – the old *Münchener Beobachter* – published by Max Amann's press empire in Berlin. This was a running mate to Göebbels' *Der Angriff* 'Attack', first put out in 1927. The masthead title of Amann's 'National Observer' was punctuated by an eagle-crowned swastika and underscored with *Editor, Adolf Hitler*. The issue of Friday, March 24 had a photograph of the editor on the front page, in his brown shirt and Sam Browne belt, addressing the rehoused Reichstag from the stage of the Kroll Opera House in Berlin. At either hand, dark-suited, butterfly-collared officials scribbled respectfully. Behind, the President of the Reichstag, Hermann Göring, surveyed the behaviour of his assembled deputies through a pair of binoculars.

The editor seemed to have little time for the duties of his chair. Glaring headlines in Gothic type announced that Adolf Hitler had been given unfettered power over Germany, by the votes of 441 deputies against 94. The paper did not mention those arrested, or prevented from entering, or the streets outside packed with Storm Troopers yelling, 'Full powers or else – !'

So the new Reichstag had stayed in business for just eighteen days. I turned the pages. Max Reinhardt was directing von Hofmannathal's *Das Salzburger grosse Welttheater* at the *Deutsches Theater,* Oscar's Elephant Review began at eight-fifteen every evening at the Winter Garden, Dr Dralle was advertising his lavender soap at 55 pfennigs a bar, and there were terrible floods in New Zealand. The puppets danced, the rain fell, the fuse was lit to blow a hole in the middle of the twentieth century.

The grey Rhineland winter was shading into spring, the gardens livened by the flower which sounds beautiful in any language – *Osterglocken, jonquille,* daffodil. The following Sunday was Dr Dieffenbach's fifty-third birthday. He had been called to a consultation in Bonn, a small town bisected by the railway in which they said only three things ever happened – it was raining, the crossing-gates were shut, or both together. He was too poor a master of his own time to arrange a party, but I gathered that we were to dine *en famille* unusually well from venison with Kärntner Serviettenklösse, savoury dumplings served in a cloth.

The doctor was indulged to be extensively reminiscent. We had been talking at table about the Oxford Union resolution passed the previous month, *This House Will in no Circumstances Fight for its King and Country.* It had been jubilantly reported in Germany as another illustration of the degeneracy of the British Empire, were one needed. Dr Dieffenbach was singularly tolerant.

'It was just a frivolity, a *jeu d'esprit*,' he dismissed it. 'Students need an occasional outrage to save them being dulled to death with work. When I went to Kiel University from the Gymnasium to take my Tentamen Physicum, the first medical examination, I was stuffed full of Greek and Latin like a Périgord goose with corn. That was in 1898, when we were properly educated.' Dr Dieffenbach was bearded, fat and jovial, resembling King Edward VII, with whom he shared the quest for excellence in food, wine and cigars, if not women. 'A couple of years afterwards, the Government flouted the opinion of us doctors and let medical students go to university before even finishing their Gymnasium, which half demolished the intellectual level of our profession. At the same time, they let women become doctors, which completed the ruination.'

I stole a glance at spirited, argumentative Gerda, across the white-clothed table between Frau Dieffenbach and her schoolboy brother Gunter. She sat submissively sipping her hock which, like indignation, turned her a delightful pink. Her father continued in English, 'Of course, it wasn't all hard work. We had our student clubs, with their coloured caps and regalia and all that. There was a good seasoning to our young lives of *saufen und raufen*.'

I could imagine the portly, jovial doctor drinking, if not duelling. He had learned my language while 'enjoying the hospitality of Old England', as he put it. He had sailed as surgeon aboard Admiral von Spee's cruiser Gneisenau, which on December 28, 1914 had the bad luck to encounter Vice Admiral Doveton Sturdee's squadron of battle-cruisers, when the Germans arrived to raid the British radio station on the Falkland Islands in the South Atlantic. The *Gneisenau*, the *Scharnhorst* and two more German cruisers were swiftly at the bottom, with their Admiral, 2000 of his men, and his two sons. Dr Dieffenbach was lucky. He was picked up by *HMS Inflexible*, and spent the rest of the war practising among his fellow prisoners in a camp of huts near Oxford.

He resumed in German, 'We had to pass in surgery and medicine, though the attitude lingered since the Wars of Liberation that the physician was learned, the surgeon a mere butcher of men. And Germany was as riddled with charlatans as a leper with sores. We doctors had to form the...what would you call it, my dear chappie?' he interjected in

English, using the awful expression from his days of captivity. *'Gesellschaft für Bekämpfung der Kurpfushertums?'*

'The Anti-Quack Society, I suppose.'

He added gloomily, 'Well, since the War they seem to be flourishing better than ever.

Dr Dieffenbach was a product of the golden age of German medicine, which produced Hermann von Helmholtz, the descendant of William Penn, who invented the ophthalmoscope to reveal the retina of the human eye. Karl Thiersch, who perfected the paper-thin skin graft. Albert Fränkel of Berlin, who discovered the cause of pneumonia. And the indefatigable Rudolf Virchow, pathologist, anthropologist and politician, who relaid the Berlin drains, studied tattooing and stood up to Bismarck. It was the age when German doctors, unlike German lawyers, interested themselves in history, philosophy and literature, and there were two orchestras exclusively of doctors in Berlin. It was the age which finished that weekend. The Nazis could not decapitate Albert Fränkel because he had died in 1916, so during that summer they decapitated his bust.

I remarked in German that my host shared the same university as Professor Domagk.

'Oh yes, he was at Kiel after the War. He grew interested very early on in the natural defences of the body against infection, and how they might be reinforced – by some drug, for instance.' He took a mouthful of the straw-coloured wine, smacking his fleshy lips. 'Then Domagk moved to Greifswald University. That would be about 1922. Next, to Münster, to follow his same line of research. After that, Professor Hörlein, head of I G Farben pharmaceuticals here in Elberfeld –' Dr Dieffenbach jerked his head in the direction of the factory – 'discovered Domagk. Exactly as a talent scout in America discovers the latest film star.'

Frau Dieffenbach, as tall as Gerda, so fair and pale she seemed to me almost transparent, broke into our conversation with, 'Perhaps we've seen the end of the quack doctors. Standards will begin to improve all round now that Herr Hitler has got the power he wanted.'

Dr Dieffenbach nodded vigorously, prodding his napkin the firmer into his butterfly collar. 'People will have to start behaving themselves, and acting with some sense of responsibility. We've had enough of this stupid fighting between bosses and workers, between one political party and another. Herr Hitler gives us the chance, perhaps the last chance, of putting our country first instead of tearing it to pieces. And Herr Hitler achieved his full powers perfectly legally and within the constitution, mark you,' he continued in my direction. 'Despite all the spine-chilling stories put about by his enemies, of Storm Troopers seizing the Reich with their fists and boots. What happened in the Kroll Opera House last Thursday could have happened in your own House of Commons in London, Herr Elgar. Which you may already know to be an institution greatly admired by every thinking person in Germany.'

I acknowledged the compliment. The Mother of Parliaments certainly enjoyed the admiration of Adolf Hitler, who confessed warmly in *Mein Kampf*, '*The dignity with which the Lower House there fulfilled its tasks impressed me immensely.*' Sir Charles Barry's buildings beside the Thames incited his wilder enthusiasm, the sculpture and paintings thrust into its 1200 niches striking the Führer as the British Empire's Hall of Fame. It was unfortunate that the British House of Commons was later burnt down on his orders, as the German one had just been on Hermann Göring's.

'There was nothing constitutional in the slightest in Herr Hitler seizing full powers.' All four of us turned a startled glance at Gerda. She made this remark staring straight ahead, pinker than ever, fingers gripping the stem of her wine glass. 'It was a put-up job. Many more than 94 deputies would have voted against him, if they hadn't been frightened for their lives.'

Her father was scowling, unsure whether to be amused or affronted. 'My dear child, Hitler was dealing with Communists, not some debating society. Force must be met with force.'

'They're all tarred with the same brush, Communists or Nazis,' Gerda said quickly, looking frightened at herself. 'They're the ignorant led by the unscrupulous.'

'Let me tell you that the Communists wouldn't give a second thought to turning their guns on people like us, if Hitler weren't there to protect us.' He leant towards her, red-faced and angry. Her mother sat upright, looking shocked, Her little brother resumed eating industriously. 'How can you say a thing like that? As a German?'

'The Communists are Germans like us,' Gerda persisted.

'If you want your life directed from Moscow, you had better live it elsewhere than this house.'

She fell silent, staring at the tablecloth, knuckles so white against the glass that I feared she would break the stem.

Her father contemptuously blew out his lips. But he continued in a milder tone, 'Who would you rely on to defend us against the Communists, Fräulein? The Socialists wear the same red shirts, washed out. As for the Catholic parties, you might as well expect a ladies' sewing circle to round up a band of Sicilian brigands. We've seen enough of politicians dancing to tunes played outside our own frontiers. Hitler has taken full powers only to set Germany free.'

There was another silence, apart from the noise of Gunter eating. I hoped for her own sake that Gerda would hold her tongue, but she said quietly, 'Free from what?'

Dr Dieffenbach held up a stubby forefinger, angry again. 'Listen to me. You are too intelligent to misconstrue the truth, so I will assume that you have not read the newspapers very carefully. Herr Hitler has been granted full powers by the Reichstag. Correct! But hardly a blank cheque. It is to be for a strictly limited period of four years. And Herr Hitler has given his solemn promise that these powers will be used most sparingly. He has promised equally that the rights of the Church shall be respected. And the right of every State which composes the Reich. And above all, the rights of the President. Surely you could have foreseen Herr Hitler's respect for the presidency, from the photographs in the newspapers? When the two men – soldier in uniform, politician in frock coat – shook a solemn handshake in the Garrison Church at Potsdam last month, there were tears in Hitler's eyes as well as Hindenburg's.'

The brief life of the new Reichstag had begun with a theatrical excursion. Its rightful home a burnt-out shell, it had assembled above the remains of Frederick the Great. Everything had been organized by Dr Göebbels. The old Field-Marshal appeared gloriously in uniform, with Pikelhaube and a constellation of medals. Hitler, hardly a regular churchgoer, looked like a dyspeptic shopwalker.

Dr Dieffenbach unexpectedly extended the arm of friendship in my direction. 'The enemies of Germany are no longer the compatriots of Herr

Elgar. What has Hitler already said? Why, that our natural ally in Europe is England! Had the old politicians renounced to England the colonies and the seas, and spared her the edge of competition from our industry, England would have in her businesslike way given us a free hand in Russia. There would have been no bloody war. No English soldier would lie under the soil of France. Our enemies today are not even the French. They are so called Germans. Jews, profiteers, debauchers, criminals. You'll soon see, Herr Hitler will set them an honest job of work, cleaning up their own filth.'

'I'll tell on you, I'll tell on you!' Gunter screeched out gleefully, pointing a finger vigorously at his sister, his mouth full of potato. 'Herr Esmarch at school said we were to report anyone at home who said anything against Hitler.'

'We've talked enough politics for one meal,' said Frau Dieffenbach hastily. 'It's not polite before Herr Elgar. The political goings-on inside other countries are always wearisome. Who is really interested in the details of quarrels in other families? The fact that they are quarrelling is doubtless interesting, but the causes are generally trivial and the arguments deployed always deadly dull.'

We all accepted this comforting parallel gratefully. Dr Dieffenbach grunted and poured himself some more wine. He turned the talk to safe, professional subjects, recounting at length the last meeting of the Versammlung Deutscher Naturforscher und Arzte – the Congress of German Scientists and Physicians, the oldest of such societies in a country much given to lofty philosophical discussion of Nature's simple mechanics.

That night I went to Gerda's bedroom.

There were three rooms in the attic. One was shared by the pair of maids, the other two up a short stair for Gerda and myself. The wall between us was so thin that we lived in an acoustic intimacy which sometimes kept me hotly awake in the freezing darkness. I could hear the squeak of her cupboard opening, the scrape of coathangers with her heavy serge clothes along the rail – a most exciting sound, creating a vision of her in stockings and underwear, though an inaccurate and flattering one, my knowledge of these garments coming perforce from ladies' dress shop windows. My students today would think me unenterprising at not broaching the intimacy of that inch or two's lath and plaster, but in 1933 the bridal dress took firm precedence over the nightdress. I was anyway terrified at rousing with creaking boards the maids, or more horrifyingly Dr Dieffenbach himself.

That Sunday night I heard her light snap out, her bed creak, I could imagine hearing her breathing and the soft rustle of her limbs. It grew towards one o'clock. Impulsively I crept from my door, tremblingly I opened hers.

She was not asleep, because she sat up at once in her black iron bed like a hospital cot, her feather-stuffed coverlet pulled round her chin .

She whispered calmly, 'You mustn't.'

I left the door ajar. I sat on the edge of her bed in my brown flannel striped pyjamas from Marks and Spencers. I saw that she wore a white nightgown of some heavy material which covered her from neck to wrist as chastely as a surplice. I whispered back, 'I admired you tonight. The way you stood up for yourself.'

She said nothing for a moment. I noticed how her eyes shone in the faint light from the window above the bed. We were seldom in such proximity even fully dressed. But neither of us touched the other. She still smelt of household soap. 'You shouldn't have come into my room.'

I started shaking, less through emotion than because it was very cold. 'I couldn't go to sleep. I had to tell you.'

She shrugged her narrow shoulders under the white nightgown. I wanted to confess my yearning for her night after night, but I feared she would be affronted, or think me stupid. I had little practical experience of women. 'I shouldn't have contradicted my father.'

'I frequently contradict mine.'

'No, it wasn't right.'

'Of course it was right,' I told her in an urgent whisper. 'The Nazis are nothing but out-of-work clerks and penniless students, with a sprinkling of ruffians and criminals. Anyone can see that. And who is Hitler? Not a man of education and culture, like Papen. He's nothing but a corporal who managed to get himself decorated with the Iron Cross, as he's continually reminding everyone.'

'I should never have questioned my father's views. Especially like that, in front of my mother and Gunter.'

'*Why* shouldn't you?' I whispered more furiously. 'You're not a child. You're a grown woman who's entitled to her own opinions. Your parents are proud enough of your being a schoolteacher, they can hardly object to your claiming a mind of your own.'

'You don't understand.' She shook her head, her hair appearing pure white in two plaits over her shoulders. 'If I argue with my father, it makes it hard for him to preserve proper discipline, to keep order in the house.'

'To keep order?' It was a mystifying conception. I said, 'Would you like to come to the cinema again?'

'You're always asking. Perhaps next month.'

'Or go dancing?' I suggested daringly.

'I can't dance. Not a step.'

'Neither can I, in fact.'

'Why are you never serious with me?'

'With my prospects in life I can't afford to be serious with women. I can only afford flirtation.'

'You forget that I have my self-respect.'

'You mean your self-distrust?'

She responded to this only, 'Someone might hear us. That would be terrible.'

'Next Sunday I'll take you to the Zoo for tea.'

'I'll see.'

'Promise?' I urged.

'I'll have to ask Mama.'

I made to kiss her, she tipped her cheek, and I dodged on to her mouth.

'*Mister* Jim, no!' she protested under her breath.

'You are so beautiful, Gerda, just like Marlene Dietrich'

I saw from the shade of a smile in the darkness that she took the compliment seriously. I stayed where I was. She whispered fiercely, 'You *must* go.'

I quoted the old Viennese saying, '*Ich leibe dich, und du schläfst*' – I love you and you sleep.

The words made her draw in her breath, as though I had cut her. 'You shouldn't speak of such serious things.'

'Come to England with me one day.'

'Now you're telling fairy tales.'

'I'm not. The War's been over fifteen years. The people of Europe must soon get tired of shouting names at one another across their frontiers. Who outside a madhouse could want another war?'

'One day, perhaps.' She repeated wearily, 'Perhaps.'

I went back to bed. The chaste excursion had so drained me that I fell asleep at once.

9

Shared intimacy between a man and a woman can be fully recalled by a glance held a second more than necessary. But Gerda never hinted that my intrusion into her bedroom was more than a dream. A month went by. We were walking towards the Schwebebahn on our way to work, at eight in the morning of the last Friday in April. She said abruptly, 'You were quite right about Hitler that night. About him being only a jumped-up corporal. Why, he isn't even German! He's an Austrian peasant from Braunau am Inn, everyone knows that.'

'I thought he was from Vienna?'

'He was only a vagabond there, shouting his mouth off that the Army hadn't lost the war, but been stabbed in the back by the civilians—'

'Which to his mind consisted only of Socialists, Communists and Jews—'

'Exactly. Anyone would have imagined him to have fought the war as a general. He picked up a following in the gutter, and wouldn't be throwing his weight about today if the Munich policemen had shot a little straighter ten years ago.'

She was talking of the famous Beer Hall *Putsch* of November 9, 1923, by then written with illuminated letters in Nazi mythology. It had been a squalid affair. Hitler had marched with General Ludendorff at the head of his Storm Troopers on the Munich War Ministry. Within half an hour, he had sixteen of his followers dead, Ludendorff arrested and himself cringing on the cobblestones. As a final indignity, the badly wounded Hermann Göring was succoured in a nearby Jewish bank.

'We've all the natural resources we need to make us rich and powerful again, any of my schoolchildren could tell you that.' We had passed the Zoo, where I had in the end taken her for tea, and were hurrying up the wooden steps to the platform. She was in her discouraging black serge, with black lisle stockings and a big black leather bag. 'But Hitler's a braggart just like the Kaiser, and he'll get us into the same trouble, you mark my words. Teutomania is too expensive a luxury these days.'

'A braggart? I've heard him called a second Martin Luther.'

'Oh, Martin Luther! He was a disastrous failure. He never settled our religious differences and united our country, like your Tudor Kings and Queens. He divided it the more. Don't forget that I am a Catholic, *Mister*.'

We reached the platform. 'Anyway, I shall have to support the Nazis,' she continued more soberly. 'I'm a schoolteacher. I'm employed by the State. If I'm thought unreliable politically I shall never see promotion, more likely I'll find myself dismissed. That's how everyone sees the situation at school. Though to tell the truth, most of the teachers needed little encouragement to become the wildest enthusiasts for Herr Hitler. And perhaps he won't turn out as bad as he seems. You've heard one of our German proverbs – Nothing is served as hot as it's cooked?'

'Yes. Almost everybody seems to be applying it to Hitler.'

'Well, what odds does it make?' she added resignedly. 'I'll raise my arm as the Nazis march past like everyone else, A good many heathens and sinners bow to the altar in church. Who wants to lose a job these days?'

We both became aware in the same instant of a young man staring at us. He was pale with a line of black moustache, in a dark suit, well-pressed but threadbare, and a curly-brimmed trilby, perhaps a clerk or a shop assistant. I was frightened by the hostility of his eyes. It was before, but not long before, everyone in Germany had to be careful what they said, indoors or out. But it was common knowledge that sharp words shot bravely against the Nazis were arrows which could provoke artillery. Doubtless the shabby fellow had no interest in us, or was reflecting on a morning row with his wife or had a hangover. But we instinctively stayed silent until the linked pair of cars slid into the station on their monorail. It was Hitler's lasting bounty that every German grew suspicious of the next.

I always threw a glance into Domagk's room as the Schwebebahn traversed the I G Farben works, but I never glimpsed him. We crossed the Wall, the main shopping street of Elberfeld, festooned with long Nazi banners. Flags were to be flown on all days of national significance, of which the Germans had many. Some brave or foolish housekeepers or shopkeepers flaunted the red, black and white horizontal stripes of the old Weimar Republic, the flag which Hitler described with a lapse of his usual prudery as, 'a bedsheet of the most shameful prostitution'. Shortly the swastika was to fly all over Germany triumphantly alone, hoisted to the peak of its flagstaff by the law of the land.

The month of April had jolted past fiercely. When the Germans recovered their breath from Hitler's sweeping up full political power, people began to say it was not dangerous, or even significant, because the Nazis were a minority party. But the Nazi rank and file were aghast that the Third Reich had gloriously dawned with the Jews still opening their shops, sitting in Court, teaching in school and even walking the streets. The Storm Troopers took over. On April 1, they organized a national boycott of Jewish shops. They pushed into courtrooms and forced outside Jewish barristers and judges. Hitler had to seize back the initiative by hastily signing the Aryan Decrees, barring Jews from the universities, the civil service, schools and the legal and medical professions. Hitler's scrawled signature abolished as easily the ancient German states and unified the Reich, surmounting the frustrations of Bismarck's whole lifetime and proving his own promises to be written on water. April had been a month to open the eyes of the Germans, had many cared to be roused awake.

'Hey there, old man! Aren't you going to introduce me?' I looked up from my seat, startled, amazed and alarmed. Standing above was Jeff Beckerman. It was a warm day, and he wore his light grey English suit with chalk stripes, on his head a floppy white linen cap with a button in the middle. I had never known him to take the Schwebebahn, though he came in every day from the black and white villa he rented at Vohwinkel, out beyond Elberfeld. I had never known him to move more than a hundred yards anywhere without his car.

'I saw you get aboard.' He had pushed his way through the crowd of standing passengers, and was grinning broadly. 'I had to take the Cord into the garage. One of the brake drums has cracked clean across, it's one of the faults with that car. I hope to God the Jerries know how to fix it.'

His eyes were pawing Gerda. She gave an unsure smile, realizing that this was the American I had spoken about so often. I stammered some words of introduction in English and German. Already I saw the long-feared consequences of her meeting Jeff, whose air of wealth and worldliness picked him from the seedy passengers of the Schwebebahn like a sovereign in a handful of pennies. Jeff seized her hand, shaking it with the enthusiastic vigour he applied to his car. 'I'm sure glad to meet you, Fräulein. I've heard a whole lot about you from Jim.'

'Fräulein Dieffenbach speaks virtually no English,' I said stiffly.

'Then she must learn! Sure she must, it's not fair, a girl like her in Wuppertal and I can't speak to her. Tell her I'll hire her a teacher.'

I translated this dutifully. Gerda put her hand to her mouth and gave an uncharacteristic giggle. I *supposed* it was a joke. I should not have been surprised at Jeff sending a professor of English ringing the Dieffenbachs' doorbell.

Gerda's stop was before ours. By then Jeff had contrived in bilingual conversation a promise for all three of us to take a spin in his car the following Sunday afternoon – if of course the brakes were working. As she disappeared with a smile through the sliding doors, he nudged me hard in the ribs. 'It was mean of you, hiding her all this time. She's a ripping girl, *nicht wahr?*'

'She's very serious, you know,' I said discouragingly. 'She doesn't find anything worth talking about which doesn't affect the lives of five million people.'

'I don't believe it. She's *schön*, she doesn't have to wear her brains like a fancy bonnet.'

'Nobody in the world takes their job more seriously than a German schoolteacher. Not even the President of the United States.'

'You're wrong, old man,' he said cheerfully. 'All women are only interested in little things, food, clothes, if it's going to rain and ruin their hair, whether a man helps them out of an automobile or takes his hat off in an elevator. That's why women make rotten politicians, they've got a proper sense of values. Anyway, I like intelligent girls.'

I grew depressed and panicky. My relationship with Gerda was insipid, but I had the comfortable feeling that she was my property, if only because I had no rival. My dislike of Sunday's expedition deepened when Jeff arrived at the Dieffenbachs' gate in bright-buttoned blue blazer and white flannels, looking readier for yachting than motoring. He grasped a huge bunch of pink, white and red carnations, elaborately arranged in a cone of frilled paper. Gerda's eyes glowed at the flowers. Her mouth opened at the Cord gleaming in the sunshine. Dr and Frau Dieffenbach came into the narrow front garden, similarly impressed with vehicle and burstingly self-confident owner. Young Gunter scurried round touching the white coachwork reverently. Even the two maids peeped in whispering admiration through the front lace curtains. I had a painful feeling of unnecessity.

It was a glorious afternoon. The sun shone from a blue Sunday sky unhazed by smoke, and Wuppertal hardly smelt at all. The streets were full of strollers in their sombre Sunday best, the walls thick with Nazi banners, and streamers with the repeated exhortation, *Honour Work and Respect the Worker!* The morrow was May Day, declared a national holiday by the new Government, there were to be parades and rallies all over Germany. Hitler was himself to address a hundred thousand pairs of ears on Tempelhof Airdrome in Berlin, plus countless more in every home and, through lamp-post loudspeakers, in every public square of the Reich. The pomp was to show the Nazis as neither puppets of the capitalists nor conspirators of the bourgeoisie, but true champions of the German worker. On the following day, May 2, Hitler emphasized this by taking over all German trade unions, occupying their offices with Storm Troopers, sequestrating their funds and jailing their leaders.

We had the car roof folded back, the warm breeze tugging the brim of Gerda's black straw hat and running its fingers through wisps of her pale hair. She wore the ankle-length blue and white striped cotton dress which I had imagined bought for my own benefit. I sat in the back, still with my Trinity scarf. Jeff drove eastwards along the river, which flowed through Wuppertal like its gut, growing progressively filthier. Beyond Barmen the grimy town fell away from us and the valley became walled with the unspoiled woods of the Marscheider Wald. We stopped amid the huddle of steep red roofs against a lake which composed the village of Beyenburg. It was overshadowed by a fifteenth-century sandstone church, barnlike without transept, which we perfunctorily inspected before Jeff found a café where we could sit outside under a brightly striped umbrella *à la française*. He ordered coffee, cream cakes and brandy. Nazi-dominated Germans enjoyed the freedom denied Englishmen of sipping spirits on a Sunday afternoon.

Gerda refused the brandy but ate several cakes. I found myself translating Jeff's compliments and gallantries, and her shy, smiling replies. When Jeff tried asking her through my own mouth to take dinner with him the following Saturday. I jibbed.

'What's the matter, old man? You're not engaged to her, are you?'

'No, but I'm rather keen on her.'

'Oh, bull! Maybe I should tell her about that little brunette in Cologne?'

'I never touched that woman.'

He looked mockingly. 'You don't say?'

'We sat in the kitchen and talked about the drugs they're experimenting with at I G Farben.'

He jerked his head across the table. 'Would she believe that? *Du lieber Gott!*'

'How about you and that tart in Berlin?'

'I keep telling you, Heike wasn't a professional.' He arrogantly stuck out his legs in their spotless white trousers. 'Anyway, women prefer a really experienced man of the world.'

Gerda was searching both our faces, puzzled and disconcerted by the tone of our exchanges. '*Genung!*' Jeff exclaimed. He commanded the waiter, '*Bitte, bringe noch zwei Glases Cognac.*' I noticed that he was beginning to use more German.

My tide of jealousy rose. My anchor was Gerda's personality. How could a level-headed schoolmistress with a mind and will of her own fall for the dash and extravagance of Jeff? What touching faith I had in the constancy of woman! The next Sunday afternoon Jeff appeared in beautifully cut plus fours with knitted brown socks and hand-made

English brogues. He invited Gerda for another drive. This time I wasn't asked.

I decided to relinquish Gerda. In love affairs I withdraw at the gentlest rebuff, like a snail in a shower. I told myself sourly that a handsome young man with splendid clothes, a feeling for flattery and with the only Cord car in Germany was irresistible. I was not wholly fair. Jeff had charm and vigour, and he was American. He brought to old-fashioned, contorted, introspective, stiff-necked Germany the fresh wind of boundless prairies, endless highways, topless skyscrapers and unlimited money. To Gerda, he was *Blondie of the Follies*.

'Herr Jim, you must have a poor opinion of me,' she confessed one evening when we found ourselves alone. I made some demurring remark. 'Jeff is very insistent. And I don't get many luxuries here in Wuppertal,' she said artlessly. 'But I feel very guilty, because you are so nice and quiet, and so much more intelligent than Jeff.'

My relations with Jeff remained amicable. They had to be. He seemed to regard his snatching Gerda only as a good joke at my expense. On May 10, Nazi students lit a bonfire from their libraries. Dr Göebbels benignly inspected the flames in the Franz-Josefplatz, while they shouted '*Brenne Heinrich Heine! Brenne Karl Marx! Brenne Sigmund Freud! Brenne Heinrich Mann!*' But both national and domestic disarray seemed trivial some six weeks later, when I thought I was about to lose my right hand.

10

On Friday morning I smashed a test-tube in the lab, and from a spot of blood saw with annoyance that I had pricked my right index finger. On Friday night it was tender, it throbbed when I woke on Saturday, and over the day grew ominously red and swollen.

I hesitated to consult Dr Dieffenbach. I had lived in a doctor's house – a King's doctor's house! – since I was fifteen, but my complaints had been always too trivial to provoke the cogitations of Sir Edward Tiplady. And by the nature of her profession, my mother had an intimacy with household remedies. Though I was never a sickly child, she would regularly apply them out of interest. I was dosed with garlic against worms, rubbed with hot roast turnip against chilblains, or with a steak to be promptly buried in the back garden against warts. My bowels never remained unmoved in the presence of senna infusions, rhubarb tea and boiled onions. I became a hypochondriac, which my life working closely with medical men has aggravated. They have an instinctive way of eyeing you for promising defects, as a knacker a passing horse. I have imagined picking up as many diseases as pieces of their jargon.

'You don't look well,' Gerda said as the maids were clearing away our evening meal. She showed increased solicitude for my welfare and comfort, I assumed through her guilt over Jeff. 'And you hardly ate a thing.'

'It's my finger.'

Her face grew concerned as I thrust the swollen tip towards her. 'You must be careful. Papa had a patient the other day whose finger started just like that. In the end he got blood poisoning, and they had to take him into the hospital and amputate his arm.'

I thanked her for the encouragement.

'You must show it to Papa once he gets back.' Dr Dieffenbach had missed his dinner through an urgent call. 'I'm sure he'll be able to stop it spreading with hot fomentations.'

I sat for a while over Hans Fallada's new novel *Kleiner Mann, was nun?* while Gerda in her glasses corrected exercise books. I knew that no infection was trivial. My father once caught his hand on a rusty nail rummaging in the dark of the wine cellar, and had been incapacitated for weeks.

We heard the doctor come home. I shut my book and followed him to his surgery at the back of the house. He was still in his Homburg, washing his hands.

'Come in, come in,' he invited in English. 'Have you ever had diphtheria, my dear chappie'?'

'No, I haven't.'

He hung his hat on the stand with a weary gesture. 'I've just seen a bad case. Membrane right across the throat and the heart affected. Its twin attack, as garrotter and poisoner. Herr Petersen's little girl, on the other side of the Zoologischer Garten, I've known him since the War. Well, it's the disease which takes four or five thousand German children to Heaven every year.'

As he neatly folded the small starched towel which he had dried his hands on, I made the remark that a physician of his skill might save the child.

'Were I the reincarnation of Hippocrates I could battle no more successfully against the Klebs-Löffler bacillus once it's on the rampage. There are but three things I can do.' He made a gesture of resignation. 'I can inject diphtheria antitoxin into the veins. I can administer strychnine to steady the heart. And I can hope for the best. If the child's breathing gets worse, I shall be called from my bed tonight to perform a tracheotomy.' He indicated with his forefinger a cut just below his voice-box. 'There're rumours going round this last year or so that they're developing the immunization against the disease, like your Edward Jenner discovered against smallpox a hundred years ago. Perhaps that will make a dent in the mortality.'

The room was small with white walls, lit by a strong electric bulb in a shade like a saucer and there was a reek of carbolic. One side was occupied by an uncomfortable-looking examination couch with a horsehair-stuffed top. Against the other stood a steel-and-glass case of instruments, on top a metal sterilizer like a chafing-dish over a spirit lamp. On the desk, a dish of instruments – scalpels, forceps, curved needles – lay marinating in reddish antiseptic. Dr Dieffenbach drew a box of cigars from the drawer and clipped one with a pocket guillotine. He smoked cigars unabashed while examining his patients, I suspected even intimately.

'Well, old chappie, you are looking at me like the unfortunate messenger from Birnam Wood in *Macbeth*.' He was fond of parading his involuntary intimacy with English literature.

I held out my finger with an apologetic air. He inspected it in silence, while the surgery filled with aromatic smoke. He pressed the pulp. I winced 'You have a cellulitis here,' he announced calmly. 'Our old friend the streptococcus has bitten you.'

'It won't spread, will it?' I asked, alarmed.

'Who can say? If the infection doesn't resolve in twenty-four hours, I can make a little cut or two and insert a rubber drain.' His unruffled professional manner at that moment struck me as incorporating the worst of British phlegm and German insensitivity. 'Sit down, and I'll take your temperature. Chin up, my dear chappie. I shall endeavour not to send you home looking like Admiral Nelson.'

It appeared that I had some fever. He prescribed kaolin poultices every four hours. All Sunday, Gerda made them in the kitchen, spreading the shiny white china clay on a square of pink lint with a spatula, then boiling it like a cabbage in a saucepan of water. With frowning seriousness she wrapped the poultice, tight and scalding, round my finger. I always winced and gasped, and she would say as she applied the layer of waterproof gauze and a bandage, 'Remember, Herr Elgar, it is for your own good.' I felt this unnecessarily schoolmistressy.

My mind became increasingly occupied with the chances of earning a living as a one-armed chemist. I had every faith in Dr Dieffenbach. He was superior to a Krankenkasse doctor, one employed by the compulsory public sickness insurance which was established in Germany in 1883, anticipating our British National Health Service by sixty-five years. And like our British National Health Service, its doctors complained that they were underpaid and overworked, its patients complained that they could not always choose their doctor, though the Verbände der Ärtze Deutschlands did its best to provide a selection. Dr Dieffenbach looked down on the Krankenkasse severely.

I stayed on my feet that Sunday, my right arm in a sling. I clearly could not go to the brewery on Monday. Anyway, Jeff was in Berlin. I awoke feeling so ill, and my hand so pained, that I could not rouse myself from my bed.

Gerda brought me some barley-water, but I was too sick even to savour her concern. About noon, Dr Dieffenbach sent a maid to summon me to his surgery. As he took off the jacket of my pyjamas, I could see clearly red streaks now reaching from my hand and up my forearm towards my heart.

Dr Dieffenbach stood smoking his cigar for the best part of a minute, inspecting the unbandaged hand impassively.

'We'll try some new pills,' he decided.

I was then so frightened I would have swallowed arsenic had he suggested it. 'Perhaps I should send a letter home,' I said shakily. 'To break the news that I am ill –'

'You are hardly in top condition for correspondence. I'll send a line on your behalf to Sir Edward Tiplady. I owe him a note on other matters anyway. But if these pills do their job properly, by the time he receives it you will be cured.'

Dr Dieffenbach went to the glass cupboard. He reached inside for the *Aesculape* Field Surgical Chest he had acquired from Army surplus after the War. It was the size of my Woolworth's attaché case, gleaming steel, canvas lined, every instrument's place outlined in black and fitted with German ingenuity and precision. For a second I was horrified that he was about to cut off my arm without more ado. But he produced a glass phial about four inches long, for which the chest was a hiding place.

'I heard only today of these tablets being used on a professional brother, who pricked his finger doing a post mortem on a septic case,' he informed me unnervingly. 'That's often a death warrant, you know. Germs become more virulent, altogether more proud of themselves, after a triumphal passage through the human body.'

He tipped some tablets into his palm. They were an inch across, reddish yellow, about twenty of them in the phial. 'These would make a horse retch, my dear chappie,' he continued with amusement. 'You must get a couple of them down you three times a day. You have quite a nasty *Phlegmone* there in your arm. The enemy is attacking up the easy roads of your lymphatic system. Well, we shall teach this adventurous streptococcus a lesson.'

'What are they?' I inspected the two pills in my hand as he filled a glass with water.

'Curiosity is a superfluous quality in the patient. It's stuff called "Streptozon", which to you can mean no more than another brand of schnapps. Now back to bed, dear chappie. You're feverish enough to boil a kettle.'

Illness abroad is doubly wretched. 'The purple wallpaper which we will grow to hate as we lie in bed with grippe,' Cyril Connolly wrote perceptively about his cheap Paris hotel. I was oppressed by *my* wallpaper, a design of violets. The sloping ceiling seemed to be descending to crush me like the torture chamber of *peine forte et dure*. The ghostlike Frau Dieffenbach brought me broth, but I wanted only water. Even the sounds of Gerda next door were no more than an irritation.

About eight that evening I descended the narrow attic stairs, grey woollen dressing-gown over my shoulders, to the lavatory on the landing below. A minute later I was hurriedly out again. I leant over the banisters shouting in panic for Dr Dieffenbach. He appeared from the living-room, napkin under chin, half alarmed and half angry.

'Doctor, I'm bleeding to death,' I cried in German.

Frau Dieffenbach and Gerda appeared behind him, wondering if I were dying or delirious.

'Bleeding? Where from?' the doctor asked brusquely.

This was awkward, in front of the ladies. 'Internally.'

'Fore or aft?' he demanded impatiently.

'Fore.'

He mounted the stairs, snatching off his napkin and mumbling bad-temperedly. He followed me into *die Toilette*, where I indicated dramatically with my good hand the bright red water in the pan of solid china, made in Staffordshire and named amid a spray of flowers in English, *The Little Thunderer*. Dr Dieffenbach's professional balance seemed shaken. 'Have you any left?' he demanded, pulling his beard. 'I need a drop more, if you can find it.'

He brought a conical flask from his surgery, into which I passed an inch of this alarmingly coloured fluid. He packed me back to bed. After a few minutes he appeared in smiling reassurance. 'No nephritis,' he announced in English. 'No septicaemic abscess, no pyelitis. I've tested your offering, my dear chappie, by the tincture of guiac method, and find it free from all blood. The colour is a harmless dye, which should have occurred to me. But a doctor never thinks at his clearest when snatched away from his dinner. I've seen the same effect in children who've gorged themselves with sweets which the manufacturers have turned pretty red colours with aniline dyes. They pass straight through to the urine, and you can imagine how the mothers get hysterics. How's the hand? Why, a great improvement already.'

I noticed that the red lines were fading. 'The streptococcus is in full retreat,' Dr Dieffenbach said with satisfaction. 'We shan't send you home looking like Admiral Nelson after all,'

He left me lying feebly on my pillow. 'Streptozon' was transparently a fancy name for sulphonamide, as 'Atebrin' was for the mepacrine hydrochloride used against malaria. I was an involuntary colleague of Professor Domagk's mice.

11

In summer, everybody thinks less. With leaves and flowers to distract the eye, skin and air making friends again, fresh fruit to eat – delicious proof of Nature's kindly abundance – people stop brooding and grow lazy and lecherous. Life looks different, a golden thread to be spun out as long as possible, not a coin to be risked for a cause. A country becomes docile towards its native politicians and completely indifferent towards foreign ones. From his first year of office, Hitler grasped this as instinctively as any other item of mass psychology.

Hitler busied himself in the sunshine to annihilate his antagonists. The Storm Troopers had for years been able to murder whoever they liked with the tolerance of the Law. It would have taken a braver witness to testify, a braver juryman to convict and a braver judge to sentence than in Ireland during the Troubles. Now they had the force of Law itself. There were rumoured to be 100,000 Germans in concentration camps, each prisoner playing the grisly double role of terrorizing those still left outside. All opponents of Hitler not behind barbed wire were under the earth, and even the wraiths of resistance vanished.

The Geleichstellung, the co-ordination of Germany, was accomplished that summer at breakneck speed. Hitler's safeguards of March were forgotten, his four-year limit not worth remembering. The Reichstag enjoyed the vestigial function of Hitler's sounding board, which it fulfilled to hear his resolve of spreading peace and light across Europe, a message accepted particularly enthusiastically by the London *Times*, the British Labour Party and President Roosevelt. Hitler was already giving the world a taste of the piecrust promises with which he was stopping the mouths of the Germans.

The German Social Democratic Party vanished. Hitler's signature dissolved it. He also dissolved the German National Party, his partner in the coalition appointed by President Hindenburg with the idea of keeping him under control. The Catholic Centre Party lasted until July 4, when Storm Troopers appeared in its offices to close it down for ever. And on July 20, representatives of His Holiness in Rome signed a concordat with representatives of Herr Hitler in Berlin.

Hitler's success in these early vulnerable months came from his genius for the deadly game of political chess, from an eye which saw deeply into the dark, timorous, mean recesses of the human heart, and from his transforming the roughhouse which passed for German society into a disciplined country where everyone knew where he stood. Hitler restored order. And the Germans loved him for it, as Gerda loved her father.

'My dear chappie, you must realize how things are for us in Germany,' explained Dr Dieffenbach, clipping his after dinner cigar a month after saving an English arm with a German drug. 'The Jews are vastly over-represented in medicine, as in the law. I sometimes wonder if we can truly call these two learned professions German at all. But I would agree that Herr Hitler is being rather hasty. He will have second thoughts, assuredly. You must expect him to be a little headstrong in the first flush of success. Besides, he has to pander a little to his most fervent supporters, who are not exactly the type of person I would invite to dinner.'

Dr Dieffenbach always evaded my questions about the nature of the pills. He did not know that I had seen a letter which Gerda inadvertently left on the pink chenille cloth when filing her father's professional papers. It was a short handwritten note from Domagk, saying they were receiving encouraging reports from 'Streptozon' all over Germany, particularly from Professor Dr Schreus at the medical academy in Düsseldorf and from physicians in Münster and Kiel. In Wuppertal, Professor Dr Klee was using it successfully at the Municipal Hospital for erysipelas and angina of the throat. I supposed I G Farben had good reasons for keeping the drug up its sleeve, though I did not think much about it. Once cured by his doctor, the patient forgets the drug and begrudges the fee.

I was already planning to spend Christmas with my parents. I certainly did not see my days in Germany as numbered. In the years ahead, there were plenty of Englishmen to visit Germany curiously and leave it enthusiastically, including Lloyd George. Nazism had a glitteringly superficial appeal, a nation as one folk, all sharing alike – even such privations as the weekly 'one pot' meal – all setting their country above themselves, all healthy, straightforward and comradely, the apotheosis of togetherness, a youth movement for all ages. I missed the full significance of the moral infection round me, as I had missed the full significance of the cured physical one in my hand.

Once a month I had to report to the Polizeipräsidium on Druckerstrasse, between river and railway, crammed together as they traversed the narrow valley. It was a painless and even an amicable episode. A citizen of the British Empire was a curiosity to break the monotony of Hungarians or Roumanians, Dutch or Danes. A scholarly-looking policeman with pince-nez made a neat copperplate entry in violet ink on the yellowish, lined paper of my file, and that was that.

I was due to appear at the end of October. Hitler had just abruptly withdrawn from the Disarmament Conference at Geneva, and the League of Nations for good measure, which particularly disconcerted the London *Times*, the British Labour Party and President Roosevelt. I was on this occasion shown immediately into a small office containing two men my own age, both in Nazi brown shirts with Sam Browne belts, swastika armbands above their left elbows, breeches and jackboots stuck under a trestle table covered with papers.

They questioned me for two hours, keeping me standing while they smoked cigarettes and drank coffee. Why was I in Germany? I protested that my work permit was in front of them. Yes, but why was I *really* in Germany? I observed that their country was most interesting and educative to visit. Had I any Jewish blood? Did I look it? I asked. Where did I learn to speak German? And why? How much money had I saved in Germany? Did I transfer money to London? What was my father's work? They wanted the names and addresses of all the people I knew in Wuppertal.

They were a pair of jacks-in-office, dressed in an authority which was neither little nor, to the world's pain, brief. But the icicles of my reserve began to melt. A citizen of the British Empire expected to be above the antics of the natives when they grew restive. I had a feeling of always being watched, in reality too dramatic a notion. The Gestapo had been in business only six months, a minor organization confined to the State of Prussia, christened by a clerk at his wits end for a set of distinctive initials among the hundreds newly proliferating in Germany.

A few days later I encountered Gerda in the hall of the Dieffenbachs' house, below a newer and larger photograph of Hitler. Her face was scarlet, her eyes spilling tears. I had often seen her indignant and sometimes angry, but never weeping. It was Jeff, she explained.

'The school say I must not mix with foreigners. If I do, they tell me I shall lose my job. It's not thought right for a German in my position to ride about in a big American car, when there are workpeople with hardly enough to keep alive.'

'What's it to do with the school, whether you ride in an American car or the Schwebebahn?' I protested, though not displeased.

'My whole life is of concern to the authorities,' she said desperately. 'Everything that anybody does has the Government nosing into it. You never know if the teacher sitting next to you is an agent for the Sicherheitsdienst.' This was the SD, the early State Security Service, under the cashiered former Naval intelligence officer Reinhard Heydrich, whose later extermination in Prague led to the elimination of Lidice and its whole population. 'There're Brownshirts and officials I've never seen before, in and out of the school all the time. I don't want to end up in the Special Court.'

I had heard plenty of the Sondergericht, with three Nazi judges and no jury, established after the March elections to deal with dissenters.

'People have been in trouble you know, quite a lot of them,' Gerda continued, hesitant and fearful of what she was saying. 'Now the police and the Storm Troopers are entitled to go into any house they like, and ferret out whatever and whoever they wish…There are people Papa knows who have just disappeared. Like that.' She snapped her fingers. 'Papa doesn't say much about it, but for all he knows they could be dead and buried. Perhaps they are. All over Germany they're keeping people as long as they like in protective custody… Protective! The camps are far worse than the detention barracks in the Army. Anyway, the Storm Troopers ransom people to be let out, it's a racket like Jeff's gangsters in Chicago.'

'I suppose some lady teacher was jealous of you with Jeff and his car, and told the Brownshirts?'

'No, it was Gunter.'

'Your own brother!' I was horrified.

'He passed the story to his schoolmaster. You know how Gunter thinks absolutely everything about the Nazis is wonderful, just because they organize camps and give him a uniform and they all sing songs round a fire. They tell him it's his duty to inform on anything at home which goes in the slightest against the thinking of National Socialism. You can't blame him. All kids are instructed to put their country first, even before their parents. He doesn't know any better.' She ended charitably, 'I expect he'll grow out of it.'

I decided to guard my tongue carefully within earshot of the young man. I noticed that Gerda took every chance afterwards to slap the cheeks of Hitler's little enthusiast.

These two incidents decided me to quit Germany. I had no knowing who might be itching to report me to the SD, and put me in serious trouble. Or perhaps my mind was already made up, they were the clicks of a shutter admitting light to a sensitized film. Jeff was nettled. He had bought a cosmetics firm in Berlin, and had planned my concocting voluptuously-smelling perfumes and powders from chemicals.

'What's the matter? Homesick?'

'You know I haven't a home to pine for.'

'I guess Germany's getting too noisy a jungle for the explorers to sleep soundly,' he agreed, after trying to dissuade me. 'These Nazis are nuts, when you come down to it. A government's job is to declare war and raise taxes and keep the railroads running, not to tell a girl who she can go out with and who she can't. Sure you've made your mind up? I guess England's just like the States right now, full of college graduates selling apples.'

I was to leave just before Christmas 1933, through Ostend again, and by night. On my last day in Wuppertal I met Professor Domagk for the second time.

Dr Dieffenbach gave a small evening party to speed me on my way. There was French champagne and spiced biscuits and *pets de nonne* – nun's farts, the name given to delicately flavoured pastries by Voltaire. Gerda wore her blue and white dress with diagonal stripes. I invited Jeff. She seemed to have accepted renouncing him as she accepted having to raise her arm when the Storm Troopers marched past. Dr Dieffenbach invited the Domagks. But the Professor arrived alone, late and agitated.

'Gertrude can't come,' Domagk anxiously explained the absence of his wife. 'It's our four-year-old girl. You heard she was ill?'

'No, I hadn't.' Dr Dieffenbach looked concerned. 'What's up with the child?'

'She pricked herself with a needle, and it went septic. It may have been contaminated with some virulent organisms which I'd brought back from the laboratory. On my clothing perhaps, one can never be sure of these things.'

'My dear Gerhard, I'm so sorry.' He grasped the professor's hand. 'What's the pathogen? Have you identified it?'

'Yes, it's a streptococcus. She's developed a suppurative *Phlegmon* on her arm.' Domagk's face, drawn with worry, passed unseeingly round the rest of us in the room. 'The poor little girl's got a positive blood culture. Septicaemia, there you are,' he said resignedly.

'But she's receiving the best treatment?' Dr Dieffenbach asked urgently.

'She's in hospital. The surgeons are trying to arrest the infection, they've already made fourteen incisions in the arm. The only hope left is amputation.'

'*Du lieber Gott*! But has the decision been made?'

'It's being made at this moment. I'm on my way to see them.'

'You should never have delayed by coming here.'

'I came intentionally. Listen –' Domagk dropped his voice, but I was near enough to hear. 'Do you suppose I should give her "Streptozon"?'

'Why not? It's been proved safe.'

Domagk frowned. 'Has it? Who can say? It's still in the experimental stage.'

'You've no alternative,' Dr Dieffenbach told him sternly.

'It's never been used on a child before, never.'

'You simply reduce the dosage, exactly as you would for any other drug in your armamentarium.'

Domagk stood shaking his head. 'Amputation might save her life. The sulphonamide might equally well kill her.'

'Give her the drug,' Dr Dieffenbach repeated firmly. 'You know perfectly well that you cannot make a proper clinical judgement within your own family. When your brain's clouded with emotion, you're like a sea-captain trying to navigate in fog.'

Domagk still demurred. I stood listening, while my host read him a lecture lit by the candid light of true friendship. 'Gerhard, you're a fool. Or rather, you're a bacteriologist, which in clinical matters is much the same thing. You sit all day in your laboratory pottering with your Petri dishes and squinting down your microscope, and you forget those beastly germs of yours infect real people, not just the mice which you use as biological litmus paper. Real men and women, who like eating and drinking and making love to one another and going to the pictures. Listen to me – I'm a clinician. You've always got to be taking chances in clinical medicine. An unadventurous doctor leaves nothing but a trail of carefully-treated corpses.' He ended revealingly, 'I didn't hesitate, when I saw that sulphonamide was the only way to prevent our young English friend from cutting the figure of Admiral Nelson.'

'Very well,' Domagk nodded several times. 'I shall exhibit sulphonamide.' He paused. 'I had already made up my mind, Otto, but I wanted to share responsibility with someone outside the family.'

'Have you the "Streptozon"?' Dr Dieffenbach asked urgently. 'I've none of the pills left.'

'I was intending to collect some from my laboratory, then go on to the hospital.'

'Why waste time? Herr Elgar here knows the way, and his American friend drives the fastest car in Germany. They'll get to the hospital with the pills before you do. Go along and see your child, and tell the surgeons what you've decided. Those gentlemen might take some persuading, they haven't got wind of sulphonamide yet.'

I was instructed to revisit Domagk's room, the one with the painting by Otto Dix. I was told that Professor Hörlein had left a phial containing twenty tablets of 'Streptozon' on the roll-topped desk. Domagk departed for the hospital. Dr Dieffenbach telephoned the I G Farben works for the night-watchman to admit me.

The expedition appealed hugely to Jeff. In 1933, motorists in neither Germany nor England were incommoded with speed limits, and we roared through the misty night with headlights ablaze and horn blaring. The only necessity for our breakneck rush was Jeff's sense of the dramatic. I left him provoking the car to angry, impatient roars in the triangular cobbled yard with the railway tracks, while I hurried across the footbridge over the stinking river, above me the brightly-lit cars of the passing Schwebebahn. A window or two was alight in the research block, indicating some engrossed scientist or perhaps just the cleaners. I reached Domagk's study door on the third floor and switched on the light.

I saw the sulphonamide at once. Two phials, not one. Each with twenty tablets. I hesitated. I should be leaving Germany within hours. I took one phial in my hand. The other I slipped into my tweed jacket pocket.

I turned to go. There was a gap among the framed photographs on the wall. I missed the amiable, bearded features of Professor Paul Ehrlich from Frankfurt-on-Main. The man who cured the infection which took the lives of Schubert, Nietzsche, Gauguin and Toulouse-Lautrec had the misfortune to be born a Jew, and therefore worthy of nothing but odium.

12

We lived in the basement. Everything we had was second-hand. Our furniture was the discards of upstairs, the carpet old and bald, the once expensive chintz sofa grown pale, split and extruding flock, propped up by *Who's Who* and Bradshaw's Railway Time Table, both out of date. Our newspapers were always yesterday's, our magazines last month's. A radiogram upstairs had given us our portable gramophone, a black musical suitcase which my father would charge with a shiny needle and play *Blue Skies* on a scratched record. Our wireless set was almost new, in a wooden cabinet as ornamental as a Victorian bracket clock. It was a gift rather than a throw-out, that we might enjoy the uplifting diversion of Sir John Reith's BBC, which every Sunday had three religious services and five religious talks. Even our food had been used upstairs, cold joints, hashed vegetables, broached pies, milk which left sour little flecks in our tea. But we enjoyed the hottest water and the best nuts of coal, because we lived beside the boiler and the cellar. Sometimes during the London summer I imagined that the air we breathed had already been exhaled by the people upstairs and generously passed down for our consumption via the drains.

My father was Sir Edward Tiplady's butler, my mother his cook. For all I know today, there are biochemists and even professors like myself who are the sons of butlers and barmen, dustmen and dog-catchers. But the educated persons of the 1930s were socially more sensitive, and the middle classes suffered a particularly painful neurosis about those who emerged to join them from 'below stairs', whose next intention was suspected as murdering them in their beds. Largely for these reasons I had been unable to find work in my own country and had gone to seek it in Hitler's Germany.

It was early evening on Monday, January 1, 1934, exactly a year after I started at the Red Crown Brewery. I had been home a week, and ached to be back with the Dieffenbachs. Surroundings which the kindly eye of familiarity had once blurred now struck me as starkly squalid. There was the same black kettle forever simmering on the black grate, the high barred window like a cell's looking on an 'area' beside the holystoned front steps, through which I would watch for hours the passing women's calves in Harley Street. I had not seen the rest of my country since returning, as it had stayed aloof behind the worst fog in memory.

'This here Hitler,' said my father. 'Strikes me more like Charlie Chaplin than anything.'

'Don't be misled by the moustache. A lot of people in Germany are very frightened of him, you can take it from me.'

'Go on.' He seemed puzzled. 'I reckon he's leading the Jerries by the nose.'

'On the contrary, more and more Germans are supporting him. Because he's successful, which you must admit is unusual with most politicians in Europe at the moment.'

My father was a cheerful, sardonic Cockney with curly sandy hair gone grey, ostentatious false teeth and terrible feet which had saved his life in the Army by keeping him out of the trenches. He was a servant always ready for a quick draw of a cigarette behind the door, or a quick swig from a forgotten glass. I inherited from him a self-confidence and realism which allowed me to climb in the world with neither humility nor pride, which are equally self-accusatory in the successful man. He was wearing a brown Norfolk jacket – also second-hand – because we were having tea. Proper tea, high tea at six o'clock with kippers my mother had fried in the huge basement kitchen, bread and raspberry jam, bright yellow cake from Lyons with coconut icing which stuck in your teeth and tea so strong it looked like liquid leather.

'I don't hold with Jerries,' my father concluded sweepingly.

'There's good and bad ones, like good and bad Englishmen, and I suppose good and bad Zulus.'

This confused my mother that there were Zulus in Germany, but I had long ago overriden any irritation at these bizarre conversations with my parents. She was not the traditional jolly, plump, floury-armed governess of the kitchen, but thin, tense, severe and silent, her dark clothes always neat, her long greasy black hair always tucked away in a linen cap. She was ten years younger than my father, and like many serious-minded people of shallow intelligence found intense satisfaction in religion. From her I inherited my orderliness and purposefulness, and by some microscopic genetic twist my brains.

'Mind you,' my father continued emphatically, 'even Hitler can't be that barmy he'd start another war. Not after the last little dust up.'

'In Germany you'd sometimes think the next war had started already.'

'Nah, they ain't got no Army, not to speak of.'

'There're men always on the march, even if they're only off to the Reich Labour Service camps and armed only with beautifully polished picks and shovels. There're always parades, bands, banners inciting everyone to be patriotic, to put their country before absolutely everything, even friends, families, husbands and wives.' My father looked unbelieving. 'Hitler will bring back conscription soon, it's inevitable. He's got the raw material for his Army half-cooked already.'

'I pray there won't be another war,' said my mother solemnly. 'I couldn't face it all again, that's for sure. It was bad enough, bringing you up with your dad in the Army and the casualties and the Zeppelins. And the flu,' she added. 'And that's not even to think of what they did to our Bertie.'

Our only decoration in the basement was our shrine, a photograph of my Uncle Albert with jaunty, spiky moustache, in khaki and twinkling brass. It shared a frame with a sheet of printed buff foolscap, with inked details like a notification of lost property, by which the War Office informed us that 5655 Private A Elgar of the City Regiment had been killed in action. It was headed CASUALTIES FORM LETTER and ended curtly in print, *I am to express the sympathy of the Army Council with the soldier's relatives,* over some distant Civil Servant's signature. We working class were of as little consequence dead as alive. Nobody even bothered advertising to us, other than cigarettes, beer and patent medicines. It was the society of master and man, officer and private, the vigorous, acquisitive, voluptuous, cruel society of the Edwardians. A society too thrustful, successful and self-confident to fall a casualty of the Great War, and was simply demobilized to become the Gay Twenties. It saw Britain through World War II, and when Mr Harold Macmillan stopped his artificial respiration in 1963 was found to have been dead for several years.

'I wouldn't let Jim go for a soldier, that's straight, not after what he's made of himself.' My father looked at me proudly, a self-indulgence he seldom allowed. 'But if you asks me, Hitler's just having us on. He ain't got no money, you see.'

'Can I have another cup of tea, please?' The fourth occupant of our table held across her large slightly chipped cup. She was Rosie, the new nineteen-year-old housemaid, who completed the household staff with Mrs Emerald the daily char and Holdsworth the chauffeur who lived out, and was anyway away with the Daimler. The Tipladys were enjoying their Christmas holiday in some huge mansion whose windows glittered across muddy, misty English fields like their hostess across the difficult terrain of London society.

I was naturally interested in Rosie, snub-nosed and bright cheeked, sharp and pert, neat waisted, promisingly plump above and below. She slept in the attic, five floors above my basement cubicle which was half-filled with chemistry books. All week she had been trying perplexedly to make me out. I was obviously a gentleman, but I mucked in with the servants. It was a contradiction beyond her grasp, an outrage to established order, like a millionaire in prison. But when I chatted to her for ten minutes or so I became depressed and disgusted. An ill-lettered housemaid was dross after a German schoolmistress. My passion for Gerda had burnt almost unfelt, like a low fever, but had flared painfully with a change of environment.

Rosie's bewilderment itself underlined my strange, uncomfortable position in the Tiplady's house. I was the frog which had turned into a prince. An extremely awkward transformation in England, where no former frog could possibly be asked to dinner.

After tea, Rosie had to air the beds, because the Tipladys were expected on the morrow. At six-thirty on the following evening, my father brought me a summons to ascend past that resented green baize door, which

separated our two families like the water-tight bulkheads between First
Class and Steerage on the transatlantic liners. I found the first-floor
drawing-room empty. I stood where I had often stood before, by the heavy
brass fender which caged a display of well-polished fire-irons, the coals in
the carved marble fireplace flickering a vigorous yellow, freshly made up
for the evening by Rosie. It was a square room, with three tall windows
looking on Harley Street, the ceiling moulded and picked out in gold, the
gold-green wallpaper striped and silken, the curtains matching precisely.
The furniture was antique and over-plentiful. There were two good
pictures, a Stubbs of well-nourished groom holding well-nourished horse,
and a William Blake God, sinewy and sea green.

As the ormolu clock on the mantelpiece tinged half past six, Sir Edward
Tiplady came in. He was always punctual, always preoccupied, but with
the doctor's knack of concentrating upon you his limitless attention for
the strictly circumscribed time allowed in his presence.

'You're a rotten correspondent,' he said at once. His hands were full of
open letters accumulated during his holiday.

'I'm sorry. I find writing such an effort I keep putting it off. Then it
seems too late to bother.'

'You sound like one of my patients excusing his failure to break his bad
habits.'

He went to the mantelpiece, taking a cigarette from a silver box amid a
forest of shiny white cards inscribed with copperplate, seeking his
attendance at social or medical gatherings. I never remembered the
mantelpiece without them. He could have accepted barely a fraction, but
I suppose stuck them up from vanity, or for self-assurance or because he
thought it churlish to chuck them newly opened into the wastepaper
basket.

'You look five years older, Jim. When did you get back?'

'Christmas Eve.'

'You knew they'd made Tommy Horder a lord?'

'Yes, that was last year, just after I left England.'

'God knows why. Pal of Ramsay Mac's, I suppose. Tommy hasn't done
anything in particular since attending the *last* King and discovering sugar
in the Royal wee.'

He was famously jealous of unpretentious, sarcastic Thomas Horder, twenty years his senior and living down the road at No 141. Horder had made his way without pushing too violently the doors of the many anterooms to medical success. Tiplady was a deft manipulator of men and their favours, and had no doubt whatever that he was a physician fit for a King. Perhaps he saw the truth which everyone whispered, that Lord Horder was the better doctor.

'Did you see this year's Honours List? Morris of the Morris Oxford now Lord Nuffield! Neither Rolls nor Royce managed that.'

Sir Edward lit the cigarette with his gold petrol lighter and threw himself into a brocade armchair, sheaf of letters on his lap. He was tall and lean, handsome, fair-haired and smooth-cheeked, in his early forties. He had as usual plunged from holiday into consultations already arranged by his secretary Mrs Packer, and wore his professional uniform of black jacket and striped trousers. He seldom changed for dinner like everyone else, his evenings always busy with patients or meetings. I noticed that he now sported a large pearl pin through his grey silk tie, and a dashing lavender waistcoat. He still wore spats, though he had abandoned the wing collar during the past twelvemonth. He always had a clinical smell about him, a faint tangy odour of antiseptic. Or perhaps he only suggested it.

He sat smiling, wrinkling the fine lines round his pale blue eyes, looking at me quizzically but fondly. He always treated me in a humorously easygoing way. He was always unsparingly kind to me and effortlessly generous. I think he found our relationship less complicated than any other which he was obliged to make in the house. Of course, it was a Platonic homosexual one. This streak in Tiplady was then unmentionable, tacitly unrecognizable, and believed to nurture the seeds of collapse of the British Empire as of the Roman.

'So you're not going back to Germany?' I shook my head. He continued, 'I suppose every young man's entitled to one voyage of adventure, even if it ends in shipwreck. You're far more self-assured,' he decided. 'Meet any nice girls there?'

'Only Dr Dieffenbach's daughter.'

'What's-her-name...yes, Gerda. She must be very grown up. She was a little thing of seven or eight when I finally got Otto out of the clutches of our military people. What's he think of our friend Hitler?'

'He's one of his most fervent supporters.'

Sir Edward looked shocked. 'I just don't believe you. A man of Otto's social position and intelligence falling for all that ranting and raving—'

'You don't understand how it is over there—' I stopped. It was becoming increasingly difficult to explain Germany in secure, easygoing, respectable, comfortable, unexcitable, insular, fogbound England. 'People like the Dieffenbachs see Hitler as their saviour against the Communists. And the man to put Germany back on the map, the map which they remember from 1914. The Nazis sit round camp fires singing patriotic songs, and the next morning batter to death anyone who disagrees with them.'

'But that's all exaggerated, surely?' Sir Edward looked pained that I should regale him with travellers' tales. 'It was exactly the same during the War, our newspapers running a serial of frightfulness by the Hun, babies on bayonets and all that. I never believed a word of it, neither did anyone else with a brain. It was all a ruse of Northcliffe's to whip up morale on the Home Front. Well, he got his Viscountancy out of it.' A large, fluffy, pale ginger cat leapt into Sir Edward's lap, its claws scratching the bundle of letters. I had not been aware of an animal in the room, but cats seem able to materialize themselves at will. He sat stroking it restlessly. 'I utterly refuse to take a single word that Hitler utters seriously.'

I did not feel that I could contradict him. Men believe what they want to believe, or dare not disbelieve. That was Hitler's secret weapon from the start. I only repeated what I had told my father, of Germany already a nation of marching armies.

'Well, we won't be able to reintroduce conscription *here*,' he said cheerfully, abruptly standing up and turfing off the cat. He always seemed to be moving. 'MacDonald and the Labour Party would have fits. We'll have to rely on the Territorials and the Officers Training Corps in the public schools to keep us out of the soup. I wager everyone will have forgotten Hitler in five years. Their Chancellors come and go like the turns in a music hall show, surely?' He pushed the bell beside the fireplace. 'I say, weren't you ill over there? Otto wrote something last summer about a lymphangitis of the arm. That must have been most unpleasant for you.'

This was the moment for me to produce, like the prize of the Saladin's talisman from the Crusades, the phial of tablets which I had stolen from Domagk's room.

'What's this stuff?' He stood with legs apart before the fire, turning the phial in his fingers without opening it.

'It's the drug Dr Dieffenbach cured my arm with. It goes by the name of "Streptozon".'

'Proprietary names mean nothing,' he interrupted impatiently. 'You can name a drug like a new sort of chocolate.'

'Chemically, it's para-amino sulphonamide. I G Farben have been making it for years, as a red dye for carpets and curtains and all that. For some reason or other they decided to try it against streptococcal infections. I've even had a look at the lab report on their infected mice.'

'How did you come by this?'

'It's a sample given me by Professor Domagk.'

'Professor who?'

I repeated the name. 'He's the fellow who did all the work on it.'

'Never heard of him, I'm afraid.' To my amazement, I had my trophy handed back.

'But aren't you interested in it?'

'Not particularly. Chemotherapy is an exclusively German fetish, because they are better at handling molecules than handling people, and they have no compunction about slaughtering droves of mice to prove some obscure and often impractical chemical point. I suppose I was a bad research worker when I was younger, because I became too friendly with my guinea-pigs.' He sat at the mahogany bureau by the window, spreading out his letters and uncapping his fountain-pen. 'Leonard Colebrook is at this very moment trying to cure ordinary puerperal fever by injecting his mothers with arsenicals – the arsenicals which Ehrlich invented against the spirochaete. With utter lack of success.'

I had not imagined this rebuff. 'It worked on my arm,' I objected.

'I'd prefer to ascribe that to your own healthy young blood, rather than a dye for carpets.' He did not even look up. 'Everyone knows how lymphangitis can clear up on its own accord. The Germans are always pressing their latest chemicals on us as miraculous cures. I've been injecting gold into my tuberculous patients for months, with no good reason except that every other doctor in London has been persuaded to do the same. I prefer to treat infections on the sound and tried principle of immunology, as preached by our mutual friend Sir Almroth Wright.'

We were interrupted by my father in his tail coat with red-and-white striped waistcoat, come to serve the evening cocktails.

'You must be pleased to have Jim home again, Elgar,' remarked Sir Edward, still scribbling.

'He uses too many of them Jerry words, sir.'

'But aren't you glad he's become proficient in the German language?'

'What's wrong with English, sir, I always say,' my father disagreed cheerfully.

He was carrying a large oval silver tray by its handles, ceremoniously breast-high. He lowered it slowly on the eighteenth-century pier table, marble topped, its legs a vulgar profusion of gilt mermaids and dolphins. Then he filled a glass with pale sherry from a square decanter and transferred it to a silver salver. All was performed with a solemnity, an exaggeration of movement, to imply that any action in Sir Edward Tiplady's personal service was of importance, or that a butler's performance of tasks as easily done by his master was worth the money.

'Edward, you haven't changed yet.' Lady Tiplady appeared almost on the heels of my father. 'You know we're going to the theatre.'

'Are we? What a bore.' He was reading a letter through his monocle. 'What's the show?'

'It's the Lunts – *Reunion in Vienna*, at the Lyric: The Rothschilds asked us before Christmas to join their box. Surely you remember?'

'I've laid out your evening dress, sir,' came from my father, who had to play the valet in the same way that my mother was obliged to double as housekeeper. The War had replaced servant plenitude with the servant problem, the ingredient of all middle-class conversation.

'Well, Jim, you would seem to have resisted the siren voice of *Die Lorelei*.'
'Lady Tip', as she was known downstairs, directed to me a voice laced with
the acid she kept for servants, tradesmen, gossip, and dinner guests either
boring or more intelligent than herself. She was tall, slim and dark-haired,
in her late thirties but looking younger, beautiful and beautifully dressed.

'Perhaps I was lucky to resist it, your Ladyship. As it is a voice reputed
to deprive a man of his sight and hearing.'

'Then the siren's voice would seem to have caught the ear of a good
many people in Germany today, by all accounts.' She took a gin-and-
french from my father's salver without glancing at him. 'What are we
going to do about Jim?' she asked her husband.

'Do?' he asked vaguely, sipping his sherry at the desk.

'I mean, he can't go on living here, can he?'

I had noticed how the upper classes frequently assumed their language
incomprehensible to the lower. There were many things which they
would never discuss before the servants. The servants' affairs they could
discuss freely over their own heads. But I was not listening. The Tipladys'
only child, Elizabeth, had come into the room.

The year which may have changed me had transformed her. I had
previously disregarded her as a household nuisance, like Sir Edward's half
dozen cats. Now she was nearing fifteen, and already developed as a young
woman. She had the same glistening dark hair, pale complexion and high
cheekbones as her mother, but her eyes were softer, her lips full and as
inviting as June strawberries, her breasts straining impatiently against the
maidenly cut of her short blue dress. Sire seemed infinitely innocent,
submissive and explosive – the look of Leonardo da Vinci. She sat on the
sofa, turning her attention idly to a copy of the *Tatler* lying on the fireside
table with three or four new novels from Harrod's library. The likes of me
were to be ignored.

'Why not?' asked Sir Edward. 'Why shouldn't he still live with us?'

'The situation has become perfectly bizarre.' Lady Tip sat beside
Elizabeth on the sofa, smoothing the sheath-like crimson silk evening
gown over her long legs. 'It was all right when he was the butler's boy, but
now he's a grown man and perfectly able to look after himself. He can't
expect us to go on feeding and housing him in times like these.'

Lady Tip hated me. She was naturally jealous of the attention and affection which I diverted from her husband. My whole education I owed to Sir Edward's urging, expense and inspiration. The ladder of learning was then steep, sharply tapering and rickety. I was lucky to be the child in ten who progressed from elementary to secondary school, and among the four in a thousand who stepped further into university. There were only three hundred State scholarships, and three hundred more from Oxford and Cambridge, fought over by every clever poor child in the country.

Sir Edward had spurred me to win one of each, he had himself coached me in Latin for Cambridge 'Little Go', his cheques at Trinity arrived for birthdays, May Week or out of the blue. Aside from the unmentionable part of our relationship, he was generous because he had no son and because he hated to see a good brain go to waste. Without Sir Edward, I should today look back on a life scribbled away as a clerk in some benumbing office. Or I should be a millionaire.

'Jim could at least get a job, and make some contribution to his keep,' Lady Tip continued.

'Perhaps I could persuade Almroth Wright to take you back at Mary's,' Sir Edward said to me. 'Though of course, Sir Almroth hates chemists in any shape or form. I'm seeing Alexander Fleming next week, I'll sound him out. God, what a bore old Flem is getting!' he broke off. 'It must be five years now since he found *penicillium* mould contaminating his Petri dishes and killing off his staphylococci. He still keeps working it into a discussion on anything whatever at the Research Club. Not of course that anyone can hear a word Flem says beyond the first two rows.'

'There's always the dole,' said Lady Tip, sipping her gin-and-french.

This annoyed Sir Edward. 'You really can't expect Jim to queue at the Labour Exchange with a lot of unemployed tram drivers and road menders.'

'Why on earth not?' she asked calmly.

Another cat, a tortoiseshell, appeared mysteriously and jumped on to Sir Edward's lap. My father impassively poured a second glass of sherry. Elizabeth continued turning the shiny pages of the *Tatler*, the unattainable eyed by the unspeakable.

13

I signed on the dole at a Labour Exchange just behind Oxford Street. The middle-aged clerk behind the grille, with his yellowish celluloid collar and dandruff, luxuriated in the same official arrogance as the two young Nazis in Wuppertal police station. I got twenty-nine and threepence a week. I paid ten shillings through my father, less as a contribution to Lady Tip's household than to her meanness. People like the Tipladys passed through the Depression as comfortably as passengers in a *wagon lit* across the bleak, peasant-sustaining plains of Eastern Europe.

Though in 1934, and in London, things weren't as bad as they were remembered. The British national income had dropped by barely a tenth, compared with the American by half. 'The Hungry Thirties' was a will o' the wisp risen from the industrially rotting areas of coal, steel and shipbuilding up north. The unemployed marched on London, but the fire had gone out of the fight since the General Strike of 1926. It was then that Britain edged the way Germany slid. 'The Organization for the Maintenance of Supplies' was a private army blessed by Home Secretary Joynson-Hicks (scourge of the decade's touchingly coy pornographers), which the various British Fascist Societies began to infiltrate. But in the mid-1930s, the unemployed were a force as submissive to authority as those who advanced at Ypres or the Somme and other names which lodged in British folk memory – like 'the dole' itself

In the land to which I returned, like the land which I had left, the political party system was suspended. Britain had a 'National' Government, created in 1931 under the threat of imminent national bankruptcy and continued until 1945 under the threat of imminent national extinction. Ramsay MacDonald had won his last election by asking for 'A Doctor's Mandate', a slogan suggested by Sir Edward Tiplady's *bête noire* Sir Thomas Horder, who breakfasted *tête-à-tête* every Tuesday with this self-doubting, self-despairing Prime Minister. Meanwhile, King George the Fifth gazed upon his subjects in or out of work with unfathomable benignity, the Prince of Wales cut a dash round the Empire and Cambridge continued to win the Boat Race.

The wages of unemployment was boredom. I was imprisoned in the basement, irritated by the ringing of the patients' doorbell to which my father continually ministered. I read books from the library and spent afternoons in art galleries and museums, obtaining a cultural education denied the usual biochemist. As summer came I tramped London from Parliament Hill to the Crystal Palace, patching the soles of my shoes with scraps of leather my father bought at a penny a bag from a kindly cobbler.

One early June evening, I was idling away watching my father cleaning the silver in his butler's pantry, which was hardly more than a large cupboard off the basement kitchen. He sat in shirt-sleeves and green baize apron, an emaciated hand-rolled cigarette dangling from his lips.

'Got your eye on young Miss Elizabeth, ain't you?' he remarked abruptly.

I coloured at the discovery of a deadly and guilty secret. When she came home from boarding school I always contrived to glimpse her round corners and through the cracks of doors, or more delightfully skipping past our high window. I could only romance about her, but our fantasies are always more solidly satisfying than our realities. As I was incapable of reply, my father added casually, while polishing a silver flower bowl, 'She's not his, you know.'

I was equally shocked and intrigued. 'What makes you think that?' I asked sceptically. I had often romanticized my own true parentage, but I bore a frustrating resemblance to my father.

'I hear things.' He continued polishing in silence. 'Fact, there's precious little about the family what I *don't* know. When I goes into a room and they clam up tight, I says to myself, " 'Ullo, something fishy here". It doesn't take much to overhear a thing or two if you're careful, though often it's not worth the bother, just a row about who they're having to dinner.'

Such duplicity increased my respect for my father. He was not entirely the simpleton I took him for. 'But whose child is she? Do you know?'

'Remember Dr Ross? Sir Ronald Ross, I should say, him of "Malaria Day"? He died a couple of years back.'

'Surely not Ross!' I exclaimed. I remembered Sir Ronald calling regularly at the house the summer we had moved in, eight years previously. He was then nearing seventy, bull necked and square jawed, wearing a grey moustache with spiked ends as might have decorated a sergeant-major. On August 20, 1897, in a small laboratory facing Queen Victoria's statue in Calcutta, Ross had discovered the parasite which caused malaria, in the stomach of the spotted-winged *anopheles* mosquito. This was the last link in the causal chain of a fever which had baffled man since it had speeded the collapse of the Roman Empire.

The day was celebrated by annual oratorical lunches at the Ross Institute for Tropical Diseases at Putney. But Ross was mostly proud of his four novels and his poetry (which Osbert Sitwell mysteriously found of unforgettable beauty). Men always flatter themselves at doing at all what they do badly, rather than easily and well. He gave me one of his books and asked when I was going to join the Army.

'Nah, not *him*,' said my father contemptuously. 'There was an Italian doctor what came with him, and what had bin aht to India and China and such places.' He knocked a spike of ash with his little fingernail into the cracked saucer which passed as an ashtray. I remembered a tall, thin, sallow lank-haired younger visitor in Ross' shadow. 'When Sir Edward was still a doctor in the Army, Lady Tip was having an affair. It was during the flu, what killed so many people.' He continued steadily applying silver powder dissolved in methylated spirits from another cracked saucer. 'Lady Tip didn't catch the flu. She caught something what's more common all the year round.'

My amazement was followed by a pleasant feeling of conspiracy in *lèse-majesté*, and the desanctification of the goddess Elizabeth. 'They still sees each other to this day. And he still gets a bit of tail of her, for all I know. Bloody good thing, keeps the bitch in a better temper. Shouldn't think she gets even half an inch out of Sir Edward. He's a sissy, you know, written all over him.'

My father dropped his voice. The pantry door was open, and from the clatter in the kitchen it seemed Rosie was laying the trays for tomorrow's early morning teas. She always seemed to create undue noise, whatever she did.

'Why doesn't Sir Edward divorce Lady Tip?' I asked simply.

'Don't be barmy. The King's physician? A divorce would be the end of him at the Palace, that's for sure. And in a lot of other respectable houses as well. He'd never live down the scandal.' The bell rang. My father cursed, pinched out his cigarette, took off his baize apron and put on his tail coat. 'Lady Tip wants her booze, I suppose. Polish that, Jim, there's a good lad.' He tossed me the chamois leather. I started clearing the film of powder from the silver bowl, ruminating on our sensational conversation. I have refrained from giving the Italian doctor's name, because it is perpetuated in a laboratory dye for bacteria, and is familiar to the meanest medical student.

I did not anticipate being alone for long.

'Give us a kiss.'

Rosie appeared at the pantry door, red-faced, bright eyed, lips pursed invitingly. She was in her black art silk afternoon dress – it was rough brown calico for the morning's cleaning – but she had taken off her lace apron and her collar and cuffs, her dark curls tossed free of a cap, giving her an excitingly undressed look. I grabbed her, she pressed hard against me, seeming to exhale the heat of the glowing fires which she was continually reviving. 'When are you going to take me to the pictures?' she asked pertly.

'I can't afford it. I'm on the dole.'

'Go on! I'll pay.'

'That would never do.'

'Why not? Lots of girls stand treat these days.' She rubbed her rough, square-nailed fingers against my cheek. As I smiled, without conceding to her, she said, 'Regular toff, ain't you?'

'I'm one of the servants, same as you are.'

'You speaks like a toff.' She slowly and voluptuously cradled my neck in her raw red arms. She had 'set her cap' at me, as they said in the paper-covered novels on greyish pages which she read beside the basement stove.

I was drawn into her soft embraces like a bee into a summer flower. In common with Gerda, she never used perfume. She couldn't afford even Woolworth's. But unlike Gerda, her body had that heady tang which the Italians call *odure di donna*. She whispered, 'If you came upstairs one night, I wouldn't mind.'

'I'd wake the whole house up,' I objected.

'No you wouldn't. Not if you went careful, up the back stairs.'

'Supposing Lady Tip found out? You'd lose your position.' Rosie wrinkled her nose, but made no reply. I had already planned the route of a tiptoe Romeo, but had refused to let myself risk it. Not through chancing Rosie the sack. But because life was humiliating enough, without taking a housemaid as a mistress. I should be letting down the toffs.

We leapt apart. The green baize door leading down to the basement creaked on its spring. Rosie was clattering at her trays again when my mother came in. She wore her best black overcoat and her black hat with a bow and black gloves. She had been to weekday evensong at Holy Trinity Church by Regent's Park, Sunday matins being precluded by the Tipladys' lunch. She stood looking through the pantry door, taking off her gloves. I was busy polishing the silver with my leather.

'Don't put them cups down so, you'll break them,' she said quietly to Rosie.

Rosie looked round sharply and irritatingly set out the rest of the crockery with exaggerated tenderness. Then she tossed her dark curls and disappeared.

'What was you two up to?'

For a moment I was about to profess amazed innocence, like a child. Then I said simply, 'It's nothing whatever to do with you.'

My mother stared at me without changing her expression. She looked abruptly at the floor. 'Don't waste yourself.' She raised her glance round the kitchen. 'You can get yourself out of all this,' she said, just loudly enough to carry the hate in her voice.

The baize door creaked, my father clattered down the stone steps. 'It was the bloody cats what wanted feeding,' he announced bad temperedly. He added in the same tone, 'You ain't got far with that silver.'

'I'm a chemist, not a scullerymaid.'

He grunted. Picking up his nipped out cigarette from the saucer, he turned away in silence. It was the first time I dared to perform the experiment which demonstrated how terrified my parents were of me.

The bruised and silent atmosphere was fortunately shortly broken by the baize door opening again and Mrs Packer appearing, in her hat and about to leave for the day.

'Jim, there you are – Sir Edward wants you upstairs.'

The secretary was definitely not of the servants. She could ring for her tea from her small white office beside the consulting room at the back of the ground floor. She was pale and gingery with freckles, she wore starched white coats tightly belted round her narrow waist. Before leaving for Wuppertal I had imagined her middle-aged, but now I realized she could not have been much older than Gerda. No one seemed to know of Mr Packer, nor to mention him.

'You saw Sir Edward's been to the Palace today?' she said proudly as we reached the hall. 'it's in the evening papers.'

I had not noticed it. 'What's Sir Edward want me about?'

'Good news, I hope. He had a meeting with Sir Almroth Wright earlier. Perhaps he's found a job for you.'

I felt indifferent to this information, when six months earlier I should have been elated. Idleness had become my life, and the arduousness and discipline of employment looked distinctly uninviting. The same spiritual enfeeblement was probably suffered by the three million Britons who shared my experience.

'I *do* hope so.' She was looking at me smiling, head on one side. 'It does seem such a criminal waste, just kicking your heels down there. I mean with a Cambridge degree, and everything.'

She always sympathized with my being trapped in the lower classes, as she would have sympathized with a convict wrongfully imprisoned. That the social structure of the country was at blame crossed her mind as little as the prospect that it could ever be altered.

I found Sir Edward in his black jacket and striped trousers, striding about the upstairs drawing-room. 'Hello! Seen the papers?' he greeted me, boasting cheerfully. 'Nothing serious with the old gentleman, but you know how panicky everyone gets after last time.'

I took my place on the sheepskin rug, the fire in summer replaced by a fan of shiny paper, painstakingly folded by Rosie and generously speckled with soot.

'The King sends for me, he doesn't send for Tommy Horder,' he continued in the same tone. 'Tommy may be a first rate diagnostician with a first rate practice – H G Wells, Thomas Beecham, Somerset Maugham and all that – but he understands illnesses better than he does people.'

He took a cigarette from a mantelpiece more crowded with cards than ever, as it was the height of the London Season. Sir Edward was a regular attendant not only at the Royal bedside but at the Royal armchair whenever His Majesty fancied himself seedy. He went down so well because of a flair, when he chose to use it, for putting medical processes into earthy terms and even the language of the stable. This appealed to a monarch with a downright vocabulary, and an ear for a broad story which was richly satisfied by his Dominions Secretary, the Cockney J H Thomas.

He lit the cigarette, throwing himself into an armchair. 'You have to keep your head among those people at the Palace. You can imagine how I felt when Lord Dawson suddenly called me in, that Christmas of 1928? Finding myself in a bedroom with my Sovereign unconscious, blue in the face and snorting like a grampus, chest sounding like bubble-and-squeak, X-rays inconclusive, needle-tap dry, my distinguished colleagues throwing up their hands and the Privy Council convening all round me to tell the Empire the King was dead.' He laughed, and pressed the bell. 'I needed inspiration to think of an abscess under the diaphragm, and even more to know exactly where the needle had to go in search of the Royal pus. But I saved him! A couple of months, and he was off to convalesce in Bognor.'

I remember even today reading a Proclamation damp on the wall, its heavy official type declaring bravely, ornately, and pathetically, *Whereas We have been stricken by illness and are unable for the time being to give due attention to the affairs of Our Realm...* The news that a Council of State was to act for the King ran through the country like a tolling bell, the churches were left open day and night and my mother prayed at the kitchen table. The germs of pneumonia were as indifferent to a crown as to a cloth cap, and there was no treatment save the skilful fingers of his nurses. After Dr Tiplady was called on the Wednesday afternoon of December 12, an internal abscess was spotted, a rib snipped to emit the pus and antiseptic-soaked gauze packed painfully into the gap. The beloved Monarch breathed easier, the Empire rejoiced, Dr Tiplady became Sir Edward and Bognor became Bognor Regis.

'Elgar, I think I've found your lad a job,' Sir Edward announced as my father appeared with the cocktail tray.

'Glad to hear it, sir. Get him from under our feet all day.'

'I saw Sir Almroth and Flem this morning. What Flem never told me before –' he continued to me. 'Not of course that Flem ever tells you anything, conversation with him is like tennis with an opponent who pockets the ball after your every shot – and what *you* never told me before, was that *penicillium* mould contaminated his Petri dish entirely through your own incompetence and carelessness.' He said this smiling good-humouredly.

'I never thought much about it at the time,' I confessed. 'I was awfully busy working for my Cambridge scholarship. And scared stiff of being blown up by Sir Almroth, if it came to his ears. So I kept pretty quiet.'

'What modesty,' he said banteringly. 'You participated in a discovery.'

One of my jobs as a St Mary's lab boy was preparing the Petri dishes, shallow circular glass plates three inches across and quarter of an inch high, with another fitting snugly over the top, faintly resembling the domestic butter dish. As even germs must feed, these were floored with jelly made from pink Japanese seaweed, laced with the same meat broth as doubtless sustained the patients they had infected.

Fleming used a loop of sterilized platignum to smear on the jelly the spit or pus which arrived in an unending stream of swabs from the wards to his tiny, awkward laboratory in a turret on the corner of the hospital, its three windows overlooking busy Praed Street. After a night in the incubator, the invisible seeds had grown by repeatedly splitting in two, forming characteristic 'colonies' which Fleming could identify as one sort of germ or another. For confirmation, he stained them with dye and inspected them down his microscope, which had a special leather guard to prevent condensation from an ever-running nose stimulated by an ever-smouldering cigarette.

Once escaped from their protective glass, germs could be as dangerous as the vipers kept safely behind the windows of the Reptile House of the Zoo. In my own memory, two of Sir Almroth Wright's 'sons in science', as he called his staff, had been killed by their work. One caught tuberculosis, another glanders, which can strike down the rider as well as the horse. My job was to sterilize the used Petri dishes in a metal bowl of strong antiseptic. But when Fleming left for his holiday in Scotland in the miserably cold July of 1928, I stacked the dishes in the bowl and completely forgot about them until the morning he returned. He summoned me, he pointed silently to the top two or three, which I had so carelessly left above the level of the disinfectant fluid, and which could have been extruding germs into the atmosphere like the breath of a sick man.

Fleming never became angry. He reminded me of another Scots doctor, described by Robert Louis Stevenson in *Jekyll and Hyde* as 'about as emotional as a bagpipe'. But his taciturnity could make you feel horribly uncertain and guilty. As I was hastily carrying the bowl away, he picked up the top Petri dish and said, 'That's funny.' *I* saw it was contaminated with a blob of greenish mould. Fleming saw that the mould was killing off the colonies of staphylococcus germs all round it.

Sir Edward started stroking a black cat which had leapt into his lap. 'I must admit, it was canny of Flem to notice his colonies of staphs turning to ghosts of their former selves. Thank God it was Flem who baptized the mysterious mould-juice "penicillin". Did you know that *penicillium* is the Latin for "a brush"?' I shook my head. 'Wright is so damn proud of his Classical education, he would have anointed the stuff with jaw-breaking polysyllables, far beyond Flem's limited powers of speech.' He took his glass of sherry from my father. 'Her ladyship won't be in to dinner tonight, Elgar.'

'Very good, sir.'

'There must have been a good many chances involved – even the weather – to let those staphs grow cheek by jowl with the mould,' Sir Edward mused. I always admired how he effortlessly switched the level of conversation from my father to myself. It must have come from handling all manner of men in his profession. 'I suppose the mould floated from Praed Street or Heaven, or the funnel of the Cornish Riviera Express in

Paddington Station, for all I know. He's kept the dish, you know. He showed it me this morning.'

It is now in the British Museum – fittingly, history being largely the record of man's lucky or unlucky mistakes.

'So Flem's ended up with a neat little laboratory toy,' Sir Edward continued. 'Do you know what he does with this penicillin?'

'Not exactly. I never heard of it again, until you mentioned it after I got back from Germany.'

'He mixes it with the agar jelly in his Petri dishes, and it kills off all the bugs causing the common diseases – you know, pneumonia, gonorrhea, diphtheria, septicaemia and all that. But it doesn't touch such odd birds as *Bacillus Influenzae*. So Flem makes his patients cough all over a Petri dish soaked in his mould-juice, and if they're incubating the influenza bacillus it will grow in lovely colonies instead of being crowded out by the other common or garden bugs.'

'That's rather neat.'

'Oh, it's a very elegant experiment. But of course Flem's one of the most stylish lab workers I've ever come across. I wish we had someone like him at Blackfriars – my own hospital suffers a very ham-handed lot in the bacteriological department. Though unfortunately the experiment is not of the slightest importance whatever.' He laughed. 'Andrews and the bright boys at the Medical Research Institute have discovered that flu isn't caused by the influenza bacillus at all. It's due to a virus.' He drained his sherry. 'No more, thank you, Elgar. That will do.'

My father withdrew, by custom turning at the door to leave backwards, as though Sir Edward were royalty rather than its medical attendant.

'So Flem goes on boring us about his wretched mould-juice at the Research Club. But I suppose Edward Jenner utterly bored his friends for twenty years over his smallpox vaccination theories. At any rate, they tried to chuck him out of something called the Convivio-Medical Club down in Gloucester. But the story may have a happy ending for you. Sir Almroth would like to see you again. He's even asked you to tea.' Sir Edward produced his pocket diary, screwing in his monocle. 'Tuesday, July 3. GBS will be there.'

He paused for me to look impressed. I knew that Shaw was a regular visitor to the ceremonial if unappetizing teas in Sir Almroth's department. 'So you'd better sharpen up your wits,' he advised. 'Sir Almroth may offer you a job, but of course I can't promise. The Inoculation Department at Mary's is hardly running with money like your German drug companies.' He pushed the black cat off his lap and stood up. 'Now I must run along, I've a hundred things to finish before I dine in solitary state. My wife is out tonight in the company of an old admirer.'

He tried to say this lightly, but in a sentence his voice plummeted down like a singer's. We both looked embarrassed. He struggled to resume in his usual manner, 'Let me give you some advice – never get married.' But he failed. Then he stroked my cheek. That was the only gesture he ever made towards me. I was frightened to discover how miserable he was.

14

I can remember today that speck of mould on Fleming's Petri dish. It was fluffy and white, its centre dark green, almost black. I remember wondering at the time if it was the same mould as grew upon the loaves we ate in the basement, too stale to set before our betters above stairs. My mother would often bandage it on my septic cuts, an old wives' remedy which sent me to school with my fingers in the form of a sandwich. The mould from a dead man's skull was apparently more effective, had she been able to lay her hands on any.

The mould had at least not lodged me unfavourably in the memory of Sir Almroth Wright. As I left for tea with him three weeks later, I daringly slipped into my tweed jacket pocket the phial of Domagk's 'Streptozon'. I decided that the King's physician had been a shade off-hand about the drug. Today I realize that Sir Edward had little faith in any treatment at all, because there was little treatment to have any faith in, even for a King. He had only insulin for the diabetic, liver for the anaemic and digitalis for the cardiac, X-rays were ghostly and the electrocardiograph a delicate toy. He used mostly his own eyes, hands and ears, dextrously assembling round the sick man a fragile scaffolding of the medicaments available until Nature cured.

I had not set eyes on St Mary's Hospital since leaving with my scholarship, after working there and enjoying free its first-year lectures. It was an exorbitantly solid building of red brick and stone, its first and second floors with verandas looking upon the passing bus tops in Praed Street. The Prince Consort laid its foundation stone in 1845, it grew amid the shrieks of engines from Paddington Station, the miasmas of the Grand

Junction Canal and the stink of a nearby carter's stables. The hospital itself was sick in my time. It was the most popular among the medical students in London, being the worst and therefore the easiest to get into. But the new dean was already effecting a cure, as in World War II he effected it with the health of Winston Churchill.

The terrace of seedy Victorian shops opposite was the same, so was the Fountains Abbey pub on the corner. But the turret which had housed the Inoculation Department, in converted poky wards and sisters' sitting-rooms, was superseded by a handsome, rectangular, five-storied building joined to the hospital by a bridge and known to everyone as 'The House of Lords'.

'Ah! Young Elgar. Been on your travels, I hear.'

I found Sir Almroth Wright in his own laboratory, at his elbow a row of metal drums packed with test-tubes plugged by cotton wool, on the bench before him microscope, Petri dishes, platignum loops, a throaty Bunsen burner, behind him shelves of chemical reagents and dyes. A bacteriologist, like an airline pilot, has to keep everything within fingertip reach.

He immediately started talking to me in German, which he had learned fifty years before as a student in Leipzig. It seemed to suit his taste for polysyllabled pomposity. Pink cheeked, white hair brushed across the dome of his head, white moustached, he had a Nordic look inherited from his grandfather, once Director of the Swedish Mint. He had a protruding lower lip, circular steel-rimmed glasses half way down a stubby nose, a dark suit with the hopelessly ill-fitting look of a growing schoolboy's, and only a wing collar to show respect for his professional position.

'It would seem that Herr Hitler's cohorts are now diverting their murderous energies more usefully against each other,' he broke off in English, after we had talked of Wuppertal and Domagk. 'Directly after von Papen — of all people — dared to speak out for tolerance, freedom of the Press, silence for fanatics, and all that. Causing Dr Göebbels to stuff his fingers very promptly into his countrymen's earholes. From my knowledge of the officer corps, I should imagine the German Army was behind the massacre at Munich. They wouldn't care for Röhm's plan to enlist a brownshirted rabble of two and a half million Storm Troopers in their ranks,'

I saw that he was not condescending to invite my opinion, and indeed events had moved so swiftly in Germany after my leaving that I could not give one. It was shortly after the 'Night of the Long Knives', when Hitler appeared at two o'clock on the Saturday morning of June 30 at the Hanslbauer Hotel in the lakeside resort of Weissee near Munich, to pull his closest friend Ernst Röhm and other top Storm Troopers from their beds, an operation simplified by many being in bed with each other. 'Peculators, drunkards and homosexuals', the Storm Troopers appeared through the monocle of General von Brauchitsch – and they were anyway interfering with the serious business of Germany's illicit rearmament.

A thousand other prominent Germans were murdered in the days which followed. Affable, portly 'Artful Dodger' General Kurt von Schleicher was shot on his doorstep with his new wife. The socialism in National Socialism was eliminated, the Storm Troopers were demoted, the black uniformed SS were freed to become the most efficient and ruthless political police in Europe's tortured history. President Hindenburg watched it all through eyes dimming with death, and the gentleman showjumper Franz von Papen, whose talent for survival approached genius, lived to fight another day, at Nürnberg.

German politics lead us on to German drugs. Sir Almroth tipped my red 'Streptozon' tablets into the palm of his hand.

'I left Elberfeld with the laboratory and the factory in my mind inseparable,' he said in a discouraging voice. 'I G Farben churns out every variety of chemical for dyes, pesticides and yarns, and Professor Domagk churns them into mice, to see if the chemical kills them, or the bacteria with which he's already infected the poor creatures. That's not experimentation. That's not even science. It's roulette – a limited mental exercise, which even with the best of luck inevitably bankrupts the players.'

I had anticipated a rebuff more readily than from Sir Edward. Sir Almroth Wright was a Victorian naturalist with a microscope, at one with the country rector classifying his lepidoptera, the holidaymaking schoolmaster chipping specimens from the Alps, the don with camel-hair brush cross-pollinating his roses. He sought the panacea with glass microscope slides, putty and dabs of sealing-wax.

'The cure for disease, the elimination of human disease altogether, lies in the intelligent application of vaccine therapy,' he emphasized to me. This was more than Wright's life work. It was Wright's life. 'Do you know what is far superior to any mouse as an experimental animal? The human white blood corpuscle. We watch down our microscopes the effect of our cures upon *that*, not upon cages of white mice.'

He handed me back the phial. I was in no position to protest, nor had I the courage. Our conversation was anyway disrupted by the sudden appearance of Dr John Freeman, tall, handsome, Charterhouse and Oxford, in his fifties but eternally energetic, said in the Inoculation Department always to 'Blow in, blow up and blow out'.

Sir Almroth gave his usual salutation, 'Well, friend, what have you won from our Mother Science today?'

They started discussing hay fever, on which Freeman was an expert. He thought this miserable complaint to be caused by the spores of moulds, and for years had scraped bedroom floors all over London for specimens of them. They were shortly joined by Professor Alexander Fleming, as different from Freeman as Burns from Byron.

Flem was not Charterhouse and Oxford, but Kilmarnock Academy and Regent Street Polytechnic. The last of an Ayrshire sheep farmer's large family, he clerked four years in a Leadenhall Street shipping office before warmer breezes of fortune brought him the windfall of a legacy, and wafted him into St Mary's at the turn of the century. He had passed the surgical fellowship with the plan of applying his nimble fingers to the profitable scalpel of an eye surgeon, but had been given a job in the Inoculation Department to retain at St Mary's his other talents as a sharpshooter in the hospital rifle team.

Their talk turned to wound infection. All three had served in the Royal Army Medical Corps during the war at No 13 General Hospital in Boulogne Casino, studying infection in the top floor laboratory, even constructing experimental wounds among the plethora from paper and spiky test-tubes impregnated with blood serum and germs. Wright had always been close to the Army. He was professor at the Army Medical School in the 1890s, resigning when the Army ridiculed his notion of inoculation against typhoid fever. Fifteen out of every thousand soldiers in the Boer War died from typhoid, then the Army thought again, and in the Great War the proportion dropped to two.

Sir Almroth had a military air about him, the atmosphere of his department was said to resemble a mess of the Indian Medical Service, and so did the language. He always talked of his 'sons in science', and if one of them had the effrontery to get married never spoke to him for six months. A Marie Curie, a Florence Nightingale, could never have found work in the Inoculation Department. He had married one of the most intelligent women in Ireland, but that blew up before Europe did in 1914, and he went home every night to a housekeeper's dinner off the Earls Court Road. That he was a homosexual was a secret which everyone knew and no one uttered.

It was four o'clock. We went through to the library, which contained a divan, some wooden chairs, a square kitchen table and a gas ring for the kettle. Tea was a daily ritual which Wright naturally dominated. George Bernard Shaw probably attended because even he was flattered to share the cabalistic confidences of medical men.

I had never set eyes on GBS, nor on a performance of one of his plays, but I had heard all about him. In the 1930s everyone in England had heard all about him, because he was continually telling Englishmen what to do about everything. I saw the famous grizzly white beard, the thick white eyebrows and neatly parted white hair. He wore a brown tweed suit with a soft collar and loosely-knotted tie. Shaw was then seventy-eight. Wright was seventy-three. Both were Irishmen. They had known, respected and misunderstood one another since the start of the century.

I had decided to write a note of the expectedly brilliant conversation, which I still have. Like lesser men, they talked of women.

'Emotional tension is intolerant of an intellectual impasse,' declared Sir Almroth, 'but not in the woman. The female intellect will fail in trying conditions, as a Baby Austin car will fail on a steep hill.' He had himself learned to drive a car at the age of sixty-four. 'She will either come to a halt, coast with ever-increasing momentum back to where she started from, or blow up and burst into tears.'

Shaw was arrogantly at ease, long legs stuck out. 'The female intellect will grasp as quickly as my own that you are reloading your guns with the same ammunition you fired against the Suffragettes. And now it's even more likely to explode in your face, with twenty years' rust on it.'

'My target has not changed. It has simply progressed a little. I wrote *The Unexpurgated Case Against Woman Suffrage* in 1913.' Everyone in the Inoculation Department had heard of the book and no one had read it. 'Today they hoist the flag of Women's Freedom, but that is the flag of financial freedom for women and financial servitude for men.'

'Any man will beggar himself for a woman, with the exquisite cheerfulness he reserves for observing somebody else beggar his neighbour.' Shaw had of course no need to wind up the watch of his wit, but the chimes sometimes had little relevance to the hour.

I noticed Fleming, perched on the table looking bored. He was a short, stocky man, with a large head, a pink complexion, pale blue eyes, a small chin and a straight mouth which turned down at each end like Sir Walter Scott's. His was that unmercurial Lowland face, to be encountered as readily in the pubs of Glasgow as the mission huts of China or the surgeries of Canada. He was clean shaven, though at the Boulogne Casino he was a Lieutenant with a neat triangular black moustache. He seldom smiled. He was often silent.

At fifty-three, his thick black hair with a quiff had grown grey. He wore his usual dark suit, with semi-stiff collar and spotted bow tie, and it was the brief period of the year which he found too warm for his grey knitted pullover. He had an enormous wristwatch. He was nearly always smoking a cigarette. I wondered if his thoughts were in his lab, or the Chelsea Arts Club where he stopped on his way home, or even further in the hills of Argyll.

Sir Almroth took a teacup from the fixedly smiling Freeman. He continued severely, 'You cannot divert attention from good arguments by bad ones, as you repeatedly succeed in doing on the stage.'

'The female physiological constitution is a matter of fashion, like all medical theories. Today's philosophy is tomorrow's absurdity, and what was rank foolishness last year is everybody's wisdom the next.'

It was the traditional fireworks display in the Inoculation Department, but the squibs were growing damp. Shaw did not die until he broke his hip lopping trees in 1950, but that afternoon in St Mary's he had everything behind him, only *Geneva* and *In Good King Charles' Golden Days* to come. It was thirty years since Wright had struck from his flinty mind the spark of *The Doctor's Dilemma*. The play was prompted by a gratified observation from Freeman that the Department had more work than it could handle, and Wright's reply to Shaw's inevitable question that the human life for the doctor to save under such pressure of strained resources was the life most worth saving. Sir Almroth had walked out of the first night at the Royal Court Theatre in 1906, not because he objected to his depiction on the boards as Sir Colenso Ridgeon, the stimulator of the phagocytes, but because in his opinion Shaw killed off the wrong patient.

Behind Sir Almroth that afternoon was his brazen declaration, 'The physician of the future will be an immunizer.' Ahead lay the bitter confession at the age of eighty to the Royal Society of Medicine, of the 'Need for abandoning much in immunology regarded as assured.' He left a heap of discredited medical theories and a book on logic, which consumed his life in the writing and again which nobody wanted to read.

As I left, Fleming handed me silently a copy of the *British Journal of Experimental Pathology*, which he inscribed on the cover *For J Elgar*, and signed. Neither he nor anyone else had said anything about a job.

15

'Jim – !'

I was just quitting the hospital under the bridge leading to the 'House of Lords'. I spun round.

'David!'

'What the hell are you doing back here, boy?'

'Taking tea with Sir Almroth Wright.'

'What? With the Holy Ghost himself? My word, you're doing well.'

'I'm on the dole.'

'Go on! Pull the other one.'

'What are *you* doing here?'

'I'm doing my clinical. I'm one of the students. Didn't I tell you I was going to Mary's, when I went down from Cambridge? I've been here a year.'

'Did you get that First in your Part Two?'

David Mellors modestly nodded away this achievement. 'What have you been up to? More work on the staining of bacteria?'

'I've had a year in Germany.'

'You never let on you were going. Which university?'

'I worked in a brewery.'

'Oh, lovely! How do I get a job like that?' He was small, dark, wiry, lively, as Welsh as a leek. He looked at his wristwatch. 'Listen, boy. I've got a five o'clock lecture. The Fountains across the road opens at six. I'll meet you in the public bar. Can you waste an hour?'

An hour seemed of little consequence when I had wasted the past six months. I idled the time away by going to Paddington Station and watching the trains.

David Mellors and I had been friendly at Trinity, thrown together by both of us being 'scholarship boys'. Thackeray's Pendennis was still up at Cambridge then. Most of the undergraduates at Trinity were from the great public schools, many were there simply to amuse themselves. They were swells who never spared their polished contempt for students with the wrong sort of clothes or wrong sort of accent or who worked too hard or had too many brains. I had spent vacations cycling with David round the Welsh valleys, where his father kept a chemist's shop and was immeasurably better off than mine. We lost touch since I quit Cambridge for Wuppertal during the Christmas vacation of 1932. The young live too immediately to recognize friendship as a precious plant worth careful cultivation.

I arrived at the Fountains Abbey as the landlord was shooting back the bolts. I sat at a small round table with half a pint of mild ale, and there being no sign of David pulled out the journal which Fleming had pressed on me. It was Issue No 10, dated June 1929, an abstruse publication which appeared every two months and which I had never before opened.

Inside was a list of its editors. I recognized only two names. J C Drummond was a biochemist like myself, a sprightly, well-liked gourmet, professor at University College in Bloomsbury. W H Florey I remembered as an Australian at Cambridge, lecturer in pathology and a Fellow of Gonville and Caius College, next door to Trinity. During my final year, Dr Florey had left to become Professor at Sheffield, and every high table chorused amazed tut-tuts.

The index of papers seemed pretty uninteresting. _Tetanus... Myxomatosis of Rabbits..._ The last of all had the title, _On the Antibacterial Action of Cultures of a Penicillium._ I had never seen Fleming's paper on the fruits of my mistake. I found it covered thirteen pages, bolstered with tables and photographs.

It told me little that I had not already heard from Sir Edward Tiplady. I noticed that twenty-five unknown St Mary's nurses, who are claimed to be the prettiest in London, had involuntarily helped the research when laid up with influenza. Their throat swabs had been cultivated on agar jelly with and without penicillin added. On the ordinary jelly, the streptococcus and pneumonococcus germs which flourish even in healthy throats grew profusely. With the penicillin, no nurse's germs grew at all. There was a photograph of the original Petri dish, which Fleming had shown Sir Edward. It made me recall something which Fleming said at the time – that he was studying the pigment which coloured colonies of staphylococcus germs, which showed best if the germs were grown at room temperature instead of inside an incubator. So that particular Petri dish happened to have been left open on the laboratory bench for the *penicillium* mould to drop on it. As Sir Edward had mentioned, the mould-juice had been squeezed from a skein of chances.

Fleming ended by mentioning that its lack of irritant or poisonous effect might recommend penicillin as a surgical dressing, or for an injection round an infection. There was still no sign of David Mellors. I rolled up the journal and stuck it back in my pocket, carefully retaining half an inch in the bottom of my glass to defy the landlord.

The pub was filling as David burst in, pile of notebooks under his arm, stethoscope coiling from the jacket of his unkempt blue suit. 'I had a practical to finish. What'll you have?'

'Half of mild.'

'Halves?' he said contemptuously. 'Pints tonight, boy. What in the world were you seeing the Holy Ghost for?' he demanded, as he reappeared with the beer.

'I was trying to get a job. I'm on the dole, honestly.'

David took a long draught. 'Any luck?'

'Not the smell of an oil-rag. Like a fool I introduced the subject of chemotherapy. That did for me.'

'Oh, chemotherapy! Wright always calls it "pharmacotherapy", anyway. Pompous sod, isn't he? Where are you living?'

'Same place. My parents still work at the Tipladys'.'

'Sir Edward did pretty well for himself, spotting that sub-phrenic abscess in the old geezer.' He was referring to His Majesty's illness. 'It shouldn't have cracked anyone's brains open. *Pus somewhere, pus nowhere else, pus under the diaphragm*, that's the hoariest of surgical tags. Perhaps Lord Dawson and the assembled pundits thought themselves above such aids to memory.'

'Where are *you* living?'

'I'm in clover, boy. With Archie Fry.'

'In London? I thought he strode over his broad acres in the country?'

'Oh, Archie's quite a man about Town, in his own peculiar way. A flat in Belgravia, doncherknow.' David tipped up the end of his nose with his forefinger. 'Very palatial, even a Jeeves.'

'What's he want to share with you for?' I asked bluntly.

'It's his socialist ideals. You know what Archie's like. It's his father's flat, but he's got the run of it, an enormous place he thinks he should fill with families of unemployed from the East End. I salve his conscience, I'm cleaner and I'm probably less trouble when I come home drunk.'

Archie Fry was my third friend at Trinity. Where other undergraduates afforded us disdain, Archie treated David and I to patronizing equality. He was a self-made socialist from Eton, like George Orwell. But where cadaverous, tuberculous Orwell took the world as his punch-bag to be pounded with muscular prose, Archie was delightfully inept at everything he grappled – writing, publishing, politics or the quest for martyrdom in love or war. He volunteered as a matter of course for Spain in 1936 and for the Guards in 1939 but succeeded in escaping harm from either.

Since I began writing this story, Archie has dropped dead on holiday at St Tropez. Age brings no pleasures, only compensations, of which the cosiest is reading the obituaries of your contemporaries over breakfast. As expected, *The Times* strewed his grave with ornate wreaths of poisoned ivy. But Archie was essentially a *nice man*, that highest of sparing, tight-lipped English compliments. And his death brings me now only the feeling of a friend who has left by an earlier train. It also finally struck off that unrusting shackle which binds two men who have shared the bed of the same woman.

'Drink up! I need another pint,' urged David. He was the cleverest student 1 had ever known, and his bucolic bounce no affectation.

'It's my turn.'

'You're on the dole.'

'I refuse to accept charity,' I said, only half humorously.

'Why not? I accept it from Archie. Look at this tie.' He held it out. 'It's his, pure silk from Jermyn Street. I think I've got his socks on as well.'

'You don't mind sponging on him?'

'It's not sponging, boy, it's socialism. He's a socialist of the pure-minded sort, which is a mug's game. Down where I come from we're all socialists, but on the receiving end. That's different.'

After the next pint – or perhaps the one after, or the one after that – David suggested, 'Why don't you batch with Archie, too? You can't go on living in the servants' hall for ever.'

'I haven't the nerve to ask him. Besides, my parents would miss me.'

'Let them. It's got to come sooner or later. What have you got in common with them? They might have found you on the doorstep. If it isn't you, I'll be sleeping among the dregs of a Mile End doss house. Archie's conscience has been troubling him a lot lately, though I'd put it down to dyspepsia and the wind.' He spotted the journal in my pocket, and frowned as he pulled it out. 'What are you doing with this rag? Even real qualified doctors can't understand it. Not the ones at Mary's, at any rate.'

I turned to Fleming's paper, and told him my part of the story. When I finished he said, 'Yes, I've heard of penicillin. But I didn't know what it was. It's the lysozyme tale all over again, isn't it? You must have seen that famous cartoon in the Mary's *Gazette*?'

Everybody had seen it at Mary's. It depicted a line of schoolboys being birched at a penny a time by some amiable sadist, over jars labelled 'Tear Antiseptic'. One winter's day in 1922, the Niobe of sinuses had mothered a scientific infant, when a drip from Fleming's nose fell on a Petri dish and dissolved the germs growing there – exactly like penicillin. 'Lysozyme,' Sir Almroth had christened the mysterious substance. Fleming found it in tears, which he evoked from his colleagues by squirting lemons into their eyes, until to everyone's relief he discovered it also in pikes' eggs. Fleming suggested that lysozyme might be used against human infections, but medical London in 1922 was not particularly interested. Medical London was becoming wary of the fine scientific horses with flowing philosophical manes which pranced in Sir Almroth Wright's stables. I heard later that

Fleming had given a couple of lectures on the idea, but doubtless these were as usual incomprehensible.

'When I worked as a lab boy, Flem had lost all interest in lysozyme,' I told David. 'That was a big fault of his, according to everyone in the Department. He was far more interested in performing an elegant experiment than in the result which the experiment was supposed to produce.'

'Still, Flem's had some jammy luck. First a blob of snot, then a blob of mould. They just happened to drop on a Petri dish growing bacteria at exactly the right time.'

'Surely there's no talent in the world as useful as a talent for luck?' I snatched back the journal, flicking it over to the last page of Fleming's paper. 'That mould! It didn't bloody drop from Heaven. I can tell you exactly where it came from.'

At the end of the paper, Fleming gave the usual courteous thanks to his colleagues. 'That's the fellow!' I exclaimed. 'The Irishman with the French name, Mr la Touche. He was a mycologist. Which means that he did nothing from morning to night except handle moulds of various sorts. Now I come to think of it, that *penicillium* mould couldn't possibly have floated through the windows of Flem's little lab up in the turret. For the simple reason that Flem never opened them. The noise from the traffic in Praed Street was terrible, and anyway he had enough germs in test-tubes on the window-sills to kill the entire British Army. Flem wouldn't have been the most popular man in Paddington if they'd dropped on the top deck of a passing omnibus.'

David drained his glass, disappointingly unimpressed.

'I remember when I worked there in 1928,' I went on, 'la Touche used to grow specimens of moulds in big open dishes for Dr Freeman to make vaccines and inject his hay-fever patients – like immunization against typhoid. And la Touche's lab was immediately below Flem's! Why, it was a fungus factory. The staircase outside must have had more moulds floating in it than any area in London. Flem's mould didn't originate from the hand of God, but from the bedroom slippers of some wheezy asthmatic or rheumy-eyed hay-fever sufferer. Do you suppose Flem would be interested if I told him?'

'I shouldn't think so. It would only indicate that he was working in filthy conditions.'

In the end, I agreed to move in with David. 'I'm prepared to pay Archie ten bob a week,' I told him.

'At Archie's you don't pay, you borrow. Let's go down the road and get some fish and chips. I'll stand treat.'

I still have the journal signed by Fleming. If I sent it along to Sotheby's auction rooms I should get a substantial sum for it. You can still see the grease mark of our fish and chips.

16

Hargraves has just come in. Today, as I write these memoirs on the top floor of Arundel College in Bloomsbury, that most melancholy of districts, where the gaily contentious ghosts of Lytton Strachey and lovely, lesbian Carrington haunt disconsolately the concrete academic groves of London University.

My Arbeitszimmer is but a quarter the size of Gerhard Domagk's in Elberfeld. It looks not upon the Schwebebahn but on British Rail. I stare down on the lines winding away from Euston Station, behind the backs of crumbly houses whose tiles were shivered by Hitler's Luftwaffe and the Kaiser's Zeppelins. I have no Otto Dix on the wall – though our country home sports a couple of Bratbys, who resembles Dix with a splash of Cockney cheerfulness. But I have the same framed photographs of fellow scientists. One is of Domagk himself, a few strands of hair brushed across the dome of his head, in plastic-rimmed glasses and the sleeves of his white lab coat still too long for him. He is working at his microscope in the room where I met the girl with the Slav eyes. It is scrawled upon barely legibly, *freundliche Grüsse Gerhard Domagk 24.12.63*. A year later he died, aged sixty-eight, at No 11 Jägerstrasse, round the corner from his old home in Walkürenallee near the Zoo. It was an infected gallbladder. 'The germs got their revenge,' people in Wuppertal said gloomily.

The photograph next to Domagk's is inscribed *To Jim Elgar. Good luck! Alexander Fleming*. Flem is silver haired and unaccountably wistful, with rimless glasses and a spotted bow tie and a herpes lesion on his lower lip. It is a studio study from the time of his second marriage in 1953 to his bacteriological assistant from Greece, Dr Amalia Koutsouris-Voureka –

who to my mind achieved even mightier distinction by being the first woman allowed by Sir Almroth Wright to work in his Department. Fleming's photograph is dated November 11, 1954, precisely a year and four months before he died from a coronary thrombosis in bed. He lies in the crypt of St Paul's, with Wellington and Nelson.

My third photograph is from the bacteriologist Leonard Colebrook (*For Professor John Elgar, Regards, Coli*). A kind scholarly face, a long mouth with a deep upper lip and protruding lower one, beetling brows and beaky nose under heavily-rimmed glasses. He died on September 29, 1967 – another coronary. The remaining one was given me by Jack Drummond, one of the editors of the journal which contained Fleming's paper. He signed it when he was knighted in 1944. He was murdered after the war by a French farmer. After such a gallery of fatalities, my wife has strictly forbidden me to sign anything for presentation to anyone.

Hargraves would certainly frame my own photograph and hang it on the wall if he thought it would reliably speed my demise. Hargraves is a coming man, and most impatient about it. I do not like Hargraves. Not that he is in the slightest unpleasant. On the contrary, he is always smiling, encouraging our juniors, joking with our students and shaking hands warmly with our visitors. He is an outstanding chemist and exceptional organizer. He has stylish hair, a fancy moustache, glistening teeth, square glasses, and his clothes always look new. At home, he has a pink plastic swimming pool and a talkative wife. He goes for holidays on baked, insanitary beaches in Spain and discusses television. I suspect that he eats breakfast cereals and drinks vodka and even applies after-shave lotion.

Hargraves had wedged his way between my filing cabinets and my desk, ostensibly to chat about my research. Nobody at Arundel knows exactly what research I am doing. I am remote in my own small laboratory, like the ageing Sir Almroth Wright, who would arrive at St Mary's after lunch and potter scientifically until released by dinner. Suddenly Hargraves threw in a confession. 'I was at the College Council meeting yesterday – they were sorry again you couldn't make it – when the pleasant suggestion cropped up that you might be allowed to round off your time here with a sabbatical year.'

He meant that he had urged them to push me out early. 'What should I do all day?'

'Travel?'

'Oh, God!'

'Well, we all know how you love your farm, Jim.'

Why must everyone use Christian names? Hardly through friendship in this age of intense mutual suspicion. To insist that we are all equal? Supposing I had called my mentor 'Almroth'?

'My wife runs the farm. If I were there all week I'd only get in the way.'

'You're being modest, Jim. She told me you were invaluable with the livestock.'

'No, I prefer to stay here to the bitter end. It's disheartening, slogging your way through a marathon and giving up at the last lap.'

'Personally, of course, I'm delighted that you're prepared to carry responsibility for the department a little longer.'

'I'm sure you are.'

Hargraves left. He will try again at the next Council meeting, unless I mischievously swallow my boredom and attend.

The summer of 1934 saw an improvement in my condition. I escaped from the basement and I found a job. For both I was indebted to Archie Fry.

I left home in the middle of July. Perhaps my parents were secretly glad to shed the puppy they had become over-fond of, which turned into a dog they had no idea what to do with. Rosie turned pale. Sir Edward had sailed to America, but Lady Tip summoned me up to the drawing room.

'I thought you might have asked to see me of your own accord, Jim.'

Elizabeth sat on the sofa beside her, just released from boarding school, bewitching in soft summer dress of cream silk. She sat looking at me wide-eyed, as though I were some queer fish dredged from the depths for her biological inspection.

'I didn't imagine that you would be particularly distressed if I failed to say good-bye, your Ladyship.' I did not know in my own mind if I were being rude or apologetic.

'I *am* distressed. Not because you didn't *faire vos adieux*, that's a matter of indifference. But you are leaving my house after *eight years* without so much as coming to thank me for sheltering you, for feeding you and for doing absolutely everything for you during that time. You went to Germany and came back again without so much as a murmur of thanks, or even asking my leave. That's exactly the same with everyone of your class. Rank ingratitude, all take and no give.'

'My parents may be your Ladyship's servants, but I'm not,' I said more boldly.

'As far as I'm concerned, I can see no distinction.'

'I can't understand that attitude. But of course, I'm so much better educated than you are.'

'How dare you! Remember your position.'

Whether through embarrassment, or fright, or simply from seeing the fun of the situation, her daughter broke the tension by giggling.

'Shut up,' snapped Lady Tip at her. But without avail. *'Shut up*! Oh, get out, you little swine,' she dismissed me.

Archie Fry's flat was the first floor of an enormous house at the corner of Belgrave Square, gloomy and rambling, full of heavy furniture and bad paintings in expensive frames, everywhere terribly dusty. David and I shared a huge room at the back, and looked after ourselves. Archie was out all day and often most of the night, running hostels for down-and-outs in the East End, or reforming the world with the Fabian Society, or nursing a north London constituency which he hoped to win as Labour candidate in the next election. (He failed.)

Shortly after my arrival, we all three contrived to dine together in the vast green and gold dining-room. Archie was eager for my impressions of Germany.

'Surely you can't condemn these labour service camps out of hand,' Archie objected. 'The young Germans may make themselves look ridiculous by shouldering arms with shovels, but there's plenty of men in this country who'd jump at the chance of doing the same for three square meals a day.'

'That's not the point. The Nazis turn even the digging of ditches into a military exercise for the glory of the Fatherland.'

'How can we blame them? The Treaty of Versailles was perfectly wicked. We couldn't expect any self-respecting nation to lie down under it. After fifteen years it seems high time to admit that, and admit Herr Hitler's right to demand parity of armaments with us and the French. In the meantime, digging ditches seems a preferable occupation for young men in uniform than digging graves.'

'But don't you understand? The Nazis don't see war as we do, something to be avoided at all costs. They see war as necessary and desirable, the great national purifier.'

'The Hegelian view,' commented Archie. ' "The moral health of nations is corrupted by unbroken peace, as tempests preserve the sea from the foulness brought by prolonged calm." Of course, a lot of German philosophy is sheer lunacy. I suppose because they're not blessed with authors like Lewis Carroll and W S Gilbert, who can write lunacy properly.'

He struggled to cut his leg of chicken. Archie was tall and spare, with a sharp nose and bony face, his eyes soft and brown, his hair dark and lank. He wore a suit of Donegal tweed with a red knitted tie in a loose collar, an outfit which other young men of his background would have thought more suitable for the butts than Belgravia.

'This chicken,' complained David Mellors across the oval mahogany table. 'I don't know what disease it succumbed to, but it's got a bad case of rigor mortis.'

'Watson, can't you do better than this?' demanded Archie of his manservant, who appeared with a dish of greyish boiled potatoes. The Jeeves was knobbly-faced, bald, tubby and flat footed. Archie proudly claimed the man never needed call him 'Sir'. The effect was his being uninterruptedly rude to all three of us.

'What's wrong with it?' Watson asked.

'We can't cut it, let alone eat it.'

David poured himself another glass of the chateau bottled claret. The food at Archie's was terrible, the drink superb and plentiful, and he never seemed to worry at our helping ourselves.

'You can't expect me to work miracles,' Watson replied surlily. 'If you wants proper vittles, you'll have to get a proper cook.'

'I'm sorry cooking is too much for you, Watson,' Archie told him apologetically. 'I'd engage a cook tomorrow, but you know how I disapprove of a house full of servants.'

'Then you'd better go out to Lyons Corner House. I can't do everything. Keeping this place clean is like dusting the bloody British Museum.'

'Of course, Watson, I appreciate all you do to make us comfortable.'

'If you don't want your chicken, I'll clear it away,' Watson said aggressively.

'No, no, Watson, we'll try.'

'I've got some bicarbonate outside, and there's a stomach pump at Mary's,' said David.

'Watson really is a little difficult,' Archie murmured as he left. 'But if I didn't employ him, nobody else would. I just can't agree with you, Jim,' he resumed. 'I cannot take the Nazis seriously.'

'You haven't seen them at close quarters. I've been interrogated by them. That was quite frightening.'

'Yes, but Germans tend to browbeat people as a matter of course. It's part of the national character.'

'That's the very secret of Nazism. They exaggerate and twist every thought inside a German head. What once passed as normal now becomes dangerous and grotesque. Love of country, respect for discipline, pride in race...even uniforms and torchlight parades and camp fires, perfectly harmless in themselves, are these days exploited to the single end of the glorification of Adolf Hitler.'

'The Germans are perhaps a *krankes Volk*, a sick people,' Archie reflected. 'But I'm perfectly certain that Hitler is simply whipping up excitement for excitement's sake, like a speedway rider or circus performer. To keep his people's minds off the economic situation.'

'You mean, Hitler's just the Daring Young Man on the Flying Trapeze?'

'Roughly, yes.'

'Oh, God. You blind fool.' I pushed away the chicken. I wasn't hungry any more, anyway. I had come back from Germany full of the dangers of Hitler and the blessings of sulphonamide. Nobody would believe me about either. I began to suspect I was in the wrong.

The following week, Archie found me my job. His father was the creator of Fry's Carbolic Soap, and a thousand other items by which the British masses removed their natural odours and substituted others. He was also a governor of the Arundel College which employs me to this day, which is akin to the Imperial College of Science in Kensington. In his secretively generous way, Archie got his father to grant a few hundred pounds for research into the disinfectant properties of various medicated soaps, and there was no difficulty in my being appointed its beneficiary.

Research in those days carried no glamorous suggestion of white-coated armies steadily advancing the frontiers of knowledge. It did not exist outside the few universities and exceptional departments like Sir Almroth Wright's. A busy Harley Street specialist might cut up a cat as spare-time relaxation, comparable with salmon fishing or hospital politics. If you needed research apparatus more elaborate than a Bunsen burner or a retort you constructed it yourself. There was nobody to manufacture it. There was anyway no money to buy it. I started that summer to examine the potency of antiseptics like carbolic, chlorine, formaldehyde or iodine against common household germs. In the end, I found plain soap to be more effective than any of them, I hope to the gratification of my sponsor.

But first I had to supply myself with germs, for which I turned to an acquaintance of my days in St Mary's, Dr Leonard Colebrook.

'Coli' – everyone called Colebrook by his bacteriological nickname from *Bacillus coli*, even himself – was reared a strict Nonconformist, frugal, teetotal, his interests only gardening and euthanasia. Like me, he was a grammar school boy. He was due to leave the Inoculation Department the year after I quit it for Cambridge, and again like me found himself without hope of a job. Coli was grateful for a salary of £100 a year to work in the research laboratory of Queen Charlotte's Maternity Hospital, which midwives know the world over. He was still there, and the hospital was just down the way from Arundel College in the Marylebone Road.

Coli often bustled into Arundel from his little open Morris Oxford, with a bag which seemed more suited for the necessities of a leisured weekend than a day's work, which he would drop while simultaneously whipping off his Homburg hat and struggling from an enormous, enveloping raincoat, in another moment deep in discussion with some member of the staff more elevated than myself. I had started at Arundel promptly at the beginning of August, and during my second week intercepted him in the marble-lined hall.

'Why, it's Elgar. What have you been doing with yourself?' he asked amiably. He was slightly built and barely five feet tall, just turned fifty. 'The last I heard, you'd got a First at Cambridge and were doing some work on staining techniques with Hopkins. Well done.'

I told him about Wuppertal. He remarked, 'How's your German?'

'It's improved, *das versteht sich.*'

'German is essential for keeping up to date in any of the sciences.' Coli matched a deep voice with a deliberate, solemn way of saying things. 'You'll remember, I took myself off to Breslau while you were working under The Lion.' He used the more flattering soubriquet for Sir Almroth Wright. The pair were so close they were often compared in the department with father and son.

He mentioned Fleming and his mould-juice. 'It was your fault, wasn't it, that the *penicillium* ever contaminated his Petri dish? Did you know that Professor Raistrick tried to purify the stuff, down the road from here at the London School of Tropical Medicine?' I had never heard of anyone interested in penicillin outside St Mary's. 'That must have been in 1929, or thereabouts. Flem sent him a sample from that original spore – Raistrick knows absolutely everything about moulds, of course. He tried growing it on a special glucose solution. It produced a sort of mat on the surface, but the potency's all in the juice underneath.'

My chemist's curiosity aroused, I asked, 'I suppose Raistrick never isolated the active principle?'

'He hadn't much luck. He ended up with a yellow pigment which he called "chrysogenin", and he tried extracting penicillin from it with ether. But unfortunately the penicillin simply disappeared into thin air. And you can't identify a chemical if it's too unstable to stay under your nose for more than half a minute.'

'No, of course not.'

'After that, I fancy Raistrick rather lost interest. They had other bad luck. One of his staff working on the mould-juice was killed in a road accident, another died. They wrote an inconclusive paper about it in the *Biochemical Journal* towards the end of 1932, if you're interested.'

Coli agreed to supply me with a mixed bag of germs from his own laboratory. The month of August passed. A peace came to me which I had not enjoyed since Cambridge. I was doing useful work, I was my own master, reasonably well paid, well housed among friends. I was out of that damned basement. I had put off calling upon my parents because Sir Edward was still abroad and I did not wish to encounter Lady Tip. Above all, I wanted to shed Rosie.

The first of September was a Saturday. About five in the afternoon I was sitting with David in Archie's flat when the doorbell rang. The surly Watson being off, David answered it. He returned after some time. 'It's your girl friend, Rosie.'

'I don't want to see her. Say I'm not in.'

'I know you don't. I tried putting her off, but it wouldn't wash.'

'Oh, God. Must I really talk to her? It's like entertaining a ghost. All that's behind me now.'

'I think you ought to have a word with her, boy,' advised David, with an unaccustomed solemnity which alarmed me.

17

I did not ask Rosie into the flat. I took her to a nearby Lyons teashop by St George's Hospital at Hyde Park Corner. She was crying most of the way. I did not want to talk about it until we were sitting down. It would give me time to collect my thoughts. I bought her a cup of tea and a shiny bun with lumps of sugar like broken glass on top. She never touched either, but went on crying.

'Why didn't you tell me before?' I demanded.

'I couldn't...I couldn't be sure.'

'But you *are* sure? Are you?'

She nodded dumbly, the cheap pink handkerchief at her eyes thoroughly wet through.

'How long has it been going on?'

'I haven't had my monthlies since last June.'

'But how *can* you be sure. There might be other reasons.'

'I can see it.'

'*I* can't.'

'When I has my wash. I can see it, plain as anything. Soon everyone will be able to.'

'You're sure it's me?'

For a moment she did not comprehend, then she exclaimed, 'How can you say that?' starting to cry again, making me feel doubly guilty, ashamed, frightened, desperate and confused.

'You must pull yourself together,' I commanded. She went on crying. People at other tables were staring at us. I felt all of them were in the secret. 'We've got to look at this coolly.' I waited until her sobs had quietened. 'Listen, Rosie – if either of us loses our heads we shall get nowhere.'

'Ow, Jim! You do still love me, don't you?'

'Of course I do. Now, who else knows about it?'

'You're sure you love me?'

'*Of course* I love you,' I told her fiercely. 'Who else knows about it?'

'No one. Not a soul.'

'Not even Lady Tip?' She shook her head vigorously. 'You must keep absolutely quiet about it for a bit. Not a word to my parents.'

'You'll stand by me, won't you, Jim?' she asked pathetically.

'Of course I shall.' I had no option.

Rosie had to go back to help with the dinner. I hurried to the flat, desperate to put everything before David Mellors.

'I haven't done my gynae yet,' he confessed unhelpfully.

'But there must be other perfectly good reasons for a girl stopping her periods, surely?'

He frowned at the eggs and bacon he was frying for himself in the grimy kitchen at the back. 'There must be. There's more than one reason for everything in medicine. Though they say in the hospital, if any female outside a nursery or a nunnery stops menstruating, she's pregnant until proved otherwise.'

I sat down on a hard kitchen chair. David forked over the sizzling bacon. The smell made me feel sick.

'Didn't you take precautions?' he asked.

'Of course I took precautions.'

'What sort?'

'I…well, I pulled out.'

He said impassively, '*Coitus interruptus*, the poor man's French letter.'

'That's safe enough, surely?' I protested.

'Obviously, it wasn't.'

'You're not being very sympathetic.'

'Sorry, boy.'

I sat staring at the pock-marked linoleum of the floor in silence. David slipped his meal on to a plate with a fish slice, sat at the scrubbed wooden table and began to eat. 'If she *is* pregnant, can I do anything about it?' I asked.

'You could find a witch in a back street with a knitting-needle, I suppose.'

'I could end up in the dock, though, couldn't I?'

'I suppose you might. You'd have to take the gamble. Mind, there's plenty of girls who come into casualty for the gynae department to finish off what they've started themselves, or someone else has. The police ask questions, but nobody tells them much. Do you want anything to eat?'

'No, no...but if I don't want to run that sort of risk, what *can* I do?'

'You can let her go ahead and have it. There's plenty of unmarried mothers in Mary's. Sister keeps a store of wedding rings and issues them out.'

'But you don't understand. The very idea of a person like Rosie producing a child which I've fathered utterly nauseates me.'

'You might grow very fond of her. I've seen that happen before. Down where I live, there's plenty of chaps who wouldn't think in a blue moon of getting themselves hitched up before they put the girl in pod.'

'You're not trying to tell *me* that I should actually marry her, are you?'

'That's something I'd never tell anyone.'

There was another silence. David went on eating. 'Of course, you're trying to tell me something rather different,' I said. 'That I've an overpowering moral obligation to marry her. Well, that's unnecessary. I'm already aware of it.'

'Was I saying that? Well, if you did marry her, you might not be doing too badly. She's a pretty thing. Whether she'd make a good wife is a toss up with any woman, but it generally works out all right.'

'But she's an ignoramus.'

David wiped a slice of white bread in his mixture of egg yolk, scarlet ketchup and fat. 'It's not the biological function of women to be brainy, no more than for the birds of the air to ride bicycles.'

'Now you sound like Almroth Wright.' I got up to leave the kitchen. At the door I turned round. 'She's *common*.'

David made no reply.

He that doth get a wench with child and marries her afterward, wrote Samuel Pepys on October 7, 1660, *it is as if a man should shit in his hat and then clap it upon his head.* I fulfilled Pepys' ludicrous picture.

Archie declared that of course I must marry her. To his mind, one of the *bourgeoisie* – even the *nouvelle bourgeoisie* – leaving a servant girl with a bun in the oven had no alternative but make an honest woman of her. My father was refreshingly cheerful and encouraging. He said it happened every day, and she was a lucky girl knowing who the father was. My mother implored with tears that I gave the child a name. Sir Edward was back home, and would of course know all about it. He sent through my father a message to call, but I stayed away, not wishing to meet the eye of Lady Tip. As for Elizabeth, I prayed the affair was too shocking to be allowed her ears.

It happened on Saturday, November 3, at Marylebone Registry Office. In a red dress and with a little bunch of brownish chrysanthemums, Rosie was blooming and bulging – dispelling my hopes to the last moment that Nature might put an end to my predicament. We had a social difficulty. She was a waif, reared in a home in Clapham. Mrs Packer volunteered to 'give her away', and appeared with a husband in a bowler and fringe of moustache, looking like Strube's Little Man from the *Daily Express*. The Registrar had a cold, which I caught. Archie was my best man, and gave me £100.

Sir Edward had charitably taken his family to the country. We had our wedding-breakfast in the basement. My mother made a superb cake. My father made a speech and got drunk. There was confetti, as we took a taxi to the pair of furnished rooms I had found in Coram's Fields, round the back of the College and not far from Doughty Street, where Dickens used to live.

I completely forget how those days of early marriage felt. I forgot whether I loved Rosie, or had any particular sensation about her. I recall only an odd awareness of possessing her totally, her plump body, her cotton petticoats, the prayer book she had kept from the orphanage, her umbrella. It was all mine. She cooked for me every night, my mother having relentlessly instructed her. I cannot remember a word that we exchanged, nor what we did to pass the time. The unborn baby dominated us. Because of the baby, Rosie rested in the afternoons, never went out in the wet, never looked a cripple in the face. Because of the baby, we shared the thin-mattressed double bed every night without the solace of each other.

The baby was to be born in Queen Charlotte's. We were delighted to have within reach so famous a maternity hospital, which had taken the name of George the Third's Queen, who had fifteen children. In the mid-eighteenth century it was providing free lying-in for married mothers, with a diet of brown and white caudle, and infant baptism by the chaplain, which was compulsory. Colebrook worked in the research laboratory attached to the isolation block, which had shed its old walls for new in the suburb of Chiswick, above an elbow of the Thames to the west. I did not see him after my marriage until the end of February, when he appeared one morning in the hall of Arundel, removing hat and damp raincoat and dropping his bag all in one movement as usual. 'I hear your wife's having a baby in Charlotte's,' he greeted me. 'When's she due?'

'In about a week's time.'

'I'm sure everything will go splendidly.' I wondered if he was doing any mental arithmetic. 'Here's something which might interest you, as you speak German.' He handed me a rolled-up journal from his mackintosh pocket. 'I got it this morning from a colleague in Breslau – he must have thought it important, posting it off in a hurry. Take a look at it while I'm in my meeting. There would seem to be something brewing in the Rhineland.'

I unrolled ii standing in the hall. It was the last edition of the *Deutsche Medizinische Wochenschrift*, the German Medical weekly, published in Leipzig the previous Friday. The issue contained special supplements on tuberculosis and medicine in sport. I was wondering why Colebrook should have recommended it, my eye running down the list of main contents on the cover. The first was *Aus den Forschungslabatorien der I G Farbenindustrie A G Werk Elberfeld* – From the Research Laboratories of I G Farben Elberfeld. Underneath came, *Ein Beitrang zur Chemotherapie der bakteriellen Infektionen* – A Contribution to the Chemotherapy of Bacterial Infections. The author of this modest title was Professor Gerhard Domagk. The following article I translated as Prontosil in Streptococcal Disease. I wondered what 'Prontosil' was. It was written by Professor Klee, and I remembered from Domagk's letter to Dr Dieffenbach that Klee had been testing out 'Streptozon' in Wuppertal. I turned over the pages, starting to translate Domagk's paper, lips moving and finger running along the lines.

They seemed to have rechristened 'Streptozon', as 'Prontosil'. But undoubtedly it was the same sulphonamide drug which had saved my hand. The world was at last learning what I had heard from a part-time prostitute in a Cologne slum the night they burnt down the Reichstag.

18

I had no chance to discuss the German discovery with Colebrook before we met in the hall of Queen Charlotte's in Marylebone Road on the early evening of Monday, March 6, 1935. He had just come through the door, bag in hand and mackintosh flapping. He greeted me, 'Hello, Elgar – had your baby?'

'Yes, this morning. Everything seems fine.'

'Congratulations. Boy or girl?'

'Girl. I'm on my way to see them now.'

'I say, those papers by Domagk and Co in the *Deutsche Medizinische Wochenschrift* are causing something of a sensation in London.' Coli strode along with me. 'They've even got into the newspapers. I wrote to Domagk for more information, but I haven't heard. I expect he's snowed under with similar requests from all over the world. And of course things are getting a little sticky in Germany, they do so seem to be turning in upon themselves. It's as though they were already at war with the rest of us in Europe.'

'I wondered why they renamed it "Prontosil"?. I had once mentioned to Coli my being one of the earliest cases on 'Streptozon'. 'Or as I suppose the Germans would pronounce it, "Pronto*zeal*".'

'Oh, I G Farben register any number of trade marks – euphonious labels for drugs as yet unsynthesized.' (The name 'Prontosil' had been registered in 1928 with the intention of sticking it on some new sleeping-draught.) 'You know what someone in my lab suggested? It's an abbreviation of *pronto* and *silentium*.' Coli gave his laugh, which could fill a corridor. He was a cheerful man behind his solemn manner and austere tastes. 'I must say, it's strange – to say the least – that Domagk kept completely quiet about his discovery for more than two years.'

'Wouldn't he want to be absolutely certain it always worked? It would be cruel to raise the world's false hopes.'

'You're being very Christian. The reason for the delay is simple. I G Farben wanted to be certain they'd got all their patents safely tied up. And they wanted exactly the right moment to market the stuff. I know my German drug industry.'

Remembering my past discouragement, I felt entitled to complain, 'Perhaps some lives might have been saved had Sir Almroth Wright seen the possibilities.'

'You can't blame The Lion.' Expectedly, Colebrook came to his defence. 'This is chemotherapy, of course. But a different sort than we've been accustomed to since Ehrlich first coined the word. It's not like the cure of syphilis or malaria or kala azar. The drug is simple, the administration is simple, and the streptococcus is no rare parasite, but flourishing upon all of us.'

'You mean, it's one of those concepts which stand out like mountains, which nobody sees because we're too busy staring at the toes of our boots?'

'You might put it like that, yes.'

We parted, as I turned towards the entrance of the ward. The baby had been born at seven o'clock that morning. Rosie had started her pains early on the Sunday, when I had found a taxi at King's Cross Station and taken her into the hospital, waiting in a room with two other husbands. A well-starched midwife had appeared after an hour or so to explain that my wife had 'gone off the boil' and the baby was not expected that day. I gathered that for the first child the labour pains provided a prolonged overture to the drama. When I returned the next morning they had been trying to find me, and I was a father.

After I left Colebrook, I found Rosie still with the radiance of new motherhood, an expression which can transform the most ordinary girl into a saint, and which I do not believe has ever been accurately caught by painters of the Madonna.

'What do you think of her?' she asked, squeezing the bundle against her breast.

'She seems perfectly all right.'

'She's *lovely*. Do you still want to call her Clare?'

'Why not?'

Rosie wrinkled her nose. 'I dunno…it's a sort of stuck-up name.'

'I don't think so. St Clare of Assisi founded the order of Poor Clares.'

'Are you sorry she ain't a boy?' Rosie was looking at me guiltily.

'Why should I be?'

'Most men like a boy first.'

'It's all the same to me.'

'We'll have a boy next time,' predicted Rosie, smiling and snuggling up the baby again.

When I returned on the Tuesday evening, Rosie was not in such high spirits, a little tired, but well. On the Wednesday, she was flushed, with a temperature.

'It's nothing to worry about unduly,' said the starched midwife. 'After all, it's hardly unknown for a mother to run a slight temp during the puerperium. Your wife's got a rather nasty discharge down below, which would account for it. We've already taken a swab for the lab.'

'Do they know the infecting germ yet?' Her reassurance had made me anxious.

'They'll have the culture tomorrow. With luck, she'll be on the mend by then.'

The following evening, a nurse asked me to wait outside the ward door. The midwife appeared with the news, 'I'm afraid your wife's rather poorly, Mr Elgar.' I felt a pang of alarm. 'Her temp's gone up, and she's rather miserable because she's having a rigor or two. The doctor's just been with her, and he thinks the infection is still localized to the birth canal.'

I was even more suspicious of her optimism. 'What was the organism? I've had some training in bacteriology.'

'It's a haemolytic streptococcus,' she said calmly.

'Oh,' I said. Rosie was seriously ill. Potentially, gravely so. I went into the ward to find her pale, shivering and frightened. I stayed only a few minutes, distrusting too plainly my own reassurances.

'The doctor wants to move your wife to the hospital isolation block out at Chiswick,' the midwife imparted as I left. 'She'll be better looked after there.'

'Can Dr Colebrook see her? You know that I'm acquainted with him.'

'Dr Colebrook sees all the patients in the isolation block.'

'Its puerperal fever, isn't it?'

'I don't think we need quite say that. It's a severe infection, but still not a generalized one. Let's hope for the best, shall we? Can we get hold of you if we want to?'

'I'm at Arundel College all day. At night you'll have to send a policeman, or something.'

The isolation block in Goldhawk Road at Chiswick had been opened five years. Its forty beds gathered puerperal fever cases from the whole of west London. The patients were nursed in separate cubicles off battleship-grey corridors and the place reeked of antiseptic. Colebrook had instituted nursing with rubber gloves, sterile gowns and face masks, like a surgical operation, but two or three out of every thousand women delivered at Queen Charlotte's still died from childbed fever, and twelve of the forty ill women in the cubicles would not leave them alive.

With characteristic kindness, Colebrook came from his laboratory to Rosie's cubicle as I was leaving on the Friday afternoon.

'She doesn't look too well, Coli.'

'The infection seems to have spread to the peritoneal membrane lining the abdomen,' he said in his solemn way. 'That's not a good sign, I'm afraid. And of course your poor wife is suffering, with the distention and tenderness.'

We started walking along the corridors towards the door. 'She was very distressed at leaving the baby.'

'The little girl will be looked after on the ward until she's better. Obviously, we can't' allow the babies here, there's too much risk of infection.'

I frowned. 'Where could this terrible streptococcus have come from?'

'Perhaps from the midwife's hands. The labour was rather long, and she had a number of vaginal examinations. Perhaps from Mrs Elgar's own nose and throat. Perhaps from the air. We can never say. Though if our precautions of gloves and so on were more widely used, the mortality rate might start to come down at last.'

We walked a few more steps in silence. I had of course felt concern for Rosie while she was having the child, but only as if she were suffering from some straightforward illness, like influenza. Now I saw she might die, I think for the first time in my life I began to develop fondness for her.

'For centuries, of course, the disease was a complete mystery,' Colebrook continued. 'It was seen as a visitation of some particular town or parish, which lifted after a month or two and let the women bear children perfectly healthily once more. For which the local ecclesiastic doubtless took all the credit. But in reality, the streptococcus was simply being passed from case to case by the midwife or doctor. *That* revolutionary idea was mooted at the end of the last century by an Aberdonian obstetrician called Alexander Gordon, who was ostracized for it and had to join the Navy – a hard fate for a midwifery expert. I suppose none of us likes being accused of possessing dirty habits.

'Didn't a man called Semmelweiss come into it somewhere?'

We pushed through a pair of frosted glass doors. 'You don't want to go into all this, Elgar. You've enough to upset you, without my lecturing about your troubles.'

'I'm interested. The doctor I lodged with in Wuppertal kept a photograph of him in his surgery. I remember he had a beautiful moustache, and resembled a Viennese opera singer, or the man on the packet of Gillette razor blades.'

'Semmelweiss was at the Allgemeines Krankenhaus in Vienna ninety years ago. There were two obstetric wards there, one used for training medical students the other for training midwives. Five of the students' mothers died of puerperal fever for one of the midwives'. It was ascribed to the poor women's shame at being examined internally by young men. But the students went to the labour ward straight from an obstetrical class in the post mortem room, while the midwives were taught everything from models. Ignaz Semmelweiss put the fever down to "cadaveric particles", made everyone wash their hands in lime water, and knocked down the mortality by two thirds. Mind, it took another fifty years before

Louis Pasteur discovered bacteria and showed *how* it worked. Meanwhile, Semmelweiss was sacked, went mad and died from septicaemia contracted at a post mortem.'

'Semmelweiss was another man who saw the range of mountains which everyone overlooked?'

'Most definitely,' agreed Colebrook.

We had reached the front door. 'What's my wife's outlook?'

He considered this for a moment. 'Her infection may well localize itself as a pelvic abscess, which can be drained surgically. But it will be a long and debilitating illness, there's no getting away from that. And one which may well leave her sterile for the rest of her life.'

'I wouldn't mind. I don't want any more children.'

Colebrook raised his heavy eyebrows but said only, 'I expect you've informed her relatives?'

'My wife has none. She comes from a home for destitute children. She's completely anonymous. She's a particle unconnected to anyone in the world except me. The circumstances of my marriage were singular, don't you think?'

'A little unusual, perhaps,' said Colebrook guardedly.

'She was a housemaid. Why do you imagine I married her? Because I got her with child. And on to her death bed.'

'You must not simply accept that she is going to die,' he told me severely.

'Of course she will.' I was anguished not through love but through guilt, which are intertwined often enough.

'I'm going to give her a blood transfusion in the morning. I've already got a donor. It will reinforce her own white scavenger cells, in the best Almroth Wright tradition.'

Transfusion was then a complicated operation, done directly with a syringe and yards of bright red rubber tubing, the donor lying on the bed next to the chalk-white desperately ill woman. I suggested. 'Couldn't you try Ehrhich's arsenicals? Sir Edward once said something about your using them.'

'I was chasing a hare. We thought they increased the ability of the blood to kill streptococci, when injected for the entirely different purpose of killing the germs of syphilis. But they don't. We're giving streptococcal antiserum, naturally. Otherwise, we must rely on the skills of the nurses, as in any other severe infection. But your wife has a sound constitution.'

'Then what about "Prontosil"?'

'The answer's simple. I haven't got any.'

'But I have.'

His eyebrows rose again. 'How?'

'I stole them. From Domagk. Twenty tablets.'

Colebrook shook his head. 'I'm afraid that's out of the question, Elgar. I couldn't give any maternity patient an untested new drug.'

'But it has been tested. One of those papers alongside Domagk's was specifically on its use in puerperal fever. From Professor Max Heinkel's clinic in Jena. Isn't that good enough?'

'No, it is *not* good enough,' objected Colebrook forthrightly. 'I have been through those papers most carefully, and a lot of the experimental and clinical work in Germany was most slipshod. As far as Domagk's lab work goes, mice are not men. Surely you remember well enough The Lion's axiom – "experimental infections in animals have no relevance to natural infections in humans".'

I thought he was procrastinating only from blind loyalty to Wright and to Wright's hate of chemical remedies and chemists. 'I can have the "Prontosil" here in half an hour,' I counter-attacked. 'Or are you going to let my wife die?'

'Please, Elgar! You should not put things like that. You are a scientist, you surely realize that emotion is a dangerous ingredient in the making of clinical decisions.'

'But why not try it, in God's name?' I pursued arguing, through rising anger against Wright and his self-satisfied bigotism. 'Surely, it can't do any harm.'

'How can you claim that?'

'There was nothing to suggest ill-effects in any single one of those German papers.'

'The cases reported were few. And the enthusiastic research worker forgets his fatalities.'

'Isn't it worth taking the risk, just for once, that the Germans should not be bigger liars than we are?'

'Do please try and contain your language, Elgar.' Colebrook was embarrassed, annoyed and impatient with me all at once. 'I don't believe any German scientist would be deliberately misleading, even in these days of Dr Göebbels. But supposing I did give "Prontosil" to your wife? And supposing she did die? You might well blame me. Or you might well blame yourself for insisting on it. Which would be the worse for you.'

'I *do* insist on it. I'll sign a paper, indemnifying you.'

Colebrook said nothing for some moments. 'Very well,' he announced resignedly. 'Fetch the drug. The paper won't be necessary.'

But Rosie died. At ten o'clock on the night of Monday, March 11, 1935. Colebrook gave her the 'Prontosil', a tablet every four hours. But her blood and her body were already overwhelmed by the infection before he started.

Rosie's death was a shock to the Harley Street house. I had told no one that she was so ill. I had the impression that above and below stairs I was held to blame for it. I felt penitent, but it was penitence only through my suffering no true feeling of grief. I am not heartless, and the bell which tolls for all mankind can never make pleasant music. But I did not know her very well. I had been strongly attracted to Rosie through 'the hot, spicy smell of dirty petticoats'. I had married her because my upbringing left me with a raw sensitivity to the opinions of the world, to be driven rather than pushing. In short, not through honour but through cowardice.

Only my parents and myself went with her to Kensal Green. But poor Rosie had one valuable legacy. On the Saturday before her death her temperature steadied, she sat up with her face suffused pink from the dye and said she felt much better. She lived long enough for Colebrook to set aside his doubts and even Sir Almroth Wright's principles. He searched Germany and France for sulphonamide, dosed his own mice, and issued his own paper on the sulphonamide treatment of puerperal fever in the Lancet in June, 1936. A year after that, the mortality at Queen Charlotte's for the disease which killed my wife had dropped from thirty-three in a hundred to under five.

There was still Clare.

I put my problem to Colebrook. The evening of the funeral I went to his home in Chiswick Mall, which was bright with daffodils from his weekend house at Farnham in Surrey – which he had characteristically bought near Sir Almroth Wright's.

'Puerperal fever is a triple tragedy,' he told me solemnly. 'Though I've no children of my own, I do my best to sort out the domestic problems of bereaved husbands. They've sometimes two or three small ones to manage somehow or other, and often enough financial troubles into the bargain. Do you want to keep the child?'

'No.'

'Adoption may not be easy.' he remarked doubtfully. 'A lot of people these days can't run to the luxury.'

'She'll have to be put in a home, like her mother.' As he said nothing, I asked, 'Am I abnormal? I don't feel particularly attached to the child.'

'I have seen too much of the relationships between husbands and wives and their newborn babies to find any variation whatever abnormal. Do you know of anyone who might take her?'

'Not a soul.'

'The Lady Almoner at Charlotte's is of course an expert on this subject. Though I'm afraid she can't perform miracles any more than I can in the wards.'

Mrs Packer saved her. She called the next morning at Arundel College. 'Jim, I have something terribly important to say,' she began earnestly as I went down from my lab to the hall. 'Can we sit down?'

I took her across to the refreshment room at Euston Station, where Clare's fate was decided.

'My husband's a solicitor, you know, and doing as well as anyone can these times,' she explained. 'As I expect you noticed at your wedding, he's...well, he's older than I am. I mean, Jim, we'd love to have her, and we can afford to look after her, and we've a new house at Hendon which is really very nice, and of course whenever you want to come and see her –'

'There's one condition.'

She swallowed, her Adam's apple bouncing in her thin neck like a ping-pong ball. 'Anything you say, Jim.'

'Clare must never have the faintest idea who her father and mother were.'

She looked flustered. 'Of course, we'd try if you really want us to. But these things do tend to slip out, and everyone in Sir Edward's house knows—'

'You must give me your promise. Your solemn promise.'

'I promise. At least, I promise I'll do my best.'

She did very well. Clare today — and Mrs Packer's is the only false name I have used in this narrative — became a bright young MP in the 1960s, but left politics to become Professor of Sociology at a university situated...shall we say, between St Louis and Oklahoma City. She is married for a second time, to an American professor who smokes a pipe, wears tweeds and goes fishing. Perhaps he wanted her to complete his English *milieu*. She has had three children, without even running a temperature. I was once about to be introduced to her at a party in the House of Commons, but I left in tears.

That summer of 1935 was King George the Fifth's Silver Jubilee. There were flags and tea-parties in working-class streets, royal processions, military reviews, vibrantly choral services of thanksgiving. In London, St Paul's was floodlit, at Spithead the Fleet was beflagged. Clever fellows who saw it all as a carnival to boost the National Government were quickly lost in the morass of emotion. On June 7, MacDonald departed from No 10 Downing Street, Baldwin returned. On June 27, two and a half million Britons voting in Lord Cecil's Peace Ballot stood against any military measures whatever to repel foreign aggression.

The following January had Sir Edward Tiplady on the front pages again. The King was suffering a recurrence of his old chest infection. Like Leonard Colebrook with Rosie, the doctors were against ransoming a King's life with an unknown German drug. At half past nine on the night of Monday, January 20, Lord Dawson's medical bulletin said only, 'The King's life is moving peacefully to its close.' The BBC fell silent, but for the ticking of a clock. The nation dropped its head. At five minutes to midnight the King died. Nobody was sure if his last words were, 'How is the Empire?' or 'Bugger Bognor'.

19

'Tonight Hitler sleeps in the Hradčany Palace in Prague. It is time to redefine our attitudes.'

Archie said this without a shred of self-consciousness. All men become caricatures of themselves, but he achieved it younger than most. It was three years later, the evening of March 15, 1939, and the four of us were eating dinner in his Belgrave Square home. Since his father's death, he had combined the huge dining-room with the sitting-room in the modern flat-dwelling fashion, redecorating and refurnishing the rest of the place with pleasing, extravagant plainness.

'The Ides of March are come,' said David Mellors, unusually gloomily.

'Ay, Chamberlain; but not gone,' added Elizabeth Tiplady, who had left school more recently than the rest of us.

'So much for Hitler's "last territorial demand in Europe", over the Sudeten Germans,' I said.

'Do you realize the significance of what's just happened?' Archie demanded of the table in general. 'By now, we're sickeningly used to Hitler invading neighbouring countries. But for the first time he's enlarged the Reich *not* simply to include expatriate Germans like the Austrians or Sudetens. He's gobbled up a foreign nation, the Czechs. Who knows who's next?'

'The Poles,' David poured himself more claret – a '34, claimed by Archie to be the best out of ten terrible years.

'Us?' suggested Elizabeth.

'What's Chamberlain going to do?' I asked, Archie being a fount of political information more immediate if not always more accurate than the newspapers.

'Nothing. Absolutely nothing. He's done all he can do already. Did you read what he said in the House this afternoon? That the collapse of Czecho-Slovakia was inevitable. That the Slovakia half of it simply declared itself independent, so we're no longer bound to guarantee its frontiers under the Munich agreement. Fancy falling back on legal niceties with the Gestapo already in Prague! Chamberlain whines about a breach of the Munich spirit, as though Hitler had omitted to send him a Christmas card. The whole business is utterly disgraceful. Poor, old, ill President Hácha has been horribly let down, just as we let down President Beneš. No wonder the Tory party's looking sick. If I was a Conservative MP today, I'd vomit over the benches.'

'What's this we're supposed to be eating?' asked David. 'Stewed pheasant?'

'It couldn't possibly be. Pheasant shooting ends on February the first,' said Archie severely. For all his socialism, he had the aristocrat's disdain for ignorance of country matters.

'It's chicken, I *think*.' Elizabeth struggled to cut it.

'I don't know the first thing about food,' remarked Archie airily. 'It's a dish which Watson seems to like cooking. I suppose because he finds it one of the easiest.'

'Do you think Watson appreciates that instead of not having to call you "Sir", he now doesn't have to call you "My Lord"?' I enquired.

'Oh, this title!' Archie complained. 'Do you realize, politically it's like those concrete overcoats in which gangsters drop their rivals into New York harbour. One simply disappeared without a gurgle. Of course, none of us expected my father to die so suddenly last Christmas. I so much wanted to make some sort of impact on the Commons before being shoved into the Madame Tussaud's of the Lords. When I think of the constituencies I've nursed!' He ended pathetically.

Archie had always seemed to be nursing a constituency since going down from Cambridge, though the foundlings were never grateful enough to elect him to Parliament. But he did good among them, helping the inadequate and the inarticulate before they were lavished with the bounty of the Welfare State.

'Can't you shed your title the way people do with their awful christian names?' asked Elizabeth. 'Or sell it to the Americans like all the nicest country houses?'

'Archie, you really ought to sack Watson,' David advised. 'He'll give you a recurrence of your duodenal ulcer.'

'I don't eat at home very much. I'm far too busy.' Archie reached towards the cluster of wine bottles. 'It is time to redefine our attitudes,' he repeated. 'I'll frankly admit, that for a while I simply couldn't take Hitler seriously. I'll admit that I thought him perfectly justified reoccupying the Rhineland in 1936, for instance. But wasn't I one of many, who asked why he shouldn't be allowed to move his soldiers about his own back yard? And after all, he was doing a lot for the unemployed, which nobody was here.'

'Do you ever hear from your friends there, Jim?' David asked.

I shook my head. I stopped writing to Gerda when I married Rosie. 'I shouldn't care to provoke a letter returned *Empfänger unbekannt*.'

' "Addressee Unknown" has terrifying implications,' Archie commented sombrely. He went on, 'It was Spain which changed my mind about Hitler.'

'Darling, it was *such* a pity that you never got there,' Elizabeth told him sympathetically.

'I couldn't help developing an ulcer.'

'It must have been terribly frustrating, it all going on and you having to lie on your back in Swanage instead.'

'I *almost* enlisted,' he told her irritably. He had recounted the story that evening in the expectation – which he should have known to be perfectly ridiculous, it being Elizabeth – of impressing my young lady. 'I'd got as far as Paris. That's why Spain decided me more than Abyssinia. Because it was possible to get involved oneself. After all, two thousand of us in Britain joined the International Brigade. And five hundred of us won't come back. Thank God the whole thing seems almost over.'

'According to George Orwell, it was all a tremendous fiasco, even for a war,' I observed.

' "I am your choice, your decision. Yes, I am Spain",' he quoted W H Auden, raising his glass. 'Then of course there's the German Jews.'

'Our Freud which art in Hampstead,' said David.

We were interrupted by Watson in his tail coat. He had become fatter and even ruder, and I thought in many respects resembled Mussolini. 'All right, is it?'

'Divine,' Elizabeth said.

'You haven't cleared away the cocktail things,' Archie told him sternly.

'I can't do everything, can I?'

'I don't think any of us want any more.' Archie pushed away the half-eaten dish. 'You may serve the pudding.'

'There ain't none. I've some fruit.'

'Open a couple of bottles of Cliquot,' Archie commanded. He added as Watson withdrew, 'Do you know what I heard yesterday? When Halifax went to Berchtesgaden a couple of months ago, he was greeted at the front door by Hitler in that usual ridiculous get-up of brown jacket and dress trousers. Our lordly cabinet minister mistook him for the footman. He was within an inch of handing over his hat and stick. Think how the course of history might have been changed!'

'Hitler would have sent his Air Force to blow us up between the soup and fish, I expect,' said Elizabeth.

'London may not be so beautiful as Paris or Prague,' said Archie, who had travelled to both. 'But like any Frenchman or any Czech I don't want wakening at dawn to the crash of bombs. That's why I was incredibly relieved by Munich.'

'Like everyone else,' I said. The iron-crossed wings of Hermann Göring's Luftwaffe overshadowed Europe. No one had experienced mass aerial bombardment, but after Spain everyone could imagine it. The German Air Force was the atomic bomb of the 1930s.

'It's Wednesday!' Elizabeth jumped from the table to switch on the radiogram beside the fireplace. 'I mustn't miss Arthur Askey.'

'It is time to redefine our attitudes,' Archie declared once again. 'I now commit myself to standing up to Hitler, whatever the cost. With Russia, all the better — if Europe hadn't been so neurotically afraid of

Communism, Hitler would never have got where he has. If not, alone with France.'

'And America?' I suggested.

'America is only interested in the World Fair on Flushing Meadow,' Archie said irritably.

'What about this champagne, boy?' asked David.

'I expect Watson's forgotten.' Archie reached his long arm for the bell. 'The question remains, what exactly can one *do*.'

'Get your blood group registered,' suggested David practically. 'They're going to need the stuff by the gallon.'

'With Spain, it was easy. One simply volunteered.' Archie often seemed genuinely to believe that he had fought on the hard-baked, blood-soaked ridges of Catalonia.

'Volunteer as an air raid warden.' I told him. 'Or a fireman. I saw in today's paper that the government wants a hundred thousand of them.'

'I'd volunteer for the Army, but what's the point when the Government are moving towards the utterly oppressive step of conscription in peacetime? Which I and every other socialist should have imagined unthinkable in this country.'

'What's the matter?' called Watson from the doorway. 'I'd like to listen to the wireless myself, you know.'

'The Cliquot, Watson.'

'You didn't mean it, did you? I didn't think this was a champagne dinner.'

'You'll find some brandy in the cocktail cabinet,' Archie told David. 'Help yourself.'

'Darling, I can't hear the jokes,' complained Elizabeth, her ears directed to *Band Waggon* on the London Regional.

'I'm having a serious political discussion,' Archie told her severely.

'You know that I've never been in the slightest interested in politics.'

'That's what some unfortunate French aristocrat protested at the guillotine. "Which is precisely why you are here", said the executioner, strapping him down.'

Archie's tart reply sprang from her teasing about Spain and his ulcer. Elizabeth stood up, pouting, and strode from the room saying, 'I'm going to powder my nose.'

She left Archie sitting gloomily at the table. I knew that he would be instantly sorry for provoking her. I had been living in the flat almost four years since Rosie died. I had discovered that Archie's was the tenderest conscience of any I dared to probe. In a way, he turned this conscience into a talent, by which he might make a political career. David handed him a balloon glass well filled with brandy. By way of making conversation, I said, 'Have you seen that travel poster put out by the Reich Tourist Office? A beautiful coloured picture of a schloss, and underneath, *Come To Mediaeval Germany*. Either the Nazis have absolutely no sense of humour, or they flatter us with an uproarious one.'

'Can't you turn that rubbish off?' Archie scowled at the radiogram.

David obliged and sat down on the sofa, picking one of the yellow-jacketed volumes from the low table before the fire, which had *The Times*, the *Daily Worker*, *Apollo*, *Punch* and other periodicals laid out in club-like precision. 'What's this bloody rubbish?'

'The Left Book Club', Archie told him shortly. 'You get a couple of books cheap on current affairs every month. Surely you've heard of it? It's been going two or three years now.'

'Who are the doctors prescribing such intellectual tonics?'

'Well, there's Harold Laski — '

'Of course,' said David.

'And John Strachey.' Archie swallowed some brandy. 'He was at Eton. They've fifty or sixty thousand members, you know.'

David sat frowning, flicking over the pages. 'What sort of people would those be, I wonder?'

'Not intellectuals particularly, but people who regard themselves as intellectuals. Schoolteachers, university students who've seen through their dons. Anybody who feels he can't make enough of himself, who's frustrated by the political and social system.'

'Exactly the people in Germany who got the Nazis going,' I said.

Archie made a grimace. 'I know what you mean. Steam escaping from a faulty boiler by one crack rather than another. Of course, the Left Book

Club's pretty Communist. It flatters a lot of people, rather dangerously, that they're more intelligent and better educated than they actually are. But I wish I'd had the idea. It would have been more useful than going to Spain, and made a lot of money.'

Archie spoke with a Bloomsbury publisher's combination of idealism and salesmanship. He had written a novel while recovering from his duodenal ulcer – *Scrannel Pipes*, criticized by James Agate as 'the minutes of a rather decorous meeting of a committee comprising Aldous Huxley, Michael Arlen and Ronald Firbank.' As nobody had leapt to publish it, Archie founded the Urn Press in a basement. At the time of our dinner party, he was losing a thousand or two a year in the business, as comfortably as any other moneyed and cultured young gentleman down from the University. He rose abruptly from the table, saying he had some telephone calls to make. 'I hope I didn't upset Elizabeth,' he apologized in my direction.

'Lord Meddish is in his self-analytical mood tonight,' I observed, smiling after our departed host. 'He wants to stop Hitler, but he doesn't want conscription.'

'Oh, Archie's mind is always as confused as an old woman's sewing-basket.' David sat sipping his brandy, the yellow-jacketed book on his knees. 'Do you suppose Elizabeth's having a good cry?'

'Elizabeth? Don't be silly.'

'You're pretty thick with her, aren't you?'

'On the contrary, she only lets me take her to occasions like this, when there are other people about. We never enjoy what Norman Douglas called 'a friendly teat-a-teat'. I don't see very much of her at all, really, as she spends most of the winter on the Riviera with her mother. She maintains a relationship of steely flippancy.'

'I don't know how you put up with it. I certainly wouldn't take that sort of selfishness from any woman. Even a stunner like her.'

'I'd take even worse from Elizabeth,' I told him soberly. 'Surely you can understand my feelings? For years she was the untouchable embodiment of everything I wanted. Not just in the feminine way, but everything in life – money, home, *savoir faire*, friends, parents. I was happy if she threw me a word, like a fish bone to one of Sir Edward's damn cats.

Lady Tip hated me, of course, and still does. She always treated me with the utmost contempt, and I didn't see any reason why Elizabeth shouldn't do likewise.'

'Why didn't she?' asked David bluntly.

'She's much more civilized than her mother. Ever since Lady Tip was once horrible to me in her presence, she's felt guilty, perhaps. And of course my elevation to work with her father must have helped. Besides, things are changing, aren't they? Our Hitler makes class warfare look a silly game.'

'Didn't you once say she wasn't his daughter?'

'That was the gossip below stairs.'

'Personally, I think she's just a high-class prick teaser.'

Elizabeth came in, recovered from her pique and smiling. Noticing the book on David's lap, she exclaimed, 'Don't say you've taken to Mr Victor Gollancz's high-minded publications? Is he supporting this thing in Parliament to abolish flogging? You know that he doesn't eat the day when anybody's hanged, don't you? Not a thing. Daddy's seen him in the Savoy. Only a glass of champagne and a cigar.'

David knocked back his brandy and stood up. 'I must go, if I want to slip into Mary's and see Margaret before catching my train. Why is the last one to Oxford so bloody early? The dons like early nights, I suppose.'

David had been a doctor about three years. He was then working as an assistant to one of the consultant physicians at the Radcliffe Infirmary in Oxford. I was to be best man at Easter when he married a staff nurse he had met while doing his house jobs at St Mary's. She had been denied the feast that evening through night duty.

'What's Archie up to?' David asked Elizabeth.

'Talking to Watson about the Test Match in Durban. Apparently it rained just as England were winning. That seems to sum up our national destiny in general, doesn't it?'

'Can I take you home in a taxi?' I asked her.

'Of course, darling.'

It was a cold, windy, showery night, handfuls of rain rattling against the cab window. 'Must you go in yet?' I pleaded. 'It's dreadfully early. I whisked you off because I saw how Archie wanted to get rid of us all.'

'I promised Daddy I shouldn't be late.'

'You mean, you don't want to be alone with me longer than it is strictly polite to allow?'

In reply, she said, 'It must be a dreadful strain living with Archie. I wonder you're not a nervous wreck.'

'I don't see a lot of him. He's always out in the evenings organizing committees, speaking at meetings, engineering interviews or buying drinks for journalists. He's a crusader with many banners.'

'Archie seems to think there's going to be a war.'

'It'll be a relief, really, won't it? After having to run our lives from one of Hitler's speeches to the next.'

'If there's a war I shall do something *useful*.'

'Cut your hair and make munitions. Lots of girls did last time.'

'I'd be a nurse. I'd be one now, you know, honestly. But of course you have to be twenty-one before they let you start.'

'Can I kiss you?'

She formally closed her eyes and pursed her lips.

I said. *'Ich liebe dich, und du schläfst.'*

'What's that mean?' I translated. 'Please, Jim, don't start getting pompous,' she protested, much as Gerda had.

'But you're quite aware that I do love you.'

'Don't he *serious*, darling. You know how being serious spoils everything.'

We lay back in our separate corners of the taxi. 'You're lucky that I'm – well, not frightened of women, but frightened of making a fool of myself over them. That happened once.'

After a moment's puzzlement, she said, 'Oh, Rosie,' rather bleakly.

'And of course, as far as you're concerned, Elizabeth, I'm still the butler's boy.'

'Why must you keep bringing that up?' she asked crossly. 'It's awfully unfair. You're like Archie, trying to make us all feel utterly ashamed of ourselves because people in Bermondsey have got less to eat for dinner than we have. Wasn't that chicken *ghastly*?'

RICHARD GORDON

'How long are you staying with your father?'

'I don't know. Mummy may remain in Monte Carlo, though of course it's dreadfully unfashionable after Easter.'

We arrived at the newly-built block of flats in Mayfair, where Sir Edward Tiplady now lived alone. Lady Tip had walked out about the same time as King Edward the Eighth abdicated. As I reached to open the cab door, she adopted again the ceremonial expression indicating that she would allow herself to be kissed.

'Come and see *Design for Living* tomorrow,' I asked temptingly. 'Diana Wynyard and Rex Harrison.'

'Darling, there's simply no *time* for going to the theatre. Tomorrow I absolutely must go to a party with Hugo Mottram.'

'Who's Hugo Mottram?'

'He's frightfully rich on the Stock Exchange. I'm having an utterly passionate affair with him. Daddy's so pleased.'

'Good night.'

'Good night, darling. You're really the most wonderfully saint-like man, and of course I completely adore you.'

The taxi drove back to Archie's. Unrequited love is painful enough, love shrivelled by frivolity can be suicidal.

20

'Jim, it was awfully good of you to waste your time with Elizabeth last night.'

Sir Edward Tiplady came hurrying into my laboratory. I had risen in the Harley Street house from basement to attic. After Lady Tip bolted he had turned the whole place into consulting rooms, which he let profitably. It was simply a doctors' shop. Our basement was now full of files and rubbish, I tested blood and urine samples in the room where I had fathered Clare. My mother had gone as cook to a small hotel in Eastbourne. My father had died shortly after the old King, knocked down by a taxi outside a pub. The house itself then had barely eighteen months to live, before being blown to bits early in the blitz.

'I know that underneath she's terribly impressed meeting someone like Lord Meddish,' he continued. 'Who's always getting himself into the newspapers.'

'We were delighted to see her. She livens us all up.' Sir Edward always placed me in an avuncular relationship to Elizabeth. It seemed sage not to rectify his impression.

'I'm sure she didn't. She bored you terribly, I expect.' He was moving restlessly as ever round the white-painted, sloping-roofed room. He was growing grey, but his figure was still spare and the lines round his blue eyes no deeper. His happiness had much improved since shedding his wife. 'I really do find it hard work, chatting to bright young things these days. They don't even call themselves "bright young things" any more, do they? There seems such an enormous gap in our ideas, in the way we look at the world. And of course, Elizabeth is really very naughty, playing the *enfant*

149

terrible. She's really too old for that sort of prankish behaviour. Have you done Mrs Cockburn's blood urea?'

'Yes, it's normal.'

'Good, the old thing's kidneys are all right after all. But I think I'll play her along. She needs a doctor to relieve her inner tensions by listening to her troubles. Her family got sick to death of them years ago. And she always pays on the nail.'

Encouraged and financed by Sir Edward, I had started a one-man biochemical and bacteriological service for neighbouring consulting rooms and the private nursing homes and clinics then multiplying in London. Mine were the coming sciences. There had been little point in identifying the germs infecting the patient, or the deficiencies of his blood and other body fluids, when the doctor could do little to rectify either misfortune. I was doing prosperously. I dressed better, I wore bow ties like Alexander Fleming. Much of my work – like Mrs Cockburn's blood urea – was to save the doctor's conscience rather than the patient's life. Cronin's *The Citadel* had been published a couple of years, and there were still plenty of physicians in Harley Street unscrupulous about treating an imaginary illness or overrating a real one, and plenty of zealous surgeons who had to cut to earn their living. It was Domagk's sulphonamide which opened an age when so many diseases thankfully became treatable that it was no longer necessary for the doctors to invent others.

'I really came up with a complaint,' He stood smiling, hands characteristically on loins, black formal jacket tucked back, monocle in eye. 'You ruined my last night's sleep. At the perfectly ungodly hour of six-forty-five somebody telephoned trying to trace you urgently. An American, of course.' I frowned, puzzled. 'He called my number, because he remembered me as the chap who'd originally introduced you.'

'Not Jeff Beckerman?' I exclaimed.

Sir Edward nodded. 'He's at the Savoy – naturally. Apparently, he got into Southampton from New York late last night. He wants to see you as soon as possible. I'd get him to stand a good dinner, if I were you.'

I had heard not a word from Jeff, nor about him, since leaving Wuppertal. Naturally, I was excited and intrigued by the summons, and telephoned the Savoy at once. Jeff sounded exactly the same. He spoke heartily but briefly, apparently distracted during his stay in London by business as multifarious as usual. He invited me for cocktail time. This apparently meant five in the afternoon, when I usually took a cup of tea.

He had a suite. It was on an upper floor, overlooking the river. He was redder in the face, his dark hair had been allowed to grow, and from my first impression he seemed twice the size. He still wore beautifully-tailored English tweeds. There was a good deal of slapping, hugging and kidding. 'Married yet?' I asked.

'Yeah, but it didn't work out. How about you, old man.'

'Yes, but she died.'

'Oh, how terrible.'

'I've got over it now.' Rosie had gone to wherever the damp souls of housemaids went. I consoled myself that her continued existence would have meant misery for three. 'Have you been back to Wuppertal?' I asked, to keep off the subject.

Sure, I have. Before Christmas. And I'm on my way back. *Ich bin ein Wuppertaler, nicht wahr?* The Red Crown Brewery remains a monument to American enterprise and capitalism, though the Nazis can hardly keep their hands off it. That cosmetics company in Berlin has turned out a headache. The Nazis don't care for powder and scent, *natürlich*. They put the girls in calf-length uniforms and awful shoes and march them all over the country. They regard women as inferior beings, only necessary for breeding. The whole of Germany's got like one big stud farm. What'll you have to drink?'

'Sherry.'

'Try a martini. Mind, I quit living there about the time old man Hindenburg died, in the July of '34. It was after Hitler had his bloodbath at Munich. I guessed it was the hour to go. I got to hear the details – say, do you know they took Röhm to Stadelheim jail, and a couple of SS men shot him in his cell? The guy in charge was Sepp Dietrich, who ran Hitler's personal bodyguard. I've seen the guy in Berlin, he's got big ears and a little moustache, he looks as though Frankenstein the monster-maker was trying to construct Clark Gable. He'll come to a bad end – I hope.' Jeff busied himself with the cocktail shaker. 'Do you know, absolutely no one in the States would touch our fine, pure spirits after they repealed the

Eighteenth Amendment. The whole country had got the taste for bathtub gin.'

I gingerly sipped the first martini of my life. 'How's Gerda Dieffenbach?' I had been wanting to ask since entering the room.

'I saw her last year. She's fine, it seems. Still a schoolmistress. I kept clear, that game has become too dangerous. But I was sick, and I called in Dr Dieffenbach. He's disillusioned with the Nazis, I guess. He thought they'd bolster the middle classes. But Hitler isn't interested in the middle classes or any classes.' Hitler was interested only in race and blood, valour and fecundity, warfare and slavery, torture and death. 'Their boy's gone to join the Army.'

'Did Professor Domagk's daughter's arm recover?' It was like talking about ghosts.

'Oh, sure. They didn't have to operate, or anything. We saw the start of big deal, old man. I've started up a pharmaceutical company in New York State, we're making this new one, sulphapyridine against pneumonia.'

'I nodded. 'The disease which used to be called "the old man's friend", but more frequently robbed him of his healthy grandson.'

Jeff topped up my glass from the shaker. I decided definitely to give up sherry.

'That guy you used to talk about, Professor Hörlein – '

'He's been to England a couple of times. He was lecturing to doctors about Domagk and his mice.'

'He's going great guns in Wuppertal. He's a member of the Nazi party, he's mixed up with the Reich Labour Front and the Reich Health Council, as well as being on the I G Farben board of directors. A big bug in the present order of things.'

'Do you think there'll be a war?' People were asking that as they used to speculate politely about the weather.

Jeff looked hard under his bar of eyebrow. 'Hitler wants his war, and Hitler's going to win it.' I could say nothing in face of this chilling opinion. Jeff flicked up a Chesterfield. 'There's only one man in the world who can stop him,'

'Roosevelt?'

'Me.'

I stared in silence through the large window at the Thames, chocolate coloured with its spectrum of oil, a string of barges heading downstream behind a tug billowing black smoke. Jeff seemed wholly serious. I wondered whether his mind had become unhinged under the pressure of business in two continents.

'Let's take a short walk,' he added, almost equally surprisingly. 'I've got my secretary Donna over here, she's out shopping at Harrods but she'll be back, and I don't want her to know a word about this. The slightest whisper to a woman, you might as well say it on the radio.'

We took the lift down in silence. Leaving by the river entrance of the hotel, we strolled in the small, delightful triangular public gardens. It was a fine evening, the red double-decker trams clanking along the Embankment, bearing the office workers home to Camberwell and Brixton. 'You know Göring's been in London?' Jeff asked abruptly.

I heard a rumour, but I didn't believe it.'

'He was here less than twenty-four hours. It was on May 11, 1937, the day before your King George's Coronation. He just showed up at Croydon with a few other Nazis. Wanted to get into the Royal act, I guess, maybe wave to the crowds from the balcony of Buckingham Palace. Ribbentrop was mad. Hitler already had an official representative for the ceremony, General Blomberg. Göring spent the night at the embassy in Carlton House Terrace, then they smuggled the *Reichmarschall* out. The crowds in the streets would have had him for dog meat.'

'What's this got to do with you stopping the war?'

'I told you about Göring so you'd know a lot of things go on across the frontiers which never see newsprint. Have you heard of General Franz Halder?'

'There're too many German generals to keep count.'

'He's Hitler's Chief of Staff, and I guess busy this moment with his pencil and a map of the county of Kent, planning the best way up from Dover. Say, who's this?'

He had paused at a bust among the shrubs. 'Sullivan, of Gilbert and Sullivan.'

'Oh, sure –' Jeff whistled a phrase from *The Mikado*. 'Do you remember what I told you during that crazy show in Cologne? How the generals hated Hitler as a Johnnie-come-lately? They reckon he's more likely to lead Germany to ruin than to glory. Halder would be very, very pleased to see the end of the Führer. So would Count von Moltke, great-grandnephew of the famous one. Also von Trott, von Schlabrendorff and Carl Gördeler, who was over here last year with his wife, ostensibly giving lectures but making contact with Horace Wilson at the Foreign Office. Do you know what's happening in London on July 18?'

'I haven't the faintest.'

'It's the International Whaling Conference.'

Jeff stopped to inspect the memorial to the Imperial Camel Corps. I had no idea where this strange conversation was leading. But he seemed to be handling important German names with assurance. I wondered how the International Whaling Conference came into it.

'The German delegation will be headed by a guy called Wohltat. He's a civil servant, from the Economics Ministry. He's close to Göring. And he's interested in bigger fish than whales. He's coming to do a deal with Wilson. Colonies, cash for Germany – a thousand million pounds. A free hand to act as they like in eastern Europe. In return, Hitler will guarantee the British Empire. Halder could tear up his map of Kent.'

'Those are terms which Britain would never accept.'

'They are terms which Britain herself suggested. Through Horace Wilson.'

'I simply don't believe you,' I said forcefully.

'Have it your own way,' Jeff told me airily. 'But those terms could be a starting point. This is my plan. If your Foreign Office told Halder they'd stick to that sort of agreement once the generals had kicked out Hitler…that they'd support the generals against the Nazi machine right up to the hilt…that they'd support Gördeler as the new Chancellor, which seems the fashionable idea…then we'd be getting somewhere.'

'The Germans would murder the rebellious generals.'

'Not for one moment. Listen – the German people have been living for the glorious tomorrow since Hitler first walked into the Chancellery. Maybe the tomorrow's getting nearer, they feel they can almost touch it. But they absolutely hate the idea of another war. And so do the generals. For the same good reason. They're afraid they might lose again. I'm going on to Germany in two–three days. I've got a contact with Halder right there in Wuppertal. It's essential I meet someone from your Foreign Office. Maybe you can arrange it through Sir Edward Tiplady? In six months, we could have Hitler in Heaven or St Helena.'

Jeff paused, lighting another cigarette. I did not know what to make of it all. Jeff was not a vain man, he did not seek importance, he did not exaggerate. He was practical, a man who would set about making a million dollars or restoring peace in the world without fuss or self-delusions. And in the six years I had known him, everything he had foreseen in Germany had come sickeningly true.

'I suppose I could try Sir Edward, or Lord Meddish, who I share a flat with. But in the present temper of the country nobody wants to smell even faintly of appeasement.'

'It wouldn't be appeasement, if the end result was Hitler's head on a spike.'

'I'll see what I can do,' I promised.

'But hurry, old man. Time's short.'

Going up in the lift, Jeff talked about Wuppertal. 'Living's tough in Germany today. Everything *ersatz*, coffee from acorns, margarine for butter, a stick of rhubarb pretending to be a lemon. Their clothes are made from *Zellwolle* substitute, their rubber from God knows what. The Germans are worse off than during the War.'

'Don't they object?'

'Under the Nazis? You must be crazy. There's some sickening things happening behind barbed wire which even the Nazis are ashamed of, because they keep quiet about it.' We reached his floor. 'You know Hitler has to wear reading glasses?' Jeff added. 'He's never allowed to be seen or photographed in them. It would spoil the superman image. He has his speeches typed in special extra-large *Führerschrift*.'

Jeff was a useful repository of information which, casually uttered, could silence a London dinner-table.

His secretary Donna was already in the suite. She was short, blonde and bubbling, twenty-two or three, with big eyes and big bosom. As she ordered Jeff to telephone about some theatre tickets, I politely asked about her volume of work. But it seemed she did not know how to type.

21

Within the hour, I was telling Archie of Jeff's scheme in the flat. To my surprise, he did not dismiss it as fantastic. 'There's quite a traffic in unofficial diplomatic activity behind the scenes. Swedes and Swiss and those sort of people. They remind me of the mice busy under the floorboards at some tremendous diplomatic reception. Well, sometimes the unexpected appearance of a mouse can make even an ambassador jump. There's somebody I know from Eton doing rather well in the FO. I'll give him a ring. Anything is worth trying in the country's present straits.'

But the Foreign Office seemed in no hurry to accept the services of the only man in Europe who could prevent the outbreak of war. The following evening, Jeff telephoned me at the flat. 'Can't you pep them up?' he complained.

'I don't think one can pep up the British Foreign Office. Anyway, on Friday nights it disperses to its country houses. That is why Hitler always makes his most violent moves on Saturday mornings.'

'I'd try calling the Embassy, but I guess Joe Kennedy's never heard of me.'

'He's probably away with the Astors, anyway. I hear his sons and daughters are well in with the Cliveden Set. It's at Cliveden and not in the Cabinet, of course, where British policies are formulated.' This was not entirely a newspaper columnist's joke. Jeff put down the telephone. He was not in the mood for kidding.

That Friday, Neville Chamberlain traversed the muzzle of British foreign policy so that it no longer aimed harmlessly at the sky, or perhaps at the British people themselves, but at Hitler's head. He had gone to

Birmingham, where his family name shone like burnished brass. Instead of plaintively protesting again at Hitler's perfidy, he changed his mind and said Britain would resist Hitler's domination of the world to the uttermost of its power. Everyone cheered. The last time they cheered him he was waving his piece of paper on Heston Aerodrome. The following week, President Lebrun of France paid a State visit. The weather stayed cold and showery. On the Wednesday, Hitler subdued Lithuania by sailing in the pocket battleship *Deutschland* from Swinemünde to Memel. His latest aggression at least had the singular variation of being committed by water.

Jeff fumed expensively all that week in the Savoy. Archie finally told me that his friend from the Foreign Office would see 'my man' on the Friday afternoon. But not within official walls. We were invited to take tea at the Travellers' Club in Pall Mall at four o'clock.

To Jeff's visibly diminishing self-confidence, we were led by a porter in bottle-green livery and brass buttons to a large oblong morning-room full of dark leather furniture, on which a pair of elderly gentlemen sat asleep. The windows looked across St James's Park to the Foreign Office, for which the club was something of a canteen. Jeff's bounce expired more with our young diplomat, who had chestnut hair, a pink plump face, an old Etonian tie and a name not double-barrelled but triple-barrelled. 'Would you prefer toast or tea-cake?' he asked politely. 'The tea-cakes are rather good.'

'Tea-cakes,' I replied for us both.

'You've some contacts among our German friends?' suggested the Foreign Office man, when he was leaning back in his deep armchair and lazily stirring his tea.

'That's right.' The casual English grandeur of the club was too much for Jeff's natural brashness. His demoralization was completed by being presented for the first time in his life with a tea-cake. He could explain only stumblingly the scheme which had appeared so exciting and straightforward in the Embankment gardens.

The diplomat spread his tea-cake thickly with strawberry jam. 'Could you give me the name of this person in Wuppertal, who's the link between you and the Reich General Staff?'

'No, sir.'

'Well, don't worry. Male or female?'

'I'm not prepared to say.'

'German?'

Jeff nodded. I wondered for the first time if it was Gerda. 'More tea?' The diplomat invited us. 'And what precisely would you wish His Majesty's Government to do, Mr Beckerman?'

'Promise the support of the British Empire for the German generals when they murder Hitler.'

'And it is you who will bring them the British Empire's message?'

'That's right,' Jeff agreed.

'Oh, Charles—' A tall, bald man caught our host's eye. 'You *are* on the committee, aren't you? The cottage pie at lunch was really rather dreadful. I wouldn't have given it to my housemaid to eat.'

The two members discussed the cottage pie. Then all four of us discussed the architecture of the club. Then Jeff and I found ourselves out in Pall Mall.

'I try to prevent a war,' Jeff said bitterly. 'And what do I get? Tea-cakes!'

Last week — last week as I write this, and can lunch in professorial dignity at the Athenaeum Club next door to the Travellers' — I invited the same diplomat with the triple-barrelled name. 'Yes, we'd looked up that young American fellow's background,' he remembered. 'Which wasn't very savoury. His family were the biggest bootleggers in New York during Prohibition, hardly more than gangsters. We were suspicious of him. We were even suspicious of Carl Gördeler, and he was a former Lord Mayor of Leipzig. Both might have been catspaws, giving Hitler an excuse to shoot powerful but inconvenient generals as British agents, without incurring the resentment of his Army.'

'Weren't you wrong about Gördeler? He finished at the end of a length of piano-wire after the 1944 bomb plot.'

'Perhaps we were. There was a half-hearted sort of plot in 1939, I suppose. Halder fussed about a bit during the final days of that August. General von Witzleben was supposed to collect some troops and chuck Hitler out by marching them to his front door. The other generals all posted themselves away from Berlin. You can't say the plotters lost heart. Their heart wasn't in it from the first place. I heard about it all from a Cambridge don, who interrogated Halder after the war. The *Generaloberst* told of an earlier plot for September 1938, but unfortunately that was the day Chamberlain flew to Munich. When Hitler called off the impending war, his popularity went up in Germany as much as Chamberlain's did here.'

'So my American friend did know what he was talking about?' Jeff *had* a contact, a surprising one in Wuppertal, whom he told me about in Munich after the War.

'Possibly,' he admitted, sipping his port.

'What happened to Herr Wohltat and the Whaling Conference?'

'Oh! An utterly disgraceful episode. Sir Horace Wilson tried to buy Hitler off. A miserable failure! He should have offered more.'

'Do you still like tea-cakes?'

My guest looked surprised. 'Yes, I often have them at the Travellers'. They're not nearly so good as they were.'

The following Friday of March 31, 1939, Chamberlain offered Colonel Beck, the Polish Foreign Minister, a guarantee of Britain's unqualified support should Hitler attack Poland. Colonel Beck accepted, between two flicks of ash from his cigarette. That evening I was taking David Mellors and his pretty red-headed fiancée to dinner at Kettner's in Soho, to talk over the wedding arrangements for the following week. As we sat down, David asked, 'Have you heard of a chap called Florey?'

'Yes, he was a don at Caius when I was up. An Australian.'

'That's right. You knew he'd been Prof. of Pathology in Oxford since 1935?'

'No, I didn't. The last I'd heard of him, he'd gone to Sheffield.'

'What do you do, boy, when you move into a department as a new broom of a professor?'

'Send your staff to the library to look out other people's unfinished lines of research,' I told him promptly.

'You're right. Get them busy picking brains, which is quicker than scratching their own. From all accounts, the Path. Department at Oxford was in a pretty ropy state when Florey blew in. About the first item he gingered up his boys and girls to investigate anew was lysozyme.'

'Old Flem's tear antiseptic!' I exclaimed. 'That's as out of date as the Charleston, surely?'

'Oh, God!' exclaimed Margaret in anguish. We both stared at her. 'I forgot to tell Daphne the other bridesmaids have decided on pink hats.'

'She can buy some dye at Woolworth's, dear,' said David helpfully. 'Next on Florey's list was another of Flem's babies which never got past the toddling stage – penicillin. You had something to do with it, hadn't you? Apparently they've now managed to isolate a grain or two of the stuff.'

'Professor Raistrick tried to isolate some at the School of Tropical Medicine,' I said sceptically. 'But I heard the penicillin kept vanishing under his nose.'

'Florey's got a pretty bright chemist working for him there. Chap called Ernst Chain, half-Russian and half-German. Apparently he used to work at the Charité Hospital in Berlin.'

I had heard of Dr Chain. 'Yes, he escaped from Hitler and went to work with Hoppy at Cambridge.'

David grinned. 'Florey got him transferred to Oxford, like Joe Payne from Luton Town to Chelsea. I don't know what the transfer fee would be.'

'No, I'll tell the others they can all wear white hats, like Daphne,' said Margaret thoughtfully.

'Where did Florey get the mould from?' I asked. 'As far as I knew, the specimen at Mary's was the only one which actually produced any penicillin.'

'They had a culture of it already in the lab. Flem sent a bit to Oxford years ago. Chain is able to grow it faster than Flem did, by lacing the broth underneath with yeast.'

'Have they brought Flem himself into the research?'

'No. Chain thought he was dead.'

I laughed. 'That would be taking Flem's habitual self-effacement to an uncomfortable extreme.'

We talked about the imminent wedding, but more about the imminent war. As two men, we had a particularly keen interest in the possibility of conscription. It arrived within a month. One hundred and forty-three MPs voted against it. 'It is very dangerous to give generals all they want,' objected Major Clement Attlee – but he was thinking of the Somme, when the generals had more men than ideas. The conscripts were afforded exceptional treatment. Unlike any previous soldiers in the British Army, they were issued with pyjamas.

22

Neville Chamberlain was a man of peace. He even went to war peacefully. He was followed by a nation of inoffensive shepherds, cheerfully shouldering their crooks. There was no nastiness. There was no undue enthusiasm. The war was very genteel. We had the blackout and the evacuees. Everyone carried a gasmask in a little cardboard box the size of a Brownie camera. Air-raid trenches were cut among the flowerbeds of Hyde Park. Strips of sticky brown paper criss-crossed shop windows, to prevent their breaking when a bomb dropped outside. The only bloodshed was a doubling of road casualties by unlit motorcars. Meanwhile, Poland was smashed between two flicks of ash from Colonel Beck's cigarette.

Our lives were not endangered, only changed. Archie was outraged to discover that volunteering for the Army was officially discouraged. He saw the chance of his duodenal ulcer returning, and spending yet another war on his back in Swanage. I waited submissively to be gathered tidily by the harvester of conscription.

I had little work nor income, because London was empty of patients and Sir Edward was busy evacuating his hospital from Blackfriars by the Thames to a vast red-brick Victorian asylum sprawling across the South Downs. Its London wards were left empty for the half-million air-raid casualties the Government secretly but confidently expected in the first week of the War. Towards the end of October, when people were still saying it would all be over by Christmas, Sir Edward telephoned me one breakfast time at Archie's flat. Could I call that afternoon on a Professor Ainsley? The address was near Marble Arch. It was important.

Mystified but flattered, I presented myself at a small block of offices, sandbagged to the first floor, not far from St Mary's Hospital, behind a cinema in Edgware Road. I waited in a bleak official anteroom, while a smartly-dressed blonde with a superior accent answered the telephone, typed and received callers with impartial bored condescension. Ainsley's office beyond seemed a store-room for battleship-grey filing cabinets, among which he had wedged himself at a cheap, bare desk with three telephones, each of a different colour. He was small, grey-haired, knobbly-faced, bushy-eyebrowed, middle-aged, solemn-looking. A likeness to Alexander Fleming struck me. He wore a plain blue suit and a red knitted cardigan, which I later found that, like Fleming, he abandoned only during the hottest weeks of midsummer. I had during the morning taken care to discover that he was the Wychart Professor of Biology at Cambridge. I did not know that this self-effacing, amiable, overworked, practical intellectual who was to control my life for the next six years came directly under Professor Lindemann, the Oxford physicist with enormous influence on Churchill. Lindemann had just moved into the Admiralty as the new First Lord's personal assistant.

'Should I make some joke about, "Let slip the dons of war"?' Ainsley asked affably. 'Like a lot of my colleagues at Cambridge, I suppose I'm sitting here working for the Government for the duration.' He looked round the room unenthusiastically. 'I gather you were out in Germany in 1933? And that you met Gerhard Domagk?'

Sitting on a hard chair opposite, I told him, 'I was in Wuppertal, working in a brewery.'

'Yes, we know all about that. Did you meet anyone else in the I G Farbenwerke?'

'Only Professor Örlein.'

'Phillip Heinrich Hörlein, born June 5, 1882, at Wendelsheim,' Ainsley recited reflectively. 'And a Nazi. I heard him talk about sulphonamides to the British Association at Nottingham a couple of years ago. Very effective he was, too. Anyone else?'

'Only the lab technician. A girl.'

'Perhaps you'd care to describe Domagk's lab, and anything else you remember in the factory. Draw a plan, if you like.'

I sketched what I could remember of the factory lay-out. Had the British Government been so interested, I thought, they could have sent a man that summer to ride up and down in the Schwebebahn. Ainsley began to question me about the Dieffenbachs. I became aware that a dossier on myself lay somewhere in the battleship-grey cabinets.

'The Dieffenbachs were a decent family who fell for the Nazi line, or thought it prudent to pretend as much,' I told him.

'Did *you* fall for it at the time?'

'Not in the least. I think I saw how dangerous the Nazis were before a lot of people in England did.'

'You've no conscientious objections to killing Germans, nothing like that?' he added airily. I shook my head. 'Nor how you killed them? I don't of course mean resorting to torture, and putting yourself on the Nazis' own level. But killing them by the deliberate spread of – shall we say – botulism or plague or anthrax?'

I hesitated. 'No. It's the same principle as dropping high explosive.'

'I'm glad to see you are a realist, Mr Elgar. Nor am I myself talking theoretical science. The Government intends to wage war with every weapon possible – we are merely returning Hitler's compliment – which includes pathogenic bacteria.' He paused, looking at me closely. 'Little or nothing is known about handling and distributing such pathogens. Or of their likely effect on the enemy population. We've a few sketchy papers on 'germ warfare', that's all. Your name was put forward by Sir Almroth Wright, no less. Sir Edward Tiplady and I both agree that your particular combination of biochemical and bacteriological skills make you the right man to direct our new unit. Of course, bacteria may never be used as a weapon in this war. Neither may poison gas. But I assure you that the enemy has for some time been investigating the possibilities of both, and we should be criminally at fault not preparing ourselves for similar action.'

I could say nothing for a moment. I was amazed, even more, flattered. I felt a flush of warmth towards Wright for at last finding me a job, if a peculiar one. I had imagined Ainsley wished only to interrogate me about the I G Farben plant, not to offer me a lever of the war machine. Perhaps they could find no one else to take it. My students today might be appalled at my accepting such inhuman work without scruple. But I had no qualms later over the Americans dropping two atom bombs on the Japanese. You could not fight the Nazis or the Kamikazes with half a smile on your face. My only feeling, as I agreed, was the job being preferable to peeling potatoes in the Army.

'Where does this research take place?'

'In Oxford. At the Fungus Institute, a small and admirably unobtrusive grey stone building just south of the Parks. The strictest secrecy is of course essential – you will have to sign the Official Secrets Act, which proscribes the most alarming penalties. As far as the University and the rest of the country are concerned, you are performing research on making valuable foodstuffs from toadstools and lichens.'

Well before that snowy Christmas, I was installed on one side of South Parks Road at Oxford, secretly attempting to breed strains of germs so deadly they could wipe out the population of Europe, while in the large building opposite Professor Florey was attempting to develop penicillin and save the world from the deadly germs which already infested it. Thus science progresses.

I wore grey flannel trousers and a Harris tweed jacket and I bought a second-hand bicycle. I found lodgings in north Oxford, that area of red-brick family dwellings embraced by the Woodstock and Banbury roads, where the lofty donnish intellect struggles daily with earthy domesticity. I had David Mellors and his new wife nearby for company. I browsed in Blackwell's and drank in the Randolph. I have never enjoyed so gentle and agreeable a life as the time I was preparing unpleasant death for millions. Of my laboratories, my colleagues and my work itself I may still write nothing. The Official Secrets Act has an infinite memory, and the world is not yet peaceful enough for dust to lie undisturbed on my deadly experiments.

In that December, when the strange war became weirder, with the Russians fighting the Finns and the British about to fight the neutral Russians instead of the Germans, I had a letter forwarded from the Harley Street house with a Swedish stamp and an affixed strip of brown paper printed, *Opened By the Censor*. Inside was an unaddressed, undated sheet with a typed message.

Dear Jim

God willing, I shall arrive in London via Stockholm first–second week December. I'm trying to fix a passage with United States Lines to be home in time for Christmas, but of course it's tricky. Call me up at the Savoy. I'm still where the railway flies in the sky.

Cordially, Jeff.

I was astounded to find Jeff still in Wuppertal, even though the RAF was dropping on him nothing more weighty than the prose of the Ministry of Information leaflets. Perhaps he was still trying to stop the war. The Savoy knew nothing of him, but it was not the time to make bookings from one side of Europe to another. I left the Fungus Institute number, and two mornings later he telephoned in high spirits

'I arrived in a Swedish plane with the Swedish ambassador, which I guess is safe enough,' he explained. 'Hey, what are all those blimps in the sky round London?'

'That's the balloon barrage. The Germans run their bombers into them.' Jeff pressed me to have dinner the following night. I asked if I could bring a girlfriend.

'Sure thing, old man. I'm lonely. There's no girls I know left in London, and Donna sailed home early summer.'

'What's it like, being a neutral in Germany?'

'Creepy. The Gestapo had their beady eyes on me round the clock. I guess they'd have run me out, if I hadn't jumped of my own accord.'

'How are the Dieffenbachs?'

'Are you crazy? If I'd waved to them in the street, they'd have ended in a concentration camp.

Jeff had the same suite as in peacetime, with blackout curtains which he claimed made opening the window like undressing a nun. I knew that Elizabeth was living in her father's flat, and imagined she would be impressed to meet a man hot from the enemy's camp fires. But it was I who felt staggered as she appeared through the door in uniform, with a Service gasmask in a haversack. 'Motor Transport Corps,' she explained. 'Do you like it? I wish I was blonde. Khaki goes so much better with fair hair. American cigarettes, divine,' she murmured, taking one of Jeff's Chesterfields.

'Where are you serving?' asked Jeff, dazzled by her.

'I'm going to Paris on Monday. There! I should never have said so. Careless talk costs lives. I'm driving ambulances and things at the British Transit Hospital, because of the French I picked up with Mummy on the Riviera, though everyone says I have the most ghastly Midi accent. Mummy thinks that Paris will be a much nicer place to spend the war in than London. Last time, they had a few shells from Big Bertha, but the food remained delicious. Mummy regards the war as a personal insult to her from Hitler,' she added to me.

There was champagne, and caviar canapés on a silver tray. Jeff wanted to express either admiration of the fighting British or appreciation at escape from austere Germany. There was no food rationing in England until the following month, and there seemed a shortage only of taxis and torch batteries. As the long-promised bombs stayed off, London had the gaiety of a fashionable garden-party spared a threatening summer storm.

'Have you seen anything of Archie?' I asked Elizabeth while Jeff was telephoning the headwaiter.

'Yes, he's dreadfully confused, poor dear. Now that Hitler's in bed with Stalin, he doesn't know if the war is an anti-Fascist crusade or an anti-Communist one. He says the British working classes went to war quite ignobly, only because they were fed up with Hitler. But fed-upness is an incredibly powerful force, isn't it, with the British? So in the end he's gone to join up as a Guardsman.' This was news to me. 'At least it will give him some peace from continually redefining his attitudes. What *are* you doing at Oxford?'

'I'm on war work at the Fungus Institute.'

Elizabeth looked nonplussed. 'I've got it. You're developing a mushroom like the Caterpillar's in *Alice*. Eating one side will make our soldiers so small they can creep on the Germans unseen, and the other will make them so tall they'll frighten the enemy to death.'

'That's right,' I told her.

Jeff explained to us how the Germans were cock-a-hoop after the Polish campaign. 'The *Wehrmacht* and the dive bombers made mincemeat of the Poles. They've a new tactic. If the tanks run into trouble, they radio the Stukas to bomb them out of it. I guess Poland hadn't a combat plane in the sky after the first day. And now they've sunk your carrier, the *Courageous*. And the *Royal Oak*, right inside Scapa Flow. You've got to take your hat off to the U-boat captains, I guess.'

'You forgot the *Athenia*,' said Elizabeth. 'Sunk without warning nine hours after the war started. Drowning a hundred and twelve people, including children,'

'And including twenty-eight Americans.'

She coloured. 'I'm sorry.'

'Anyway, the Germans believe that Churchill sank the *Athenia*, to do another *Lusitania*. It's a crazy idea, but nobody dare deny it. Say, you remember your Professor Domagk? He was arrested by the Gestapo.'

I raised my eyebrows. 'All I heard about Domagk was his turning down the Nobel Prize.'

'I'll give you the real story. It's all round Wuppertal.' Jeff produced a sheet of flimsy paper from his pocket with a triumphant flourish. 'I had that sewn into my overcoat. As I was travelling with a Swedish diplomatic party, I decided the Gestapo wouldn't be too nosy.'

It was the carbon of a letter from Domagk at I G Farben in Wuppertal, dated November 3, 1939, to Professor Dr Gunnar Holmgren, Rector of the Karolinska Institute in Stockholm. It started with the appropriate academic greeting, *Magnifizenz!*, its twenty-odd lines of German expressing Domagk's honour at accepting the 1939 Nobel Prize for Medicine and Physiology, and his readiness to visit Stockholm on December 10 to receive it.

'Don't ask me how I got that letter,' Jeff said proudly. 'But mine weren't the first prying eyes to read it. The Gestapo intercepted it, of course. Domagk must have been overconfident, or maybe didn't see what went on under his own eyes. A lot of intelligent Germans don't want to. You remember Karl von Ossietsky, the German who won the Nobel Peace Prize in 1934?'

'And promptly disappeared into a concentration camp.'

Jeff nodded. 'To a mind like Hitler's, a Nobel Prize of any sort carries a political sting. The story is that Hitler ordered Domagk's arrest himself. On a Friday night in the middle of November, a couple of guys in plain clothes knocked at Domagk's house near the Zoo there and said they were Gestapo officers. They arrested him, searched his place, confiscated all his correspondence. Then they locked him up in Wuppertal Jail. In the morning they ordered him to clean out his cell and offered him a cup of coffee, to both of which our professor gave a dignified refusal. A top SS man from Düsseldorf came across to interrogate him, but by then there was a hell of a row going on. The chief of the civil police was demanding to know why their distinguished citizen was behind bars.'

'With the Gestapo, he wouldn't get an answer.'

'That's right.' Jeff poured more champagne into Elizabeth's glass. She was sitting in an armchair with her gasmask on her knee, listening in fascination. 'They kept him there eight days. They let his wife bring some food, and they moved in a couch instead of a plank bed. When one of the warders asked what he'd done to get arrested, Domagk replied, "I won the Nobel Prize". The warder went round the other prisoners saying, "We've got a madman in there".'

We laughed. 'Then a week later Domagk got himself arrested again,' Jeff went on. 'It was at an international medical congress in Berlin. You know how suspicious the Nazis are of foreign contacts. They wanted him to sign a declaration that he wouldn't make a speech or mix with the guests. Domagk refused. So inside he went. In the end, the SS took him to the Ministry of Education, and gave him another letter to sign addressed to the Karolinska Institute, refusing the Nobel Prize.'

'He signed that?' asked Elizabeth.

'If he hadn't, the world would have heard that Professor Domagk had suffered a fatal heart attack. But do you know what the Nazis did? They sent the letter to the police at Wuppertal, so it would be posted to Stockholm with a Wuppertal postmark. These trivial bits of thoroughness are what make me feel most frightened of the Germans.'

Three waiters wheeled in a trolley with our dinner. 'When's America coming into the war?' asked Elizabeth.

'Who can tell what's in Roosevelt's mind?' Jeff stubbed out his cigarette. 'If Joe Kennedy here at the Embassy had anything to do with it, I'd say never.'

'Archie says this Kennedy chap has written Britain off already,' Elizabeth told him. 'And I gather Kennedy is highly delighted at the prospect.'

'You can't expect the Boston Irish to stroke the British lion,' Jeff observed.

'Perhaps the Germans will get rid of Hitler themselves,' I suggested. 'After all, they nearly blew him up in that Munich beer cellar last month.'

'That bomb was a put-up job, to put public sympathy right behind Hitler.'

'But half a dozen Germans were killed by it,' exclaimed Elizabeth.

Jeff snapped his fingers. 'What's six or seven lives to the Nazis? Even German ones? Let's eat.'

It was the last good meal I had in England for fifteen years. It occurred to me that Elizabeth must have been seeing a good deal of Archie.

23

'Of course, it was Dr and Madame Trefouël working at the Institut Pasteur in Paris who made sulphonamide therapy on any scale possible at all.' Dr Henri Lamartine, beside me on a deck chair in the afternoon sunshine early in a beautiful summer, produced another blue and gold packet of *Weekend* cigarettes. It opened like a book. He had been in Oxford six days, without exhausting his supply brought from Paris. He refused English cigarettes, because they gave him *la toux sèche.*

'Isn't that a little sweeping?'

'No, I don't think so, *mon cher confrère.*' He spoke excellent English, in a dry, precise way which matched his appearance and, as far as I could tell from a week's collaboration, his character. He was of middle height but lean, his dark hair well greased and brushed back, with a small woolly moustache and many thin lines round the angles of his mouth. His complexion was yellowish, and his long-fingered hands had many moles on the back. He wore a smart chalk-striped blue suit, a dark shirt and plain silk tie. He was ten years older than me, my opposite number at the Institut Duhamel in Montparnasse, though his position in the French military and bureaucratic cat's cradle was more complicated than mine. He was ending a week's exchange of information and opinions. I was to pay a return visit to Paris in the autumn.

'Oh, well left alone, sir,' I interrupted.

Lamartine frowned deeply. 'I do not understand why you acclaim a player for missing the ball.'

That Wednesday of May 8, 1940, we were enjoying a cricket match in the Oxford Parks. 'It's simple. The bowler made the ball veer at the last moment. Had the batsman not spotted it, he would have been caught off the edge of his bat and sent back to the pavilion. You see?'

'I think you have to be an Englishman of many generations to comprehend this mysterious game.'

'It's really simple but with delightfully subtle variations, like a Mozart symphony.'

'Why could they not *all* have bats?' Lamartine wondered. 'It would make the game much livelier.' He resumed his argument. 'I G Farben waited two years before presenting "Prontosil" to the world, while countless millions continued to die from blood poisoning, meningitis, etcetera. They wanted their patents watertight, that's all. Well, *c'est logique.* But it was the Trefouël, with Dr Nitti and Dr Bovet, who found the "Protosil" dye was broken down in the body, and only the sulphonamide part of it did the work of killing the bacteria. As sulphonamide was discovered by Gelmo of Vienna in 1908, I G Farben couldn't patent it. We made the Germans look fools. Farben must have known all the time that only the sulphonamide in "Prontosil" was active. They manufactured it with a red colour to mask the truth.'

'Taking pure sulphonamide instead of "Prontosil" at least saved the patients turning bright pink and passing alarming pink urine.

'It's over?' asked Lamartine, as the players abruptly trooped from the field.

'No, the captain's declared.'

'Declared what?'

'It doesn't matter. Let's have a cup of tea.'

It was towards the end of the phoney war, the *drôle de guerre* as Lamartine called it. A month previously, Chamberlain announced that Hitler had missed the bus. But unfortunately it was still being driven by the Führer in whichever direction he cared, at an unstoppable pace. Denmark and Norway had been swiftly overcome, though Lamartine assured me emphatically that the French expected little trouble from the Germans for the rest of the year – 'Hitler was forced to strike up north. He will be somewhat more prudent before letting fly at the Maginot Line.' Lamartine was returning to Paris in the morning, and I solicited Professor Florey to invite us that night to dine in Queen's College.

High table life continued, as it had when Charles I was conducting another war from Oxford. Sitting on either side of Florey in his long-sleeved MA gown, we inevitably fell into the argument whether Chamberlain would go and Churchill come in.

'I am sure the change is very necessary,' Lamartine gave his opinion. 'Just as it was very necessary for France to get rid of Deladier as prime minister six weeks ago. Paul Reynaud has brought a much more invigorating atmosphere, you can feel it in Paris already.'

'He seems a sprightly sixty-two,' agreed Florey guardedly.

'Indeed, Professor. He bicycles, and does the gymnastic daily.'

'I think barnacle Chamberlain will survive tonight's vote,' I said gloomily. 'The Conservatives will flock into the lobby behind him, because it's part of the public school spirit. If Labour has the guts to force a division at all, with the prospect of exactly that happening.'

'In what research are you engaged, Professor?' asked Lamartine, politely directing the conversation to his host.

'Have you heard of a substance called penicillin?'

'Never.'

Howard Florey was then aged forty-one. He had thick dark hair parted carefully just left of centre, and an impassive deliberative look. He often smiled, but never widely. He wore soft collars with plain ties and dark suits, and rimless glasses. His quiet voice still showed its salting in the air of Adelaide. He could be aloof. He distrusted England and the English since arriving in Oxford as a Rhodes scholar in 1922, but he had mellowed like the Oxford stone and was tipped to emerge from donnish intrigues as the next Provost of Queen's. I thought during the war that he bore a resemblance to the bandleader Glen Miller. But perhaps it was only the glasses.

'It's the juice of the mould *Penicillium notatum*, which has been found to kill staphylococci in the lab,' Florey explained.

'Staphylococci, which are resistant to sulphonamides,' reflected Lamartine. 'Might it be used on patients?'

'It's wretchedly difficult stuff to extract. All we've got is a few grains of brownish powder. But we've found it's completely non-toxic to animals, which is encouraging.'

'Might I be allowed a specimen of this mould?' Lamartine asked. 'It sounds quite interesting.'

'If you wish,' Florey said amicably. 'Drop into my labs before you go, and I'll let you have some reprints of the published papers and a note on our work in progress. The mould travels excellently.'

That night in the House of Commons, Labour found the courage to force a vote. According to the Oxford History a quarter of a century later, Labour's mind was made up by the female MPs of all parties, who decided in their room to divide the House if nobody else would. I hope the story is true. I have long believed women more practical in misfortune than men. I bade farewell to Lamartine on the Thursday. On the morning of Friday, May 10, the elderly maid in my north Oxford lodgings brought early tea with the news that the wireless said Germany had invaded Belgium. 'Just like last time,' she added. 'They'll never learn.'

Holland was invaded, too. That Holland was conquered in five days was bemusing to Britain. We all thought the Dutch needed simply to open the dykes for the Germans to be bogged down or drowned. Prime Minister Churchill offered us blood, toil, tears and sweat. But the fighting was still, as Chamberlain had said of the Czechs, comfortably in a far away country between people of which we knew nothing. About eleven in the morning of Wednesday, May 22, Professor Ainsley appeared at the Fungus Institute unannounced.

'It's this bloody man Lamartine,' he began as I poured him a cup of tea. We sat on laboratory stools, alone amid sufficient germs to depopulate Oxfordshire overnight. 'Elgar, you've got to go to France.'

This was hardly cheering news. The fighting was then round the names graved on British war memorials – Arras, Cambrai, Bapaume. That very morning the *Wehrmacht* panzers had reached the Channel near Etaples, our base in the Great War, its geometrical grey forest of British headstones washed with the salty winds across the estuary of the River Canche. 'Sugar?' I asked.

'No, thanks. Given it up for the duration. My kids have my ration. You seem to have dropped something of a danger, Elgar. I passed on to Sir Edward Mellanby at the Medical Research Council what you told me about giving Lamartine a specimen of penicillin mould. Obviously,

Mellanby's interested in Florey's work across the road – though I must say he doesn't seem to give it much urgency. But he doesn't want a bit of the mould, plus full instructions for growing it and extracting the penicillin, floating round France at this particular moment.'

'Isn't Mellanby being overdramatic?' I felt resentful, because it was Florey's fault Lamartine had left with the specimen, not mine. But it seemed no moment to argue. 'Penicillin is hardly another sulphonamide.'

'Yes, but unlike sulphonamide, it's active in the lab against the staphylococcus and the causative organism of gas gangrene,' replied Ainsley forthrightly. 'So who knows its potential in war wounds? Anyway, some high-up politico has been informed – most foolishly, in my view – and ordered us to get it back.'

'But can't you simply telephone Lamartine? Or somebody at our Paris Embassy?'

'That's exactly what we can't do. He seems to have disappeared'

'How extraordinary.'

'Things seem somewhat disorganized at the Institut Duhamel,' he continued drily. 'I suppose we can't blame them, if they're at panic stations. But you know about penicillin, Elgar. And you know Lamartine by sight. You've got to cross the Channel and stop the mould falling into the wrong hands.'

'German hands?' I looked even more surprised.

Ainsley gulped down his unsugared tea, his expression wry from more than its bitterness. 'Your friend Lamartine is a bit of an odd fish. We've just found out that he was once mixed up with the Croix de Feu – Colonel de la Rocque's outfit, French-style fascism. Lamartine should never have been allowed to reach the position he did. He may have gone to earth, waiting to hand over his little present when the Nazis arrive.'

'They won't penetrate to Paris, surely?' I objected. 'They didn't last time.'

'They did in 1870. And the parallel with the Franco-Prussian War may be closer than with the last one.' Ainsley glanced at me sideways. 'A couple of days ago, the Cabinet decided we might have to pull Gort's army out.'

'Bring them home?' I was shocked. 'The French didn't care for that, surely?'

'The French don't know. I was let into the secret because we may have to open our bag of tricks.' He nodded round the lab.

'But what about the Maginot Line?'

'The Maginot Line is as irrelevant to the progress of this war as Napoleon's tomb,' Ainsley replied shortly.

When Ainsley had left in his official car, I crossed the road to the Sir William Dunn Laboratories (there was an Oxford variety as well as a Cambridge one). I had never before intruded on Florey there. I gathered that he was a good professor, captaining his team as well as initiating its research, understanding his staff's problems inside the laboratory, and out – which were often the most important ones for successful work. He shunned publicity, but enjoyed that sublimest of professorial gifts, of being able to raise money easily and in large quantities. I found him sitting in his room in his white coat.

'Doesn't look much like a weapon of war, does it?' he said quietly when I had explained Ainsley's visit. He picked from his desk a conical flask stoppered with cotton wool, the fluffy, greenish-white mould inside lying like felt on the dark fluid of its broth,

'You haven't even tried it as a cure for infected mice yet, have you?'

'I'm going to this weekend. Fortunately, I didn't let on to Lamartine. I've a difficult job, judging the right dose. Did you know, the Americans gave sulphonamide with quinine for pneumonia at New Rochelle University back in 1919? It didn't work, so they abandoned it. They fixed the dose too low, I suspect. We haven't much penicillin here to play with, but if I inject too little I won't get a decisive result. Then no one outside these four walls will have any further interest in penicillin, and won't be prepared to give us hard cash to keep up the work on it.'

'Domagk was lucky never to have that problem.'

'It's a hard thing to say at this particular moment, but without Domagk's sulphonamide our mental sights would never have been adjusted to see the potentialities of penicillin. Fleming certainly didn't see a future for penicillin in 1928. Or he didn't think it worth practical steps, beyond using it in a local way once or twice for an infected sinus and an infected eye among his colleagues at St Mary's.'

'Are you working on it full time?'

'Oh, Lord no. Penicillin's only one of our research projects. We've hardly had time to come to grips with it at all these past couple of years. I've a depleted staff, like everybody else with a war on, and we've all the routine work, teaching medical students and all that.' He paused to give a smile. 'Unlike you, who can devote yourself to developing your edible fungi across the road. I hope you can get a mushroom to taste like a turkey. It'll be handy at Christmas.'

Florey understood perfectly well what I did in the Fungus Institute. That he never acknowledged as much was one of his jokes. He made few of them. Some people called him a cold fish. But perhaps Oxford professors lose the facility on appointment, like Trollope's bishops the ability to whistle.

I had two days before travelling to France during the Friday night. Late on Thursday I was summoned to the communal telephone in the hall of my north Oxford lodgings. It was an enormous house built for fecund Victorian dons, as the grey-spired church of St Philip and St James opposite had been raised for their family worship. The hall always smelt of sour milk and cabbage, and the telephone like everything else you touched was coated with a thin layer of grease.

It was Sir Edward Tiplady. He had heard from Ainsley of my expedition. I had discovered they were close friends, serving for some years on a committee planning scientific warfare, of which I had no inkling. 'Jim? You know already, don't you, that Elizabeth's been posted to France?'

'I didn't know she was still there.'

'Would you look her up? She's billeted with a French doctor. A Professor Piéry, at No 6 rue Lascut. That's near the Bois.' He gave the telephone number. 'Just to see if she's all right, don't you know. Things look a little sticky over there. Her mother's bolted back to London. Give her my love. I'm sure you can look after her, should she need it. Good luck, Jim.'

He was trying to be his usual casual, cheerful self, but it did not work, no more than when the old King lay under his care desperately ill. I wondered if the below stairs tales of Elizabeth's parentage were false, or inspired by Lady Tip from hatred of her husband.

24

I sailed from Newhaven to Dieppe in an ordinary cross-Channel steamer, painted grey, blacked out and escorted by a destroyer. There were crates lashed to the decks, the only passengers a hundred or so Servicemen of all ranks, even a red-tabbed general. The journey proved less disturbing than my storm-tossed crossing towards Wuppertal. There were no submarines, no aeroplanes. I found the French blackout lacked the puritanical gloom of our own, where the narrowest chink brought an air-raid warden banging on the front door with that already most tiresome enquiry, 'Don't you know there's a war on?' A comfortable express took me to the Gare St Lazare. I arrived in Paris shortly after eight o'clock on the morning of Saturday, May 25, about the same time as Major-General Spears arrived on Churchill's instructions to put some heart into the French Government – and to convince them that the British Army was *not* following its traditional tactics in trouble and making a dash for the nearest blue water.

I took a taxi past the Madeleine to the British Embassy in rue du Faubourg St Honoré. I never forgot my first impression of Paris, the smell of coffee and Gitane cigarettes, the advertisements everywhere for *Dubo...Dubon...Dubonnet* and the lugubrious Nicolas wine man with his fistfuls of half a dozen splayed bottles, the noisy traffic and shrill-whistling policemen, the green buses with people hanging over the taffrail, the pavement cafés with everyone reading their morning papers. The more important statues and doorways were sandbagged, as in London. There were a good many Army lorries. I noticed at once the sauntering, lost-looking groups on the pavements with suitcases and bundles, refugees which had been pouring into Paris all the past week from Belgium and north-eastern France.

An Embassy official with a retired soldierly air expected me, but could offer little help. 'I suppose you could try the NAAFI in the boulevard Magenta,' he suggested gloomily when I asked about a bed. '*What* did you say you'd come to Paris for?'

'To collect a bit of mould.'

He looked lost. The war was becoming too complicated for him.

I decided to make straight for Elizabeth's billet. Another taxi took me between the green billows of chestnuts in the Champs-Elysées towards the Arc de Triomphe. The professor's was one of the tall, grey, brown-shuttered confluent houses overlooking the sunken railway line near the Porte Maillot. As I went to ring the bell of the highly-varnished front door, Elizabeth herself stepped into the sunshine in her uniform.

'Darling! My God.' I had never before seen her disconcerted. 'But what *are* you doing in Paris? Were you just leaving?'

'On the contrary, I've just arrived.'

'From England? But everybody here is getting ready to fly for their lives.'

'Surely it can't be as bad as that?' I asked, though feeling abruptly uneasy.

'Haven't you seen this morning's paper?'

'I can't speak a great deal of French.'

'The Belgians are on the point of giving up. The whole French Government has been to Notre Dame to pray for Divine inspiration. That's a terribly bad sign, isn't it? Some people say the panzers will be parked in the Place de la Concorde in a couple of days. But of course Paris has been buzzing with rumours for weeks, the French High Command tells people absolutely nothing. I suppose they're far too ashamed of themselves.'

Remembering Sir Edward's charge, I asked, 'How about yourself? Are you getting out?'

'I can't, until I'm ordered to. It's such a lovely relief, not having to make decisions, isn't it? Where are you staying?'

'Nowhere. My arrangements seem a little disorganized.'

'Then you'd better sleep here.' I protested against such intrusion. 'The professor and madame won't mind a bit,' she assured me airily, being always light-hearted in the disposal of other people's hospitality. 'But what *are* you doing here, instead of growing mushrooms at Oxford?'

'It's rather complicated, but it's to do with an experimental drug which mustn't fall into the hands of the Germans.'

'How thrilling. Jim darling, you are dressed rather peculiarly, aren't you?'

I was wearing my Harris tweed jacket with grey flannels, carrying my flapping umbrella and a small suitcase. 'This is my usual holiday outfit.'

'Jim, you're a darling. I forgot to say how utterly wonderful it is to see you.' She came nearer and kissed me. For the first time she did not make her ceremonial pouting face.

Professor Piéry had left for work at the François-Xavier Hospital, madame was out. I left my bag, explaining to Elizabeth that I must be at the Institut Duhamel before that Saturday noon. 'I'm walking across to my hospital in Neuilly, I'll put you on the right bus at the Porte Maillot,' Elizabeth told me. 'It's so much cheaper than a taxi, and almost as quick. Get off at the Jardin du Luxembourg. Dinner's at eight. I'll explain everything to the professor in French. If the air-raid warning goes, you follow the arrows marked "Abri".' She had the calmly practical approach to the war of so many Englishwomen. It must have been a sizable national asset. As we walked in the warm morning along the rue Lascut she talked about her father and mother in England with the simple eagerness of a schoolgirl. 'Archie's still in England,' she told me. 'And he's a *sergeant*. Isn't that grand?'

The bus took me along the arcaded rue de Rivoli, with its tiny expensive shops still selling articles of supreme uselessness, past the sandbagged statue of Jeanne d'Arc, then across the Seine and the Ile de le Cité. The Institut Duhamel was a small square brick and stone building overlooking the Luxembourg gardens. I had an introduction to a Dr Champier, who had worked in the French Hospital in Soho and spoke good English. He sat at an untidy desk in a cubicle of a room, the tall window tight shut, hot and stuffy and smelling of French cigarettes. He was a short fat man with bushy black hair and a large moustache, in a blue suit with a legion d'Honneur rosette in the buttonhole. He wore an expression of worry which I hoped was habitual.

'Why are you so anxious to trace Lamartine?' he asked.

'I must apologize for not being at liberty to tell you.'

'But surely, among *confrères*...?' He spread his pudgy hands.

'Times are abnormal, as you appreciate.'

Seeming to accept this he folded his hands on his paunch. 'Whatever your reasons, I cannot help you much. Lamartine has left here. Between ourselves, he should never have been appointed. But there are political influences in this country which can put almost any man in almost any position.'

He produced a packet of Gitanes, which I refused. 'No, the battle didn't start at dawn on May 10, my friend.' He jerked his head in the direction of the front line. 'It's been in progress since the end of the last war. Never again should the Germans invade us, we said. That was logical. We had a million and a half dead, a third of our country devastated, and we were flat broke. But unfortunately it became "Never again" to war of any sort. Our nation has lost its soul. There're plenty of Frenchmen who wouldn't mind Hitler in the Elysée Palace if it would save their own skins, take it from me.'

I made some reassuring remark that Hitler still had a long way to come. 'Has he, Mr Elgar? I hope you're right. A hundred kilometres isn't much when we haven't an Army equipped or trained to stand up to him. What can we expect? After a couple of decades of changing our government almost every weekend, of corruption and swindling, of every man out for himself whether he's boss or worker, of riots and indiscipline – remember the Stavisky affair?' He struck a pink-coloured match. 'Stavisky was that devious financier supposed to have committed suicide. Any medical man could tell from simply reading the newspapers that the police shot him. Dead men tell no tales against people in high places. So we had barricades in the streets. The Government did nothing but resign. No wonder now *les cartes se brouillent*.'

He blew out a cloud of pungent smoke.

'I'll tell you something. Lamartine has indiscreet contacts with the Croix de Feu. That's one of those parties like Action Française. All admirers of *nos chers amis* Hitler and Mussolini.'

'I know.'

Champier grunted. 'His home address is a top floor apartment in the avenue Pierre Premier de Serbie, by the Trocadero. But you'd be more likely to find him at No 22-bis rue des Brouettes – Wheelbarrows Street,' he translated for me. 'That's off the boulevard de Clichy in Montmartre. It's where he has his mistress. She's very pretty. I saw her once when they were dining together at the Mere Catherine. Or perhaps he has gone on holiday to the Côte d'Azur,' he ended with a smile. 'You will understand that people have better things to do at this moment than look for errant bacteriologists.'

'Is he spying for the Germans?'

Champier considered this for some moments. 'I don't think so. But he might sell his secret knowledge of germ warfare for the conquerors' favours – if they arrive.'

He had extinguished my remaining doubts about the trouble and risk of my expedition.

'Should I not find Lamartine in a day or two, may I come back to you?'

'If I am here. There are rumours that Monsieur Reynaud and his Cabinet have already labels on their bags for Tours.' We stood up and shook hands. 'What is it that Lamartine has of yours?' Champier tried again. 'Some strains of botulism so deadly that the entire population of the world will be erased, Hitler included?'

I conceded, 'It's an antibacterial drug which is very experimental and may never work.'

'In that case, you would seem to be taking a lot of trouble to capture a mirage.'

I consulted a map over the nearest Métro entrance, and caught a train from Notre Dame des Champs station to Pigalle. It was noon, and everyone was coming out for lunch. Apart from the speckling of uniforms, it might have been a peacetime Saturday. I sat at the nearest café table and ordered a beer. I managed to achieve sketchy directions from the waiter to the rue des Brouettes. The man drinking Cinzano at the next table was reading an early edition of *L'Intransigeant*. *'Les Allemands a Ypres'*, said the headline.

Twenty-two-bis was a seedy looking building, a small block of flats. Just inside the open front door, I spied through a hatch the traditional French concierge in her black bombazine. I had lost enthusiasm for my quest. I was hot and hungry, and I had no idea what Lamartine's mistress called herself. I said earnestly, 'Dr Lamartine?' and to my surprise she replied at once, '*Cinquième étage*,' holding up five fingers for my further edification.

I climbed a narrow stone stair amid tasty smells of cooking. The door was opened by a pretty, short woman in her early thirties, fair haired with a snub nose and big green eyes. She had a Japanese kimono loosely round her, she was untidy and unmade up, and startled to see me.

I asked for Dr Lamartine as best I could. She stared blankly, clearly careful to hint no connection with him to a stranger. I asked, '*Parlez vous anglais?*' She shook her head. '*Sprechen Sie Deutsch?*'

'*Ja, ja. Ich lerne Deutsch in der Schule.*'

'I am an English scientist from Oxford,' I explained in German. 'Dr Lamartine came to visit me earlier this month. My name is Mr Elgar.'

The dourness in her face disappeared. Lamartine had been talking about me. 'Yes, you went to watch a game –'

'Cricket,' I said in English.

'Henri very much enjoyed his stay.'

'Can I see him, please?'

Her glance wavered. 'He's not here.'

I said resolutely, 'May I come in?'

She had a moment's hesitation. 'All right.'

The flat was small, my mouth watered at the overpowering smell of simmering onions. The living-room was cramped and untidy, the table littered with newspapers and popular magazines, *Le Figaro, Le Temps, Match and Marie-Claire.* There were a good many books about in the bright yellow paper French covers. On the wall was a Picasso reproduction – then uncommon – in the corner a treadle-operated sewing machine, against the window a desk with a large typewriter surrounded by sheets of foolscap. I got the impression of an intelligent, independent woman. Of Lamartine there was no trace, not even a hat.

I explained that I had come from the Institut Duhamel, and had urgent business with Dr Lamartine connected with the scientific work we both followed. I wondered how much she knew of this. I suspected from my assessment of her intellect a lot.

'I haven't seen Henri for over a week, I've no idea where he is, none whatever.'

She looked as though telling the truth, though for all I knew he was listening behind the closed door of the bedroom. 'If he should come here, would you ask him to telephone me urgently?'

I wrote down Professor Piéry's address and number. She agreed readily, though I felt only to be rid of me.

'I shall be returning to England within a week or so.'

'To England? I hope that you'll be able to make it.'

'There are plenty of ports besides Calais,' I told her confidently. 'And the front will have to stabilize some time, won't it?'

She made a face as though tasting something disagreeable.

Discouraged by this call, I took the Métro in search of Lamartine's family nest in the avenue Pierre Premier de Serbie. It was a tall grey building with well painted black shutters, all folded back except for three pairs on the top floor. These turned out to be the rooms of his flat. After ringing and knocking without avail, I returned to seek the concierge. Madame Lamartine and the children had left for the Dordogne *à cause de la guerre*, it appeared.

I had not got far after Florey's penicillin. And the Nazis seemed to be bearing down with their usual panache. Truly, he that the devil drives feels no lead at his heels.

25

'One still must eat,' said Professor Piéry gloomily in English. 'It is necessary.'

He was tall, spare, lined, dyspeptic-looking, in his late fifties, with thick grey hair brilliantined and brushed back, a slim grey moustache and a grey suit with a black band across the lapel for a relative recently dead (from peaceful causes, he explained to me). He was a physician, a specialist on the liver. I later discovered all French physicians to be specialists on the liver, an item of the self which the Frenchman is inclined to confuse with the soul.

Despite his lean and sickly appearance Professor Piéry was a hearty and fastidious eater, complemented by the most enthusiastic and finicky of cooks. We sat in the large downstairs dining-room, which was stuffy and full of Second Empire furniture. It was relieved only by a large garish colour photograph in a gilt frame of their only son Jean-Baptiste in khaki. He was a lieutenant in Intelligence liaising with the British Army, and nobody knew if he was captured, in Ramsgate or dead. We started our *potage aux légumes*. A Frenchman who cannot start family dinner with soup imagines his world is coming to an end, which indeed that Monday evening of June it was.

The only British troops left in France were mostly prisoners. About ten miles inland from Dunkirk, the Colme Canal flows parallel to the sea. Nearer the beaches, the Moëres Canal forms an arc, with its base a third canal, the Dunkirk-Furnes. To the east lies the River Ijzer, to the west the River Aa. These waterways made a box from which the Germans were fended while 215,000 of 250,000 British soldiers, and 125,000 of 380,000 French, were ferried away in a week by 850 freakishly variegated ships.

185

It was a box which could have been smashed, had not Hitler himself halted his panzers on May 23. Perhaps he wanted to spare from utter destruction the British Empire he so admired, and which might still be useful for him against the Americans. Perhaps Hermann Göring boasted he could do the job less costly with bombs. The notion would have pleased Hitler, because the German Army may have been the royal infant of Frederick the Great, the German Navy the Imperial child of Kaiser Wilhelm, but the Luftwaffe was the young Hercules of National Socialism. Luckily, the crooked shadow of Nelson was cast long in the Empire's sunset. Dunkirk was a British defeat, but it was a defeat, which defied disaster, for our modern politicians eternally to invoke with clarion calls on their tin trumpets. It also occurred during the week when Howard Florey found that penicillin kept alive mice infected with the staphylococcus germ, which defied the sulphonamides.

Paris was full of refugees, everywhere in the streets, pathetic and desperate, sitting on their bundles with nowhere to go. The air was flecked with the soot of burning oil tanks, the fashionable area smoky with incinerated Embassy secrets. The air-raid sirens had sounded during the night, with a more tuneful gallic wail than the lugubrious London ones. And there was still no trace of Lamartine.

During the week I had no reply at his mistress' flat – she may have spied my coming – while Champier at the Institut Duhamel was plainly impatient at my adding to his more alarming problems. He gave me half a dozen addresses of Lamartine's friends in Paris, but these achieved nothing but the absorption of my time. I had no justification to call the police, amid I am no policeman myself. I might as well have stayed in Oxford. It was harrowing to feel a failure, particularly one which I knew might be held severely against me for the rest of my career.

Yet those days of Dunkirk were the happiest of my life. My desires, my fantasies with Elizabeth were realized. Compatriots in danger, we huddled like two children in a thunderstorm. The defences of steely gossamer which she had wrapped round herself melted to nothing. In a French professor's house with a battle raging a hundred miles away, she gave herself to me. I use the now archaic expression deliberately, because Elizabeth could never be blown by the storm of her emotions from the course set by the compass of her mind. And there was another factor. She retained the tinselled glitter of her conversation, but her determined frivolity had been shrivelled by the war.

In the morning, she was to drive her little official Austin two hundred miles to Cherbourg, where we were assured by the Embassy that a ship of some sort would be ready to take British personnel across to Southampton. I was going with her. I had no official permission, but official permission for anything was becoming increasingly irrelevant. Meanwhile, as Professor Piéry pointed out, it was necessary to eat.

'I suppose Mussolini's going to declare war any minute now,' I observed, hardly lightening the gloom over the vegetable soup. 'The jackal on the heels of the red-mouthed lion.'

'All is not lost,' Professor Piéry declared morosely. 'The British soldiers which you took off the beach can surely remuster in England? They will return to the fight through Brest, or St Nazaire. Remember, the Germans got even nearer to Paris in 1914. We must hope for another miracle of the Marne.'

'I hear that Madame de Portes has already selected her bedroom at the Château Amboise,' remarked Elizabeth rather acidly, referring to Countess Hélène de Portes, Prime Minister Paul Reynaud's mistress.

'The Government sees no necessity to take a holiday among the chateaux of Tours,' she was rebuked tartly by Madame Piéry, dark-haired and sharp-nosed, sitting opposite her husband. 'It is our duty to disbelieve pernicious rumours.'

Elizabeth smiled charmingly. 'Like the passengers aboard the *Titanic*, I suppose, madame? The captain and officers are incompetent, but if they say we shan't hit the iceberg we sleep happily in our bunks.'

As two red spots appeared on his wife's cheeks, the professor said even more gloomily, 'It is not very pleasant of you to express such lack of faith in the French Government, Mademoiselle Tiplady.'

'We have surely passed the time for politeness,' returned Elizabeth evenly. 'All they have presided over so far is three weeks of headlong retreat.'

'Well, they shall be stopped, as last time. *Ils ne passeront pas.*'

He slapped the table as he used the words of Marshal Pétain, who had become vice-Premier in May, and who with the Commander-in-Chief General Weygand had a combined age of one hundred and fifty seven. Madame Piéry busily rang a shrill little handbell for the *côte de veau*. Our conversation degenerated into perfunctory scraps. We were laying our cutlery on the *porte-couteaux* for the meat plates to be changed for the vegetables in the French fashion, when our meal suffered an unimagined interruption. The maid burst in, wide-eyed and open mouthed. '*Madame, c'est monsieur…*'

Jean-Baptiste appeared in the dining-room on her heels. I immediately recognized him, though he was not in the bright colours of his photograph. His uniform was dishevelled and caked with mud, a tear in the sleeve. He had his revolver, and carried a steel helmet instead of his *kepi*. He was pale faced, haggard, with several days' growth of beard. Madame and the professor leapt to embrace him, both weeping.

As we recovered from the surprise, I tugged Elizabeth's sleeve, but the parents insisted on introducing us, saying we should stay, we would have a party. The son sprawled at the table while madame fussed with the maids to prepare him a meal. Meanwhile, he cut segments of a large *brie* cheese lying in its mattress of straw, gobbling them in his fingers and gulping down a bottle of burgundy. Professor Piéry asked, '*Mais ton régiment? Il est actuellement à Paris?*'

In reply, the lieutenant snapped his fingers. '*Mon regiment, c'est fini. Kaput.*'

The professor looked amazed, alarmed and then horrified.

Jean-Baptiste stared at Elizabeth and myself, and said bleakly in English, 'You imagine I've run away, I suppose? I could hardly have done so, even if I'd had the inclination. I had no regiment to run away from. To put it more explicitly, my regiment had run away from me. *Bien sûr*, the whole division had run away. We left our artillery, stores, ammunition, petrol, everything. The men threw their rifles in the ditches and set off for home.' He cut himself a length of bread, digging up a blob of cheese with the crust.

'Our English friends look shocked,' he continued sarcastically. 'Had you been at the front yourselves, you might have felt more charitable. Our soldiers didn't fight, because they didn't see the point of it. The Germans were going to walk over us, obviously. Whether they walked over us alive or over us dead was a matter of indifference to them. It was also a matter of indifference to the outcome of the war. It was not, however, a matter of indifference to us. *C'est logique, hein?'*

He had brought the horror of the battle into the room. 'It was rifles against tanks, an equation which does not offer much difficulty in the solving. Their planes were at us all the time. Messerschmitts strafing us, Junkers, Stuka dive-bombers. We never saw a plane of our own.' He turned a harder look at me. 'Nor of the RAF, monsieur.'

I returned, 'The RAF was operating in a different area, doubtless.'

'The RAF was not operating at all. Your planes were all sitting at home. Churchill would not send so much as a squadron to save us. Do you know why I am sitting here now, instead of fighting honourably with my comrades?' he asked angrily. 'Because you English have run away faster than us. We were expecting you to attack the enemy with us in Flanders. But Lord Gort marched his troops in the opposite direction. And when they got to the sea, the French had to hold off the enemy while the British embarked for home.'

'I just don't believe that,' objected Elizabeth sharply.

'You may not like to, mademoiselle, but that is the truth. The British soldiers were taken aboard the ships, the *poilus* left on the beaches, kept there by the muzzles of British rifles.'

'The poor boy is distressed,' said the professor.

'That *must* be untrue,' I insisted. Though it was not entirely untrue. The Welsh Guards fixed bayonets against French soldiers scrambling towards British boats.

Jean-Baptiste shrugged. He said quietly, 'We shall see, after the war. If any of us are left alive.'

During this episode I was aware of the telephone shrilling in the hall. As everyone in the house was too distracted to notice, Elizabeth slipped out to answer it. She came back saying it was a Madame Chalmer, wishing to speak to me urgently. That was the name I had found from the concierge in the rue des Brouettes of Lamartine's mistress.

26

The story of Madame Brigitte Chalmar's life was singularly uninteresting, particularly when recounted in German and the French which Elizabeth translated for me while driving. Early on the next morning of Tuesday, June 4, we had picked her up near the Bois de Boulogne at Porte Dauphine Métro station, at the end of her line from Clichy. Madame Chalmar wore a smart flower-patterned cotton dress, silk stockings, a wide-brimmed hat and white gloves, embellished by an umbrella, a hat box and a bulging suitcase secured with a length of rope. Lamartine was at Tours, and she promised that she would face me with him in return for being taken safely from Paris.

'I was in Hamburg and Berlin, after I had finished at the Sorbonne,' she explained in German, sitting in the back of the small car. 'I was perfectly disgusted with the Nazis, so I wrote about them for such intelligent periodicals as *La Liberté*. In the end the Gestapo expelled me. That was before I married Monsieur Chalmar, but of course the Nazis would soon find me if ever they installed themselves in sight of the Arc de Triomphe. If you are running a police state you develop a skill in keeping files on absolutely everybody. My husband was a nincompoop,' she continued with the calm severity a Frenchwoman can apply to men. 'Then I met Dr Lamartine, who was of quite different character, an intellectual, a man I could talk to. Of course, his views on the Nazis are not mine, but perhaps he is more sophisticated. He sees how you must keep strict order in a country these days to have any order at all. Look at all the strikes and riots we've had in France! Henri always thought a dose of Hitler would have done the French a lot of good, and perhaps he was right. *Vous permettez, mademoiselle?'*

She took a packet of Weekend from her large and shabby brown handbag. 'Henri was saying things like that at the time of the Popular Front and Léon Blum, when everyone in France with a little money put by was far more frightened of the Communists than of Hitler, I assure you. In those elections of 1936, Léon Blum was beaten up and spent the campaign in hospital, but he won. Though everyone continued to go on strike, nevertheless. Of course, now I only write articles for the women's magazines, I've changed, it's only natural, a girl calms down and becomes a serene woman, otherwise she would tire a man out in a fortnight. *N'est ce pas?* And that swine Lamartine has left me in the lurch,' she added with abrupt sourness, 'he doesn't care if I end up on Luneberg Heath in a concentration camp.' She removed her broad-brimmed hat and fanned herself with it. '*Ah, c'est effroyable, cette vague de chaleur.* But it's preferable to the trains, which are unbelievably crowded.'

They were even more crowded the following week, when crammed expresses whisked thousands of Parisians from under the nose of von Küchler's 18th Army with an efficiency commendable to the Societé des Chemins de Fer Nationale. After the French government had fled down the same Route Nationale Ten we were then negotiating, our successors on the road were less fortunate. It became choked to immobility with men, women and children, the sick, the old, the pregnant, Frenchmen, foreigners who had once already escaped Hitler's clutch, all pouring from Paris by car, lorry, bicycle, on foot, with barrows, carts or perambulators, without provision, without destination. We could still buy petrol, though Elizabeth had prudently stowed cans in the boot. When a week later vehicles ran dry of fuel, or crawled and boiled to a halt, they were pushed by their desperately impatient followers into the ditch. Girls prostituted themselves in barns for food, and the peasants sold water at a franc a bottle. Everyone then was ill-tempered, frightened and crying, the Luftwaffe bombed the crossroads and strafed the unending pathetic columns as they wished, every now and then police motor-cyclists ploughed the way for a column of black limousines with horns blaring, as officials raced for safety faster than the people they had left without it.

Our traffic was already heavy, and seemed to increase as we went along, all the cars with luggage and bundles piled on the roofs, several bearing

Belgian number plates. At Chartres, the traffic was jammed right through the town, everyone pounding their horn buttons in anguished impotence. A gendarme slowly worked his way along, examining all travellers' papers.

'*J'ai mal à la tête,*' Madame Chalmar informed him bad temperedly through the window. '*Je suis à l'agonie.*'

'*C'est la guerre, madame.*'

Outside Vendôme there was an air-raid warning, another gendarme on a bicycle blowing his whistle and waving at us furiously.

'Should we get in the ditch?' asked Elizabeth half-heartedly, coming to a halt.

'Far too dirty.'

'They're always false alarms, anyway.'

'*Je meurs de mort naturelle,*' asserted Madame Chalmar, holding her head resignedly.

Tours is like a filleted fish. Its backbone filled the long straight rue Nationale, from which run short side-streets. It is only 140 miles from Paris, but it took us twelve hours before we crawled in the unending line of traffic over the Pont Wilson, which crossed the Loire at its head. Madame Chalmar's excitement seemed to have expelled her headache and sensations of impending death. She directed us to the house of her friend Monsieur Perronet, a lawyer, her informant of Lamartine's whereabouts. We found him a fat, affable gingery man with a pudding-faced amiable wife, who at once offered to put us up. He seemed still an enthusiast for the British, or at least expressed no hostility. Or perhaps he was like the Good Soldier Schweik, with a placid nature proof against the cruel vicissitudes of Europe.

Lamartine had been in Tours a week, he assured Madame Chalmer, staying at a small hotel behind the station. He had come to Perronet *toucher un chèque*. I had the strong impression that the lawyer disliked him. I wanted to beard the doctor there and then, but Madame Chalmer declared herself prostrate. Elizabeth and myself were worn out, and took the excuse to postpone an embarrassing confrontation. We had planned to spend one night in Tours before driving due north to Cherbourg. I felt no urgency. The Germans were no longer attacking, but consolidating their front along the Somme. They were likely to be in the same place at Christmas.

I certainly could not conceive their tanks shortly racing for the Pyrenees with the speed of peacetime touring cars.

Elizabeth and I shared the best spare bedroom, which was full of massive old-fashioned furniture, its curtains faded sharply where they had caught the sun, and as inhospitable as a museum. 'The sheets are damp,' said Elizabeth as she got into bed.

There was an air-raid warning during the night. Monsieur Perronet banged on the door in agitation, but we preferred to stay where we were. We lay holding each other tight in the particularly intense blackness of French shutters.

'That fleeing lieutenant last night—' she said. When we had left that morning, Jean-Baptiste was still asleep. 'Do you suppose he'll be shot as a deserter?'

'The French can't shoot half their Army.'

'He didn't like us a bit, did he?'

'The French think that we got them into the war.'

'They hadn't the guts to get themselves into it.'

'You know what the German propaganda leaflets make of the situation — *England Will Fight to the Last Frenchman*.'

'I suppose people will believe anything if it's repeated often enough,' Elizabeth decided. 'Even that Bovril prevents that sinking feeling and Skegness is so bracing.'

'Newspaper readers can be divided into three groups,' I quoted. 'Those who believe everything, those who believe nothing and those who examine everything critically. The first group is by far the largest, the third regards all journalists as rascals.'

'What nasty cynic said that?'

'Hitler, in *Mein Kampf*. Would you have imagined five years ago that we should be lying in bed in the middle of a French provincial town discussing the psychology of the masses?'

'Would you have imagined five years ago that you'd have taken my virginity?'

'That's putting it a little far, isn't it?'

'It's the principle of the thing.'

'Five years ago I was the butler's boy.'

'It's very strange, darling, to think that I'm in bed with the father of my housemaid's baby.'

'Was that remark necessary?'

We had become aware of the drone of a plane. We heard in the distance the unmistakable crump of bombs. 'Five,' counted Elizabeth. 'Do you think he's carrying a round half-dozen?'

'No ack-ack fire,' I observed.

'All the ack-ack guns are in the Maginot Line.' We lay silent, both wondering in secret fear if the plane would turn towards us. But it droned away like an irritating wasp. 'Will you promise me something, Elizabeth?'

'Is there anything left?' she asked in a simple voice.

'That you'll never again treat me with that awful bright-young-thing manner.'

'That was my defence. If I'd treated intensely any single one of the men who were after me, then I should have found myself in love, and desperately miserable because I felt bound to rebuff all the others. I'm very *sérieuse*, you know.'

'I was the only one of your adoring little circle who did know that all along.'

'And if I had taken them *all* seriously, I should have won the reputation of a nymphomaniac, which would only have aggravated the problem.'

'I thought you were falling in love with Archie.'

'Oh, Archie! Good heavens, no. He's not nearly intelligent enough.'

'I'm assuming you're in love with me?'

'Only assuming? Isn't that a rather indelicate – even an insulting – remark in the circumstances?'

I held her tighter. 'Your mother wouldn't approve of it. Nor your father, I think, either.'

'He isn't my father,' she said bluntly. It was the first time she had mentioned this. 'Do you ever see your daughter?'

'Never. She's evacuated somewhere safely, I suppose. I could have kept in touch with Mrs Packer, but I wanted to pretend the whole episode hadn't happened. People at Oxford think I'm a donnish bachelor.'

She snuggled closer to me. 'I'll come to Oxford, darling, just as soon as I'm given leave.'

'Oxford looks lovely just now.'

The all clear blew. 'I wonder who got the sixth bomb?' asked Elizabeth sleepily.

When we came downstairs in the morning, the TSF was playing loudly in the salon. Maurice Chevalier was singing *Ma Pomme*, followed by advertisements for coffee, hair tonic, cream cheese and brassières.

'Ssh!' said Madame Perronet, leaning close to the set, finger to lips.

'*Ici Radio Paris...*' I could not understand the news bulletin, but Madame Perronet's expression served well enough. At four o'clock on that morning of Wednesday, June 5, the Germans had attacked with a vast flash of artillery from the mouth of the Somme to where the River Aisne met the River Ailette, 125 miles away near Reims.

'*Les Allemands on mis la balle en jeu,*' she said grimly, shrugging her plump shoulders.

'I suppose we *are* going to get home all right?' remarked Elizabeth.

'We'll get back from somewhere, even if it's from St Nazaire,' I told her confidently. 'The whole of France can't simply collapse in front of the Nazis.'

Madame Chalmar was so devastated after yesterday's drive that she had to eat breakfast in bed. She appeared about nine, dressed as though going on her honeymoon. She wore a small close hat with a feather, a low cut green silk dress, silk stockings and shoes with very high heels. She still had her white gloves and umbrella, she was brightly made up, and the vivacity of her smile indicated full recovery from her exhaustion. As she started on foot for Lamartine's hotel, chattering feverishly to Elizabeth and myself, it dawned on me that she expected to find him there with another woman, with luck in bed. The rival would have to look pretty good that morning to bear comparison.

The small hotel was like so many in France, an indistinguishable slice of a street-long block of tall, shuttered stone buildings. In the hall, a harassed porter in a yellow-and-black striped waistcoat with alpaca sleeves guarded a bank of pigeon-holes with dangling brass keys. He was arguing fiercely with half a dozen travel-worn men and women standing amid cheap suitcases and bundles, desperate for a roof. Madame Chalmar asked in a sweet, social voice, '*Dr Lamartine, s'il vous plaît,*' to which the porter shouted distractedly, '*Numero trente-cinq.*'

We all three crammed into the rickety, creeping, lattice-sided lift. Lamartine responded to our knock at once. He must have been expecting someone. He was in trousers, braces and a white shirt without its collar, a towel round his neck and flecks of lather on his cheeks. He stared blankly at us. Madame Chalmar broke into sobs.

We held a confused conversation in French and English. Commendably recovering himself, Lamartine embraced Madame Chalmar, whose carefully prepared face now had red blotches with the mascara starting to run. He agreed to see me alone in half an hour's time at the café next door.

He appeared punctually, sitting down with an affable, businesslike air, as though we were still in Oxford. 'You've had some difficulty in finding me, Mr Elgar,' he apologized. 'Well, I've permitted myself some rather irregular behaviour. When a man sees a risk to his life, he becomes impatient with the influences which normally direct his movements.'

I felt this excuse inadequate for my trouble. 'But *why* should your life be in danger?'

'The lives of all Frenchmen are in danger. The Germans must have thrown 100 divisions into their attack this morning. Weygand has 40, 45 at the most. I've good contacts in the War Ministry. And that leaves out of the calculations the Nazi air force. France is finished, my friend. We shall be asking for an Armistice before summer is out.' He turned to order some coffee.

I suspected him of playing the alarmist for his own ends. 'But even the Nazis don't kill their beaten enemies.'

'I should have expected you, of all Englishmen, to be realistic about the Nazis. My particular speciality would hardly endear me to them. They know all about me, I can be quite confident of that. They know all about you too, I'm equally sure. I advise you and your young Miss to get out of France before they come and arrest you.'

This gave me a horribly sickly feeling.

'Though I doubt if they would shoot me out of hand,' he continued calmly. 'The Germans would want my knowledge, and the SS would be only too happy to extract it from me. I certainly couldn't guarantee, sitting here in the sunshine, that I would never give in to threats I knew were far from empty. That I would never collaborate with the Germans to produce bacterial weapons for use against you British and the Russians –'

'The Russians? But nobody attacks his own allies.'

The cup of black coffee appeared. Lamartine tore the paper off his cube of sugar. 'Wait and see, as you say in England. You've read *Mein Kampf*, I believe? Hitler said then that an alliance with Russia would be the end of Germany. If he has changed his mind since he wrote it, he has certainly changed his mind about nothing else. And the steppes of Russia always have had an irresistible fascination for European conquerors. But of course, no sane man waits to be faced with the tormenting choice between his own painful death and treating with the enemy,' he continued more reflectively. 'Therefore I am shortly going to Marseilles and then to Africa. I have friends organizing my arrangements. I am speaking to you in the greatest confidence, Mr Elgar. I still hold a commission in the Army.' I had never known this. 'So I could be shot for desertion. Life is very difficult.'

'You haven't asked why *I* put myself in such danger to follow you here.'

'Brigitte said you wanted the papers given me by Professor Florey.' He jerked his head towards the hotel, where Elizabeth and I had left Madame Chalmer alone with him. 'I destroyed them before leaving Paris. All I have is up here.' He tapped his forehead.

'But have you the mould?' I insisted. 'We simply can't give the Germans a chance to develop it. Florey's penicillin is highly experimental, but there's at least a likelihood that in a few years' time – if the war's still going on – it could be used on casualties.'

'I saw its possibilities at once,' Lamartine said quietly.

'Well, where is it?' I asked brusquely.

'In a safe place.'

'Not safe from the Germans, though.'

He drained his shallow cup of coffee. 'I'll be frank with you, *cher confrère*. In my desperation, I had been looking upon that mould as my saviour with the Germans.'

'I thought as much.' I was unable to keep disgust from my voice. 'If you're prepared to hand over your bacteriological knowledge to the Germans, you might at least give the penicillin back to France's own allies.'

He lit a Weekend. 'You can save your indignation. I told you, everything is changed. I shall soon be across the Mediterranean, perhaps tomorrow night. You shall have your precious mould.'

I did not trust him. 'I want it now, this very morning,' I insisted. 'We too must be on our way urgently, you just said as much yourself.'

'It will take a little time to recover. I shall have to use my car and my precious petrol. A day will make no difference.' He gave a slight smile. 'Hitler is hardly in that hurry. Meet me at my hotel, nine o'clock tomorrow morning. Now I must hurry back to look after Brigitte. She is unhappily suffering from *une crise de nerfs*.'

27

We spent not one night in Tours, but six. Madame Chalmar's *crise de nerfs* evaporated rapidly. During the afternoon she called at the Perronets' for her luggage, to move into the hotel with Lamartine. 'I don't really need my heavy clothes,' she informed me archly in German. 'This winter we'll be sitting where it's hot and safe.'

I appeared at the hotel at nine the next morning. In response to the porter's telephone call Madame Chalmar came downstairs, still radiant and overdressed. 'Henri says will you please come back tomorrow,' she announced in German, dropping her voice to a whisper in the crowded lobby. 'He has had to leave for the day on urgent business connected with our departure.'

'Tomorrow!' I exclaimed impatiently. 'But we've got to get back to England while the going's good –'

'Ssh!' She laid a hand with long scarlet nails on my arm. 'It doesn't do to be heard speaking German. We could be taken for spies, and lynched on the spot. There're Nazis everywhere, you know how the wireless keeps warning us about the Fifth Column. How do you suppose the German tanks would have got so far, if there hadn't been plenty of agents to stop the bridges being blown up?'

Elizabeth asked when I got back, 'Do you think we should give up the idea of this beastly mould?'

'To be perfectly clearheaded, *I* should be more use for the rest of the war in Oxford than the mould would be.'

'We can hang on for another day or two, I suppose,' she said sulkily.

'I think we must. I just hate the idea of Lamartine and his awful girlfriend getting away with anything.'

During the next two days Madame Chalmar reappeared several times at the Perronets'. She was always smiling, always calm, always explaining that Henri was occupied with urgent business, that she would quite certainly bring the mould within twenty-four hours. I had the depressing feeling that the safety of Elizabeth and myself depended on the domestic arrangements of Lamartine and his mistress. 'It's always me who runs his life,' she explained serenely. 'Henri is far too intellectual for practical affairs. He has learned to do absolutely everything I tell him.'

The Germans were then attacking violently in the Champagne area east of Paris, and General Rommel had reached the Seine south of Rouen – but this time, the bridges were blown up under his nose. Le Bourget aerodrome was repeatedly bombed, and Tours was full of rumours that the Government were leaving for the châteaux of the Loire. 'I hope the châteaux are on the telephone,' said Elizabeth morosely. But General Weygand was full of confidence. 'My orders are still for every man to fight without thought of retreat,' he declared. 'The enemy will soon reach the end of his tether. We are on the last lap. *Tenez.*'

On the Sunday morning, the Germans were in Soissons, 75 miles from Paris. We decided to go, mould or not. We would make for St Nazaire, Cherbourg being uncomfortably near the battle. The Germans already had their hands on Dieppe. Incredibly, I had sailed into it with perfect safety only a fortnight before. We shared the feeling of everyone else in France – when Hitler's finger-tips brush the nape of your neck, you jump from the nearest window.

We went to the hotel in a last speculative, unconfident chance of catching Lamartine. '*Parti,*' snapped the porter in the striped waistcoat. When Elizabeth asked where, he swore at her and said '*Inconnu*'. As he turned to defend himself against newcomers imploring accommodation, Elizabeth calmly reached across for the key of number 35.

The room was a mess, and smelt of shaving soap, face powder and feet. There were newspapers everywhere, full ashtrays, an empty cognac bottle. Strands of Madame Chalmar's blonde hair decorated the pillow of an unmade double bed. Our search revealed a forgotten jar of

Coty's face cream and a 25 centime piece with a hole in the middle, which I still have.

'I suppose they've bolted for Marseilles,' said Elizabeth, as we stared at one another dourly.

'We'll have to follow them.'

'We'd never find them.'

'We could ask at the shipping offices.'

'Really, Jim! They're not booking a Mediterranean cruise.' I noticed a scrap of paper on the floor by the commode, which bore on its cracked marble top the ancient, decorative telephone in its spindly cradle. Pencilled in writing which I recognized as Lamartine's was *Bordeaux 45–444*.

'Of course, the number could be one of his relatives, or another doctor or another girlfriend,' I suggested. 'But surely it's worth ringing, just to find out?'

'We'll have to go a little carefully, darling, with everyone utterly hysterical about spies. And even in peacetime, the telephone system was not one of the glories of France.'

We tried telephoning Bordeaux from the Perronets'. There was a six hour delay. 'I think we should *go* to Bordeaux,' decided Elizabeth after listening to the news bulletin on the TSF. 'The further we are from the front, the better our chance of getting home all in one piece.'

Our Bordeaux call came through. Madame at the other end announced herself to Elizabeth as the Hôtel d'Avignon. Elizabeth asked for Lamartine. No, the doctor and his wife had not yet arrived. Elizabeth slammed the telephone back on its stand triumphantly. We decided to start early the following morning, a 200-mile drive without headlights along a Route Nationale Ten choked with traffic daunting even Elizabeth.

During our next day's crawling passage past garages chalked *Pas d'Essence*, Mussolini announced from his usual perch in the Palazzo Venezia in Rome that Italy had declared war against the plutocratic and reactionary democracies of the West. And the French Government announced it was leaving Paris for Tours. At midnight, Monsieur Reynard and General de Gaulle were sharing the same car to quit Paris by the Porte de Châtillon. On their heels came several million of their fellow Parisians.

Elizabeth and I were somewhere between Poitiers and Angoulême, a hundred miles from Bordeaux, and the car had broken down.

We pushed the car on the verge between the poplars, with a press of cars, lorries, carts, bicycles and walkers in the darkness on the cobbles behind us. The torrent which burst from Paris forced trickles along every country road in France, even those reserved as strategic highways by the Army. We decided to spend the night in the back, huddled under Elizabeth's khaki greatcoat. She discovered a month-old *Times*, and insisted on doing the crossword in the light of a torch.

About seven in the morning an Army lorry came hooting importantly upon us. Elizabeth leapt into the road. A pretty girl in a British uniform was sufficient to bring any military driver to a halt. Our only possessions in our pockets, we were dumped at Angoulême station. There were still trains to Bordeaux, all arriving crammed from Paris. 'Then we shall have to travel on the buffers,' said Elizabeth, and I was not confident that she was joking.

We climbed on the train about one in the morning of Wednesday, June 11, jammed rigid in an unlit corridor. The engine puffed away from the station purposefully enough, but soon halted with screeching brakes in the black countryside. 'I do so want to leave the room,' complained Elizabeth. I thought of Lamartine, cosily in bed with Madame Chalmar.

We crossed the river Dordogne about six in the morning, and were shortly tipped relievedly into the Bordeaux railway terminus against the banks of the Garonne. Elizabeth and I had been almost isolated from news for two days, though the train was crawling with unpleasant rumours like a beleaguered trench with lice. We heard that the Germans had already smashed into Paris – which was untrue, for a couple of days. And that Mr Churchill was in France – he was, flown to Briare on the River Loire escorted by a squadron of Hurricanes, to tell the French Government at the Château de Muguet firmly, even fiercely, that the RAF stayed on its airfields behind British coasts.

Lamartine's Hôtel d'Avignon was between the famous Esplanade des Quinconces, leading down to the river, and the Jardin Public. It was much like the Hotel he had fled. We arrived there about half past eight. The woman in black behind the reception desk telephoned my name, said '*D'accord*' into the instrument, and told us to go up.

Lamartine was fully dressed, waiting in the open doorway of his bedroom. With a short bow, he invited us inside. It was larger than his last, with coffee-coloured wallpaper and a big brass bed. Madame Chalmar was sitting in the only chair, upright, attired as if about to grace some fashionable social function.

'Would you mind sitting on the bed?' invited Lamartine, lighting a Weekend. 'There would appear to be nowhere else.'

'Why didn't you give me that penicillin mould at Tours?' I demanded. I was angry, though biochemists are peaceable beings and I have the most placid of temperaments, for which my wife continually expresses gratitude.

'I would not seem very respectful of your intelligence, Mr Elgar, if I did not tell you bluntly that I have no intention of giving what you want.'

Madame Chalmar sat looking closely at her scarlet nails. 'You are going to give me that penicillin!' I was surprised to hear myself shouting.

'Mr Elgar, I must ask you to take a more compassionate view. My situation has changed since I talked to you last Wednesday in Tours. The situation of France has changed. Then, I was pretty certain that Brigitte and I had a clear run to Algiers. Mussolini coming into the war rather upset the...what do you upset in English, Shaw used it in a play?'

'Apple cart,' said Elizabeth.

'Exactly. So I shall stay here, with the famous mould. Mr Elgar, you would not leave me defenceless against the Gestapo? That's not very amiable of you.'

Elizabeth broke in, 'We know you're mixed up with the Croix de Feu. You can hardly wait until the Germans appear to give them your loot. They'll probably pin a medal on you.'

'I hope that mademoiselle is being more fanciful than offensive.'

This remark incited me to grab him by the lapels. 'Give me that penicillin.'

'Take away your hands! This is no way to treat a colleague–'

I shook him. I had never been so furious with anyone in my life before, apart from Elizabeth's mother. '*Merde...*' He snatched himself away.

Madame Chalmar gave a scream, quickly choked. Lamartine produced from his armpit a small black automatic pistol, pointing it alternately at Elizabeth and myself.

'*That* is certainly no way to treat a colleague,' I told him.

I was frightened. The experience accepted without undue consternation in films and television is in reality utterly demoralizing. It was horrifying to feel my life within a twitch of Lamartine's finger.

'Keep away from me,' he said, his voice shaky.

'I should not have expected a professional man to carry firearms,' I returned, somewhat primly.

'These are abnormal times.'

'Jim, stay where you are, don't do anything, don't move,' came Elizabeth's voice.

My brain resumed functioning. 'You don't seem to think highly of your own neck, Lamartine. If you shoot us, you'll be arrested by the nearest gendarme. You'd be guillotined.'

'The Germans will be here long before the necessary legal processes could be completed.'

'The Germans would hardly encourage Frenchmen to be murderers.'

'You may safely leave the Germans to me, Mr Elgar.' He was still pointing the pistol. It struck me that he was in fact a German spy, or at least in their pay. Then to my relief he tucked the gun back in its holster. 'I have made my point, I believe? You see that I am prepared to use bullets to protect my possessions. Now will you please leave us in peace.'

I looked at Elizabeth. She was white, but seemed as composed as usual. 'I shall tell this tale when I'm back in London,' I said to Lamartine. 'The war can't go on for ever. You'll have some very nasty questions to answer at the end of it, take my word for that.'

'*Je m'en fiche de cela.*' He stubbed out his Weekend and opened the packet for another.

'If you have second thoughts, you can get hold of me through the British consul. If you give me back the mould, I'll keep quiet about what's happened in this room. I promise that.'

'It is a great disadvantage of you English that unlike we French you can never see when you are beaten. You are simply not realists.'

He struck a match. Madame Chalmar still sat staring in fright, fingertips to lips. Hand in hand, Elizabeth and I escaped.

'Darling, you were utterly wonderful, you handled him perfectly,' she said.

'He's not dangerous, he's only frightened,' I said modestly. 'Everyone's frightened, just look round you.'

We decided to make straight for the British consulate. Bordeaux was full of rootless people, as Paris had been the week before. The streets were jammed with newly arrived cars, in which the occupants had no choice but to sleep and live. The cafés were all crammed, the food shops all sold out. The consulate lobby was full of British civilians in the same plight as ourselves. The weather had become oppressive, and everyone strained to curb their temper. There was no official in sight, but from the conversation the chances of a boat home were slim.

We spent an hour leaning against the wall holding hands, discussing the chances of being locked in the same cell with Lamartine and Madame Chalmar. Then a voice came unexpectedly, 'I say – Elizabeth Tiplady.'

I turned to find a young pink-faced man with the zig-zag braid of a Royal Navy Volunteer Reserve lieutenant.

'Why, it's Hugo,' she exclaimed.

'The uniform suits you.'

'How sweet.'

'What on earth are you doing in France?'

'I was posted to the British Hospital in Paris.'

'Really? That must have been no end of fun until the balloon went up.'

'Yes, it was, awfully.'

'Then why have you come to Bordeaux?'

'I'm trying to get home.'

'But what about your unit?'

'I seem rather to have lost it. Do you suppose I'm a deserter?' He laughed.

'I say, old thing, can you do anything about a ship?' Elizabeth asked. Under the shiny, forged steel of this conversation, which might have occurred in Gunter's tea room in Mayfair, I could detect her nervousness.

'Well, I'm in a destroyer which is sailing tonight. I expect I could get you aboard her.'

'Oh, super.'

'How's Sir Edward?'

'He seems very well. Jim, this is Hugo Mottram. Don't you remember? I was going out with him when you wanted to take me to the theatre. Hugo, this is Jim Elgar, who's coming to England with me.'

'Sorry, Elizabeth. The Navy can't transport civilians.'

'Don't be ridiculous, Hugo. You can't fuss over .red tape with the Germans likely to come round the corner any minute.'

'King's Regulations are hardly red tape.'

'Anyway, Jim isn't a civilian. He's a chemist on vital war work, and we're engaged to be married.'

Hugo stared hard at my crumpled styleless clothes, my grubby semi-stiff collar, my dusty shoes and grimy, stubbly face. I still had my umbrella, which had become tattered. 'I'm so pleased,' Hugo said limply.

'Did you mean that?' I asked, as he disappeared amid the crowd.

'Do you suppose I'd say anything as serious as that on the spur of the moment? Over this past fortnight, I've simply assumed it to be the case.' I leant to kiss her. 'Darling, *please*! I'm in uniform.'

Shortly afterwards, one of the consular staff appeared to announce that we should both be taken off that night, and advised us to stay in the building for further orders. Our relief at this news rendered a day sustained by cups of tea and four squares of Motoring Chocolate perfectly tolerable.

I was too tired and uncomfortable to express elation at Elizabeth's admission. I was dejected at leaving France, like the British Army, in frustration and defeat. But I was overwhelmingly comforted at the prospect of the pair of us reaching English soil, the U-boats and Luftwaffe permitting. About four in the afternoon, I was amazed to see Madame Chalmar appear, carrying a bulky foolscap envelope. Elizabeth translated for me excitedly. 'She says the doctor is neither a fascist nor a traitor, just very stupid in the practical affairs of life. He should never have acquired a revolver, he's never fired one in his life. He doesn't even know how to reload it.'

I did not believe this, but asked quickly, 'She's got the penicillin?'

From her large handbag, Madame Chalmar produced the flask I had last seen in Florey's room at Oxford. I noticed at once that the mould was still alive. The Germans could simply have seeded out fragments, and grown as much as they liked. 'How awfully uninteresting it looks,' said Elizabeth in disappointment.

We all shook hands, Madame Chalmar said as she left, '*Enchantée, monsieur*,' as though breaking up a party.

'How did she manage to get it out of him?' I asked Elizabeth, looking at the flask unbelievingly.

'She said she shamed him into it. I always thought she wore the trousers in that *ménage*. Lamartine is a weak character, isn't he? Utterly puny, you could tell that by all his lies when he'd no intention whatever of giving you the stuff back.'

'Even so, she was forcing him to disgorge something which might have saved both their lives.'

'Surely, darling, you know that women who suffer terrible *crises de nerfs* over trivialities can be absolutely indomitable over fundamentals?'

I took Florey's papers outside and burnt them on the pavement. The passers-by took no notice. People were up to all manner of odd things in Bordeaux during those few days. I was desperate to destroy the mould completely, as quickly as possible, and without trace. When I got back to the consulate, Elizabeth was pink faced and swallowing hard, her khaki handkerchief to her lips. 'I've eaten it,' she announced. 'Like a good spy with a secret message. The broth stuff and all. It tasted utterly horrible. You said it was quite harmless, darling, didn't you?'

Our passage of 500 miles was stretched by detours into two and a half days. The weather broke for the first time since the sun warmed the armour of Hitler's tanks as it rose on the morning of May 10. Behind us in France, Prime Minister Paul Reynaud implored President Roosevelt to declare war on Hitler. But without success. So he resigned in favour of Marshal Pétain. We disembarked in Plymouth on the Sunday afternoon of June 16. We went to a big hotel for tea, sitting among the plants with elderly couples impassively reading their Sunday papers while eating fingers of buttered toast and cress sandwiches and complaining about the shortage of sugar.

About seven-thirty the following morning, we stood under the clock at Paddington Station in London, suddenly shocked that we should be torn from one another.

'You do mean it?' I asked her timorously once again.

'You don't surely imagine I should have abandoned myself like that in France, if I hadn't already decided to marry you?' She said this in a hurt voice. 'I told you, Jim darling, I'm *sérieuse*.' She promised to come to Oxford as soon as she could. 'Though I shall probably get into the most frightful hot water about losing that car.'

The red buses traversed Piccadilly Circus with an air of elephantine security, policemen as stolid as suet puddings in uniform halted them for the march of men in bowlers armed with umbrellas. The cinemas were opening for the afternoon performance and St James's church was advertising its next Sunday's preacher. The evening papers announced that the French were suing for an armistice. A French delegation was escorted by General Kurt von Tippelskirch to the clearing in the Forest of Compiègne where Foch had dictated his terms in November 1918. They found Hitler sitting in the same railway coach, shifted by German Army engineers to the same position on the rusty tracks. Such petty details made the Nazis so frightening, like sending Domagk's letter for posting in Wuppertal.

28

I did not see my fiancée for a month. I reconciled myself that separations are the saddest undertones of war. Then Elizabeth wrote from her transport depot near Norwich that she was bored to death, and would be coming to Oxford on the Saturday of July 20 by the midday train. It was awfully tedious, but she couldn't spend the night.

The German jackboots which had trampled over France now seemed likely to crunch upon English shingle. But the Luftwaffe which had smashed or scared from the sky the air forces of six nations, and paralysed European statesmen for five years, was for the first time tasting a well-mounted and well-directed adversary in the Spitfires and Hurricanes which Churchill had refused the dying prayers of the French. I was working day and night developing murderous germs to spatter any invading Nazis, who themselves seemed the most pernicious bacilli on earth. The technical details were exasperating. You can turn loose wild germs as you can turn loose a wild dog, but you cannot guarantee they will bite only the right persons.

The morning of Elizabeth's visit. I fell in with Florey as he was walking across the tree-dotted Parks, in sight of the jubilantly Tractarian red brick of Keble College. He always walked to the Dunn labs from his home in Parks Road.

'If the Germans do get as far as Oxford, which God forbid,' he said sombrely, 'we'll destroy everything to do with penicillin in the Department, except just enough mould to smear on our jacket linings. A few of us might escape to carry on the good work.'

'Escape to where?'

'That's the question. Perhaps to Canada. I've heard that the Fleet and the King and Queen are ready to go there in the last resort.' Florey's face lightened under the curly brim of his trilby as he began to talk about his successful experiment with mice during the week of Dunkirk. 'It was really most conclusive. I used eight mice, and you wouldn't have imagined that the ones injected with penicillin had ever been infected. Our untreated controls all died within twelve hours. The problem now is production. We've only enough penicillin for another twenty-five mice, and when I ask the big drug manufacturers for help they explain they're busy on war work. It's most infuriating.'

'What's the chance of being able to use penicillin on humans one day?'

'The step from mouse to man is a big one,' Florey said warily. 'Literally – a man is three thousand times mouse-sized. At this rate, I don't know when we'd ever have our hands on enough to treat a single case.'

'Have you written your work up yet?'

'There's a short preliminary paper appearing in the *Lancet* next month.' I missed at the time the significance of this casual exchange. We had reached the gate leading from the Parks to the rear of Florey's Pathology Department. 'Would you like a look at the national penicillin factory?' he invited. 'I've ten minutes before lecturing. The medical students still have to be taught, and the rest of my time seems to be absorbed filling in forms.'

He led me to a smaller building against the main laboratories. 'The animal house,' Florey explained. 'We're making use of its post mortem room.'

It was small and filled by an extraordinary apparatus the height of a man in the middle. Four large upturned bottles on the top were connected by rubber tubes and glass pipes to half a dozen smaller ones below, the whole cased in an open-fronted stand of polished mahogany. It resembled one of the preposterously logical drawings of Heath Robinson's – perhaps a machine for getting quarts into pint pots.

'It's the brain child of my ingenious young assistant, Norman Heatley.' Florey explained how it worked. 'We suck out the broth – which of course has all the penicillin juice in it – from under the growing mould, replacing it with a fresh supply. You can do that a dozen times, the mould doesn't seem to mind. Then we cool the broth with ice, acidify it with phosphoric acid, and let it drip from those inverted lemonade bottles on top through the glass columns of amyl acetate. That's a good solvent for penicillin. Our final result is a few grains of brown powder.'

An electric bell rang and a light flashed on a makeshift panel to the right of the machine. 'One of the lemonade bottles needs replenishing,' observed Florey mildly.

'That's a beautiful piece of woodwork.'

'Yes, it's one of the shelves from the Bodleian Library.'

I asked him if he was still growing the mould on Fleming's original nutriment of meat broth. 'We tried all manner of chemicals to increase the yield,' Florey told me. 'Glucose, glycerol, thioglycolic acid. In the end, we found brewer's yeast did the trick. Then we needed something bigger than the ordinary lab flask for growing the felt of mould, but fortunately the right sort of receptacle was in good supply and near at hand.'

'Pie dishes?' I guessed.

'No, bedpans.' He gave his slight smile. 'It's very improvised, isn't it? And very British.'

It was largely improvisation, from one end of the country to the other, which that summer of 1940 saved our skins.

Elizabeth's train was as usual half an hour late. She was in uniform, running down the platform like a schoolgirl. 'Darling Jim, how wonderful, how absolutely wizard! I'd almost forgotten what you looked like. I really must see round the colleges, Christ Church and Balliol and places, I'd never been to Oxford in my *life*.'

'The colleges are full of Civil Servants, who were evacuated from London with the children and expectant mothers.'

'And the river, I must see the river. Do you suppose we can still hire a punt?'

'I expect so.'

' "Stands the church clock at ten to three? And is there honey still for tea?" '

'That was Cambridge.'

We went to a pub. There was only beer and sloe gin to drink. We sat at a table in a dark beamed nook. 'Did you get court-martialled or anything about the car?' I asked.

'What car?'

'The one we abandoned at Angoulême.'

'Oh, that! The whole French adventure seems just like a dream to me now. Doesn't it to you? Do you suppose they've got any cigarettes? It really did bring the war home to me, not being able to buy a packet of fags when I felt like it.'

I returned from the bar with ten Woodbines. Elizabeth was slightly pink and staring straight ahead of her. 'Jim, darling, I was intending to be ever so flippant and stupid, and pass off everything in France as a trivial joke which of course neither of us could possibly be expected to take seriously.' She paused. She continued in a crushed voice, 'But I can't. It couldn't possibly be a joke to you, I know. It doesn't look very funny to me, however hard I try.'

I had already suspected her cursing herself as a bigger fool for giving me her hand after giving me her body. 'Are those your own feelings? Or are your mother and your father behind it?'

She shook her head vigorously. But I insisted, 'I'm still the butler's boy. God!' I exclaimed. 'With Hitler just across the Channel. Nothing in this country is quite so indestructible as its snobbery. We'll go down with the ermine ensign fluttering bravely on our stern.'

'Jim —! It's nothing to do with that. I can't marry you because I'm going to marry Archie.'

'Archie!' I sat bolt upright, almost cracking my head on a beam. 'But you can't possibly marry Archie.'

'I can,' she said meekly.

'But Archie's a fool.'

'He's a very intelligent writer.'

'That doesn't make him more intelligent than I am. You told me so yourself.'

She made no reply, but performed the extravagantly wasteful gesture of stubbing out her half-smoked cigarette. 'Well, I'm going to marry him, and that's that,' she concluded in a matter-of-fact voice. 'I'm sorry, Jim. That's absolutely all I can say, isn't it?'

'It's his title, I suppose?'

'It helps,' she answered frankly.

There was a long silence. 'Well, if you love Archie – '

'I do, I do,' she said quietly. 'Ever since you first introduced him, I think.'

'And if you've arranged to marry him – '

'Soon, now he's likely to be posted overseas any minute.'

'Overseas? There's nowhere left to go.'

'It's terribly secret. Somewhere hot.'

'Then there's nothing whatever I can do about it, is there?'

She laid a hand on the arm of my tweed jacket. 'Darling Jim! I knew you'd understand.' I have never heard words uttered with more intense relief.

I was invited to the wedding. I decided that my absence would afford Archie more gratification than my presence embarrassment. We gathered together in the sight of God in St Giles, Belgrave Square, on the Saturday of September 7. It was an unhappy choice of wedding-day. Hermann Göring had failed by a hair's breadth to eliminate the fighter stations amid the fair fields of Kent, and lost 225 of his aircraft to the Hurricanes and Spitfires the previous week. The feared Stuka dive-bomber was a flop, needing ten thousand feet of clear visibility, with which the skies of Britain were not generous. Göring had not planned the Luftwaffe for night bombing, but to work with the Army as the tanks came rolling over the rubble. So he sent his Heinkel Dornier and Junker bombers with swarms of protective Messerschmitts to attack London in broad daylight.

The air-raid warning sounded. After a whispered discussion with the happy couple at the altar, the vicar announced in canonical tones that the ceremony would continue. Archie declared that he would have Elizabeth as his wedded wife. The Vicar asked her, 'Wilt thou have this man – ' and a stick of bombs fell nearby, I thought right on Buckingham Palace. 'We shall adjourn to the crypt,' he said hastily.

In the stone-vaulted crypt with Sir Edward and Lady Tiplady and a hundred people I did not know, I found myself on a bench against the wall next to Archie with Elizabeth. He was still a sergeant in the Brigade of Guards.

'I honestly didn't expect you to come,' he said to me, sounding offended. Leaning away from Elizabeth, he added in a lower voice, 'I'm sorry about all this.'

'Do you think we should shake hands like gentlemen?'

'No, no, not now!' he said in alarm. Another bomb fell. 'I suppose this old church is safe?'

'You're not afraid, are you?'

'Of course I am.'

'I'm not.'

'Then I congratulate you on your courage.'

'It's not a matter of courage. I don't care any longer if I die.'

The reception was in a restaurant in Sloane Square. There was an iced cake and champagne. Sir Edward talked archly to me about fungi. Lady Tip pointedly avoided me. It came time for the happy pair to leave. There was a hired limousine, even confetti. At the door I found myself in a knot of guests and relatives close to Elizabeth. She looked up at me with bright eyes. 'It *was* because of the butler's boy,' she whispered. 'I'm telling you that because it's cruel, but not nearly as cruel as…as the other. Jim, darling, I love you.'

They left for Llandudno. That was Elizabeth.

29

My own wedding day was Wednesday, February 12, 1941.

I realized that I was getting on. I had turned thirty in the New Year. We had only a few air-raids on Oxford, but the previous summer, after Elizabeth had thrown me over, we were taking the warnings seriously enough to troop down to the lodging-house cellar at night. In such informal, half-dressed intimacy I made the acquaintance of Jean. She was a medical registrar at the Radcliffe Infirmary, like David Mellors. She had qualified in Scotland, she was slim and sandy, with delicate skin and freckles, she had blue eyes and wore tweed skirts with a silver thistle brooch on her blouse. She radiated homely comfort like pre-war Mr Therm of the Gas, Light and Coke Company.

'How did you come to meet Sir Edward Tiplady?' she asked.

We were engaged. We were walking through the grounds of the Radcliffe Infirmary, one of the most beautiful places to lie sick in. It was built in the eighteenth century with a bequest from Dr John Radcliffe, and a little on the side from the Duke of Marlborough. You could still recognize the original country infirmary of thirty beds, one operating theatre and its own beer house, in the grey stone Georgian building facing a quad with a chapel, like a college.

During the war, Lord Nuffield from Cowley was following the Duke of Marlborough from Blenheim by pouring his profits from motorizing the nation into its wards. Jean and I were passing Wren's Radcliffe Observatory, built to resemble the Athenian Temple of the Four Winds, and providing the most charming view from any operating theatre in the world.

'My father was his butler.' She stared at me. 'Why are you so surprised?' I asked.

'I suppose one never thinks of butlers as having sons, somehow,' she replied, flustered.

'I assure you they breed, like other mammals.' She said nothing to this, seeing that she had hurt me. I added, 'Don't worry, I was long ago reconciled to the butler's supreme unimportance in the society he moves among. I suppose that's a quality he shares with the eunuch.'

'It doesn't mean a thing to me, honestly.' She did not see how uncharitable this was. 'I'm not a snob, you know that. And anyway, nobody in Scotland has a butler, except the dukes.'

I thought I should mention something I had overlooked. 'By the way, I was married once before.'

She made an angry response. 'This is a fine time to tell me.'

'I'm sorry. It's always rather embarrassing to bring out. I was waiting for the right moment, but of course right moments never arrive. When we were laughing it was too serious, and when we were glum it would only have deepened the gloom.'

'You seem to take a rather light-hearted view of matrimony.'

'It was over six years ago,' I excused myself. 'It seems longer, because the war's broken the perspective.'

'What happened to her?' Jean began to recover her temper and enjoy a womanly interest.

'She died.'

Jean looked shocked. 'Oh. I'm sorry,' she said apologetically. 'What was it from?'

'My wife died in childbirth at the beginning of 1935. She was the very first patient Leonard Colebrook treated for puerperal fever with sulphonamide. But it didn't do the trick. I had only a few tablets which I'd smuggled out of Germany, and when they ran out we just had to watch her die.

'What about the child?'

'She survived all right. I had her adopted.'

'So you've a daughter aged six about the place somewhere?'

'Yes.'

'I'd never have thought it of you.' I wondered if she meant this as a compliment. 'What was your wife like?' she asked inevitably.

'She was Rosie the housemaid.'

'I see.'

We walked in silence until we reached the hospital rear gate leading to the Woodstock Road. 'Do you want to call it off?' I asked.

'Oh, no. I don't suppose it makes any difference.'

We were to marry in the Radcliffe Infirmary chapel. My mother came from Budleigh Salterton. When Hitler's *Wehrmacht* had appeared opposite Eastbourne, my mother's hotel closed down and she went as companion to an old lady in South Devon, though I had never thought of her as the companionable sort. My mother had grown grey, wrinkled and more religious than ever, for which the war to date had offered much encouragement.

Jean's family seemed all doctors and nurses, and looked about them with Scots severity. David Mellors was my best man. We both wore hired tail coats. The bride was late, and David himself hurried into the church only when the organist had started repeating his repertoire.

'Where the hell have you been?' I asked in an angry whisper as he joined me on the front pew.

'Sorry. I was giving a hand to Charles Fletcher.'

Dr Fletcher was working at the Radcliffe Infirmary as a Nuffield research student. 'Today he's trying some penicillin for Florey on a patient,' David whispered.

This was clearly of greater interest to David than my wedding. 'I didn't know Florey had enough to treat a case,' I whispered back.

'He may *not* have enough, boy. The patient's pretty sick. He's a middle-aged policeman who's been in for a couple of months already, with staphylococcal septicaemia. All from a scratch at the angle of his mouth while pruning his rosebushes.'

'None of the sulphonamides touched it. I suppose?'

'Not a hope. By now, he's got abscesses everywhere, osteomyelitis of the head of his humerus, an abscess perforating his eye. So we're risking trying penicillin on him by intravenous drip. He wouldn't have lasted much longer, anyway.'

'You mean, you're not absolutely certain that penicillin itself is non-toxic to the human?' The organist paused and changed his tune. The congregation was shuffling and coughing.

'Fairly certain. Charles Fletcher tried it on a volunteer last Monday,' David informed me, still in a whisper. 'There was panic stations over that – she threw a temperature. Luckily, it turned out the effect of an impurity.' The organist broke off, playing a triumphant chord. My bride had arrived. We stood up. I realized that David had been working with his morning suit under his white coat. 'Florey's extracting the excreted penicillin from the patient's urine, of course,' he told me. 'Every drop helps. We have to rush the bottles across to the Dunn Labs.'

'How?'

'On the handlebars of my bicycle.'

I had to turn my attention to personal matters.

The policeman died, as Rosie had died. After five days they ran out of penicillin. A fortnight later Florey tried again, in a boy with an infected leg bone. 'It brought his temperature down to normal,' my wife told me in the small, awkward flat I had taken in north Oxford. 'Florey's going to concentrate on treating children.'

'That shows a nice humanitarian approach.'

'Oh, no. They need smaller doses.'

Between February and May, four more cases of overwhelming infection with the sulphonamide-defying staphylococcus were treated with penicillin at the Radcliffe. Three were children. One died. He had a brain infection which normally killed swiftly, but the post mortem (which my wife attended) showed that penicillin was killing off the germs. The others were cured of infected bones and infected urine. So was a labourer with a carbuncle.

The hospital did not hold its breath and look on admiringly. It was a busy place, everyone had his own work to do, and new drugs were always being tried and forgotten. Florey and the people in the Dunn Labs were anyway thought tedious academics, curers of mice and guinea-pigs, always an intrusive nuisance among the practical doctors. As the forgotten father of the mould, I was naturally interested that after 13 years in the lumber-room of science it might after all have a practical use – if Florey could produce enough of it. Apart from recovering penicillin from the patients' urine, every flask and syringe was carefully rinsed, while the Heath Robinson apparatus in the animal house was now complicated with milk churns, milk coolers and a discarded domestic bath-tub.

'A bronze letter-box comes into the process somewhere,' Florey explained to me when we met one evening in South Parks Road.

It was the end of June 1941 and the blitz had stopped – though Britain had by then lost more civilian dead than Servicemen. Hitler had turned on his Russian allies, exactly as Lamartine had foreseen. 'I've at last persuaded a little chemical firm in the East End to grow the mould, and send up the juice in more milk churns,' Florey imparted. 'We're getting to look like prosperous dairy farmers. But a single bomb any night could put an end to *that* contribution.'

Florey asked if I had read his penicillin paper in the recent *Lancet*. I nodded. It was not over-informative. Florey and Chain stated simply that after their work on Fleming's lysozyme, penicillin seemed promising to investigate. They described its purification as a stable brown powder, its killing various germs in the test-tube, and more significantly its saving the lives of twenty-five infected mice. The *Lancet* had added a short and tepid leading article.

'I suppose you realize that copy of the *Lancet* will be opened in Stockholm?' I could not prevent myself asking. 'The conscientious German intelligence service will snip out your article, and in a few days a translation will be sitting on Gerhard Domagk's desk in Wuppertal. If the Gestapo now feel they can trust him.'

'Perhaps we should have done everything in secrecy, but it's difficult,' Florey said resignedly. 'We'd no encouragement from the Government to hush our work up. If it comes to that, we've had precious little encouragement from the Government about anything. They seem to have lost all interest, since risking your life in France for it. I suppose they've plenty of other things to worry about.'

'Did publication of your paper produce any result?'

'Yes. Flem appeared in Oxford.'

'I heard he'd come up for the day. At least he's proved that he's alive.'

We had reached the Science Library at the top of South Parks Road. Florey was going to dine in Queen's, I was going home. I asked, 'Does Flem really think that penicillin has possibilities?'

'Oh, yes. He thinks it could oust the sulphonamides.'

'That's rather grandiose, isn't it?'

Florey cautiously made no reply.

'Is Flem bitter at all over your success with it?'

'I think he's envious that I've got Chain on my staff here. Chain discovered how to purify it only after so many chemists had failed. Raistrick, and so on. But you know, Jim, if Flem really had faith in his discovery in the 1920s, he'd have nagged the chemists, or searched for one with the right trick up his sleeve. After all, Flem wasn't working in some isolated lab in an attic. He had all the resources of the Inoculation Department at St Mary's at his beck and call.'

'Don't forget Sir Almroth Wright couldn't stand chemists at any price.'

'Well, Wright was getting doddery by then,' Florey said realistically. 'Flem would have got his own way, if he'd pushed hard enough.'

'He missed the bus, as the late Chamberlain said about Hitler?'

'I hope I'm not being vain, but penicillin would be unknown today if I hadn't decided to reinvestigate it in 1938. That delay of ten years was perfectly inexcusable. Old Flem missed the significance of his own paper.'

We parted. As I walked home, a half-forgotten fact impishly tickled my memory. I looked out my signed copy of *The British Journal of Experimental Pathology* containing Fleming's paper. I read again the list of editors. They included H W Florey. He had missed the significance of Fleming's paper, too.

30

The following morning I had a telephone call from Ainsley inviting me to dinner at his London club (clubland, like high table, was undaunted by the war). He had never before issued a social invitation, nor even offered me a drink. I wondered what was up.

Ainsley's club in St James's had the lower floor sandbagged, the roof blown off, and the front windows replaced by boarding. He led me to a small smoking-room in the rear, where an oval table stood with glasses and bottles. 'Most of the club servants have been called up,' he grumbled. 'So we help ourselves and sign for it. We're allowed one whisky a day, but a lot of the members cheat, particularly the ecclesiastical ones.' I asked for a glass of chablis. 'Thank God the wine committee had more sense than Chamberlain in 1939, and anticipated a long war.' He sniffed. 'I could swear that's a cigar. Someone must have found a box in the cellar.'

We sat down, inevitably discussing Hitler's invasion of the Soviet Union. 'Did you know that Hitler invaded Russia on exactly the same day as Napoleon?' Ainsley passed a hand over the bald patch of his grey head, a characteristic gesture. 'June 22, 1812 or 1941. Obviously, *plus ça change, plus c'est la même chose* applies equally to megalomaniacs.'

'Do you suppose the Russians will hold out?' Everybody was asking this.

'If they can hold out till winter they can hold out for ever. But I'm afraid the *Wehrmacht* will go its usual devastating way. Still it gives us a useful breathing space. And it makes the tediously anti-war *Daily Worker* look silly. Or it would have done, if Morrison hadn't banned it.'

'And what do we do when we've drawn our breath?'

'God knows.' Ainsley gloomily sipped his whisky of the day. 'We're not a great power any more. Churchill has to pretend that we are, and everyone in the country believes him, or has to pretend to believe him, because there's no alternative. We weren't a great power before the war broke out, but I don't think even Hitler saw that.'

'The Empire – '

'The Empire is a bolthole for the Fleet, that's all.'

'What about the Americans?' I was arguing to keep my spirits up, like whistling in the dark. 'Roosevelt's "Lendlease" idea in March was surely a significant gesture, not just a business deal to eke out our stock of dollars?'

'Listen, Jim – this is very secret. Churchill's meeting Roosevelt some time this year. I don't know where, except it'll be somewhere in the States. Probably Boston. Some sort of grand, bland declaration will be named after the venue.' (The pronouncement came in August as the 'Atlantic Charter'. President and Prime Minister met afloat off Newfoundland, in Placentia Bay. To have so named their joint statement might have given it an obstetrical ring.)

Ainsley glanced sadly at his empty, unrefillable whisky glass. 'I'll tell you something else secret. Staff talks were held between us and the Americans during last February and March, and naturally there are unannounced contacts between various branches of both countries' Services. The upshot for you, Jim, is that Lindemann wants you to fly to America for a few weeks on Friday.'

The abrupt news of Churchill's adviser directing me to escape from our beleagured island left me without speech. I listened bemusedly while Ainsley prosaically explained that I was destined for the small town of Warsaw in Colorado, where there was a counterpart of the Fungus Institute. 'You must keep this expedition dark, even from your wife,' he added earnestly.

Jean knew I was working with lethal bacteria, not fungi. But she let patriotism stifle curiosity. It must have been the same for the wives of research workers on the atomic bomb.

'How?' I asked.

'Tell her you're going on a month's course, rock-climbing with the Royal Marines. The better to search for unusual variants of bacteria.'

Ainsley stood up, looking at his watch. 'We'd better eat, or there'll be nothing left.'

As we made for the dining-room, I said, 'So Roosevelt doesn't intend to let the British Empire disappear off the face of the map?'

'On the contrary, I think that's precisely his object. America will come out of this war as the only country to be reckoned with in the world. Plus Russia, if only she can manage to stave off the Nazis till November. And without America firing a shot, if she's clever. It's much more sensible to step into the ring when all possible challengers have knocked themselves out.'

I could not bring myself to believe this. 'But supposing the Japs attack America?'

'That would be interesting. Hitler might well inflict himself on the United States as an ally. After all, the Japanese are hardly Aryans, are they?' After this horrifying prospect, he speculated, 'I wonder if there'll be any meat tonight? How remote seem the days when I used to cut all the fat off my roast beef.'

I went to America on the Friday. I let my wife into the secret. I instructed her to pass around that I was on a deep-sea diving course with the Navy, too many of my acquaintances knowing that I had no head for heights. An RAF car driven by a pretty WAAF took me through signpostless England to an airfield near Salisbury, where a small Anson was waiting to fly me to another.

Only when aloft it occurred to me that I had never flown before. I could not identify the RAF station I arrived at. I still cannot today. There were a lot of seagulls about, I noticed. At dusk, I climbed with a dozen other civilians into an aeroplane with black paint on the windows. Someone whispered that we were bound for Lisbon. If we evaded the cannons of the Luftwaffe, I thought. There was also the possibility of the device in my brief-case disrupting in the lowered atmospheric pressure and infecting us all with bubonic plague. Beside it lay a test-tube of penicillin mould, which I had cadged as an afterthought from Florey before leaving South Parks Road.

We arrived in the early hours. We saw a city street lit with lamps. We marvelled.

I had two days in which my stomach, enfeebled by British rations, collapsed under the weight of peacetime menus like an old lady in a crush. On the Monday morning I left in a Pan American flying boat for New York.

I found Jeff's name everywhere. *Beckerman Beer, Beautifully Brewed,* said the hoardings and electric signs, the girl sipping her foaming glass with an ecstasy deserving more worthy stimulus. I was to spend two wonderful days in this Aladdin's Cave before travelling to Warsaw, Colorado. I telephoned Jeff's office.

I was greeted with an explosion of delight. That evening, Jeff appeared at my small hotel in a chauffeur-driven Cadillac with two girls, both of whom struck me as far prettier than the ecstatic one in the advertisement. The car was stuffed with presents – a case of bourbon, boxes of Spam and peanut butter, whole tinned hams, bars of chocolate, packets of chewing-gum. He seemed to think I needed feeding up. Jeff himself had grown much fatter in the eighteen months since I had seen him in the Savoy. He had also grown much richer.

'I'm turning out about a quarter the sulphonamides used in the United States. I got new plants opening every three–four months,' he declared proudly within a couple of minutes of our meeting. 'Chemicals, textiles, pharmaceuticals, I'm operating right across the country, even into California. That's apart from the old brewery at White Plains, here in New York State. I'm opening another brewery this fall in Wisconsin – you see, old man, everyone in America just forgot how to make real beer during Prohibition.' I asked about the Red Crown Brewery in Wuppertal. 'The Nazis grabbed it. But they paid for it!' he exclaimed triumphantly. 'I guess they didn't want to upset the neutrals.'

'I hope the RAF have now blown it to bits,' I suggested cordially.

'Well, it was still there last week despite the RAF. Wuppertal's a boom town, you know. German industry today is stronger than ever.'

'We're led to believe that German industry is on the point of collapse.'

'Then you can forget it.'

Jeff leant back in the corner of the limousine. We were driving along Fifth Avenue. He was dressed with commercial sobriety in a lightweight blue suit and white shirt. I reflected that he must have burst out of his

Savile Row wardrobe, and noticed that he still wore handmade English shoes. He had given up Chesterfields, but lit a cigar. The two girls occupied the jump seats, dutifully providing him with an air of adoring incomprehension.

'The Nazi economy's in better shape than any time since Göring offered Germany guns instead of butter,' Jeff reasserted, 'Hell, they're getting all the butter they want from France and Holland. A lot of Frenchmen and Dutchmen are going to starve to death before the first German feels hungry. But don't get me wrong, old man. Unlike almost all my countrymen, I've had the doubtful privilege of seeing the Nazis close to. I'm one hundred per cent for Britain. Any sane man last summer would have asked Hitler for the best terms he could get. Thank God that Churchill's insane, just like the Nazis say.'

'There'll always be an England,' said one of the girls.

'Even Joe Kennedy sang a different tune when he came home for the election last fall. That was after Roosevelt laid hands on him. I guess no one will hear of Kennedy again, once the war's over. Nor Lindbergh. I'm disappointed with Lindbergh.'

'Say, did you ever meet the Duchess?' asked the other girl eagerly. I looked blank. 'You know, Mrs Simpson.'

I apologized that our paths had not crossed.

'Have you got yourself married again?' Jeff asked. I nodded. 'So have I. But that didn't work out, either. Was it that pretty dark thing in uniform you brought along to the Savoy?'

'No. She married a friend of mine, who's been discharged from the Army with an ulcer and works for the Ministry of Information. He's one of the people who keep telling us that the German economy is finished.'

'Why aren't *you* in the British Army?' asked the first girl, I thought bluntly.

'Flat feet.'

'You must be hungry,' Jeff said to me. We arrived at a huge restaurant with a loud band, exuberant chorus girls and enormous steaks. Jeff began reminiscing about our night out in Cologne. Our two companions grew bored. Some time after midnight we shed them. I went back to Jeff's apartment – luxurious rooms, apparently unending, high above Park

Avenue. 'Take anything you like from the closets,' he invited. 'Even your clothes are rationed now, I guess?'

I helped myself to a tie. A negro in a white jacket brought highballs. Through the big window I could look down on the feverish lights of New York. We talked about Wuppertal and the Schwebebahn. 'Hitler was crazy, shoving Damgk in jail,' Jeff commented. 'He should have let the Professor go ahead and receive his Nobel Prize, turn out the band when he got home, and have Göebbels proclaim the magnificent benefits to all mankind hatching from Nazi Germany. That's why nothing, nothing at all, will ever come out of Nazism,' he added in disgust. 'It's a nihilistic creed. When the Nazis have wiped out everything that's good and decent in the world, they'll have nothing to replace it, except more oppression. When there's no one left alive on earth for them to oppress, they'll start cutting one another's throats. For the simple reason that Nazism can't exist without aggression. Imagine Hitler snipping the tape to open a new hospital!'

His remark made me remember the test-tube in my jacket pocket. I had left Jeff mystified at the real reason for my mission to Colorado, and he had swallowed his inquisitiveness.

'What in hell's this?' He turned the test-tube in his fingers, sprawling in his chair, his heavy bar of eyebrow puckered.

'Ever heard of penicillin?'

'Never.'

'It's a drug produced by that mould.' Jeff did not find it an intriguing exhibit at that hour of the night. 'It hits staphylococci and gas gangrene and diphtheria, which aren't touched by your sulpha drugs. An extremely efficient Oxford professor called Florey started using penicillin on patients, only eighteen months after beginning his experiments to find exactly what it was. Imagine even Henry Ford achieving that with the automobile.'

Jeff grunted. He rolled the test-tube round, looking more interested. 'I guess Churchill knows all about this?'

'They've hardly enough to treat a couple of kids with blood-poisoning, let alone an Army. They have to grow the mould in bedpans, because they can't get anything else. They have to extract the penicillin juice with lemonade bottles and milk churns, fixed in a lovely bookcase from the

Bodleian Library. Perhaps penicillin could be our secret weapon. But its production is strictly a cottage industry. I thought you'd be interested to look at it. The mould loves nothing better to grow on than brewer's yeast.'

'Brewer's yeast you can't get your hands on.' Jeff scratched his chin with his thumb. 'You could grow it on corn-steep liquor, I guess.' I had never heard of this. 'When you crack corn to get the starch,' Jeff explained, 'you steep the grain in sodium sulphate. You end up with thousands of gallons of stuff like molasses, which you can't even give away. Out West, they're trying it out for fermentation processes of various sorts. You could grow this mould on it, like any other mould.'

He fell silent, continuing to revolve the test-tube in his fingers. 'Supposing Mr Churchill came to me and said, "Jeff, old man, we want penicillin by the ton, and tomorrow". Do you know what I'd do? I'd buy a few loads of corn-steep liquor – I wouldn't need to buy it, they'd pay me for taking it away. Then I'd shut down a section of the brewery out at White Plains, and I'd grow penicillin in the vats. You know how these contaminating moulds love to grow in breweries.'

I laughed. 'A brewery's an advance on lemonade bottles, I suppose. It's imaginative, anyway.'

'Sure, it's imaginative,' he said seriously. I finished my highball, and sat tinkling the ice in my glass. 'It's only by being imaginative that I've made my money. So what's the problem? Growing a mould and extracting a chemical from its juice.'

'Florey used amyl acetate for the extraction process.'

'There you are. The principle's established, it's only a matter of nuts and bolts.' He got up to fetch a foolscap pad and pencil from his leather-topped desk. 'Let's try sketching out the production line. See here, I've got the vat...'

The interest of us both warmed, glowed, and broke into a flame. The floor round Jeff became covered with sheets of pencilled plans. I watched over his shoulder, giving a chemist's advice and replenishing the highballs. The New York lights were fading in the summer dawn when we plummeted down the elevator. Jeff picked up his Cadillac from the sidewalk and we drove through the sharpening light to White Plains. Beyond the city, to one side of the highway stood Jeff's chemical plant, to the other the Beckerman Brewery. He turned the car towards the brewery, roused the watchman, strode with the drawings under his arm towards the vast building with the fermentation vats, and pacing distances with his feet began the plan which flooded a wartime world with penicillin.

31

All bad things come to an end. The European war and my marriage finished on the same day.

It was never much of a marriage. My second wife was perfectly correct the day I enlightened her about my first. I did have a casual approach to matrimony. But in wartime, everyone seemed to be getting married with a desperate light-heartedness.

I still cannot walk through the front door of the Radcliffe Infirmary without a sickening feeling at my own foolishness. The greater event of that wedding day is recorded just inside. A plaque acclaims 'The first systematic use of penicillin', which all medical people wrongly take as a misspelling for 'systemic'. There is another plaque outside the Botanic Garden at the foot of Magdalen Bridge. Fleming is mentioned on neither of them.

I had turned to Jean as to the comfort of a glowing fire after the icy wind which had pierced me from Elizabeth. But a warm fire sends you to sleep, when you wake up there are only uninteresting ashes. Jean had lived a narrow life of high teas and earnest conversation. I had shared the easygoing, amiable hard-heartedness of Archie's circle. I had been browbeaten by Hitler's Storm Troopers. Our similar occupations were a disadvantage. We were both more interested in our work than each other. We were both rather duller than our jobs. We had a large number of bitter rows, though they were pardonably about socialism, van Gogh, ITMA and T S Eliot. Then a pink-faced young doctor called Fred appeared, and she went to live with him. 'I say, I really am most frightfully sorry about this,' he kept apologizing, as though he had inadvertently gone off with my umbrella.

On a Friday morning a week after VE-Day in May 1945, I had been called urgently to Ainsley's office off the Edgware Road. 'What do you know about FIAT?' he asked at once.

'It's a make of Italian car.'

He gave an uncharacteristic gesture of impatience. 'These damned initials are sprouting everywhere – ALSOS, OSRD, TIIC, and so on. Now FIAT has just been created by SHAEF.'

I knew at least that SHAEF was Supreme Headquarters Allied Expeditionary Force. The others were a secret cypher to my ears. 'OSRD is the Office of Scientific Research and Development, and TIIC the Technical Industrial Information Committee,' Ainsley explained. 'I have completely forgotten what ASLOS stands for, but it's the brain-child of General Marshall. I believe there's also something called CIOS, which must be...let's say, Combined Intelligence Objective Subcommittee. FIAT is Field Intelligence Agency bracket Technical bracket.'

He stared for some moments gloomily across his desk. 'I imagined in my innocence that the war would become less complicated when the enemy surrendered, rather than more so. But we are now responsible for the entire German population as well as our own. FIAT's an Anglo-American show, but of course the Americans are running it, building up an enormous staff in Germany with secretaries, dictating machines, doubtless its own PX and cinema. We're just sending across a few odd bods. I'd like you to be one of them.'

I was attracted at the prospect of escape from the rubble of my domestic life. And I could not prevent an immensely self-satisfied feeling at the notion of returning to Germany as a conqueror. Ainsley continued by reading from a typed paper on his desk, ' "FIAT is an intelligence service for identifying targets, subjects and personalities which may be of technical interest to British government departments or firms." In other words, they want you to grab as many German trade secrets as possible, and as many Germans as might know how to make better mousetraps than we do. It's the Ministry of Supply's baby. Frankly, I'm not interested in it.'

'You'd want me to nose round the I G Farben works at Wuppertal?'

'That's right. Domagk's still alive, we found that out.'

I wondered about Gerda.

'Have you turned up any evidence of the Germans producing penicillin?' I asked.

'Not so far. Hitler was flinging a few Iron Crosses about for penicillin research, but that means nothing, of course. I hear Montgomery's HQ have just sent some phials of penicillin they discovered, but they were probably one or two of ours picked up by the Afrika Korps.'

Nearly every molecule of penicillin used by the Allied Armies had been manufactured in America. The penicillin from Florey's animal house had been tried only experimentally in the summer of 1942, on fifteen wounded men in the North African desert. The supply was so meagre that it was powdered upon the wounds themselves, or injected into them through little rubber tubes – a ghost of Sir Almroth Wright's irrigation of wounds with salt solution in the Boulogne Casino. The experiment was so successful that they wanted to make Florey a general.

'It was rather ridiculous that the Germans could read all of Florey's case reports in the *Lancet*,' I complained. The policeman who pricked himself on a rose bush, the boy with the brain infection, all appeared in the *Lancet* of August 1941, embellished with a leading article of masterful caution which ran second to *Care For Home Guard Casualties*.

Ainsley agreed. 'Admittedly, we were a bit late officially suppressing information about penicillin. But look at it another way. If Fleming had developed penicillin in 1928, the whole world would have been making it. Including Germany. As it turned out, our valuable weapon was denied the Nazis.'

'A point which most certainly escaped Wright when he wrote to *The Times*,' I commented.

When penicillin had seeped into the newspapers in the middle of 1942, Sir Almroth claimed forthrightly that Fleming deserved the honour of discovering penicillin, and of the first suggestion that it promised an important use in medicine. The letter predictably had a Latin tag stuck in the middle.

'It's a wonder to me that Sir Almroth didn't write to *The Times* claiming he discovered penicillin himself.' Ainsley gave his slow smile. 'We all know Wright, don't we? He'd put his name to anything he possibly could. While telling his 'sons in science' their discoveries were far too important to be published by an unknown research worker, and would create far more attention under the stamp of his own authority. Pretty cool of him, I always thought.'

'I got the impression when I visited Mary's last month that Fleming doesn't at all mind playing the Greta Garbo in the penicillin drama.'

'And I don't suppose St Mary's minds, either,' Ainsley said emphatically. 'They want to raise money from the public, like every other hospital. How's Wright reacting to Fleming's new knighthood?'

'He gave no indication of his feelings, apart from persistently referring to him as *Doctor* Fleming.'

I had another interview that day which held greater promise of fascination. I was having lunch with Archie. I had not set eyes on him since he left on his honeymoon. He took me to a small cheap restaurant near the Ministry of Information offices in Bloomsbury, where he said they understood his diet. He still suffered from his duodenal ulcer, and had a special ration book, of which he seemed proud, as some distinction amid wartime uniformity. He had lost so much weight that his eyes seemed larger, staring from a skull-like head. He was pale and he stooped. He wore a suit of brown corduroy.

'How's Elizabeth keeping?' I asked as we sat down.

'She's very well. She's stationed at the War Office. I heard you'd got married?'

'It didn't last.'

'I'm sorry,' he sympathized briefly. 'I know all about you and Elizabeth in France, by the way.'

'Those were exceptional circumstances.'

'Oh, yes, highly exceptional.'

'Does it worry you?'

'Of course not.'

'Isn't it like our being members of the same good club?'

'I don't think that's quite the way to describe Elizabeth,' he said, quite severely.

Archie had invited me because he was writing a propaganda article on Anglo-American co-operation with penicillin. He asked closely about Jeff

Beckerman. 'Elizabeth tells me that she actually met this fellow with you before the war. He seemed to her a rough diamond, hardly the type of man to become a public benefactor.'

'Jeff doesn't want to benefit the public. He wants to make money out of it. At first they thought he was crazy, using profitable brewing capacity to grow the contaminants which all the other brewers were doing their damnedest to remove. Then Florey's paper describing his successful cases at Oxford got into the New York papers. Jeff's competitors quickly put two and two together and decided it made four or five million dollars.'

'Haven't the Americans got some enormous penicillin factory out in Illinois, or somewhere?' Archie sipped his glass of dried milk.

'Yes, by accident. The US Department of Agriculture had just opened a new fermentation research lab in Peoria, south of Chicago. That was about the time that Florey himself was sent out to the States. Did you know,' I told Archie proudly, 'that until Pearl Harbor all the penicillin mould in the world were descendants from the blob I let fall on Flem's Petri dish in the summer of 1928? But of course, the Americans do everything so much more thoroughly than we British. They got their Air Force to fly samples of soil home from all over the world. They analysed thousands and thousands of specimens at Peoria, until in the summer of 1943 they discovered an absolutely new superstrain of mould. It was named *Penicillium chrysogenum*, and it produces five hundred times the penicillin of the old one.'

'Where did they find it?' asked Archie.

'On a canteloupe melon in the gutter of the market in Peoria.'

'But there's more to the process than growing a mould on molasses in a brewery vat, surely?'

'Indeed. You have to grow it in completely germ-free air, which is a job enough in itself. If Florey got one of his bedpans contaminated with germs, he just threw the penicillin down the sink. You can't do that with a fifteen thousand gallon vat. Then they had to design agitators for the vats, and invent a new drying technique. We could never have managed it here, especially with the bombs and the U-boats.'

'But aren't we in Britain making a lot of money out of this, too?'

'Not a penny.'

'Surely, the professor in Oxford could have patented penicillin? Like the sulpha drug you stole in Germany?'

'I mentioned the possibility to Florey. He said that you simply can't patent medical discoveries in Britain, even in wartime. It would be unethical. He would be struck off the Medical Register, as though he had committed adultery with a patient.'

Archie frowned towards his cottage cheese omelette made with dried egg. I was enjoying a Spam fritter. 'That's something the Government's got to change. Those profits shouldn't be pouring into the pockets of American capitalists. They should be used for the good of the entire British people.'

'You're still a Socialist?'

'More fiercely than ever. Did you know there's going to be a general election quite soon? I was on the telephone this morning to Blackpool.' The Labour Party conference was convening to replan the world in the Empress Ballroom. 'Clem Attlee's going to break up the Coalition. I know that for sure.'

'Then Churchill will have a walkover.'

'I'm resigned to that. But Labour will at least make some sort of impact on the country as a separate party, instead as part of the administration running the war. I intend to do some vigorous electioneering, though it's difficult for a peer. The wretched public do seem to think that you live in a castle and spend every day fox-hunting. Could I rope you in to help?'

'I've abandoned Socialism. In this country, you are born either to work for other people, or have others work for you. No political doctrine can absolve you of either original sin.'

Archie seemed shocked. 'When did you first think that?'

'The day you got married.'

'I shall of course return to publishing once the election's out of the way,' he went on hastily. 'It was hardly my fault that my firm went bust. A lot of London publishers were rather sharper than me, getting their hands on a wartime quota of paper which they didn't deserve.'

'I'm off to Germany on intelligence work.'

Archie looked puzzled. 'I didn't think that was your sort of line. Don't you just mess about with fungi?'

'My job was singular in Oxford, to create disease not to cure it. I have just invented a method of wiping out Germany with bubonic plague. Now my five years' work is completely wasted. It's very disappointing.'

He stared at me, half-disbelieving. 'You never gave the slightest inkling you were engaged in that sort of horrible war work.'

'Elizabeth knew,' I told him airily. 'Didn't she mention it?'

'If Labour *should* win the election,' Archie resumed, scraping up the last morsel of his leathery omelette, 'at least we've men with experience of Government. Attlee, Morrison, Bevin, Cripps, Greenwood, all members of the War Cabinet. No one can lay the old charge of Labour being short of ministerial talent.'

'If Labour did win, it would be a national disaster. They would use their energy to institute Heaven run on bureaucratic principles.'

'Perhaps you're right,' he conceded, looking gloomier than ever.

I could hardly blame myself for failing to see that in a couple of months Archie would be a Minister of the Crown.

32

'The problem of the Nazi is essentially that of Caliban,' said Dr Harold Greenparish in his quarrelsome little voice. 'To all intents and purposes, your Nazi has been raised in complete isolation from the rest of the world. His standards are those of his dam Sycorax, his worship directed to her god Setebos – the Nazi state and the late Adolf Hitler,' he explained to me. 'He has simply no yardstick of conventional morality to measure his behaviour, none whatsoever.'

'I think that's rather an oversimplification.'

He looked pained, annoyed, a little shocked. It was the first time I had contradicted him since we had left London. 'No, I don't think so. I've talked to some of these SS chappies in the prisoner of war camps. They're puzzled – to say the least – suddenly to find the world regards them as absolute monsters. By their own lights, they were simply doing their duty. In war, one is required to kill one's fellow man, whether he is the enemy without or the traitor within. The more of either category one disposes of, the more patriotic one is esteemed to be. Surely you take my point? That's how the SS people see it, I assure you.'

'Traitors? Jews, Slavs and Czechs? And a lot of other defenceless men, women and children who did nothing wrong except to be themselves?'

Greenparish's expression indicated forbearance of my tediousness. 'Essentially, yes. In the framework of Nazi doctrines. One must be clear-headed about this, Elgar. The Nazis in their private dealings could be as clean-living, as honest, as decent, as religious as the rest of us. Your Nazi mind was terribly shuttered. They performed what we regard as utterly ghastly deeds, because they saw them as perfectly natural, and even essential, under the Nazi Darwinism of survival of the strongest. The fact that it was an insane doctrine is surely beside the point? It was the only one they knew. And of course, the lurid light of war does rather tend to encourage human excesses.'

'What about the still small voice of conscience?'

'Conscience? Does it exist, in the popular sense? I am strongly inclined to the Freudian view of conscience.' Pudgy finger-tips together, he leant back on the comfortable if worn upholstery of our first-class *wagon lit* dining car in the immense self-satisfaction of specialized knowledge. 'Freud explains conscience in terms of the super-ego, equating it with the judgements passed down to the child from the parents. But the all-pervading Nazis were of course the parents. The German people were their docile children. Particularly, of course, the younger ones, who did most of the damage. I'm sure you must agree? Human morals are not bestowed by God – about whom Freud is equally interesting. And human behaviour is by and large instilled by the methods of conditioning.'

'You mean, we learn to distinguish right from wrong as Pavlov's dog learned to salivate at the sound of its dinner-bell?'

'Fundamentally, yes,' he said with crushing assurance.

I was beginning to dislike Greenparish. We had first met less than twelve hours previously, on the departure platform of Liverpool Street Station. He had stuck out his hand and said, 'I'm Greenparish.' He was about my age, short, stout and balding, standing amid a cluster of suitcases, bags and boxes. We both wore battledress, without badges of rank. I had a red FIAT flash on my shoulders, which seemed to set me above the Red Cross but below War Correspondents. Greenparish's job was denazification. ('Dreadful word,' he would say with a shudder.) He was a psychologist who had written books and articles about the Nazi mentality from the snugness of a Cambridge college. The only Nazis he had met in his life had been sitting safely behind British barbed wire.

I made my second arrival in Germany on the Monday of August 6 in the summer of 1945. Everyone was wondering how to clean up the abattoir of Europe, while the sun warmed our delusions of permanent peace and promptly returning prosperity. The war had ended in Germany with a whimper, in Japan with a bang. A tribunal was to sit in Nürnberg to try the important Nazis, whose photographs as shabby and sagging men I could still hardly believe in the newspapers. Only Hitler's joke, Franz von Papen, achieved any style, with a Tyrolean hat and a wry smile under the eves of a steel-helmeted American military policeman.

Holland was flooded. Germany was flat. Large towns had vast open spaces with no wall higher than a man, small ones had disappeared altogether. People lived in the rubble like maggots in a corpse. Fraternization with Germans, just speaking to them, was strictly forbidden us. Even the objective Nazi Albert Speer thought this inhuman conduct in any victor. But the concentration camps had been overrun, and if Hans Frank, Hitler's Governor-General of Poland, was to write before he was hanged, 'A thousand years shall pass and this guilt of Germany will not have been erased,' there would have been nobody that summer to disagree with him.

We reached Cologne after nightfall. I had heard that the Cathedral survived, and saw excitedly the twin spires soaring against the sky. Greenparish fussed over his luggage. 'Surely there's somewhere one can get a meal?' he kept complaining, searching the ruined Hauptbahnhof. We had been given bully beef sandwiches and tea on the train. 'After all, the Army is responsible for us, and I don't see why I should be subjected to the inconvenience of hunger.'

We set off in a jeep driven by a British corporal, making a long detour to cross the Rhine. Cologne in the darkness of its bumpy, bomb-cracked cobbles seemed in reasonable shape, and only when returning in daylight I found it a skeleton, every building roofless and gutted. The autobahn took us past the Bayer pharmaceutical works at Leverkusen, once with the huge blue advertisement which I had noticed from Jeff Beckerman's Cord. The factory was intact, spared by the Allied guns after Field Marshal Model changed his mind about using it in the final scramble as an artillery base.

'You gents got any cigarettes?' the corporal asked cheerfully over his shoulder.

'Neither of us smokes,' replied Greenparish coldly.

'You'll be entitled to a ration, or you can scrounge some. Fags is gold-dust in Germany. You can get anything for them. Listen, Governor – ' The expert on the Nazi mind winced. 'You can get anything at all,' the corporal insisted. 'A bike, the family wireless, a grand piano.'

'I have no necessity for such luxuries,' said Greenparish.

'Length of cloth for the wife, bottle of schnapps, nice suite of furniture.' He drove single-handed, lighting one of his own inestimable valuables. 'You can get a Fräulein for ten Woodbines.'

'I do not indulge myself with young women,' Greenparish told him severely.

'Well, her mother then, if you prefer it,' the corporal returned accommodatingly. 'Best keep your heads down, gents. The Jerries sometimes has the habit of stretching a steel cable across the autobahn. It's their Resistance Movement, what they calls the Werewolves. Though I don't think it adds up to much. A lot of them is as glad to be rid of Hitler as we are. Still, a wire would make a nasty mess of your haircut, wouldn't it?'

Greenparish glared at me uneasily.

We approached Wuppertal from the Düsseldorf road. The streets were unlit and shattered, and I recognized nothing. But as we turned right, my excitement burst out with the cry, 'Why, it's the Zoo!'

'I reckon they've eaten all the animals,' said the driver, jumping out as we were halted by a sentry.

'That fellow's not very respectful,' complained Greenparish.

'He probably fought his way here from Normandy. We're only useless civilians.'

'I really don't understand why I should do without my dinner. After all, the war *is* over.'

I discovered the next morning that Wuppertal too was mostly demolished. The brewery had gone. The final air-raids had created a hurricane of fire which had boiled the tar from the streets. Like other embattled towns, parts of it were almost untouched. The Allied Armies had commandeered the entire fashionable area where twelve years before I lodged – furniture, paintings, grand pianos and all – simply evicting the inhabitants. We messed with the British Army, in a stone-built mansion which I faintly remembered. It had later belonged to the rich owner of an 'aryanized' textile works, everywhere now scratched by boots, filled with the sound of American Forces Network from Munich and somebody always playing ping-pong.

I went eagerly in search of the Dieffenbachs, but their house was one of the unlucky ones, blank eyed, burnt out, dead. I stood wondering sombrely what had happened to the family. Then I noticed the centipede's legs astride the river Wuppern, and one of the familiar cars sailing peacefully beneath them. Having survived the Kaiser, the Schwebebahn had outlasted Hitler. I thought that Greenparish might be able to draw some parallel with German politics and German technology.

The first man it was my duty to interrogate was Gerhard Domagk.

I had been in Wuppertal a fortnight. One of the nearby commandeered houses had been turned into offices, with trestle tables and filing cabinets and metal-framed chairs. There were red-capped military policemen stamping about with revolvers, but I managed to shoo them away. Domagk had not changed greatly. His close cropped hair was no greyer and no thinner. He still wore his neat triangular bristle of moustache. He had lost weight, but so had everyone in Germany. He was poorly dressed, but he had worn old clothes even when the shops were full of new ones.

'You are Gerhard Johannes Paul Domagk?' I started reading formally in German from a manilla file. He stood facing me across the trestle table with understandable wariness, 'You were born at Lagow, in the Province of Brandenburg, on October 13, 1895? Your parents were Paul Domagk, schoolmaster, and his wife Martha, maiden name Reimer?'

He nodded silently. I motioned him to sit. 'You don't remember me?' I asked unsmilingly.

He stared, but shook his head. 'How is your daughter? She must be about sixteen now.'

Domagk looked at me with even more suspicion. It occurred to me that he imagined I was about to screw information from him by threatening his family. It was a fear well-justified by the rule just lifted from Germany. In the last stages of the war, the whole families of deserters were shot as a matter of course.

'Her arm recovered, so I heard,' I continued. 'Yes, I heard that after our countries were at war. I heard at the same time that you were arrested by the Gestapo.'

His blank stare was followed by a look of amazement and a slow smile. 'You and that American with the beautiful car—'

'You remember? Herr Elgar. I visited your labs.' I nodded in the direction of the I G Farben works. The factory had been bombed, but the research department was almost intact. 'I went in the American's car to fetch the 'Prontosil' tablets for your daughter. Now I can make a confession. I stole a second phial of the tablets which I happened to find there.'

He was hugely relieved at being faced by an enemy he knew. 'I don't think the loss was noticed in the agonizing circumstances,' he replied.

The atmosphere thawed as we talked for a while about his child's illness. I offered him a Woodbine. 'I remember how I feared for my daughter's life,' he reflected. 'It still amazes me how the world now accepts complete recovery in such cases as a matter of course.'

'My loot ended in good hands. Yours was the first "Prontosil" ever used by Colebrook to treat puerperal fever. Though unfortunately without the success of your daughter's case.'

'Of course, I read everything Colebrook had to say about sulphonamide. His work at Queen Charlotte's Hospital was most impressive. The progress of his patients was closely checked by the bacteriological laboratory, which we never achieved with our earlier trials here in Wuppertal.'

'Have you still your painting by Otto Dix?'

Domagk smiled again. 'Otto Dix…he was called "subversive" by the Ministry of Propaganda, though I heard he went away somewhere and continued to paint exactly as he felt. Yes, I kept that picture from my laboratory. It remained discreetly in my home, even after my arrest. Though what has happened to the painting now…

He had been evicted from his house in Walkürieallee. When I had strolled to inspect it, half a dozen bored GIs were amusing themselves playing football in the garden, one of them wearing over his combat dress Domagk's evening tail suit.

Domagk stared with interest round the room which he could not leave without my permission. But before starting my interrogation, I had a more pressing question. 'Is Dr Dieffenbach still in Wuppertal?'

RICHARD GORDON

The answer was a look of horror. 'But didn't you know, Herr Elgar? Dr Dieffenbach and his wife were both taken away by the SS. It was in 1941, about Christmas time. They both died in a concentration camp.'

'Oh, God! And the daughter —'

Fräulein Gerde kept her post in the school throughout the war. But last March or April, when everything started to disintegrate, she disappeared. Where she is now, who can say? Families are separated all over Germany. There are plenty of people here in Elberfeld whose relatives are in the Russian Zone, and there's no knowing if they'll ever meet again. I heard a rumour that she had been arrested by the British. But there are rumours everywhere about everyone. The boy was killed you know. In the attack on Liège in 1940.'

I sat savouring these bitter dregs of war.

'But why should Dr Dieffenbach be arrested? I remember him as a Nazi supporter.'

'I understood it was for behaviour prejudicial to the State, and making subversive remarks. They were common charges, when the SS wanted to do away with somebody.'

'Then what made him change his opinions about Hitler?'

'Like many professional men, he found the Nazis no friends of the middle classes. The Nazis wanted to create a society where all men were equal — equal under the domination of their own officials. The Nazi Party was a duplicate state in Germany, you know. I was certainly never a member of the Party. I never supported Hitler. I acquiesced, I agree. Through prudence, and through fear. You will understand that, Her Elgar?'

Domagk laid his hand on the bare table with a resigned gesture. 'My country was at war, and I backed the war patriotically. My work was on drugs of no military significance. Drugs which may benefit all mankind. I spent my time trying to extend the range of the sulphonamide drugs to tuberculosis, though unfortunately without success. So I turned my attention instead to the thiosemicarbazones, which as you know are related to the sulphonamides. Have you heard of Tb-I 698? I found that to have a definite action against the tubercule bacillus. And all through the

242

war I continued my work on natural and acquired immunity to tumours, and on drugs against cancer.'

'Do you know about penicillin?'

'Oh, yes. A Penicillin Committee was set up in Berlin last year. We began to grow a little of the mould, in the way described by Florey. Had the war continued another year, I'm sure that German chemistry would have produced plenty of it.'

Domagk stubbed out his cigarette. I noticed that he had pronounced arthritis of the hands. 'Will you answer a question which I have been wanting to ask all the war, Professor? Why precisely did you concentrate on the sulphonamide dyes against streptococci? In the I G Farben works you had an enormous choice of chemicals to experiment with.'

'I was testing about three thousand different chemical compounds a year,' Domagk agreed. He thought for some moments, his head inclined to one side, as I remembered him. 'I started with the notion that bacteria were destroyed by the natural defences of the body very much more easily if they were damaged somehow first –'

'That was in the reprint you gave me for Sir Gowland Hopkins. He told me recently that – rereading your paper – it made inevitable your becoming the discoverer of modern chemotherapy.'

Domagk accepted the flattery with a smile.

'Hopkins is still alive?'

'A spry eighty-four. He only retired as Professor during the war.'

'My first attempt was to damage the invading streptococci with mild heat – it was only for demonstrating the reaction to students, using the living mouse. Then instead of heat I turned to various chemicals – gold, acridines, finally the azo dyes synthesized by Dr Meitzsch and Dr Klarer, one of which damaged the streptococci so thoroughly that the mouse could completely overcome the infection. That became our "Prontosil".'

'You have not entirely satisfied my curiosity. Who suggested to your chemist colleagues Meitzsch and Klarer that they turned their attention to these particular azo compounds? After all, as you just said, there were thousands of different ones pouring through their hands every year. To put it technically, who exactly suggested introducing the sulphamyl group in the molecule, and thus turn a dye into a drug?'

'That decision belongs entirely to Professor Hörlein,' Domagk imparted 'He was my superior, in charge of the whole Elberfeld plant. My own position in the laboratories was not administrative, but entirely technical. Professor Hörlein had made a comprehensive study of these azo dyes, and he was convinced that they could have some medicinal effects. He had noticed that similar dyes could arrest infection with the trypanosome parasite in mice.'

'So it is to Professor Hörlein we must be grateful as the true originator of the sulphonamide drugs? And so opening the eyes of Florey, that he might see the potentialities of penicillin? Well, that's very interesting. Isn't Hörlein the real father of modern chemotherapy? And the father of other and perhaps more remarkable drugs of similar sort yet to be created?'

I noticed Domagk stiffening in his chair and starting to fidget as I said this. I wondered if I had perhaps offended his vanity, though he had little enough of it. I asked, 'Is Hörlein still alive?'

Domagk's lip trembled. 'Haven't you heard? He was arrested last Wednesday. By the Americans. He is in prison somewhere, I think in Düsseldorf. Charged with the most terrible things. With killing people, with mass murder...' Domagk looked at the floor, then suddenly back at me. 'Professor Hörlein was on the board of I G Farben, and on the board of its subsidiary company, Degesch. That firm made chemicals...poisonous gases, "Zyklon-B". You've heard of it? The SS used it for killing their prisoners in the concentration camps, killing them by the thousand upon thousand. I assure you, Herr Elgar, that of these matters I knew nothing, nothing.'

We fell silent. So the man responsible for modern chemotherapy was also responsible for the gas used in genocide. A sickly paradox. But perhaps Hörlein had not seen it as a paradox? Drugs to cure and drugs to kill are still only chemicals. When to do either the one or the other is equally laudable, who is the technician to object? Such moral autism was the secret of the Nazi power. I wondered if Greenparish would have understood it.

'Have another cigarette.' Domagk and myself had said enough for one day. 'Take the packet.'

'You must excuse me if I unashamedly accept your generosity. Defeat reduces us all to a common denominator.' As he inspected the gift I translated the name, '*Geissblatt*.' He nodded. 'They have a good taste, more to my palate than the much prized Lucky Strike.'

33

Greenparish was giving a party.

I had been in Wuppertal all autumn, and I had grown dreadfully bored. I had questioned over and over again all the scientists and technologists of the I G Farben works, most of whom I felt could be of no interest to the occupying powers, and little even to their friends.

SHAEF had been dissolved. FIAT was under the British Control Commission, co-operating with ASLOS, OSRD, CIOS, TIIC, OMGUS and JIDA. We were all concerned in Operation Overcast and Project Paperclip, to whisk five thousand top German scientists into the United States, by way of detention camps near Paris and Frankfurt, named somewhat savagely Backporch, Ashcan and Dustbin. The bodies behind these initials naturally quarrelled fiercely with each other, with the United States Army and with Washington. By the end of November, only three scientists had reached American soil, and they were sneaked out for their own use by the United States Air Force, which was thought most unsporting. Many I interrogated showed little zest for a new life across the Atlantic. So little, they got on their bicycles and disappeared from official view forever.

I was comfortable and well fed. We lived isolated in an Anglo-American town near the Zoo, protected by sentries and road-blocks. We had our own shop, cinema, library and discussion group. Greenparish lectured the troops on the psychological background to Hitlerism, to their mystification and boredom, but at least it was warm and they were allowed to smoke and there was nothing else to do.

I saw something of David Mellors, who had become a Lieutenant-Colonel in the Royal Army Medical Corps, stationed at the British Hospital in Bad Godesberg, where Chamberlain once met Hitler beside the Rhine. On the far side of black, cold, ruined Wuppertal at Barmen, the Royal Artillery were blowing up the enemy's ammunition. The Grenadier Guards were up the hill, in a brand new German Army barracks. Greenparish and myself, and some uniformed nutritionists in UNRRA, shared the mess of an armoured regiment. His Majesty George VI filled almost exactly the outline left by Adolf Hitler over the fireplace. I had grown used to the clockwork of ping-pong, there were plenty of copies of *Life* and *Look*, and we got Bourbon from the Americans in exchange for British duffle-coats.

But I grew uncomfortable, playing a part in Hogarth's picture of Calais Gate, his fat friar fingering the immense raw joint of English beef while the ragged and skinny populace enviously sup their bowls of thin soup. I was forbidden to exchange a friendly word even with my German batwoman, who cleaned my room, polished my shoes, laundered my clothes and neatly mended them.

She was a handsome blonde who reminded me of Gerda, and I discovered that she was a Luftwaffe general's daughter, glad enough to earn the wages of the conquerors. It must have been the first employment of her life – two and a quarter million British misses and madams put their hair in snoods and went to work making tanks and aircraft, but Hitler refused Albert Speer at his Ministry of War Production to let Nazi womanhood dirty her hands with machine oil. The Führer's notion that woman's place is in the home helped lose Germany the war.

'I hear there *is* some fratting with the Germans,' Greenparish said to me in the mess. 'Among the other ranks.'

'They use the word to mean another very similar.'

He wrinkled his nose. 'At least the powers that be have taken my point sufficiently to relax the rules for my little conversazione. One's problem of re-educating the Nazis is of opening sufficient windows. Hitler was to them simply the idealized embodiment of their group-identification. Surely you agree? One must let them know that other standards prevailed outside Germany. Not, of course, that there seems a single Nazi left in

Germany today,' he added resignedly. 'They would all seem to have vanished from the face of the earth, like the swastika flags and SS uniforms and those ghastly muscular neo-Classical statues of pagan dimwits.'

The party was for the Saturday evening of December 1. Greenparish had transported a don from his own Cambridge college to lecture on English Literature, to be followed by Greenparish explaining the relationship of man to society. The don was a short, jumpy, birdlike man with large round glasses, always shaking hands and smiling and apologizing for his presence. Our colonel recognized it all as the familiar politicians' lunacy, but allowed use of a room with crystal chandeliers and cream and gold moulded walls, now badly knocked about. Greenparish had invited about thirty guests from the re-emergent Elberfeld Literary Circle. They were mostly middle-aged and elderly, and uncertain whether to be submissive, arrogant or frightened. All arrived dressed in their best, though everyone's best right across Europe was growing threadbare after six years.

On a long table against the wall were set bully beef sandwiches, sausage rolls, bottles of hock and cigarettes in glasses. Greenparish meant refreshments to be taken during the discussion of points raised by the speakers, in the manner of those spirited, sly, chattering little parties of Grange Road, Boars Hill and Hampstead. But the guests fell on the food at once, slipping sandwiches into handbags and pockets for their families, helping themselves to the wine, baring the table in two or three minutes.

'This isn't what I intended at all,' muttered Greenparish crossly. 'I honestly felt that tonight would see an achievement of mind over stomach. Look how those cigarettes simply *vanished*!'

I stood in the corner, neither eating nor drinking. In those disordered times in Germany, you developed a suspicious eye for anyone who looked out of place. I had observed aloof from the others a man with the double distinction of being young and having an air about him. He was fair, pallid, sharp faced, with pale blue eyes, in a green high-buttoned sportsman's jacket, check trousers and stylish brown and white shoes. He caught my eye. After a minute or two, he approached and said in English, 'Mr Elgar, I believe?'

'How did you know my name?'

'A lot of people in Wuppertal know you, Mr Elgar.' He spoke with the singsong precision of a man who has learned a language in a lecture room. 'You were a visitor in an earlier age.'

I noticed the thin hand which held his cigarette had fair hairs on the back, and I thought his nails were manicured. As the surviving young were all prisoners of war I asked curtly, 'Why aren't you in the Army?'

'A question which obviously needed asking. I worked for the Ministry of Propaganda, which first afforded exemption from military conscription. Later, I was too valuable for cannon-fodder.'

I saw that he must have been at least thirty, though he had a boyish look which I suspected he cultivated. But I did not believe him. There were plenty of SS men in Germany who had thrown their uniforms into the nearest ditch. 'May I introduce myself,' he continued. 'Herr von Recklinghausen. It should be "Count", but I dropped it in boyhood, the Hitler Reich not being...well, shall we say, you never knew exactly where you stood with titles. It was most amusing, to see senior members of the Nazi Party exhausting themselves in a struggle between their natural envy and their natural respect for our aristocracy. You noticed perhaps that I did not click my heels when introducing myself? So Teutonic a gesture would, I'm sure, be frowned upon in the state of affairs we now live in. *Autres temps, autres mœurs.* I try to adapt. I'm generally called Rudi.'

I felt greatly offended by this self-assertive harangue. 'If you worked for the Reichspropagandaministerium, you must be a member of the Nazi Party,' I said accusingly.

'How could I deny it? My file and party number will be among the others discovered on some country roadside by the Americans. But I have convinced Dr Greenparish that I am harmless. What a charming fellow he is! Most cultured. When I learned I was to be interrogated, I expected to be confronted with a beef-faced man smoking a stinking pipe, with his riding-crop and revolver on the table, the sort who would shoot a dozen Indian natives before breakfast. These national stereotypes! Well, they're the fault of us propagandists, I admit. But propaganda as a weapon of war has at least the virtue that it has killed nobody yet.'

He offered me his own packet of Lucky Strike, a gesture in the circumstances of nonchalant ostentation. I have never been able to hate anybody for long, even Lamartine and Archie. I began to be amused by Rudi. He was probably a deserter, perhaps a crook, disguising himself in an elaborate but transparent garment of respectability. 'What are you doing in Wuppertal?' I asked in a less unfriendly tone.

'I escaped from under the very moustaches of Josef Stalin. My home is in Schönebeck on the river Elbe, which unfortunately is in the Russian Zone. My family is extremely well known there.'

I noticed Greenparish talking animatedly in German to an elderly couple with a well-scrubbed looking, pink cheeked, plump daughter of thirty or so, blonde hair in long girlish plaits down her back. He was providing Wuppertal with its first evening party of completely unafraid conversation since the advent of Hitler. But the others were not chattering about the intellectual treat in store, rather about food, cold, queues, transport and poverty, like everyone else.

'Would you perform for me an act of mercy?' Rudi asked unexpectedly. I noticed he smelt of perfume. I supposed Germany was flooded with it after the fall of France. 'It is to save the life of a sick child.'

'Can't you get hold of a doctor? Things haven't broken down to that extent in Germany.'

'The greatest doctor in the world could do nothing. She is the little daughter of an old friend of my family's, who lives out in Beyenberg.' That was the eastern district of Wuppertal, where Jeff had taken Gerda and myself in the Cord for cakes and cognac that bright Sunday afternoon.

'He is a good man, not a Nazi, who was congratulating himself on coming alive through both the war and the Hitler Reich. Though of course like all of us he is penniless. His daughter has the meningitis.' Rudi tapped his forehead. 'She is infected with the *Staphylokokken*. You will understand, I think, Mr Elgar? You were not sent to Wuppertal to interrogate Professor Dr Domagk for nothing.' I wondered how he had nosed out information about my duties. 'The disease cannot be touched with sulpha drugs. She must have some penicillin.'

'How did you get to hear about penicillin?'

'Everyone knows about penicillin, conversation buzzes about it in the food-queues. People have always grown excited over wonderful cures since the days of Christ and his miracles. But as you know, we Germans have no penicillin at all, no more than we have chocolates or new shoes,' he ended in a tone of self-pity.

I supposed this Anglo-American achievement had been paraded in the German newspapers before my arrival. It did not occur to me then that penicillin would become one of the most valuable goods in the German black market. I thought of it as a rare drug, with a rare use outside the battlefield. But I had the sagacity to reply, 'I have formed the opinion, mein Herr, that you are not wholly honest.'

He seemed to take no affront. 'Honesty in present conditions has become a little hard to define. So many day to day transactions necessary to remain alive are unlawful. Your soldiers don't mind going without a wash or a smoke to exchange soap and cigarettes for a bottle of brandy or half an hour with a pretty girl. The Woodbines so kindly provided by Dr Greenparish this evening will in the morning be bartered for turnips or sewing-needles or tooth-powder, or with luck a little butter. How bizarre our times, when cigarettes are far too valuable to smoke! But without the black market we should have no hope of the most meagre comforts and many essentials, and the problems of you people would be much greater.'

'I don't believe for one moment your sentimental story of the ill child.'

'I hardly expected you to,' he replied blandly. 'I wished to afford you an excuse for selling me some penicillin. I don't care for commercial affairs. I'm a writer, formerly art engineer. But *on doit travailler pour vivre*. I perform a useful function as middleman in various transactions. If you let me have some penicillin, I give you my word it would go only to the most deserving of sick persons. I shouldn't like to make a pfennig out of such a commodity.'

'I can obtain penicillin no more easily than you. But let me assure you that had I a kilo at my disposal, not a milligram of it would get into your hands. You can also take it from me that the rest of the British personnel would tell you exactly the same thing.'

'Are the Allies to continue their practice of killing German children into peacetime?'

I do not think Rudi calculated this as an insult. That would have been against his interest. But rather a way of shaming me somehow into scrounging some penicillin. I replied by turning my back. Undaunted, he said, 'In case you should change your mind, Mr Elgar –'

He thrust a slip of pasteboard into the neck of my battledress. It was an embossed visiting card with Count Rudolf Ernst von Recklinghausen in Gothic print, an address somewhere in Barmen, and in the corner Übersetzer, translator. I wondered how he had acquired it. Getting printing done in Germany was as difficult as getting a watch repaired or finding new bicycle tyres. Though for 100,000 marks a German could buy a new' identity card, a new employment book and ration cards, an Army leave pass or even discharge papers, a Hungarian or Italian passport. In short, a new existence for a frightened Nazi. I suspected that Rudi knew his way to a forger's.

The don lectured apologetically about English Literature, ending by seeming to apologize for winning the war, and even for starting it. Afterwards, he sat with Greenparish and myself in the mess, apologizing for drinking our whisky.

'It went very well,' Greenparish said with self-satisfaction. 'I can even see this evening as the beginning of an entirely new phase in Anglo-German relations. Though next time I shall take care not to bring in the food before I've finished.'

I mentioned Rudi. 'Oh, yes. A most interesting young man. He was one of Göebbels' bright boys, you know. And however ruthless that mendacious propaganda machine, one must admit it was tremendously effective. Your German was still believing it while his roof was being blown off by advancing troops. And perhaps even his head.' Greenparish was amused at the joke. 'He's an interesting educational background. Before joining the Göebbels outfit, he took a degree in engineering at the University of Wittenberg.'

'Which is in the Russian Zone, like his home town of Schönebeck. And so neither can be checked.'

'He's perfectly above board, I assure you. He's far too intelligent ever to have been a wholehearted Nazi.' I was aware of Greenparish looking uncomfortably at the don, who immediately apologized for keeping us up and went to bed. When the pair of us were alone, Greenparish took my sleeve and whispered, 'That Recklinghausen chap is hot stuff. You've heard of Operation Backfire?'

'These ridiculous names only confuse me.'

'That's the show at Cuxhaven with the V2 rocket engineers. You must have heard of a man called von Braun?'

'Never.'

'He was the top scientist at Peenemünde, and was captured with about four hundred others on the launching site. He's been in the United States since summer, doing something important with their guided missile research at a place called Fort Bliss, which appears to be somewhere in the middle of Texas. Our Count was sent to Peenemünde by Göebbels himself, to handle the propaganda side. He knows absolutely everything about the place. The Americans are *very* interested in the Count.'

'I suppose there's no chance the man's telling a pack of lies?'

Greenparish looked offended. 'Of course not. He has the fullest documentation to back him up.'

I decided to go to bed, letting Greenparrish make his own mistakes. At the door, I asked, 'But why should the Americans continue to be the slightest interested in missile research? They've won the war.'

'Dear boy,' Greenparish sighed. 'You don't imagine the Russians think they've won *their* war yet, do you?'

34

I was to go home before Christmas. My nose had smelt enough of the putrefying corpse of Nazi Germany. I had a career and a divorce to resume. I was delighted with last minute orders to travel by way of FIAT HQ in Paris. The pulse of Paris, I learned from American officers, had missed a beat or two during the occupation but was now bounding as joyfully as ever.

Two days before my departure in mid-December, I found a pair of familiar faces on the 'front page of the British Forces newspaper. Fleming, Florey and Chain were in Stockholm. The Karolinska Institute had been suffering the same confusion as many old-established bodies gazing across the rubble of the post-war world. Penicillin was eminently worthy of a Nobel Prize, particularly as its discoverers, unlike Professor Domagk, were on the winning side. The Swedes' intention to award it to Fleming got into the London newspapers, raising so much academic dust the Institute had to think again. They gave half the Prize to Fleming and shared the other between Florey and Chain. This raised the dust chokingly, so they ended by splitting it three ways. The trio were in tails and white waistcoats, Fleming looking like President Truman, Chain with a Groucho Marx moustache, and Florey resembling the then vanished band-leader more than ever.

'You know those fellows, I suppose?' asked Greenparish, reading the paper over my shoulder in the mess.

'I know Fleming and Florey quite well. I was wondering how they were enjoying each other's company in Stockholm. They've never worked in the same lab, nor collaborated in anything, nor even shared the same lecture platform. They're strange bedfellows in the cradle of success. People say they're enormously jealous of each other, though of course under a conscientious politeness.'

'It is a sad failing of us academics to gossip with the well-rehearsed and well-relished maliciousness of beautiful actresses.'

'I suppose Fleming was the discoverer of penicillin, like a sheik who discovers oil in the desert and uses it to light his camp fires. Florey was the prospector who extracted it.

'Then how do the Americans come into it?'

'They made the money.'

'With both products,' Greenparish observed. 'Elgar, I had a message to give you last night.' Spotting a new issue of *Lilliput*, he grabbed it and took the armchair opposite. 'It came in a roundabout way from an ancient medico I was interrogating – he's a perfectly clean record, now the poor old thing's trying to cope single-handed in what's left of the local hospital. Apparently he's got a patient in there, he said someone you'd remember, one Gerda Dieffenbach –'

I dropped the paper. 'What's the matter with her?'

'A very common feminine complaint, I fear. She's had a baby.'

I exclaimed, 'But she must be at least thirty-five –'

'Really? I had the impression she was a young girl. Like a lot of people in Wuppertal, she knows you're here, and what you're about. She'd like to see you. It's up to you, of course, if you want to risk disobeying standing orders.'

'Do you know anything of the husband?'

'Alas, she has no such encumbrance. She was raped by some SS man, when things began to break up earlier in the year. I wouldn't go near her if I were you, she obviously wants to get something out of you.' Greenparish started reading his *Lilliput*.

I was appalled at this casual revelation. I knew that in Nazi Germany, where personal feelings were as irrelevant as leaves blowing across a battlefield, SS men who made any Nordic type of female pregnant faced nothing but the congratulations of the State. But a woman of Gerda's sensitivity and intelligence, and with her whole family killed...

'I might warn you that we arrested her,' added Greenparish, without looking up from his magazine. 'Someone denounced her because she was a Nazi schoolmistress. But in the end we let her out. She claimed she had to strike a compromise with her conscience under Hitler. Don't all the women? I expect even those blonde maidens who scattered rose-petals before the tyres of Hitler's Mercedes, when he came home from the surrender of France. So dreadfully vulgar, the Nazis.'

I stood up and walked in the fresh air of the small garden. I could not face Greenparish a second longer. But he was right. Why should I go against my country's orders and risk seeing Gerda? She was cared for in hospital, better off than the millions of Germans living on bomb sites. She had been raped, but millions more had been killed. But she had asked to see me. And the war had left me perhaps the person nearest to her in the whole world. That evening I put on my duffle-coat and walked to the same hospital where the earliest cases had been treated with Domagk's sulphonamide.

It had been bombed, its windows replaced by boarding. Inside was dim and cold, and you could see the marks on the wall where Hitler's portraits had been removed.

'I'm from the Control Commission,' I said to the middle-aged woman in an old-fashioned folded nurse's cap, who was sitting at a table with neatly arranged piles of forms in the hall. She gave me a hard look when I asked to see the doctor attending Fräulein Dieffenbach. She clearly did not approve of unmarried mothers.

The doctor was wizened, bent, white-haired, in a patched white coat with a stethoscope sticking from the pocket. I explained briefly who I was, and what I knew.

'Yes, Fräulein Dieffenbach was delivered safely of a daughter four days ago.' He clasped his bony hands together. 'You knew about her parents? That was terrible, terrible. Dr Dieffenbach was one of our most esteemed practitioners, and did enormous good here in Wuppertal.'

'May I see her?'

'I think that would be inadvisable. She is very, very ill.'

I asked in alarm, 'What's the matter?'

'Puerperal fever,' he told me starkly. 'We try to keep infection down as much as we can, but it is difficult with the sterilizing plant worn out like everything else.'

'You're treating her with sulphonamides?' I asked at once.

'Unfortunately not with the effect I should have hoped,' he replied wearily. 'She may be infected with the staphylococcus – we cannot tell, with our restricted facilities. Culturing pus to identify the infecting germ is a luxury we must forgo. And of course the sulpha drugs don't touch the staphylococcus. I have to use my clinical nose —' He tapped his nostril.

'What about penicillin?'

He sighed. 'Ah! That is not for us Germans.'

'Her life's in danger?

'That's undeniable. Of course, much depends on her natural strength. But none of us is bursting with health these days.'

'I must see her. I knew her family well before the war. It might put heart into her, to fight the illness off.'

I went up an ill-lit stone staircase in the company of the doctor and the memory of Rosie. Gerda lay in a bed at the end of a small ward, separated from her neighbour by a white screen. She had not changed as much as I had feared. Her hair was two long plaits of pale gold, tied by the nurses with a pair of bows made from bandages. She was flushed with fever, thin, her face lined. Her mouth was a little open, and looked as soft as ever.

'Oh…!' She lay against a pile of pillows staring at me, no expression on her face at all.

I smiled. 'Remember how we went to work together on the Schwebebahn?' I asked in German.

'Herr Elgar…'

She stretched out her hand. I clasped it, hot and damp. I suddenly recalled *Blondie of the Follies*.

'You know why I'm here?' she said in a whisper.

I nodded. 'I know all about it. I'm enormously sorry for you.'

'It was something sudden, unexpected. I never thought it could happen to me.' She dropped her eyes, the effort of looking up at me too much. 'I often thought about you during the war, hoping that you were all right. And that American with the big white car… I wondered if he was alive or dead. He had so much money.'

'He's alive, and has even more.'

She made a feeble smile. 'I'm not very well. I have a fever which sometimes complicates this state. But the child is all right, thank God.'

I felt simple astonishment at her affection for the cause of her pitiful state. Then it struck me that a man can never understand such emotions. And that Gerda was one of those women who long for motherhood but are frightened by its means. 'You'll get better soon.'

She made no response. Turning her eyes to me again, she said, 'I'm not a Nazi, you know. I never was. I had to say and do certain things which I was ashamed of. But the alternative…'

Mindful of the old doctor in the background, I said, 'You mustn't strain yourself. I'll come and see you again. I'll bring you some chocolate.'

'We'll have so much to talk about, Herr Elgar.' For a second she had a shade of her old vivacity. 'The war was such a pity, such a pity. The Nazis spoiled life for everyone in the world, not only for their own people. I should have gone to England with you, shouldn't I?'

We went downstairs. The doctor remarked, 'Perhaps we should try Ehrlich's intravenous arsenicals?'

'That's useless, useless.' I strode into the gloom of the winter evening, fastening the toggles of my duffle-coat, realizing that I was facing a choice more agonizing than Florey's over the disposal of his meagre, early supplies.

Gerda needed penicillin. It was denied the German population. I could have tried squeezing some from David Mellors, but the drug was scarce, carefully checked in the British and American military hospitals, a serious offence to give away. I had heard recently from Greenparish of some ampoules stolen and fetching enormous prices on the black market. It would be useless asking David, I quickly decided. And unfair, forcing him to choose between the chance of a court-martial and offending an old friend.

I returned to the mess, and sat in my luxuriously furnished bedroom trying to decide where my obligations lay. There were big risks and bigger principles involved. I shied from making up my mind, though I sensed my thoughts were irresistibly carrying me towards resolution. I opened my file of personal letters and took out Rudi's visiting card.

The address was on the north edge of the Elberfeld valley, up one of the long flights of stone steps. I climbed them counting – there were two hundred and sixty-four. At the top was a tall grey house, falling like a cliff on the steep slope. There were more stairs inside, unlit. I had to strike matches to read the number of Rudi's flat on the top floor. I hanged a brass knocker fashioned like a Notre Dame gargoyle.

There was silence. Then someone shuffling behind the door. 'Who's there?' demanded a German voice, not Rudi's.

'Herr Elgar. From FIAT. I'm known to Count Von Recklinghausen.'

More shuffling, more silence. I waited patiently for several minutes. Bolts were slipped back and the door opened. In the light of a further door standing ajar, I found myself facing a fattish man of about sixty, with a boyish red and white complexion and hair dyed bright blonde. He nodded towards the other door. 'Rudi's through there,' he said sullenly.

I entered a small room crammed with elaborately decorated antique furniture – a dresser with carefully arranged pewter platters, a cabinet of painted crockery, a hefty pear-shaped coffee-pot, the *Dröppelminna*, a local curio. All indicated that the owner had come down in the world. It was freezing cold, like all German houses, the paraffin stove reeking in the corner clearly newly lit for my reception. Rudi wore a red and black dressing gown of quilted silk over his sportsman's jacket.

'This is a pleasure,' he greeted me in his sing-song English 'Though not an unexpected one.'

35

'Would you like a cup of coffee? It's real.'

'No thank you. As you suspected, I've come on business. I want to get it over as soon as possible.'

Rudi began to dissertate infuriatingly, 'What do you think of the furniture? It is in the baroque style created by Count von Berg, who was once a big noise in the district. The flat belongs to Hans, who let you in. I'm lucky these disturbed times to find a roof over my head.'

'I've come about penicillin. I want to buy some.'

'To buy? But you of the master race have penicillin enough.'

'It's for a German.'

'I see.' He offered a packet of Lucky Strike, then lit one himself. 'What are you prepared to pay?'

'What's your usual charge?'

'You can have five days' supply for fifty pounds.'

'I haven't got fifty pounds.'

'Then I cannot help you.'

'I could have you imprisoned for these activities, remember.'

'Isn't that an empty threat? You would not dare to implicate yourself. I'm sure you can raise sufficient pound notes or dollars.'

'You know we're not supposed to have any currency except occupation marks.'

'I know that is a regulation often broken.'

There was silence. Rudi continued smoking unconcernedly. 'Your penicillin's stolen, I suppose?' I asked.

'You do me an injustice. It comes from a most respectable source – the kidneys of the Americans. The precious fluid is collected from the big Army hospitals round Frankfurt, the penicillin reclaimed by a chemist from I G Farben here in Wuppertal. At first I thought the process utterly revolting, then merely bizarre. It recalls our name for the weak beer during the war – "Hitler's bladder irrigation".'

'You steal the urine, then?'

'You really have a low opinion of me, Mr Elgar. A man who steels urine cannot stand very high even in the fraternity of criminals. The Americans are glad enough to give it to my friend the chemist for official distribution. Only a little of the fruits of his labours comes my way.'

The story rang true. Florey had used the same method with his first cases in Oxford. And the re-extraction of penicillin needed apparatus no more elaborate than the Heath Robinson equipment in the animal house.

'You see, we Nazis can't be as black as you paint us. You still turn to us if you're in sufficient trouble.'

'My God, you're conceited,' I told him.

Rudi was unmoved. 'You British are great preachers, and so lay yourselves open to the suspicion of being great hypocrites. Such indignation in your newspapers! But to paraphrase Clausewitz, genocide is the continuation of racial policy by other means.

' You were well taught in the Göebbels kindergarten, I see.'

'Göebbels, Himmler, Hitler – they've all been exalted, far too flatteringly, in your demonology. Herr Hitler was just another German statesman like Bismarck, or even Bismarck's completely unmemorable successors, Caprivi and Hohenlohe. Hitler was more unscrupulous than Bismarck, but no less opportunistic. Perhaps he was more skilful, more adept at bluff. That was Hitler's game, you know. He did not want war. I see that I bring the colour to your cheeks, Mr Elgar. But Herr Hitler got almost all he wanted by only threatening war. And you must admit that a war won without fighting is better for both sides than victory and defeat.'

'He bluffed, we called his bluff, and the result lies all round you,' I told Rudi shortly.

'Herr Hitler miscalculated. He believed that you would rat on the Poles in 1939. After all, he had reason enough. You ratted on the Czechs at

Munich in 1938. You are looking at me angrily, Mr Elgar, not because I am telling the truth, but because I am the only German in a position to tell it to an Englishman.' Rudi reached for a black leather briefcase on the dresser with the pewter dishes. He drew from it a sheet of paper. 'We are yoked in the harness of an illegal conspiracy, Mr Elgar. So you shall see how much I trust you.' He said this without irony.

It was a letter from the *Wolfsschanze*, the Wolf's Lair, Hitler's Russian Front Headquarters at Rastenburg in East Prussia. It was dated July 14, 1944 – less than a week before the bomb plot misfired. The brief typewritten text commended Herr Recklinghausen for his work at Nordhausen in Thuringia. I knew that Nordhausen had a factory for flying bombs, that it was manned by slave labour and that the Americans found so many of them dead their rows of bodies floored the huge barbed-wire compound. Hitler's spiky signature at the bottom gave an icy feeling in my heart. The man had actually touched the paper I was holding.

'This wasn't anything to do with propaganda,' I told Rudi.

'In wartime you have to take many jobs and do as you are told.' He took the letter back. 'That piece of paper could land me in Nürnberg. But I know that you must keep the secret as well as I. You British and Americans cannot blame Herr Hitler for all that has happened in Germany, you know. Nor can we Germans, though naturally we make him our scapegoat. Hitler gave the German masses what they wanted – uniforms, processions, marching soldiers, order, discipline and revenge for our shame in 1918. You may raise the Jewish question, but anti-Semitism in Germany was not mobilized by Adolf Hitler. It was another Adolf, Stocker, a protestant clergyman, Wilhelm the First's court chaplain. He founded the Christian Social Party in 1878, when the politics of the masses first began in Germany. The German Conservatives soon joined in the game. An enemy is necessary for any political party, otherwise it starts looking responsible for its own mistakes. What enemy more convenient than the Jew, who is everywhere and mixed up with everything? Besides, there is malice in every human heart, a cudgel for every human fist.'

Now it was Rudi who had coloured, as though speaking to a room of brownshirted cronies. 'Ignoble emotions are more easily exploited than noble ones. Your British cynicism must tell you so, Mr Elgar? And Herr

Hitler had a knack for exactly that. He assumed mock fury in dramatic speeches, and flattered Germany with spectacular leadership. Though in fact he thought the German people just as stupid as the masses of any other nation.'

'I know,' I told hint coldly. 'I've read *Mein Kampf*.'

'It is pleasant to think we share a common taste in literature,' Rudi said calmly.

I wanted to escape from the room. 'If I raise the money, will you have the penicillin? It's urgent. And anyway I'm leaving Wuppertal for good the day after tomorrow.'

'Come back at noon.'

Hans with the dyed hair was waiting in the hall. I hurried back to the mess. I had ten pounds in sterling notes hidden in my room. The rest I borrowed from Greenparish, who I had suspected of hoarding currency from selling his cigarette ration. I climbed the cascade of stairs to Rudi's flat again the following morning. By then I was full of doubts over the unsavoury transaction. The penicillin might be under-strength, or unsterile, so worse than useless by augmenting the infection.

Hans answered the door. He told me that Count von Recklinghausen was out. I waited until Hans returned with a foolscap envelope, which I tore open on the spot. It contained a squat bottle with a screw top, the sort used in laboratories the world over. Gummed across the stopper was a reassuring printed label saying *unfruchtbar*, sterile. It was half full of brownish crystals, like the early penicillin I had seen at Oxford. I handed over the money, which Hans counted carefully. He said '*Danke*' curtly and shut the door.

In the hospital, the nurse with the flowing hat was not at her post. I walked up and down impatiently. After some minutes the old doctor appeared, still in his mended white coat.

'How is Fräulein Dieffenbach?'

He shook his head gloomily. 'The news is bad. She has suffered a spread of the infection to her blood. I had hoped that it might have remained localized, but in her present physical condition it was just too much for her. We must hope that she has enough reserve of strength to overcome it.'

I held up the bottle proudly. 'I have some penicillin.'

He took it silently, turning it in his thin, white fingers. 'It's not American penicillin?'

'American penicillin is impossible to obtain. You know that.'

'There are ways. I've had a few ampoules here, stolen from the military hospitals. Might I ask where you got it?'

'That's out of the question,' I told him shortly. It did not seem the moment to inspect the teeth of gift horses. Then I added, 'It was extracted from urine.'

'Yes, I know of that technique. But the source may still be of importance,' the doctor said musingly. He held the bottle towards the light. 'Sometimes it is not penicillin at all, but any sort of crystals, perhaps brown sugar, or water coloured yellow.' He abruptly broke the sterile seal, tipping some of the powder into his palm. 'No, that's not penicillin.' He sniffed it. 'It has a distinct scent. It is bath salts, ground up in the kitchen.'

I had gone a couple of streets towards Rudi's flat before realizing the pointlessness of again climbing the flight of stairs. Hans would certainly not open the door to me. I could do nothing against Rudi without landing myself in the same jail. He knew that I was leaving Germany for good the next day. He would just laugh at me. Which would be intolerable.

I hurried back to the mess. I told the orderly sergeant that I wanted a jeep and driver at once. It was not until mid-afternoon that transport could be produced. It was dark when I arrived in Bad Godesberg.

It was a modern Luftwaffe hospital, serving the airfields scattered thickly across north-western Germany. Like everything else provided for Hitler's Forces, down to their boots and braces, it was of better quality than afforded German civilians. A corporal on duty told me that Colonel Mellors was in the wards. I sent my name, with a message that my visit was urgent. Within a few minutes David appeared, in battledress and carrying a stethoscope, bubbling as usual.

'Can I have a private word with you?' I asked tensely.

'You've chosen a fine moment, boy, We've just got a couple of cases of typhus, which is putting the DDMS into a fine flap, typhus having been officially eradicated in this part of the world. I expect they're sitting up there saying I'm a bloody fool who's made the wrong diagnosis.'

He led me down a long low-ceilinged corridor into a room with his name on the door, containing a desk, a pair of metal and canvas chairs, some filing cabinets and a refrigerator.

'Got the clap?' he asked amiably.

'Certainly not!'

'I imagined that to be the case, from the secretiveness of your approach.'

'You remember, I worked out here in Wuppertal before the war? I stayed a year with a German family, the father was a doctor.' I told him quickly the story of Gerda, and of her present suffering.

'You say she's got puerperal? Just like your wife?' I nodded. David began to look uneasy. 'What do you want me to do about it, boy? Is she being treated properly? I know a squadron-leader who's a gynae man looking after the WAAFS at Celle, up near Hanover. I could get him on the phone.'

'I want some penicillin.'

I wondered if David would be angry, but he just said resignedly, 'Look, boy—'

'I'm sorry. I've put you on a spot.'

'I'm continually getting these pleas, you know. From the men, who've been fratting with girls. It's always the old father or mother who are dying. To tell the truth, I don't believe one of these heart-rending stories is true. The girls want to sell it on the black market. I can't get enough for my own patients.' He jerked his thumb towards the refrigerator. 'That's half full of penicillin, but I could use twice as much if I had it.'

Feeling deflated, embarrassed, and foolish, I asked, 'You can't spare an ampoule, even for me?'

He shook his head slowly. 'I just can't break the rules, can I?'

'I didn't really expect that you would.'

'That's flattering, I suppose.'

'I shouldn't have come here. It was all on an impulse.'

'This woman's pretty sick?'

'The doctor said she'd developed septicaemia.'

'She's likely to be a goner, then?'

'You'd know better than me.'

David sighed. 'It's her bad luck to be born a German, isn't it? But we didn't start the war. And we didn't lose it, either. No, I'm sorry, Jim. I'm sorry.' He got to his feet. 'I must get back to those typhus cases.'

'And I'm sorry to make a nuisance of myself.'

'Not a bit. You'd every right to bring me your problem. It's the Army which doesn't allow me to help.'

We exchanged a few commonplaces. At the door, David jerked his head and said, 'I've got to go in this direction. Can you find your own way out?'

I nodded. 'Shall I see you in London over Christmas?'

'Yes, let's make a night of it.'

David hurried round the corner. I waited ten seconds or so. I went back to the office and switched on the light. Inside the refrigerator were cardboard packs like cartons of American cigarettes. Each was labelled, 'Penicillin – 50 Doses'. For the second time in my life, I stole.

36

Paris after Germany was as delightful as Offenbach after Wagner. Its smell was unquenchable. It still reeked of coffee and Gauloise cigarettes, though both were hard enough to come by. The breath of the Métro stations still blew as dry as a biscuit. There were GIs everywhere. Good Americans, having escaped death, went to Paris.

FIAT had first gone into action in Paris. Our vanguard of eleven scientists, with an escort of three armed American officers, landed in France just after D-day. They had entered Paris in a pair of jeeps with the leading tanks of General Leclerc's liberating division. There was good reason for the rush. They wanted to question Professor Joliot-Curie. He was married to the daughter of Madame Marie Curie, and the couple had shared the Nobel Prize for studies in radioactivity. FIAT wanted to know if the Nazis had the atomic bomb.

I had a room in a commandeered hotel on the rue de Rivoli, previously occupied by the Gestapo. I shared with two ebullient American officers, who promised to show me the delights of 'Pig Alley' – Pigalle. I had orders to report without delay to an office near the Place d'Etoile. But as often happens with military arrangements, the officer in charge had no news of my coming, no knowledge of me in his life and no interest in me whatever. As I had travelled overnight, I was in the street well before midday, at a loose end. At the next corner, I found the road crossed by a narrower avenue, Pierre Premier de Serbie. It was the home of the only man during the entire war to threaten me with a gun. I strolled to the block of flats, and saw with some excitement LAMARTINE against one of the numbers displayed in the hall. The lift was out of order, like most in Paris. I walked upstairs, full of curiosity.

My ring was answered by a plump, middle-aged woman in black, sleeves rolled back on pink arms, unwelcoming, alarmed at confrontation with a stranger in British battledress. She said in reply to my enquiry, '*Je suis madame Lamartine*'. So this was the wife he had deserted for the talkative Madame Chalmar. I had taken her for the maid. 'Are you a British officer? I speak some English.'

'I met Dr Lamartine during the war. I have a friendly interest in his whereabouts, that's all.'

'Dr Lamartine is dead,' she told me curtly.

I exclaimed, 'What happened?'

'My husband was killed in the big air raid by the RAF on March 3, 1942. He was living across at Montmartre. He had sent me and the children away from Paris when the war started.'

'I'm very sorry, madame,' I consoled her.

'*C'est la guerre*,' she said briefly. 'When did you last see him, monsieur?'

'In Bordeaux, during the summer of 1940.'

She looked at me suspiciously. 'What was your business with my late husband?'

'You've heard of penicillin, I expect?' She nodded. 'Dr Lamartine had a specimen of penicillin mould, which I was sent from England to recover before the Germans could get their hands on it.'

'Henri would not have given it to the Boches,' she said promptly. 'He was not a collaborator, whatever people say. But there's no use talking about it now.' She started to shut the door. 'You knew Madame Chalmar? She was killed by the same bomb,' Madame Lamartine added with satisfaction. 'To be exact, the firemen found her with my husband's body, very hysterical. She died suddenly shortly after. I do not think she was a very healthy woman.'

'You knew her well?'

'No. I would not have wished to meet her.'

I walked slowly back to the street. I never had any liking for Lamartine. But I thought him stupid rather than sinister. For him to be killed by a British bomb struck me as a rather unnecessary exaggeration of irony. My experience stimulated my curiosity to call on Professor Piéry, his house being not far away by the Bois.

He had the same maid, puzzled at being unable to place me. He was at home, and received me in the dining-room with the same lurid colour photograph of his son, the fleeing lieutenant. He looked much older and even thinner. His cook's art had become the most pointless in France.

'My dear Mr Elgar –' He shook hands powerfully but solemnly, holding mine in both his. 'What terrible experiences we have suffered, since you last left this house. With the young Miss Tiplady –'

'Miss Tiplady is very well, and now married.'

'*Eh, bièn*...we wondered if you ever got home safely to England. Those days of 1940 brought no credit to any of the Allies. Not to us French, because we ran away. Not to you British, because you snatched back all your planes. Not to the Americans, because they should have declared war on Hitler there and then. But you have heard of Jean-Baptiste? My son?' I shook my head. 'He was shot. By the Germans, as a hostage.'

I was so appalled that I could say nothing. I had noticed that the professor still wore a black crepe band across his lapel. His was a suffering of which I had often heard during the past few months, but never encountered face to face. He waved me to a chair. 'We are getting over it now. We see him as dead for the honour of France, like any other soldier killed in action.'

'But when did this happen?'

'In 1942. Of course, in 1940 my son had to report back to the Army, and was immediately locked up by the Germans. He had a hope they might release him, because of his English – to interpret the broadcasts of your BBC, something of that nature, but the Boches had enough interpreters of their own and weren't inclined to trust a Frenchman. I got him out early in 1941, on what they called *en congé de captivité*. Jean-Baptiste had been working in my laboratory at the Françoise-Xavier, and the Germans were releasing in a conditional way *le personnel sanitaire*, as well as men to run the railways, the electricity and gas, and so on. My God, he was better off then than millions of others captured in the fields, or even sitting in their barracks, some of them kids just called to the colours, who'd never even had a rifle in their hands. Do you know what these were saying at the

Armistice? That it obviously meant demobilization for everyone, they'd be back in their homes in a fortnight. Instead, they were marched off to Germany, without food, sleeping in fields, and kept for the rest of the war securely behind *les barbelés*.'

He paused, leaving me to feel the pain of his silence for almost half a minute.

'Then in 1942…at the beginning of August. Things really started to become very bad in Paris that summer. The German General Schaumburg had been killed, a bomb was thrown at his car. The Nazis were getting nervous, which was a very dangerous state, as I'm sure you know. Of course, they ascribed the attack to "Jews and Communists", but it was the work of the Resistance. Jean-Baptiste was arrested by the SS. Why they should pick on him I don't know, I don't know…'

The Professor sat in his chair slowly shaking his head, still in tragic bewilderment. 'Perhaps it was because of my position in the medical faculty of Paris. There were plenty of my son's fellow-officers after the Armistice who were left completely unmolested. He was kept in the Fresnes prison, we never saw him nor heard from him. Then a German officer was shot dead in Molitor Métro station, near the racecourse in the Bois de Boulogne. The Polizeiführer, the SS General Oberg, announced that one hundred Frenchmen would be shot if the assassin was not handed over by the population to the French police in ten days. Well, the assassin was not. My son was shot with the others on the morning of August I, by the little barracks at the Carrefour des Cascades in the Bois. He was allowed to write a letter first, which I have in that desk. As an additional punishment, General Oberg shut all Paris theatres and cinemas for a week,' he added with a contemptuous snort. 'Which shows how the Nazis equated the value of a hundred human lives.'

We sat without speaking for some moments. I could not console him, because consolation is a charity which can outrun the power of words.

'Yes, my son died in action,' Professor Piéry repeated wearily. 'Had that assassin been denounced, do you know what would have happened? All his male relatives – including his brothers-in-law and all his cousins over eighteen – would have been shot. Yes, shot, all of them. Their wives would all have been sent to concentration camps. Their children all taken to a prison-school. This Teutonic thoroughness was made completely clear to us by a proclamation from General Oberg when he took up his job. The General claimed his measures were necessary for the calm and security of the Parisiens. And they say the Nazis had no sense of humour,' he ended bitterly. 'That letter of my son's will be passed down in my family, it shall never be destroyed.'

I was relieved that a knock at the dining-room door broke the tension. The maid appeared, remembering me now and smiling. She left on the table a brass tray with two minute glasses and a bottle of reddish *apéritif* which I noticed from its encrusted neck had been in use for some time.

'We are still obliged to be frugal,' Professor Piéry explained, pouring out two drinks. 'But things are naturally better than during the occupation, when we had alternate *jours avec* and *jours sans* – of wine, you know.'

I asked something which had often been in my mind the past five years. 'What happened in Paris in the days immediately after we left for Tours?'

'Oh, the Germans showed their noses early on June 14. They came along the rue de Flandre from the porte de la Villette, in the north-east. There was nothing in their way except unarmed policemen to direct their traffic. I saw a column of them about six-thirty, driving towards Neuilly from the Invalides. Soon we had posters plastered everywhere, a kindly young fellow in field-grey without his helmet, holding up three French kids who were eating his bread-and-butter ration. *Abandonnées, faites confiance au soldat allemand!* Göebbels at his most expert. Göebbels graced us with a visit in July. Hitler appeared at once, of course. Things resumed an appearance of normal. The tide turned, everyone came back from the roads to see if their belongings had been stolen, a consideration hardly in their minds before departure, I assure you. I could never have left Paris, of course, because of my patients. The cinemas and cafés reopened. So did the *maisons closes*. I remember we had Faust at the Opéra, and the *Folies Bergère* started again. We even had *Sainte Jeanne* by your Bernard Shaw that winter. There was a swastika flying from the Eiffel Tower and the Germans took over the Rue de Rivoli completely, from one end to the other. At noon every day they paraded up and down the Champs-Elysées with a brass band.'

The Professor took a tiny sip of his *apéritif* 'We had to settle down to some sort of life. The Germans requisitioned all our cars, we had wooden soles to our shoes, we had nothing to smoke and we went about on bicycles. Everybody kept rabbits, and they dug up the Jardin du Luxembourg to grow vegetables. There was a curfew, and any *retardataires* who missed the last Métro had to spend the night squatting in a police station.'

'Didn't you manage to get any encouragement from the outside world?'

'Listening to foreign broadcasts meant the concentration camp, but of course most of us risked it. The papers all presented the war after 1941 as a struggle between the European Forces and the Bolsheviks. That was the Pétain line. Laval had the effrontery to make a speech here about the immense German sacrifices to this end on our own behalf. They founded *La Gerbe* – "The Sheaf" – which was supposed to be a balanced intellectual weekly, *pour les hommes de bon volonté de tous les partis*. But it was all Nazi hypocrisy, its disappearance was a minor joy of our Liberation.'

'What about de Gaulle?'

'They called him a tool of the Jews. Whom they collected in the *Vélodrome d'Hiver* – the indoor cycle race-track – and deported to the concentration camps.'

The door opened. Madame Piéry appeared, dressed in black. She started crying as she greeted me, through association with her son. 'He was not alone,' she said. 'Now that everything has come out, the Germans shot 29,660 French hostages.'

The news of death never seems to come singly, or perhaps the first blow makes us more sensitive to the others. I reached London the week before Christmas, where I had booked a room at a small hotel in Cavendish Square. Among my waiting letters was a telegram sent the day before from Budleigh Salterton, saying that my mother was 'seriously ill'. By the time I arrived there, she was dead. She had just turned sixty and had suffered a stroke. 'She was so loyal, so devoted and so hardworking,' the old lady kept repeating in a heartbroken voice. 'One simply doesn't find servants like that any more.' My mother left me £200, the savings of a lifetime. It was useful to buy a second-hand pre-war car. My only emotion was a ghost of the liberation I felt so guiltily on the death of Rosie.

I had a lonely Christmas, but I hate obligatory jollity. In the New Year I won my expected job at Arundel College, Senior Lecturer with the old professor only three years to go. I should be 37 when I succeeded to the chair, exactly the age when Florey had burst into Oxford. I had decided that, like Florey, I should set my staff searching out unfinished lines of research. But for the cure of cancers, not infections. That was the next exploration for man's restive mind.

I never had so much confidence in my science and myself as that New Year of 1946. Perhaps the Millennium being enacted by Mr Attlee's government had something to do with it. But cancer is still uncured. And I ended up as a professor as futile and frustrated as most of the others. My divorce was more permanently rewarding. I consulted a jolly, chubby, bearded solicitor just released from commanding a submarine, who peppered his advice with expressions about surfacing, crash diving and depth charging. 'There are three times the petitions as before the war,' he said with satisfaction. 'Couples who married in the Forces discover a terrible shock, living together for longer than a fortnight's leave at a time. Without the duty-free cigarettes and drinks, too. Got another target in your periscope?'

The following week I opened my *Times* to find that Sir Edward Tiplady was dead. I telephoned Archie, who seemed insistent that I join Elizabeth and himself at the funeral.

It was a dull and drizzling afternoon at a crematorium on the edge of a vast estate of little red-brick council houses at Shepherd's Bush. I went by Underground in my new utility suit. I arrived as Lady Tip in a mink coat was stepping out of Sir Edward's angular 1935 Rolls Royce. She had spent most of the war living in Claridge's Hotel, with several exiled kings and Alexander Korda.

Archie was looking gaunter and gloomier than ever, Elizabeth lovelier. She wore a smart black costume, the straight skirt reaching half way down calves in black nylon stockings, her dark hair in a small round black hat with a deep frill of stiff black muslin. The Packers were there, but said nothing about Clare, though I saw how they were bursting to. I barely remembered what my first wife looked like, until I found among my mother's effects a small photograph album annotated in her copperplate hand with the dates of unmemorable outings. It struck me how happy I looked, but perhaps I was obliging the camera

Archie offered me a lift in their small car, elaborately excusing his use of official petrol by some imminent meeting in the Ministry. 'I happened to come across one of your reports from Germany on industrial intelligence. Not at all badly done,' he observed to me, I thought most condescendingly. 'Cripps, Dalton and Bevin are very interested in that particular exercise, I hope you realize. I had a special meeting with them at the Board of Trade last August.'

'How are you enjoying revolutionizing the country?'

'I'd be enjoying it much more if my ulcer didn't play me up. It's all tremendously hard work. But tremendously exhilarating. This time we're setting methodically about building a just and equal society in Britain, instead of shouting vaguely about "A Country Fit For Heroes To Live In", like Lloyd George.'

'You don't seem to have got very far yet,' I told him. There was continued rationing of everything from bacon and butter to soap and shoes, a scarcity of everything else, and nightly gloom from street lights left unlit to save electricity.

'Of course we have. We've already the date for nationalizing the coal mines,' he told me, sounding offended.

He was dropping Elizabeth in Belgrave Square. 'Come in and have a cup of tea,' she invited me. Archie did not seem to object. 'Don't forget we're dining with Mummy at Claridge's,' she instructed him, as he drove off.

The flat was undamaged, and much as I remembered it from the beginning of the war. 'Do you know who poor daddy called in when he had his heart attack?' Elizabeth asked me. She entered the kitchen at the back, still with her frilled hat on. 'Lord Horder. He wouldn't have anyone else.'

'Your father was immeasurably good to me.'

She lit the gas under the kettle. 'At heart he was a pansy, wasn't he?'

'Yes.'

'Did he make advances towards you?'

'Not physically. He would never have dared. And it would have repulsed him. He was far too sensitive.'

'I thought that pansies had just as much sexual drive towards each other as men and women?'

'That's true. But there're a number of men who love women and find physical sex repugnant.'

'Hand me that teapot, there's a darling.'

'Archie's left us alone in the flat? Without even a servant on the watch?'

'Why shouldn't he?'

'Isn't that typical of Archie. He always does what he thinks he should, rather than what he wants. It's a form of self-honesty, I suppose. And *that's* so much rarer than honesty towards other people.'

'It's why he became a socialist. Because he thought he should. He could have fulfilled himself much better by spending his money as dutifully as any other millionaire.'

'It's why he let me play the parasite on him so long. And kept that awful man Watson.'

'Very *cordon noir*, wasn't he? Did you know that Watson was a crook? He'd done the most awful things, killed someone and escaped with his neck. He learnt how to cook in prison. I wonder what happened to him?'

'Probably got a job as catering officer in the Army.'

She laughed, pouring steaming water to heat the silver pot. 'It's why Archie married me. Because he saw it as exactly what he *should* do, as the best thing for both of us.'

'To save you from the unspeakable disgrace of marrying the butler's boy?'

'You should never have let me get away with it. You should have carried me off and married me when we escaped from France. I'd have gone willingly, darling, honestly.'

'I shied away because I was afraid of being hurt. Surely you of all people can understand how I grew up with an inferiority complex? It's kept me from a lot of delicious things in life. Perhaps even from claiming the fame for discovering penicillin.'

'I hope you don't take sugar? We've used all the ration.'

'You've never been happy with Archie, of course?'

'Not really.'

'If you would really have married me in 1940, why were you such a bitch to me before the war?'

'I was frightened. Don't forget, I'd grown up with you as unattainable to me as I to you. Then my mother bolting, and realizing that my father was a pansy. I felt insecure, so I played the bitch. A lot of girls do that. Women appear to be unfeeling, when they're only frightened of their feelings. During the war I wasn't frightened of anything at all. It was the same throughout the country, wasn't it? Everyone had something more important to think about than their complexes. All the madhouses were empty.'

'When's Archie likely to be back?'

'Hours. Poor dear, he thought he would spend every day bringing justice and light to the world. Instead, he passes all his time in a beastly office at the Elephant and Castle, arguing over details of pensions and things with lawyers.'

'He's left us alone because he thinks he should show how he trusts us.'

'Oh, Jim, you are exasperating. He left us alone because he thinks I deserve a little adultery.'

In the bedroom she threw off her hat and a pair of orange laced-edged silk French knickers. But we were both so eager she fell on the coverlet in the rest of her outfit. I enjoyed Sir Edward's daughter while she was still in her mourning clothes from his funeral. Not bad for the butler's boy.

The fourth death could have been my own. The next day I called at Ainsley's office, which had files stacked everywhere and a busy air of closing down. 'This might interest you,' he said, sorting through a sheaf of photographs on his desk and flicking one towards me. It showed the page of a printed book, a column of names and addresses, each entry numbered, resembling a telephone directory. My own name struck me at once.

'Elgar, John,' the entry started in bold type. '1911. geb., Chemiker, London W1, Harley Street, RSHA IV E 12, Statpoleit Düsseldorf.'

'That's from the Gestapo's Sonderfahndungsliste GB, Special Search List for Great Britain,' Ainsley told me cheerfully. 'Our Field Intelligence unearthed it. It contains about two and a half thousand names, put together by one of Himmler's boys called Schellenberg. You're in

276

distinguished company. There's Noel Coward, David Low the cartoonist, Rebecca West, Gilbert Murray, Bertrand Russell…those figures after your name are the number of your file in the Reichssicherheitshauptamt.' That was the Reich Central Security Department. He folded his hands across his red knitted cardigan with a smile. 'They were going to establish Gestapo headquarters in London, Liverpool, Birmingham and so on.' Then for the first time I heard Ainsley laugh. 'Just think of the people you'd have to be seen dead with! I think Nöel Coward made that remark about it.'

'I'm flattered the Nazis thought me so important in Wuppertal.'

Ainsley tossed another photograph across the desk, of a round-faced bespectacled nonentity in SS uniform, not unlike Himmler himself. 'That's SS Colonel Dr Franz Six, former professor of economics at Berlin University. He was to have been in charge of the fun. Instead, he had to content himself with the mass murder of Russians with his Einsatzgruppen. At the moment, thank God, we've got him locked up at Nürnberg. Looks a nasty piece of work, doesn't he?'

'And thank God Hitler's Operation Sealion never came off.'

'I can console you that the invasion would have been an unmitigated disaster for the Nazis.'

'Because the RAF won the Battle of Britain?'

'No, my dear fellow.' He gave me a wise look. 'Because the Fleet was anchored at Scapa Flow. The Germans had no ships, and we could have blown their barges out of the water. Britain always wins wars by sea power. I fancy that Hitler's famous intuition told him that, as the man didn't know a bowsprit from a barnacle.'

37

It was almost two years later. I was having dinner with Jeff Beckerman at Munich in the middle of December, 1947. He had been driven in a US official car 150 miles from Stuttgart to meet me.

'Seeing you here's saved two precious days,' he declared jovially. 'Now I can cancel the Savoy and pick up the *Queen Mary* from Cherbourg.'

'So Britain's not worth visiting any longer?'

'Commercially, no,' he replied frankly. 'Attlee's government may be swell for the British working man, but it doesn't exactly encourage anyone to try making any dough.'

Jeff lit a cigar between courses. He was still fatter, in a civilian suit like myself, with a flashy tie. We were both staying the night at a hotel run by the American Government for the flock of officials and businessmen at the time gently cropping its way across Germany. It was a warm, comfortable, well-stocked oasis in a city still dark, cold and damaged.

Our table was by an upstairs window, and I could look over the Marienplatz by the Munich Rathaus, where about noon on November 9, 1923, Hitler and his Brownshirts picked up Julius Streicher on their way to the Feldherrenhalle, where the Nazi revolution came to grief under the muzzles of the police carbines. In his triumphal days, Hitler ceremoniously retraced the route, Goring, Ribbentrop and the rest all marching in jackboots along the tramlines.

I recalled the official photographs Ainsley had shown me, taken at Nürnberg in the early hours of October 16, 1946. The same Nazis were lying on top of plain black-painted coffins against a background of brick, the cut nooses still round their necks, each body neatly labelled with an

278

adhesive strip. Ribbentrop wore a dark striped suit and stylish tie, Keitel's face was a mask of blood, Frick wore the sporty tweed jacket he had affected during his trial, and Goring having pre-empted the hangman lay on an Army blanket with his right eye a little open, looking at the camera with a wink of death.

We talked about pre-war days in Wuppertal. I told him of Gerda, with a child from some unknown SS Schütze. She could never know that I had brought her the penicillin. But she had written effusively thanking me for the bar of chocolate. 'Did you really have a contact with the German generals before the war?' I asked Jeff with curiosity. 'You remember, when you would have prevented the whole thing if the Foreign Office man hadn't fobbed you off with teacakes.'

'Sure I had.'

'Was it Gerda herself? I often thought so.'

'No, but you know him. Herr Fritsch.' I frowned. The name meant nothing. 'The manager of the brewery, who always wore a wing collar.'

'But he was a nonentity!'

'He'd have liked you to think so, for safety's sake. He'd dropped the "von". He was related to Werner von Fritsch, who was Army Commander in Chief before Hitler got rid of him in the spring of 1938. He resigned after some homosexual scandal had been cooked up by the Nazis. Who knows? If they'd taken me seriously in London, you and I might be sitting here now amid scenes of peace and prosperity.'

I was still mystified over Jeff's urgency to see me. 'I'm flattered you drove all this way,' I told him.

'You needn't be. It's a matter of business. I came to Munich with a specific purpose. To ask if you'll work for me again.'

'But I've already got a job. I'm going to be a professor.'

' "Professor"!' He did not hide his contempt.

'Besides, I can't possibly move to the States. For domestic reasons.'

'The job isn't in the States. It's right here in Germany. I'm restarting operations in a big way. You think I'm crazy?'

'Of course I do. Germany's just a scrap heap from the North Sea to the Alps. They're even talking of demolishing what's left of the factories and turning the country into the biggest farm on earth.'

RICHARD GORDON

'Sure. But Germany can't go on being the poor-house of Europe for
ever. Germany's a country with a future. Look what's happened already.
We re-established the Länder, putting back the calendar to the peaceful
days of little kings and cuckoo-clocks before Bismarck. We found enough
Weimar politicians who'd somehow kept out of trouble under Hitler –
there weren't any left alive who'd stood up to him. We even put up
Communists, for God's sake. Then we let them have elections, back in
1946. Nothing like starting training in democracy early.'

'Hitler was democratically elected,' I reminded him.

'He would not be elected again. When your guts are ripped out, you're in
no mood to try charging the enemy. Listen, it's going to be like this. The
Four-Power Council has been deadlocked for months. Right? The Russians
would like to extend Communism to the Rhine, we'd like to extend
Democracy to the Vistula. Those are two impossibilities. So the Russians
will eat their share of the Germans like cannibals. We shall invite our share
to sit down and halve the goodies. The western Länder will have to combine
into a new Republic sooner or later, just to face up to the Russians.'

The German orderly in a white jacket brought our steaks. 'And that
German technology!' Jeff murmured admiringly. 'I suppose you knew the
US division of your FIAT collected 200,000 pages of trade secrets from Leitz
Optical alone? And 600,000 pages on dyes, synthetic rubber, plastics and so
on from I G Farben? Truman has ordered the information sold to US
industry at nominal prices. Our FIAT had a budget of almost four million
bucks, but I reckon it was money well spent. You British didn't really get
into it,' he admonished me. 'I guess it's your old trouble. War is OK, but
trade is ungentlemanly.'

I asked what the job would be. 'Organizing my interests. I trust you.
You speak German. You know the Germans.'

'Can't the Germans organize themselves?'

'They couldn't under the Nazis. Hitler's organization was terrible, just
a lot of overlapping agencies all at each other's throats, with no directives
but a vague idea of carrying out the Führer's will. I expect they'll improve
on it when they haven't to worry about a knock on the door at four in the
morning. The salary could be about what your Prime Minister gets, old
man.'

'I'm sorry. But I'd rather stay at home in the British Empire.'

Jeff looked exasperated. 'What British Empire? Roosevelt wanted to see the end of it, and he did. You British have ended the war with no money, no power, and no influence. Only thousands of millions of coloured people who want to see the back of you as soon as possible. And you're putting up a statue to Roosevelt in Grosvenor Square. That's gentlemanly to the limit!'

Like most Britons, I still did not see the truth which Ainsley had prophesied in his club. Nettled, I said, 'Well, we still count in Europe.'

'The whole of Europe's now just little kings and cuckoo-clocks. There's only two powers in the world, the Russians and us. And we've got the bomb.'

'Besides, I'm getting married,' I added as an unanswerable objection.

'I thought you were married?' Jeff grumbled.

'I got divorced. I'm marrying that girl with the soldier's gas mask I brought to the Savoy. The one who married a close friend of mine. It's all very gentlemanly.'

'Think it over. Telephone me in New York if you change your mind.'

'Honestly, I'd rather be a professor.'

Jeff grunted. Suddenly remembering, he took out his pocket-book and handed me a newspaper cutting. 'Did you ever come across that guy in Wuppertal?'

The cutting came from a recent *New York Times*, headed *German "Scientist" Gets 5-year Term*. It was a short, bald story of Count von Recklinghausen, a rocket engineer from Wuppertal, who had been cleared of Nazi guilt by the Allied Control Commission and been flown to America with several hundred other scientists. He was in trouble through selling New Yorkers' shares in his non-existent family engineering business, and found to be neither a count nor a scientist but a journalist from Hamburg with a police record for swindling. He had apparently reached the United States through forged documents and exploiting the rivalries between various Allied organizations. I hoped that Rudi's flattering letter from Hitler was a forgery, too. I decided to post the cutting to Greenparish anonymously.

'What shall we do for the rest of the evening, old man?' Jeff asked me. 'Go find some women wrestling in mud?'

I left early the next morning in a US Army jeep for Nürnberg. I was going to renew another old acquaintance.

Since the previous May I had been following the trial of 23 top men from I G Farben. It was an all-American show, in the Nürnberg Palace of Justice, where the Nazi bosses had been tried expediently, if not entirely logically. I recognized the courtroom at once from the photographs in the newspapers during 1946. To the left of the dock was a booth for three or four young men and women, the interpreters, every word spoken having to pass from microphone to earphones, through their heads. To their left stood the witness chair, opposite it across a dozen yards of bare floor the desks of the lawyers. Facing the dock, raised well above it, sat the four American judges in their black gowns – Shake, Moms, Herbert and Merrell. Everywhere stood armed American military policemen in their white-painted steel helmets, the 'snowdrops' who had become as familiar in a hundred grimy and remote British towns as the bobby.

I spotted Hörlein at once among the dark-suited prisoners. Fourteen years of war and 28 months of imprisonment had scarred him less than I expected. He was then 65, he had lost some weight, and when he turned his head I noticed that he had shaved off his moustache. He still wore his round glasses.

The Court was Military Tribunal Six, the trial the United States of America v Karl Krauch *et al.* I had seen a copy of the indictment in London. Through Archie, our affairs being *very* gentlemanly indeed. But his marriage was dead, and he was relieved to keep the divorce between friends. He would have found some stranger intruding into Elizabeth's affections deeply hurtful.

The charges were sweepingly formidable. The first count was the planning, preparation, initiation and waging of wars of aggression and the invasions of other countries. The second, plunder and spoliation. The third, slavery and mass murder. Four, membership of the SS. Five, conspiracy to commit crimes against the peace. Professor Hörlein escaped only count four.

I had timed my arrival at Nürnberg for Hörlein's own turn to face the music. That was Thursday morning, December 18, 1947. I found quickly that he had an excellent German counsel, Dr Otto Nelte. His first point to the judges was of Hörlein's relative ignorance about his fellow-directors' business. 'The administrative structure of I G Farben was so decentralized as to render it virtually impossible for an individual member of the board to be informed of the activities of the others,' the lawyer insisted. The judges were not over impressed.

'Ever since 1933, Professor Hörlein was in opposition to the Party,' Dr Nelte asserted. 'Especially to Streicher, who supported the fanatical adherents of treatment by natural remedies in their attacks upon pharmaceutical firms. Moreover, he became a victim of a campaign of defamation, because he took part in the fight for freedom in the field of science against the plans of Hitler and Göring to prohibit vivisection for scientific purposes.'

I did not think the judges were impressed with this either. But it rang true to me. The Nazis were fervent health cranks. That Hitler was appalled by vivisection was another paradox matching that being untangled before me.

It was strange next to hear the lawyer refuting the charge I had first heard from Colebrook in 1935 – of I G Farben withholding the sulpha drugs from the world until certain that the lining of its pockets was safely sewn up with patents. 'Through the discoveries made in the Elberfeld works, which were organized and managed by Professor Hörlein,' he declared for good measure, 'every year millions of human lives were saved, and through drugs like the antimalarial atebrin, health restored to hundreds of millions of human beings.'

Then he came to the Zyklon-B.

The defence was simple. Hörlein did not know what was going on. Degesch was a subsidiary company of I G Farben at Frankfurt, its full title Deutsche Gesellschaft fuer Schaedlingsbekaempfung. But Hörlein did not know that Degesch was supplying Zyklon-B to the concentration camp at Auschwitz. He did not know that Zyklon-B was for the gassing of human beings. Hörlein was admittedly a member of the Degesch Verwaltungsrat – its management committee – but several links were missing in the chain of evidence. 'The assertion that the management committee knew of the business transactions involving Zyklon-B is unsupported. No transcript of such meetings has been submitted, no evidence has been introduced to prove that Hörlein had obtained knowledge of it in any way whatever. He did not take part in any meetings of the management committee at the critical time. He did not receive reports disclosing that Zyklon-B had been supplied to Auschwitz or the terrible use made of it at Birkenau.'

These missing links were a year later to stimulate the curiosity of the *New York Times*.

Domagk's name came up for the first time. Dr Nelte was arguing that new drugs were never allowed to leave the Elberfeld works until exhaustively tested by the latest scientific methods. From my knowledge of Domagk's character and talents this was transparently true. But his reason for labouring the point soon became clear.

'Professor Hörlein had no influence in, and therefore no responsibility for, the selection of doctors to whom the Elberfeld drugs were given for clinical testing. There was no correspondence or direct association between Professor Hörlein and Dr Vetter, who at one time worked in Dachau, where the prosecution accused him of experimenting with various preparations. Concerning allegations of experiments in the Buchenwald concentration camp, the prosecution has linked Professor Hörlein with the therapeutic experiments with methylene blue, supposed to have been carried out by Dr Ding there in January 1943.' I knew this to be another dye, used as a urinary antiseptic. 'The prosecution state that in September 1942 the defendant Hörlein urged the testing of methylene blue on typhus. But no evidence has been produced.'

Dr Nelte ended by stressing Hörlein's good character. 'I shall submit numerous affidavits from German Jews and persons of foreign nationality,' he promised. 'The result will be a picture of a man who, during the bad years after 1933, preserved a courageous and noble heart. A man to whom great injustice is done if one calls him, as did the chief prosecutor, a "sickly spirit" and an "architect of the catastrophe".'

He ended with a curious irony which had already occurred to me. 'In the *Neue Zeitung* I read yesterday of the ceremonial award of the Nobel Prize in Stockholm. Dr Gerhard Domagk, director of the pathological laboratory of the Elberfeld works, appeared for the presentation of the Nobel Prize awarded to him in 1939 for the discovery of the medical effects of sulphonamide. Professor Domagk worked with and under Professor

Hörlein in the Elberfeld I G Farben plant. Whereas the world pays tribute to Professor Domagk and thus also to the Elberfeld plant by presentation of the highest scientific award, Professor Hörlein, who was given honourable mention together with Professor Domagk by North American newspapers for work on the sulpha products, stands at the same time before this Tribunal as a defendant.'

The story on which Hörlein's life depended took more than a day in the telling. I was billeted on the Americans, spending my spare time in Munich watching the mending of its fragmented university. When it came Hörlein's turn to testify in his own defence, he spoke with dignity, with respect and with effectiveness.

'Mr President, Your Honours. As a layman in legal matters, I believed that the prosecution would give facts which – at least, in their own opinion – gave them the right to claim individual guilt. Instead, they merely mentioned my name in connexion with the general charge of criminal medical experiments. It is so simple to make charges, but it seems to be very difficult to acknowledge errors.'

He talked about a life spent solving health problems of the whole world. 'I worked for humanity, for the honour of German science, for the benefit of the German economy, for my firm and for my family. There was no conflict of interest, and no conflict of conscience, in all these goals.'

Hörlein claimed that he would never have changed his job of running the comparatively small Elberfeld works. He had once refused a bigger one in I G Farben, because his task at Elberfeld was directed to humanity's greatest benefit – health. 'Hundreds of thousands of soldiers *of all nations*,' he emphasized, 'in this war have had their lives and health preserved by atabrine.' That was the drug discovered under his influence at Elberfeld as an improvement on quinine. 'Millions of people may in the future be saved from death by malaria, a disease from which a third of mankind is suffering, by this invention of the Elberfeld laboratories which can be produced in any quantity desired.'

He ended, 'I am proud that before this Court many scientists of international reputation have paid tribute to my work.' That was all in Dr Nelte's affidavits. 'The prosecution, however, in their opening statement called me and others of my colleagues a "damaged soul". They accused me of crimes against humanity, and tried to prove this monstrous statement. I hope that the Tribunal has been convinced by the presentation of evidence by my counsel that these charges are unfounded. I am, therefore, awaiting your decision with calm and confidence.'

The decision was long coming. The judgements were not given until the last days of July 1948. By then, the Berlin airlift had been flying a month, the German currency reform had laid the foundation stone of a palace of prosperity, I was married and Elizabeth was pregnant.

Life in post-war Britain was still threadbare. But it was enlivened for me by the delightful Gilbert and Sullivan situation which had developed between Fleming and Florey. They seemed to know as vaguely as the Karolinska Institute, or anyone else, who deserved the credit for penicillin. Sir Howard Florey took the Heath Robinson apparatus in the Oxford Dunn labs as a ladder which raised him to become Provost of Queen's College in Oxford and Chancellor of the National University in Australia, to a peerage and the Order of Merit. Sir Alexander Fleming used his interpretation of the penicillin mould in St Mary's to savour the adulation of a film star.

The inaudible, diminutive, shy deadpan Scot was taken equally to the warm heart of American lecture audiences and the icy one of the American Press. From the whole world he gathered academic medals and academic gowns. He was particularly fond of the Spanish one, so gorgeous that he was said to be mistaken in Madrid for the new cardinal. Madrid named a street after him, where appropriately parade the *putas* – he suspected that he would he remembered as the man who made vice safe for the masses. He would distribute small medallions of the famous mould to his eminent new acquaintances, such as the Pope. 'God wanted penicillin, so he invented Alexander Fleming,' he was supposed to have told an American lady. But it was an impossible utterance from a man like Fleming. He never used a sentence of more than half a dozen words in his life.

I was too busy at Arundel College to revisit Nürnberg that summer. I only read a transcript of the Military Tribunal's verdicts. (From Archie again.) The Presiding Judge, G C Shake, had declared, 'The defendants now before us were neither high public officials in the civil government nor high military officers. Their participation was that of followers and not leaders. If we lower the standard of participation to include them, it is difficult to find a logical place to draw the line between the guilty and the innocent among the great mass of German people. We find none of the defendants guilty of the crimes covered by counts one and five, of preparing and waging war.'

I skipped through the typewritten pages until I found Hörlein's name. 'We cannot impute criminal guilt to the defendant Hörlein from his membership of the I G Farben board of directors. He is acquitted of all the charges under count two of the indictment.' That covered plunder and spoliation. The Judge continued with count three, slavery and mass murder.

'The evidence does not warrant the conclusion that Hörlein had any persuasive influence on the management policies of Degesch, the organization proved to have supplied Zyklon-B gas to concentration camps, or any significant knowledge of the uses to which its production was being put. We are of the opinion that the evidence falls short of establishing his guilt on this aspect of count three. Concerning the evidence of inhumane experiments, we may say without going into detail that the evidence falls short of establishing guilt on this issue beyond a reasonable doubt. Applying the rule that, where two reasonable inferences may be drawn from credible evidence, one of guilt and the other of innocence, the latter must prevail, we must conclude that the prosecution has failed to establish that part of the charge.'

So Hörlein was free.

But one of the four judges dissented. Judge P M Herbert had said, 'The responsibility for the utilization of slave labour, and all incidental toleration of mistreatment of the workers should go much further. And should in my opinion lead to the conclusion that all the defendants in the case who were members of the board of directors are guilty under count three.'

In the New Year of 1949 Judge Herbert told the *New York Times*, 'The destruction of important Farben records at the direction of certain of the defendants probably deprived the prosecution of certain essential links in its chain of incriminating evidence, and leaves one with the feeling that the result might have been different if the complete Farben files were available to the war crimes prosecutors.'

The *New York Times* unearthed that one of the defence lawyers had been charged with improper action over the disappearance of records, but had been cleared. Some of Hörlein's fellow defendants had sentences of imprisonment, finally confirmed by the Military Governor of the US Zone on March 4, 1949. Hörlein himself went back to Wuppertal. Perhaps he was doubly lucky. 'For being in a position to know and nevertheless shunning knowledge creates direct responsibility for the consequences,' wrote the ghost who stepped from Spandau, Albert Speer. Hörlein enjoyed for five years a life of expanding prestige and prominence, as chairman of the new Farben company to run the works which I had first entered on the cold Saturday of January 1933.

Last summer I went back again. Like all slim blondes, Gerda has not aged too emphatically. She still coaches a few private pupils. She is still unmarried. Her daughter is another pale blonde, busily running an advertising agency with her husband in Frankfurt. Gerda told her she was the daughter of a gallant Army officer, whom she had met, loved, and lost without trace in the explosion which blew the Nazis into history.

In Wuppertal I heard one bat squeak in the black caverns of the past. I came across the affidavit sworn by Gerhard Domagk for Hörlein's defence at Nürnberg. 'When in October 1939 I was awarded the Nobel Prize, Professor Hörlein called to my attention that Hitler had prohibited that German scientists accept this prize. He advised me to approach the Ministry of Culture. I took the warning by Professor Hörlein that serious difficulties might arise for me out of this matter not seriously enough. It did not prevent me from writing several letters of thanks which I considered necessary. The result was that in November, 1939, I was arrested by the Gestapo. When Professor Hörlein learned about this incident through my wife he went to great pains to obtain my release.'

Domagk signed that in Wuppertal on January 20, 1948, six weeks after he had at last been presented with his Prize in Stockholm. His evening tail suit, essential for the ceremony, was never the same after the GIs had played football in it. Domagk wore the ancient tail suit he had been married in twenty years before, which through the privations of recent years still fitted him. He refused the offer of a new suit tailored in Stockholm. He wanted to appear a true representative of post-war Germany. He received the medal and the decorative folder signed by King Gustav. But under the Nobel regulations, the additional 30,000 dollars, if unaccepted at the time of the award, returns automatically to its funds. He never got the money.

38

Today I retired. The afternoon of my sixty-fifth birthday saw a pleasant little ceremony in the great hall of Arundel College, where I was presented with a leather-bound book of congratulatory essays from my colleagues. The affair was managed by Hargreaves, both efficiently and enthusiastically. Elizabeth looked charming, and even our two sons managed an air of amiable sufferance.

The swords forged in the decade of the thirties were sheathed or shattered in the next. Now we have much better ones. I have seen only three truly significant happenings in my lifetime. The Nazis, and the toppling of their *horrid king, besmear'd with blood Of human sacrifice, and parents' tears.* Secondly, the invention of drugs to kill the germs which have prowled so dangerously round man ever since he evolved to intrude into their atmosphere on earth. And atomic fission, which keeps the world alive by frightening it to death. There is nothing like war as a stimulant of technical progress.

In Bunyan's day, tuberculosis was the Captain of the Men of Death. But whenever their captain falls, he is replaced by another. 'Malignant Fever' carved on old tombstones has been replaced in our ignorance by 'malignant disease'. I might myself have achieved the fourth significant event by producing the cure for at least some cancers. But I lost my enthusiasm for cancer research. It was replaced by doubt that the prolongation of life in our overcrowded and quarrelsome planet was an activity as saintly as we thought. Domagk felt the same about sulphonamides in the days of Hitler. Florey did about penicillin in the war.

The cubs of Hitler now purr in well-fed contentment. Himmler's death mask has a glass case in the Black Museum of Scotland Yard. We British become our old selves again when an excavator discovers a forgotten Nazi bomb, when we can evacuate our houses, drink tea together, and sing songs of happy cheer like William Blake's child on a cloud. And what do I conclude, who have been close enough to kiss the smiling and murderous faces of our century?

I can only agree with a voice of the 1930s, Susan Stebbing – *Human beings are too fine in their highest achievements to justify despair.*

Leaving the hall afterwards, David Mellors came up to me, grinning. 'Do you remember in Germany after the war, when you desperately wanted some penicillin? You pinched it from my office when I left you alone for a minute. I did that on purpose, you know. I'm not such a fool as I look, boy.'

RICHARD GORDON

DOCTOR IN THE HOUSE

Richard Gordon's acceptance into St Swithin's medical school came as no surprise to anyone, least of all him – after all, he had been to public school, played first XV rugby, and his father was, let's face it, 'a St Swithin's man'. Surely he was set for life. It was rather a shock then to discover that, once there, he would actually have to work, and quite hard. Fortunately for Richard Gordon, life proved not to be all dissection and textbooks after all... This hilarious hospital comedy is perfect reading for anyone who's ever wondered exactly what medical students get up to in their training. Just don't read it on your way to the doctor's!

'Uproarious, extremely iconoclastic' – *Evening News*
'A delightful book' – *Sunday Times*

DOCTOR AT SEA

Richard Gordon's life was moving rapidly towards middle-aged lethargy – or so he felt. Employed as an assistant in general practice – the medical equivalent of a poor curate – and having been 'persuaded' that marriage is as much an obligation for a young doctor as celibacy for a priest, Richard sees the rest of his life stretching before him. Losing his nerve, and desperately in need of an antidote, he instead signs on with the Fathom Steamboat Company. What follows is a hilarious tale of nautical diseases and assorted misadventures at sea. Yet he also becomes embroiled in a mystery – what is in the Captain's stomach remedy? And more to the point, what on earth happened to the previous doctor?

'Sheer unadulterated fun' – *Star*

RICHARD GORDON

DOCTOR AT LARGE

Dr Richard Gordon's first job after qualifying takes him to St Swithin's where he is enrolled as Junior Casualty House Surgeon. However, some rather unfortunate incidents with Mr Justice Hopwood, as well as one of his patients inexplicably coughing up nuts and bolts, mean that promotion passes him by – and goes instead to Bingham, his odious rival. After a series of disastrous interviews, Gordon cuts his losses and visits a medical employment agency. To his disappointment, all the best jobs have already been snapped up, but he could always turn to general practice...

DOCTOR GORDON'S CASEBOOK

'Well, I see no reason why anyone should expect a doctor to be on call seven days a week, twenty-four hours a day. Considering the sort of risky life your average GP leads, it's not only inhuman but simple-minded to think that a doctor could stay sober that long...'

As Dr Richard Gordon joins the ranks of such world-famous diarists as Samuel Pepys and Fanny Burney, his most intimate thoughts and confessions reveal the life of a GP to be not quite as we might expect... Hilarious, riotous and just a bit too truthful, this is Richard Gordon at his best.

RICHARD GORDON

GREAT MEDICAL DISASTERS

Man's activities have been tainted by disaster ever since the serpent first approached Eve in the garden. And the world of medicine is no exception. In this outrageous and strangely informative book, Richard Gordon explores some of history's more bizarre medical disasters. He creates a catalogue of mishaps including anthrax bombs on Gruinard Island, destroying mosquitoes in Panama, and Mary the cook who, in 1904, inadvertently spread Typhoid across New York State. As the Bible so rightly says, 'He that sinneth before his maker, let him fall into the hands of the physician.'

THE PRIVATE LIFE OF JACK THE RIPPER

In this remarkably shrewd and witty novel, Victorian London is brought to life with a compelling authority. Richard Gordon wonderfully conveys the boisterous, often lusty panorama of life for the very poor – hard, menial work; violence; prostitution; disease. *The Private Life of Jack The Ripper* is a masterly evocation of the practice of medicine in 1888 – the year of Jack the Ripper. It is also a dark and disturbing medical mystery. Why were his victims so silent? And why was there so little blood?

'…horribly entertaining…excitement and suspense buttressed with authentic period atmosphere' – *The Daily Telegraph*

Please allow for postage costs charged per order plus an amount per book as set out in the tables below:

	£(Sterling)	$(US)	$(CAN)	€(Euros)
Cost per order				
UK	2.00	3.00	4.50	3.30
Europe	3.00	4.50	6.75	5.00
North America	3.00	4.50	6.75	5.00
Rest of World	3.00	4.50	6.75	5.00
Additional cost per book				
UK	0.50	0.75	1.15	0.85
Europe	1.00	1.50	2.30	1.70
North America	2.00	3.00	4.60	3.40
Rest of World	2.50	3.75	5.75	4.25

PLEASE SEND CHEQUE, POSTAL ORDER (STERLING ONLY), EUROCHEQUE, OR INTERNATIONAL MONEY ORDER (PLEASE CIRCLE METHOD OF PAYMENT YOU WISH TO USE)
MAKE PAYABLE TO: STRATUS HOLDINGS plc

Cost of book(s): —————— Example: 3 x books at £6.99 each: £20.97

Cost of order: —————— Example: £2.00 (Delivery to UK address)

Additional cost per book: —————— Example: 3 x £0.50: £1.50

Order total including postage: —————— Example: £24.47

Please tick currency you wish to use and add total amount of order:

☐ £ (Sterling)   ☐ $ (US)   ☐ $ (CAN)   ☐ € (EUROS)

VISA, MASTERCARD, SWITCH, AMEX, SOLO, JCB:

☐☐☐☐☐☐☐☐☐☐☐☐☐☐☐☐☐☐☐☐

Issue number (Switch only):

☐☐☐

Start Date: **Expiry Date:**

☐☐ / ☐☐   ☐☐ / ☐☐

Signature: ————————————————

NAME: ————————————————————————————

ADDRESS: ————————————————————————————

————————————————————————————

POSTCODE: —————————

Please allow 28 days for delivery.

Prices subject to change without notice.
Please tick box if you do not wish to receive any additional information. ☐

House of Stratus publishes many other titles in this genre; please check our website (**www.houseofstratus.com**) for more details.

TITLES BY RICHARD GORDON AVAILABLE DIRECT
FROM HOUSE OF STRATUS

Quantity		£	$(US)	$(CAN)	€
☐	THE CAPTAIN'S TABLE	6.99	11.50	15.99	11.50
☐	DOCTOR AND SON	6.99	11.50	15.99	11.50
☐	DOCTOR AT LARGE	6.99	11.50	15.99	11.50
☐	DOCTOR AT SEA	6.99	11.50	15.99	11.50
☐	DOCTOR IN CLOVER	6.99	11.50	15.99	11.50
☐	DOCTOR IN LOVE	6.99	11.50	15.99	11.50
☐	DOCTOR IN THE HOUSE	6.99	11.50	15.99	11.50
☐	DOCTOR IN THE NEST	6.99	11.50	15.99	11.50
☐	DOCTOR IN THE NUDE	6.99	11.50	15.99	11.50
☐	DOCTOR IN THE SOUP	6.99	11.50	15.99	11.50
☐	DOCTOR IN THE SWIM	6.99	11.50	15.99	11.50
☐	DOCTOR ON THE BALL	6.99	11.50	15.99	11.50
☐	DOCTOR ON THE BOIL	6.99	11.50	15.99	11.50
☐	DOCTOR ON THE BRAIN	6.99	11.50	15.99	11.50
☐	DOCTOR ON THE JOB	6.99	11.50	15.99	11.50
☐	DOCTOR ON TOAST	6.99	11.50	15.99	11.50
☐	DOCTOR'S DAUGHTERS	6.99	11.50	15.99	11.50
☐	DR GORDON'S CASEBOOK	6.99	11.50	15.99	11.50
☐	THE FACEMAKER	6.99	11.50	15.99	11.50
☐	GOOD NEIGHBOURS	6.99	11.50	15.99	11.50

ALL HOUSE OF STRATUS BOOKS ARE AVAILABLE FROM GOOD BOOKSHOPS OR
DIRECT FROM THE PUBLISHER:

Internet: www.houseofstratus.com including author interviews, reviews, features.

Email: sales@houseofstratus.com please quote author, title and credit card details.

TITLES BY RICHARD GORDON AVAILABLE DIRECT
FROM HOUSE OF STRATUS

Quantity		£	$(US)	$(CAN)	€
☐	GREAT MEDICAL DISASTERS	6.99	11.50	15.99	11.50
☐	GREAT MEDICAL MYSTERIES	6.99	11.50	15.99	11.50
☐	HAPPY FAMILIES	6.99	11.50	15.99	11.50
☐	LOVE AND SIR LANCELOT	6.99	11.50	15.99	11.50
☐	NUTS IN MAY	6.99	11.50	15.99	11.50
☐	THE SUMMER OF SIR LANCELOT	6.99	11.50	15.99	11.50
☐	SURGEON AT ARMS	6.99	11.50	15.99	11.50
☐	THE PRIVATE LIFE OF DR CRIPPEN	6.99	11.50	15.99	11.50
☐	THE PRIVATE LIFE OF FLORENCE NIGHTINGALE	6.99	11.50	15.99	11.50
☐	THE PRIVATE LIFE OF JACK THE RIPPER	6.99	11.50	15.99	11.50

ALL HOUSE OF STRATUS BOOKS ARE AVAILABLE FROM GOOD BOOKSHOPS OR
DIRECT FROM THE PUBLISHER:

Hotline: UK ONLY: 0800 169 1780, please quote author, title and credit card details.
INTERNATIONAL: +44 (0) 20 7494 6400, please quote author, title and credit card details.

Send to: House of Stratus Sales Department
24c Old Burlington Street
London
W1X 1RL
UK

TITLES BY RICHARD GORDON AVAILABLE DIRECT
FROM HOUSE OF STRATUS

Quantity		£	$(US)	$(CAN)	€
	THE CAPTAIN'S TABLE	6.99	11.50	15.99	11.50
	DOCTOR AND SON	6.99	11.50	15.99	11.50
	DOCTOR AT LARGE	6.99	11.50	15.99	11.50
	DOCTOR AT SEA	6.99	11.50	15.99	11.50
	DOCTOR IN CLOVER	6.99	11.50	15.99	11.50
	DOCTOR IN LOVE	6.99	11.50	15.99	11.50
	DOCTOR IN THE HOUSE	6.99	11.50	15.99	11.50
	DOCTOR IN THE NEST	6.99	11.50	15.99	11.50
	DOCTOR IN THE NUDE	6.99	11.50	15.99	11.50
	DOCTOR IN THE SOUP	6.99	11.50	15.99	11.50
	DOCTOR IN THE SWIM	6.99	11.50	15.99	11.50
	DOCTOR ON THE BALL	6.99	11.50	15.99	11.50
	DOCTOR ON THE BOIL	6.99	11.50	15.99	11.50
	DOCTOR ON THE BRAIN	6.99	11.50	15.99	11.50
	DOCTOR ON THE JOB	6.99	11.50	15.99	11.50
	DOCTOR ON TOAST	6.99	11.50	15.99	11.50
	DOCTOR'S DAUGHTERS	6.99	11.50	15.99	11.50
	DR GORDON'S CASEBOOK	6.99	11.50	15.99	11.50
	THE FACEMAKER	6.99	11.50	15.99	11.50
	GOOD NEIGHBOURS	6.99	11.50	15.99	11.50

ALL HOUSE OF STRATUS BOOKS ARE AVAILABLE FROM GOOD BOOKSHOPS OR
DIRECT FROM THE PUBLISHER:

Internet: **www.houseofstratus.com** including author interviews, reviews, features.

Email: **sales@houseofstratus.com** please quote author, title and credit card details.

TITLES BY RICHARD GORDON AVAILABLE DIRECT
FROM HOUSE OF STRATUS

Quantity		£	$(US)	$(CAN)	€
	GREAT MEDICAL DISASTERS	6.99	11.50	15.99	11.50
	GREAT MEDICAL MYSTERIES	6.99	11.50	15.99	11.50
	HAPPY FAMILIES	6.99	11.50	15.99	11.50
	LOVE AND SIR LANCELOT	6.99	11.50	15.99	11.50
	NUTS IN MAY	6.99	11.50	15.99	11.50
	THE SUMMER OF SIR LANCELOT	6.99	11.50	15.99	11.50
	SURGEON AT ARMS	6.99	11.50	15.99	11.50
	THE PRIVATE LIFE OF DR CRIPPEN	6.99	11.50	15.99	11.50
	THE PRIVATE LIFE OF FLORENCE NIGHTINGALE	6.99	11.50	15.99	11.50
	THE PRIVATE LIFE OF JACK THE RIPPER	6.99	11.50	15.99	11.50

ALL HOUSE OF STRATUS BOOKS ARE AVAILABLE FROM GOOD BOOKSHOPS OR
DIRECT FROM THE PUBLISHER:

Hotline: UK ONLY: 0800 169 1780, please quote author, title and credit card details.
INTERNATIONAL: +44 (0) 20 7494 6400, please quote author, title and
credit card details.

Send to: House of Stratus Sales Department
24c Old Burlington Street
London
W1X 1RL
UK

Please allow for postage costs charged per order plus an amount per book as set out in the tables below:

	£(Sterling)	$(US)	$(CAN)	€(Euros)
Cost per order				
UK	2.00	3.00	4.50	3.30
Europe	3.00	4.50	6.75	5.00
North America	3.00	4.50	6.75	5.00
Rest of World	3.00	4.50	6.75	5.00
Additional cost per book				
UK	0.50	0.75	1.15	0.85
Europe	1.00	1.50	2.30	1.70
North America	2.00	3.00	4.60	3.40
Rest of World	2.50	3.75	5.75	4.25

PLEASE SEND CHEQUE, POSTAL ORDER (STERLING ONLY), EUROCHEQUE, OR INTERNATIONAL MONEY ORDER (PLEASE CIRCLE METHOD OF PAYMENT YOU WISH TO USE)
MAKE PAYABLE TO: STRATUS HOLDINGS plc

Cost of book(s): ———————— Example: 3 x books at £6.99 each: £20.97

Cost of order: ———————— Example: £2.00 (Delivery to UK address)

Additional cost per book: ———— Example: 3 x £0.50: £1.50

Order total including postage: ——— Example: £24.47

Please tick currency you wish to use and add total amount of order:

☐ £ (Sterling)　☐ $ (US)　☐ $ (CAN)　☐ € (EUROS)

VISA, MASTERCARD, SWITCH, AMEX, SOLO, JCB:

☐☐☐☐☐☐☐☐☐☐☐☐☐☐☐☐☐☐☐

Issue number (Switch only):

☐☐☐

Start Date:　　　　　　**Expiry Date:**

☐☐/☐☐　　　　　　☐☐/☐☐

Signature: ————————————

NAME: ——————————————————————

ADDRESS: ——————————————————————

——————————————————————

POSTCODE: ————————

Please allow 28 days for delivery.

Prices subject to change without notice.
Please tick box if you do not wish to receive any additional information. ☐

House of Stratus publishes many other titles in this genre; please check our website (**www.houseofstratus.com**) for more details.